The Guardian

BY

Lyle Aryn

Dedicated to the memory of Jim Torgerson

I would like to take a moment to thank all the people who have contributed to this book.

First, to Beulah, Sylvie and John.

To my wonderful Mom, who has always believed in me.

A special thank you to my niece, Mahealani. That's her on the cover! Isn't she a doll?

Love and peace to all of you,

~~LA

In the darkness, all I could hear was her breathing. The exhalations came short and shallow – the panting of someone in pain. A soft glow seemed to come from everywhere and nowhere. Dimly and just to the point where the eyes could barely make out vague shapes.

In this dim light, her breathing quickened. I could just make out the curve of a bare shoulder; the glint of steel. The hard metal was dark with rust and formed the links of a massive chain that seemed to disappear into her shoulder. The light grew again, brighter, yet still misty darkness.

In the pale light her breathing became quiet sobs. I could just make out the shape of the girl, suspended by the rusted steel. Dark hair flowed down, hiding her face, the black strands of it brushing the floor tiles a few feet below her. Along with the chains were clear tubes pumping dark fluids. The light grew.

In the weak glow, a wordless plea escaped her lips. The girl hung naked, hands bound behind her at a painful angle. Heavy drops falling from her body, hitting the plastic tiles with a muffled pitter-patter. On the other side of the room stood a dark, featureless shape. The thin light revealed the sheen of vinyl gloves, the glint of surgical steel, but no more. The light grew, painful bright now. Surgically cold. Ruthlessly illuminating.

In the fierce white light her breath stopped completely. Her head turned, first to the dark shape, and then to me. For the first time I saw her face, though it was still mostly hidden by her tangled raven hair. Her lips trembled, her eyes wide, green, with a red run of tears marking her pale cheeks. With mounting horror, I realized that the chains weren't rusted at all. The stainless steel was coated with blood. I struggled uselessly to go to her, to say something, to do anything to comfort her.

The light vanished.

In the darkness, she screamed.

"Timothy Kines, wake up. You have work to perform." A feminine voice pulled me from the nightmare. In the dim light that made it past my curtains I wondered if this was just another layer to the dream. However, the throbbing in my head quickly dispelled that illusion.

The hands that shook me were surprisingly strong. Her shaking nearly dislodged the bedding off on to the floor, and me along with it. As I focused my gaze at last, her appearance served to dispel the lingering effects of the troubled sleep I had been in. I pushed her hands away roughly and rolled off the bed. Pure instinct guided my motions as I stood to face her; awake and entirely confused. *This is impossible.*

The fact that a stranger stood in my room was insignificant next to the woman herself. My room was lit brightly by a bluish light that emanated from the woman. Or, to put it more precisely, from where her eyes should have been. Two coldly blazing blue orbs seemed to serve in their place. These points of starlight blue rested in caverns of black, as if the light had cast a shadow.

When I could tear my gaze away from hers, I noticed that the woman herself seemed to be a creature of bewildering contradiction. Though her features were smooth, with nary a wrinkle to mark them, she still seemed to portray the very image of eternity. Her face was harsh, but perhaps that was only a trick of the eerie light. Her mouth was turned down into the permanence of terrible sadness. Once I had wondered what it would look like to be immortal; Now I knew.

She was dressed simply in a white cloth gown. The shabbiness of the rag was magnified by the brilliance of her light. Iron shackles circled each wrist, though no chain ran between them. Even so it was clear that she was someone's prisoner. She wore her years of enslavement prominently.

"Who are you?" I asked, the only question to escape my befuddled brain. *Not a bad start.*

"That is not important to you. Soon I will be gone... I am only nothing. You are Timothy Kines? The son of Jonathan Kines?"

I nodded, noticing then that the 'gown' she wore was actually just a thin bed sheet. One of mine in fact. It seemed obvious now why she hadn't turned on the light. The fabric was rather sheer.

"Where are your clothes?" I asked nervously. Quickly I tried to think if I had any friends that might hire someone like her for a joke. It didn't take long though, for me to come up with nothing. I was a bit of a loner. *What the hell is this?*

"That isn't important either. It was hard enough getting us both here as it is." I couldn't be sure, but it seemed that she flushed a pale scarlet. That single reaction served to pinpoint her humanity in my mind. Strange as she was, she was still flesh and blood.

"What is that supposed to mean? We are standing in my room. You haven't taken *us* anywhere."

"I wasn't speaking of you. Now listen quietly. I haven't got that much time here."

"All you are doing is speaking in circles. Unless your purpose here is to drive me mad with senseless ramblings." I let an edge of authority into my voice. Even though I knew very well that I was just about as commanding as a kitten.

Somehow it seemed as if her face softened. Her lips twisted into an expression that was almost apologetic. A deep sigh escaped her pale lips.

"You have a very special job to do. I thought that much was already clear." She stated, stopping again.

"I had guessed that you would make a request of me. The much seems to be implied by your presence here. However, I cannot read minds, and I would ask that you kindly tell me exactly what it is you would have me do. What do you want from me?"

The whole thing was absurd. I could have believed I had fallen into another dream, except that the blue light made my eyes hurt.

"Very well then. Perhaps I am no longer accustomed to dealing with people bound to time in such a linear fashion." She took a deep breath.

"Behind you in your bed is a young woman. Your job is to take care of her, and to keep her safe. He will be coming for her, and you must make sure that he doesn't take her away from you. Understand?"

"No." I didn't dare look. The woman sighed dramatically.

"Her name is Sobely Blossom. She is your age, or near enough. She has no memories, but considering everything she's... *experienced,* that is probably for the best. Poor thing. Her time here may be short, yet I trust you'll make it pleasant." She picked her words out like crumbs from glass.

"What are you talking about? Is this some kind of joke?"

"Am I laughing? I was told to expect something like this, but I had hoped your father would have said *something* to you about all of this."

The mention of my father increased the power of the throbbing headache. Anger welled up inside, turning my stomach to steel. I felt my ears burn, my hands clench. My arms shook. The cobwebs burned away, leaving only the cold rage.

"My father is dead. It would be kinda difficult for him to tell me all about the woman with light bulbs for eyes that would break into my room and speak in Gibberish."

"Then maybe he *was* fallible after all. Hmm. Just because he's dead doesn't mean he can't still alter the course of events to come. It is just unfortunate that his son isn't accepting the task being laid out before him."

"I haven't said no."

"Nor would a negative answer affect the decisions that have been made. Either you will protect her, or you will fail." She said ominously.

In the uncomfortable silence that followed this exchange, I hazarded a glance behind me. Another woman, this one definitely young, lay asleep atop the covers. The fact that she too was naked almost went unnoticed. One look at her face changed everything. Though I felt even more confused than before, I understood that my world, my priorities, had shifted.

The girl had been the regular occupant of my nightmares for as long as I could remember. Always the victim of unspeakable horrors.

One look at her sleeping face, and the world had flipped. Dream had become reality, and the shadows now contained monsters numerous and terrible. It was as if gravity itself had shifted. As if I were a planet that just discovered the sun.

For the first time since my father died, I could feel the beat of my own heart. It beat a furious tempo, pounded like war drums. The hairs on my arms stood straight up, and I could feel strength pour into lethargic limbs. It took me a long moment before I realized the cause. *Adrenaline. When was the last time you felt the surge of it?*

"I can only hope that Mr. Kines had his reasons for keeping you completely in the dark about all this. None of us knew what he was thinking even when he was still around to tell us. All that is left is to leave her here, in your hands. If you have any sense at all, you will run at the first glimmer of trouble. Run as far as you can for as long as you can, because he'll never stop hunting you." The woman whispered. I turned to question her further, only to catch her vanishing in a flash of blinding blue light. The bed sheet fluttered to the ground. So complete was her disappearance, one could almost believe she had never been there at all.

Though if I needed proof of all that had all happened I needed to look no further than my own bed. I stared at her as she slept, marveling at the delicate shape of her face, the oddly beautiful length of her ears. Her face was smooth in peaceful slumber and surrounded by a lush pile of hair as black as charcoal. Every feature, from the pixie-like cheek bones to the impossibly shaped ears, served to draw my eyes to her own, closed though they were. I knew even with them shut that they would be green, and just as impossible as her ears. Yet also completely *right.*

The world should have felt surreal, for surely this was some kind of waking fantasy. Yet it was also, clearly, reality. I had entered a realm of impossibility, and I now had to act within it.

I had no idea what I was going to do.

A glance at the clock drew my attention to a more pressing problem. Any moment now, Mom would walk in to tell me good morning and good-bye. This simple morning ritual had become an anchoring point in our lives and was how we got each day started. It was a reminder that there was someone else with us in the swirling uncertainty that the world had become.

However, the discovery of the strange naked woman lying in my bed would *probably* derail things. Just a bit.

I pulled on my slippers and stepped out my bedroom door, closing it a little too quickly behind me. Twenty feet separated my room from the house proper. My 'room' had in fact served my father once as an office.

My mother already stood on the gravel path that ran between the back door of the house and my room. Another minute and I would have been too late.

She was almost as tall as I and had barely a wrinkle to show for her forty years. She was strikingly beautiful, which sometimes caused her annoyances with the men at work. Three years had passed since my Dad died, but she still lived as if she would hear the thundering rumble of his Charger coming down the street. That he was simply, perhaps, on one of his trips.

Though the cut of her business suit was proper and formal, she still managed to make it seem flirtatious just by wearing it. Her chestnut hair was worn up, her make-up minimized. Certainly, it helped her for her job to look nice, but that wasn't her intention with it. She wasn't a woman who was concerned with vanity.

I sometimes caught her staring out the window at night, looking for the car that would never come home. Listening for a voice that would never again call her name.

Her dark eyes were full of compassion or fire, depending on who was trapped in their gaze. And in rare unguarded moments, such as now, they were full of infinite sadness. Her heart knew that dressing up was just an act, that it was just patchwork to keep the cracks from spreading. Wallpaper to hide the signs of the quake that had shook both our lives.

I had the urge to tell her everything, to just blurt it out. Yet at the same time I still had no idea what I would say. *Nobody explained it to you, either.*

"Good morning Mom." I said cheerfully, pretending not to notice her moment of sadness, and covering my momentary hesitation.

"Well good morning, Tim. You're up early." She replied, her face becoming the mask of false smiles.

"I've got some things I needed to do today, so I thought I would get an early start." I replied casually.

"Oh. Can I give you a ride into town, then?" She asked, her eyes asking a very different question.

"Nah. I feel like walking. I need to eat something first anyway." I answered, not volunteering an answer to her unasked question. I had none to give.

"Well... okay then. Umm... I am working late tonight. My boss needs me to stay after hours again, to make sure all the paperwork for the merger gets done today." She hugged me and kissed my cheek.

"Mom..." *Prepare first, remember?* "Uh, don't work too hard. You've been putting in a lot of late nights lately."

"I know I am sweetie. I'm taking some time off after this is done. Maybe we'll go on a trip or something."

A trip sounded like a fantastic idea to me, though I knew it would be a little more than just a weekend vacation.

"That sounds like a good idea to me, Mom. Have a wonderful day, okay?" I released her.

"You too, honey. Be careful." She caught herself before asking what I was up to, and I felt relief that I had the sort of Mom that respected my privacy. She spun on her tasteful two-inch heels and strode around the house. I waited until I heard her car pull away before returning to my room.

On the other side of the door stood the girl, now awake. Her eyes were wide with alarm, and her mouth opened to scream, though only a tiny squeak escaped her lips. The sun shone bright upon her through the open door. For several seconds we just stared at each other, stunned into a brief shared silence.

They remind me of the eyes of a cat...

I shut the door, catching a glimpse of her turning around before it snapped shut. My brain was thrown into complete disarray. All my priorities just scrambled, the only clear thought was of her.

She was all of five-foot two, maybe. And thin. Though I had dreamt of her for a long time, the foggy memory was nothing next to the reality. Her skin was as pale as cream, her hair as black as a crow's wing. Even now she seemed so unreal. Surely no one could actually be that beautiful, that lovely.

The impossibly long ears arched outward, twitched with surprise. The only thing I might compare them to were those described by Tolkein, when he spoke of elves. Only I had always imagined those to be much shorter and pointed straight up, tucked tight against the skull. Hers were graceful, curving away from her skull in line with the arch of her cheek bones.

Even through the terror on her face, her eyes had pierced right through me. They were the impossible green I knew they would be. I had never *seen* eyes that green. The brief flash of bright light had caused the pupils to rapidly shrink into slits, like the eyes of a feline.

One panicky gaze had been enough to capture a piece of my heart. One glance to make it beat as it had not done for years.

Finally, everything shifted back to their proper order. I felt a burning shame. Yes, she was gorgeous, strange; but she was also scared. The woman had said she would have no memories. She must have been frightened out of her mind, and I had panicked out of mine. *You're not the one that ought to be afraid.*

I took a deep breath and re-opened the door.

My heart caught in my throat. She had dived under the blanket, leaving only a tangle of black strands visible. The bed shook as she sobbed pitifully, the sound one I could never forget. My embarrassment lost all its power. Here was a girl with nothing. I was the only one that could help her. For some reason I was expected to step up, because of who my father had been.

Yet, that wouldn't be the reason I did anything. I would step up for *her;* because it was the right thing to do. Because I could not help it. She'd been haunting my sleep already.

"I apologize, miss. I didn't mean to frighten you." I said, as gently as I could. I drew near the bed and paused, unsure of what to do, or what to say. Unsure of whether or not she would even understand me.

The blanket moved, and those green eyes peered out. The skin around them was red and swollen from tears. I sat down on the edge of the mattress, *needing* her to not fear me. I resisted an urge to pull her into my arms and hold her. To give her comfort that she might not desire. The last thing I wanted was to make her feel more terrified than she obviously was.

The quilt inched down a little more, revealing her rose-colored lips quivering like leaves caught in the wind. They were cracked slightly, though whether from thirst or from biting I could not tell. Above them rested a nose to match everything else, the perfection of its delicately formed shape something any super model would envy.

"Who... who are..." Though her sobs had quieted, she had no breath, could not speak around her trembling lips.

"My name is Timothy Kines. Do you know who you are?" I asked kindly. Her eyebrows, thin black lines above impossible eyes, knitted together and she shook her head.

"Your name is Sobely Blossom. I was told that you probably wouldn't remember anything. Please, don't be afraid of me. I promise that I'm not going to hurt you."

"Where..." Her voice was a little steadier.

"You are currently in my bedroom. You haven't been here very long though. As for where you're from, I don't know."

She sat up and held the blanket out like a shield. Her eyes darted around the room, taking it in cautiously. I had no idea what she thought of the room, with its walls lined with bookshelves and a massive oak desk dominating the center. The bed was tucked into its own little nook, a curtain drawn to one side to expose it to the rest of the room. A door across the room led into a modest bathroom.

The room had become my safe refuge, and I hoped some of its musty warmth would be apparent to her.

She relaxed suddenly, and dropped the edges of the comforter, which pooled around her waist. If nothing else, the total lack of modesty was an indicator that her mind *was* truly empty. For my part, I felt proud that I didn't tense up, or feel my cheeks warm.

"Timothy." Her voice no longer shook. "I... I do not know who I am. I do not know why I am here, or even what sort of place a bedroom is. What is it I should do?" Her voice, though barely above a whisper, was like a melody. She spoke formally, her words were accented oddly, and the result was lovely. I struggled not to shake my head. *Get your mind focused here. Do something to reassure her!*

"I don't have any answers. The one who brought you here didn't give me much information." I apologized. *That wasn't very reassuring...*

She sank beneath the blanket again, began to shake again.

"How can I know what words are, and not even know my own name?" She whispered.

Tears leaked from her eyes, and then she was sobbing again. My heart broke for her, and I wondered what could be so bad that *this* would be better than remembering.

"I'm your guardian now. Your shelter. I promise you that I will keep you safe. I won't let any harm come to you." I said quietly, still resisting the urge to touch her.

But then she surprised me by sitting up. With barely any hesitation, she leapt across the bed, throwing herself against me. Her arms were crushed against my chest, and her sobs gained force. I reacted the only way I knew how; gently encircling her with my arms. Providing strength to counter her fears.

"I am scared." She sobbed. I realized then that it was a touch that she had wanted all along. She wanted more than just comforting words and gallant promises. *She has nothing. She awoke to a dark room, silent and empty, with a head just as silent. She is barely able to function above her basic instincts. She is scared, and she needs to feel safe. I can do that. I can make her feel safe.*

I rubbed her back softly, my fingers roaming carefully in a discrete tactile examination. What they discovered was shocking and revived the anger that had died down within me. Rough, upbraided skin twisted down her back in a series of scars. The more my fingers traced, the more they found a pattern that would be gruesome to witness in its entirety. More disturbing was how old some of them were, and how fresh, others. Four, in particular, still traced a heated course along her spine, barely healed.

All were confined to the narrow field of her back. Everywhere else, there was nothing but flawless skin. Save for her wrists. As I held her out momentarily to confirm that she was without current injury, I noticed the pattern of raised, calloused tissue around her wrists. I concluded that wherever she was from she had been kept with arms bound together, and then whipped repeatedly. To what end, I couldn't begin even guess at.

"You *are* safe now. I will do my best to make sure that no harm will ever come to you again. I promise." I whispered, wanting desperately to be able to ease her discomfort.

"I am empty inside. I have nothing. How can I not remember anything? How is that even possible?" Her questions echoed in my head, and my own memory tried to make sense of it. Knowing just how badly her back had been scarred, it almost did seem a blessing that she couldn't remember. Her own mind might have been shielding her from the trauma. It fit. Almost.

If it hadn't been a consistently inflicted trauma. Pain inflicted upon her for years, at the hands of someone that had been carefully cruel. That sure knowledge forced me to only one conclusion regarding the loss of her memory.

She had been deliberately erased. More than likely, she had been erased by the woman that had brought her to my care. If you had the power to just vanish like that, then it seemed probable she could have the power to delete her memories at will. Sobely had been deleted like a computer and left with only the most basic of operating functions: The ability to speak. It was perversion, a sick and twisted action. Unthinkable, even. And yet here she was. I felt a bit ill. *Why not let her know who she is? Surely there had to be something* before *the torture.*

"I wish there were a way for you to remember. Even if a memory is painful, no-one should ever be forced to forget it. To not even know who you are..." I bit off a growl. *Who is it that would make her suffer so much, and then empty her? As if she was someone's personal plaything? Just what exactly* is *going on here?*

Who knows what it is she may have lost.

Who she may have lost...

We remained silent for several minutes, each in our own contemplations. I pulled the blanket up around her shoulders, hoping that she may fall asleep. She seemed so tired and frail. I concentrated on letting my seething rage for some unknown enemy dissipate. There wasn't a thing I could do about them. Not at the moment, anyway.

"You are so very warm. I think I was cold... before." She whispered. Her hands curled into my shirt, and I held her just a little tighter. She was so lost, so scared. A child in the dark. I could almost relax, could almost forget the fact that there wasn't a stitch on her. I marveled at how much nervousness, how much mental anguish could be caused just by someone being naked. In the bigger picture, it hardly seemed important at all.

She needed comfort, and I was providing it. I felt content, knowing that just my presence seemed to be enough to calm her. *If all hell breaks loose, this won't always be so easy.* In the back of my brain, a nagging fact tickled at me. As much as I may have wanted to, we couldn't stay here like this all day. I had a feeling that life would become very interesting very quickly.

Action delayed is just as bad as no action taken at all.

She needed to be made ready to run.

"I don't want to, but I need to get up now and find you something to wear. I think there may be something in the house that will work. We will need to get some things done today. Just curl up and take a nap under the blanket, and I'll be right back." I said, trying to get up. She clutched me tighter, her limbs trembling.

"Please do not leave me here alone. Take me with you? I do not want to be alone... again." She whimpered.

"Uh..." Thoughts whirled. "Alright. I just need to find you something to put on in the meantime."

"Why? What for?" Her confusion was clear on her face. I honestly had no idea how to explain the concept of clothing to her. *Hard to not get noticed if I'm walking around with a naked woman under normal circumstances. She'd draw attention even fully clothed.*

"Everyone wears clothes. We will want to be able to blend in, so you'll need clothes as well. We can't afford to have someone question us." *Going to need some kind of hat, too. A bit warm for a stocking cap. Sunglasses might be a good idea, too, though people might just assume she had in exotic contacts.*

"I do not seem to have any clothes." She replied. She seemed to be pretty smart, but I didn't know how I could teach her the complexities of a modest society in only a few sentences.

"Yeah, I know. That's why I need to see if I can find something in the house that you can wear."

"I also need something just to go with you now?"

"Yeah..." Twenty feet separated my room from the house proper, and there wasn't a fence to block the view. To top it off, the neighbors were very nosy. With the way my luck seemed to be going, walking her naked into the house would be noticed, reported, and discussed at length.

I eyed the bed sheet worn by the other naked woman I had seen today and dismissed it entirely. In the dark it was fine enough, but in the sunlight it would hide nothing. A towel wouldn't be much good either.

"Alright..." She said, releasing me. I turned to my dresser with an idea. From a drawer I pulled out a T-Shirt. I was a lot taller than her, and I guessed that it would easily hang down far enough to be considered decent. I tossed the green shirt to her, and then turned around to give her a measure of privacy.

After a few moments spent trying not to imagine what I wasn't watching, a small hand touched my shoulder. I jumped slightly, startled. When I turned towards her I choked, my throat trying to both laugh and sigh and sob all at the same time. She had put on the shirt inside out, and the tag stuck out beneath her delicate chin. *I suppose I ought to feel grateful that she got it on at all.*

LYLE ARYN

"Well, there is something I hadn't really considered. You don't really know *how* to dress yourself, do you?" I shook my head, feeling both amused at her earnest attempt, and worried that I was going to have to show how it was done right. I wasn't exactly a pervert or anything, but I was finding that I also wasn't entirely immune to all the effects the sight of a naked woman had on the male brain.

Get over it. It isn't her fault that she doesn't know how to do anything yet. What exactly are you afraid of? It's a perfectly reasonable thing to do. Are you afraid that you're going to become someone other than who you are? The voice in my head felt like my father's.

I felt calm for a moment. *I* knew I was a decent person. *I* knew that I was probably much more in control of myself than the majority of men my age. I wouldn't hurt her. *It's like taking care of a child that also happens to be an adult. Children need help getting dressed, eating properly, and taking baths...*

I quickly stopped my thoughts. She looked up at me in confusion, no doubt wondering about the mix of expressions that had crossed my face.

"Umm. Did I do something wrong?" Her bottom lip trembled, and she dipped her chin. If this had been a bit on a sitcom, I would have probably been laughing. It wasn't quite so funny in real life.

"Yeah, but only a little bit. Shirts don't go on quite like that."

"Oh. I guess I better try again." She reached for the bottom hem of the shirt, and I fought the almost knee-jerk reaction of turning away. She would need my help, so I put out a hand to stop her.

"Umm, if you turn around, I will help you this time." *And probably every other time she needs it. Or even just asks. No matter what the reason may be, I can't exactly refuse her anything.* Obediently she turned her back to me, arms held loosely at her sides.

"That's good. Now, arms up!" I said, trying not to sound weird. *Just like dressing a kid. Except she is beautiful, and the neighbors wouldn't think twice about it if I were helping a child get dressed. Well, maybe the Johnsons...*

Her arms went up, and I gently pulled the shirt off.

Then I hesitated. It was easy to keep my gaze from drifting downward inappropriately, but that was because of the scars. There were more there than I had felt with my fingers; and the pattern even worse than I had imagined. The fresh ones were angry red crisscrossing faded white lines. I had to fight to keep control, to keep my anger from resurfacing. I could not imagine what sort of monster it took to torture someone like this.

I knew that if I ever met that monster, I wouldn't be able to keep myself from becoming a bit of a monster myself. *Death would be too gentle for such a person.*

I took a deep breath and turned the shirt right-side out, then pulled it down over her head, covering those hateful scars. I tucked the tag in nimbly, and then gently turned her back to face me.

"Better?" I asked.

"Yes. Much better. It does not feel like it is choking me now. Although that little flap kind of itches." She said, smiling shyly. I returned the smile, lost a little in her steady green gaze. My rage had been safely buried for the time being. *At least she can be made to understand why it is worn a certain way, even if you can't quite explain the necessity.*

"You get used to it. If you remember to keep that little tag in the back, on the inside of the shirt, then it will always be on correctly. You'll get the hang of it."

"You will help me get it right if I mess it up again?" She bit her bottom lip.

"Of course." I agreed. Truth be told, I would dress her every day if that was what she wanted.

She radiated an innocence. A pureness of self that could not be faked. It was as if her spirit had been buried beneath a mountain of nothingness, bits of it shining through despite the rubble. It drew me to her, that pureness. I was becoming more 'hers' with every passing moment.

And she had no idea.

She *was* sufficiently covered now, and yet that was almost worse. Instead of remaining bag-like, the shirt clung to her curves. The fabric was thin, and I realized that it really wasn't much better than the sheet. Her wildly tangled hair pooled on her shoulders, framing the neckline that hung too low on her. While I was tall enough that my T-Shirt could act as a makeshift dress, the best it could really do was ease her into the idea of wearing clothes.

Maybe it will be more concealing from a distance.

Yeah, right. And the neighbors would think nothing of me leading a girl out of my bedroom wearing one of my shirts.

Screw what others think.

That's the spirit.

02

I had carried her over the sharp gravel and hadn't felt the need to set her down once we got inside. Instead, I carried her all the way up the stairs and into my mother's room. Only the fact that we were there on a mission stopped me from continuing to hold her. She hadn't protested the action, nor questioned it. She simply put her arms around my neck and nestled into my chest.

"I'll set you down now, and we'll see if we can find something that you can wear." I told her, following words with action. She then sat on the edge of the bed, watching me with curiosity.

One look in Mom's closet destroyed any hope of finding anything. Hanging loosely were seven nearly identical business-type suits. My Mom believed firmly in clothes fitting precisely, so all seven were exactly her size. This meant that everything would be much too big on Sobely. Mom was close to a foot taller and didn't wear any belts. She didn't need one to hold her pants up and didn't care about being fashionable.

Dad used to say that a good suit would never go out of style.

Her one indulgence were her shoes. Several different styles, but in a very small range of colors. She loved shoes but didn't see the point of buying anything that couldn't be worn to work. It was clearer to me now just how much she was still hiding from the pain of Dad's death. Three years ago, the closet would have been stuffed.

Now, it seemed, there wasn't a point.

"Well then, there goes that idea." I muttered.

"What do you mean?" She asked.

"There isn't anything here that you could wear, even temporarily. The most we could use is a pair of socks."

"What do I need clothes for?" She asked. The question was still complicated, but I felt safe in only answering what was relative to our current situation.

"So we can get to a store to buy you some things that will fit."

"Am I not dressed now? What is wrong with this?" She plucked at the shirt with her fingers. I felt heat enter my cheeks, as the motion pulled the neckline down still further. *It isn't her fault. She doesn't understand, and you're being childish.*

"There isn't anything wrong with it..." *Stupid. That's not what you mean.* "Rather, there wouldn't be anything wrong if we were just staying home all the time. But we can't do that. It's not good for either of us. You've got a lot of catching up to do if you want to fit in." I felt the answer was reasonable, even if I was avoiding the fact that we were probably in danger if we stuck around anywhere for very long.

"Anyway, that isn't something you could wear around other people. It isn't much better than not wearing anything."

"Why is that such a problem? What are all these clothes *for*?" She repeated.

Clearly just answering for what was the immediate concerns wasn't going to cut it.

"Clothes protect you. Both from the weather, and from bad people. It is rather complicated and will take a lot of time to explain. Best thing to focus on is that fact that they *are* needed. Okay?"

She nodded, obviously unsatisfied with my answer. Again, I looked her up and down, thinking of what we could do for more appropriate clothing.

I turned back to the shoe rack, thinking furiously. After a careful inspection I noticed that there were a pair of shoes one and a half sizes smaller than the others. Judging from the age, I guessed they must have been Mom's from when she was much younger. Why she kept them I had no idea, but perhaps they would fit Sobely, or at least stay on her feet long enough to walk to the store. Picking them up, I felt a spark of inspiration.

I turned to Sobely.

"I think I have an idea. It may look a little odd, but I think it would get us to the store all right." I said, taking her hand. I led her up a set of narrow stairs into the attic. One corner of the stuffy room held an old steamer trunk, which was stuffed full of older clothing. These had all belonged to my grandmother. Though she had died long before I was born, I had seen pictures of her. She was a smaller woman. And she liked to wear dresses.

Leaving Sobely to stand in the stairwell, I opened the trunk and rummaged through it. Thankfully it did not take very long to find something that would be suitable for Sobely to wear. Though it would need to be washed to be rid of its mustiness, the dark green velvet dress would go with well her eyes. Pinned to the fabric was a ribbon sash to cinch the waist. Even if it was still too big, it would be a better fit than what Mom had.

My streak of good fortune seemed to hold, as I discovered a bag full of the scarves of the type that ladies used to wrap around their head. Silk, cotton, even flannel. These I removed from the trunk as well, feeling a surge of satisfaction that at least one of our problems had a solution.

When I shut the trunk, and bounced the bag of scarves against my thigh, I felt the hard edge of something within the bag. Further exploration of its contents revealed a pair of beautifully preserved sunglasses, of the style movie stars wore. Grandma certainly seemed to dress with some class.

Next, I led Sobely down the stairs, then down the next flight, and then finally down a third, into the basement. The dress and scarves went into the washing machine, and I stood for a moment just feeling proud of my cleverness. Soon enough she would have proper clothing to wear.

Sobely drew close to me, watching the washer spin with rapturous wonder. It was then that I noticed a low growling noise coming from her stomach. Once again, I felt a like an idiot. *Who knows when she last ate? She probably doesn't even realize what that slight pain in her belly even means. And here you are feeling self-satisfied that you'll be able to get her into a dress that was probably sewn by hand sometime during the Vietnam war.*

"Come on, I think we should go and find you something to eat. Sounds like your tummy wants some food." I took her hand once again and led her back up the stairs, into the dining room.

"You should probably sit here while I fix you something to eat." I gestured to a chair, and then retreated into the kitchen.

The meager contents of the fridge reminded me of just how often Mom and I ate out. I couldn't even remember the last home cooked meal either of us had made. All that was on hand to feed Sobely were a couple pre-made burritos and various condiments. Briefly I considered making the grocery store one of the stops we would make today.

However, I didn't think we would be around for very long. The more the problem festered in the back of my mind, the more I knew that we would be taking off sooner rather than later. If she had been sprung from some captor, that captor would come looking. Judging from the cruelty shown to her, they wouldn't be too happy with anyone that got in their way. The woman's warning to run at the first sign of trouble was sound advice, only...

We weren't likely to have any warning.

Shaking the heavy thoughts from my head for the moment, I placed the two burritos in the microwave and heated them up. It wasn't much, but at least the expiration date claimed they were still edible.

She looked at the burrito. Her nose worked delicately, no doubt taking in the smell of it. One hand carefully reached out and poked at the steaming tortilla-covered junk food. Then she sat back and looked at me expectantly. Granted, it didn't look all that appetizing to me, either. I knew they were actually pretty good, though. Maybe all we had was junk food in the fridge, but we also didn't scrimp on things. So, it was flavorful junk food, and was at least somewhat less likely to give you heart disease if you decided you were going to live off of them long term.

"What is this?" She asked.

"Oh. It's a burrito. Food. You eat it."

ET phone home...

"Umm." Her face scrunched slightly. "And what should I do with it?"

Only then did it dawn on me. She might know how to speak. She didn't necessarily have to know what all the words meant. My English teacher in high school was fond of saying that most of the time, language was entirely dependent upon context. To her, having no memory of ever eating a meal before, the words 'eat' and 'food' meant little.

"Pick it up." I instructed, picking up my own. Carefully, she lifted hers off the plate, then looked back at me, waiting the next instruction. I was really hoping she wouldn't mind the taste.

"Good. Now, go ahead and put one end in your mouth. Not too much of it, mind you." I pantomimed the motion, so I wouldn't be talking with my mouth full.

That was the magic trick. Once she had put a corner of the burrito into her mouth, natural instinct took over. She bit down, started chewing automatically. Her eyes shut as she experienced the sensation and flavors. Her head even tilted backward slightly as if in pleasure. After that first taste, she wasted no time tearing into the burrito, tearing off big wolfish bites. If she hadn't been savoring every gooey bit of it, I might have worried she would choke on it. I was glad that I hadn't cooked them quite as hot as I normally would, as she would have doubtless burnt herself.

Sitting beside her, it occurred to me that this was the first time since Dad had died that more than one person sat at the table. Unbidden, the memory of the last meal I shared with Dad there began to play in my mind...

All of a sudden, I didn't feel very hungry. I plopped my burrito onto her plate and leaned back in my chair to watch her eat.

I found it oddly satisfying. The words to a song my father used to sing came to me then. *There's nothing quite like feeding a hungry soul.*

The two burritos quickly disappeared from her plate, and I wondered again how long it had been since she had eaten. After she finished chewing her last bites, she looked up at me suddenly, as if realizing that I was still there.

"What do we do now?"

"I reckon we get you dressed now. Then we have to get down to the store and buy you some of the other things you'll need." I replied, standing up and taking her hand in mine. She stood, and as we moved towards the hall she tripped on the leg of the chair.

I felt myself twist without conscious thought and caught her in my arms. Something like a jolt travelled through my skin at the impact, and I found myself stifling a gasp of shock. I experienced a flurry of emotions, with no order to them. That simple act had made me aware of just how much my world had changed in so short a time. I liked having her there, pressed against me. She was warm, and she was soft and most importantly, I knew that I wasn't *just* falling for her.

To fall would have meant starting from a point that I could fall from. But that wasn't the case at all. She had filled my dreams just as she now filled my arms, and I was *already* hers. It seemed a tad ridiculous – after all, I hardly even knew her.

But on the other hand, she hardly knew herself.

Conscious of the fact that she was staring at me, I cleared my throat.

"Are you okay?" I asked.

"Yes. I believe I am. Your arms feel very nice. Did you know that?" Her smile was warm, her lips as tempting as a flower to a bee.

"I do now." I replied, shaking the thought. "Come on. Let's go get that dress dry so we can get out of here, shall we?"

"If you say so." She answered.

After waiting for the dryer to complete its cycle, we then set about the task of getting the clothing on her. When I handed it to her, she set it down and started to remove the T-Shirt she had been wearing. Quickly I stopped her, deciding to try again to teach her the importance of modesty.

"I want you to go into that room over there to change." I said, indicating the bathroom tucked into the corner of the basement.

"Why? What is wrong with putting it on right here?" She asked.

"Well, I am here. You should dress in private, where no one can watch you." I said, taking deep breaths.

"I do not understand. You... do not want to watch me put clothes on?" Her brow was again wrinkled in confusion. While she was frustrated, I found the expression to be adorable. I also knew that I would likely be seeing it quite a lot.

"That is not quite what I meant. It isn't that I wouldn't *want* to watch you get dressed, but that I *shouldn't* watch you dress. It is... wrong." I answered, struggling.

"Am I... horrible to look at? Is that why you keep looking away from me? Is that why you want to cover me with all these clothes?" I could hear fear in her voice. She was afraid I found her ugly.

Which would be something akin to looking at the Grand Canyon and comparing it to a mud puddle.

"That isn't it either. You notice that I am wearing clothes, right?" I said, painfully aware that I had slept in these clothes. The nightmares had really messed with my sleeping patterns.

"Yes. Though, I do not know why. I do not think you are unattractive." She said, her innocence making the compliment into a simple statement of fact.

"Well, clothes aren't used just to make a person more attractive, or to cover up ugliness. They also protect you, both from weather and from other people." I knew I was probably red in the face, but bravely pushed on.

"Clothes protect you from people? I still do not understand. Would I be harmed if you saw me without clothes? You have already seen me naked."

"I told you, I will never hurt you. But seeing someone naked can cause some people to do bad things. It is hard to explain, and it doesn't even make sense to *me,* but it is important. Please believe me." I begged, hoping she would let the issue drop for now.

"If you will not harm me, then what is the harm if *you* want to see what I am under the clothes?" Her question burned a furrow through my mind, and defied easy answers. Not only that, it hinted at the possibility that she was also dealing with her own confusing desires.

"I... it isn't simple. What I would like, and what is proper aren't the same thing. I find you to be lovely, and part of me, most of me in fact, longs for nothing more than to gaze upon every bare inch of you. But that isn't right. It..." I ran out of steam, seeing nothing but confusion on her face.

"So... because you want to see me without clothes, I should not undress in front of you?" I was stunned at her conclusion. It was so close to what I had been trying to say, I felt a glimmer of hope. Maybe it wouldn't be that hard to teach her how to fit in.

Wait until you try to explain why she needs to wrap a piece of cloth around her head.

Well, she was still very attractive. People would notice her, even if we hid her more 'unique' attributes.

Sigh.

"That is very nearly it. Let's just leave it at the fact that you should dress in private." I said, relieved.

"I do not really know what you are talking about, but I will try to... obey..." Her face went blank, and her words became monotone, "I promise I will be good. Please..." She shook her head, the spell broken. Shame again made my face burn. For a moment, I had glimpsed what she had been, what she had been reduced to. Her confusion had manifested as fear of what I might do if she did not do as I say.

I felt like such a fool, making a big deal out of nothing. What did it matter if she dressed herself? What right did I have to expect her to obey without question?

She seemed to miss the pain on my face as she picked up the dress and took it into the bathroom, shutting the door behind her. In the silence that followed, I wondered how I was going to do this. I was going to pieces just trying to get her into some clothes. What would I do if some *real* trouble cropped up?

And when the door opened again minutes later, I realized that teaching her to dress was far more important right now than teaching her modesty. The dress was inside out except for one sleeve, which her arm missed entirely. This pulled the neckline down diagonally and left her right breast completely exposed.

This would be a long day.

"You know what? Never mind what I was talking about before. Let's just focus on teaching you *how* to wear clothes for the time being." I said, trying to smile cheerfully.

"Okay. I am sure that this is not on right. It feels way too tight." She said. With a bit of difficulty, I helped her out of the dress and deftly turned it right-side out. Then I pulled the thin fabric back over her head, guiding her arms to where they were supposed to go.

No matter how you slice it, hormones are hard to control. As I worked my hands under the dress to get it settled on her slight frame, I could feel the skin on my face grow warm as it reddened with a blush. Despite her vulnerability, the close contact was *still* having an effect on me. And if I were going to be perfectly honest with myself, her openness only seemed to enhance that effect.

Standing behind her as I tied the ribbon around her waist, her neck seemed inviting. Idly I felt some sympathy for a vampire. It was easy to see the temptation of an exposed neck, skin so pale and soft. Her clavicle seemed to exert a force that drew my lips towards it.

Abruptly I broke off my motion, and quickly completed the bow I had been laboring on. Sobely remained unaware of the danger she'd been in, though I now burned even hotter with shame. *Get it together, Tim. You aren't that kind of person.*

With a flash of insight, I knew that her openness and vulnerability was going to make her a target. I was going to have to keep a close eye on her. If I could feel such a strong temptation, I could only imagine what someone with fewer morals might attempt.

"All done. Why don't you turn around so I can get a good look at you?" I gasped, oddly out of breath.

Hard work tying bows.

She turned, and I stepped back. For several moments I was speechless. As I thought it would, the green dress made her jade eyes pop. The thin fabric contrasted sharply with her pale skin, making it seem to glow. In a single word, she was stunning, even if the fashion was a little dated.

The whole morning I had made an effort to keep myself from just looking at her, but now that I did...

"Is it still wrong?" She asked, her lips trembling invitingly.

"Not at all. You are very pretty. That dress suits you." My sentences came out in short bursts. For the first time in my life I understood what poets meant by breathtaking.

"Oh," She looked down at herself. "I cannot really tell what I look like."

Gently I took her hand and led her back into the little bathroom. I pulled the sheet from the little-used mirror and turned her around to face her reflection.

"That is you. Right beside me, where you will always be. I don't exactly know why you were brought here, but I can tell just by looking at you that you must be very precious indeed. With even a simple dress, you look just like a princess. Someone has gone to great lengths to get you to me, to get you to safety. While I don't know who would want to harm you, I do know that they are going to have a hard time getting past me."

Sobely reached her hand out to touch the mirror. Her jaw went slack as she felt the wonder of being able to see herself. Something that most people take for granted, Sobely had no mental image of who she was. Being able to put a face on herself seemed to settle her body tremors. As if that single act shot a dose of self-confidence into her.

"I see you beside me, and that is all I care about. I do not know who I was, but I do know that it does not matter, either. Someone threw me away, Tim. I just want to live my life." She grabbed my arm.

"And I want to live it with you."

03

Having arrived at the local boutique-style clothing store arm-in-arm with Sobely, the true task before me proved to be daunting. There was no way around it – she would need her own clothes. Unfortunately, I hadn't the foggiest notion of what sizes she would be able to wear. The current summer blowout sale also brought to mind another problem I hadn't even given any thought to yet.

While I was pretty sure I could figure out her pants size, which in turn would assist in choosing the right size for the panties, one look at the tag attached to a sporty-looking bra made it abundantly clear that selecting the correct one was another matter entirely. Trying to read the tag was like trying to decipher some secret message – only I didn't have a decoder ring.

Somehow, I doubted they would allow me to accompany her into the fitting room with an armload of different sizes.

Apparently standing in the middle of an aisle looking completely confused was an excellent way to attract attention. A smartly dressed saleswoman soon approached, a smile firmly fixed upon her face. The name on the badge she wore was "Cindy" and while her smile was somewhat reassuring, somehow it seemed as if it showed too many teeth.

"Can I help you?" She asked, making eye contact, rather than the typical once-over I usually experienced. Considering the poor fit of Sobely's dress, I read sincerity in the saleswoman's voice, rather than instant judgment.

"I hope so." I answered reflexively. It was a little late to coach Sobely on some kind of cover story.

"I need clothes of my own to wear." Sobely offered shyly, tucking her small frame in close to me.

The saleswoman's smile widened, losing the pasted-on toothiness and making her seem far more friendly than she had been just moments before.

"Well, we have a wide selection of clothes in all sizes! I'm sure we can find something lovely for you to wear!"

"Umm... we don't really know what her sizes are..."

At this statement, the woman's expression tuned quizzical, and her eyes began to blink rapidly.

"Beg your pardon?"

"We don't know her sizes. What size clothing she would wear. It's... complicated."

"I don't have any memories." Sobely chimed in.

I guess is isn't really that *complicated...*

"Uh-huh. Is this some kind of joke?" Cindy asked, annoyed.

"Not at all. If you could just help us figure out what size clothing she needs, we will take it from there. I promise. This is far too awkward to be funny."

Maybe it was the sincerity in my voice, or the open expression on Sobely's face, but Cindy's smile shifted again, subtlety. Now it was fully genuine, and earnest. Sympathetic.

"Well, I suppose it isn't like this something outside my realm of expertise. Would sure make for an interesting story to tell the other girls, later. Right this way." The saleswoman gestured towards the fitting area.

I took Sobely's hand in mine and we followed the lady to the kiosk placed just to the side of the hallway that led to the fitting rooms. From a drawer she retrieved a roll of measuring tape and a pad of paper.

"Keep the hat and sunglasses on, alright?" I whispered to Sobely. While her hat was nothing but a large silk scarf tied over the back of her head, it was doing an adequate job of hiding her ears from view. Of course, I had totally forgotten to explain to her exactly why she was required to wear it. She looked at me with a questioning look, but Cindy started talking again.

"Reminds me of a wedding party I helped once. One of the bridesmaids argued for an hour that the clothing was fitted wrong. It wasn't until I showed her the measurement on the tape that she shut up about it. Even then she insisted on buying a dress a size too small for her. In your case…" She looked over Sobely again. 'We may find that our selection is a bit limited. You are such a tiny little thing!"

"Is that bad?" Sobely asked. Cindy blinked a few times in astonishment, and then burst into laughter.

"Heaven's no! Honey, there are girls that would *kill* for your dainty figure."

At this proclamation, Sobely again tucked herself in close to my side.

"Why would they kill? Who would they kill?" Her voice was wavering, meek. I put a comforting arm around her shoulder, even as Cindy broke into a fresh peal of laughter. Upon noticing the visible tremble of Sobely's body, though, she had the sense to stop.

"I'm sorry. It's just an expression. It just means that other girls would be envious of you. You're quite lovely, truly. Now if you will step over here, I will run just this tape around and we'll sort out your sizes in a jiffy."

Hesitantly, Sobely stepped forward and allowed herself to be led into one of the dressing rooms. Like a sentinel of old, I crossed my arms and leaned against the wall. A perfect position to both watch the store for trouble and listen to what was going on behind the curtain.

"Hmm. I think this will be easier if you get out of that dress. Humph! You weren't kidding about needing clothes! Have you been walking around this whole time without underwear? My goodness!"

I cringed a bit at that.

"Underwear?" Sobely questioned.

"Yeah. You really must have amnesia… I imagine the young man was probably too embarrassed to… Oh my God! Who did this to you?"

"Umm… I don't know… is this how I look?"

I recalled that most dressing rooms had a three-sided mirror setup, so the occupants could check the "fit" from multiple angles. Sobely would be able to clearly see her whole body...

"Did that man do this to you?" Cindy asked, her voice rising in volume.

"Tim? No! He would never hurt me." Sobely's voice was fierce.

"How can you be so sure? Maybe he beat you up, and that's why... Hey!"

Sobely exited through the curtain, completely naked, and fairly threw herself at me. Trembling like a leaf caught in the wind. The only other person within eyesight was a female shopper, and her jaw dropped open in surprise.

Gently I lifted Sobely and carried her back into the dressing room, away from prying eyes. Cindy stood there frozen in shock – and after catching sight of the expression on my face, perhaps just a little fear.

"She thinks you hurt me." Sobely whispered.

For a long moment I pierced the saleswoman with a thundering gaze. The room went quiet as a grave. It even seemed as if the temperature dropped by degrees in the silence. Despite this chilling sensation, beads of sweat appeared on Cindy's brow.

"Sobely has been through a lot of abuse, Ma'am, but it wasn't done by my hand. I am her sworn protector. Her guardian. It is my job to keep her away from the people that hurt her. To keep her away from *anyone* that would hurt her. What is *your* job?"

I did not yell at the woman. In fact, my voice was barely above a whisper. My tone was even. My eyes never left Cindy's.

And she was terrified.

She gulped air in like someone saved from drowning and tried to regain her composure.

"I.... I'm sorry." She bowed, "I was out of line. I'd never seen such scarring before. Please... forgive my rudeness." She broke eye contact, unable to maintain it any longer.

"I'm inclined to. Can you please just do your job?" I let some of the steel out of my voice and set Sobely down.

"Of course! Right away, sir!"

Cindy took the measurements without further comment; the only sounds were the gentle rasp of vinyl tape on bare skin and the scratchy sound of a Bic on a yellow notepad.

When she finished, I helped Sobely back into the dress, and took the sheet of paper Cindy offered.

"I am sorry I over-reacted earlier, sir. I will leave you two alone now." Cindy said, bowing again sharply before fleeing the small room.

I glanced at the sheet briefly. The saleslady had written two columns on the page. The left-hand column seemed to be the actual measurement in inches, while the right side contained what the equivalent was in clothing sizes. I couldn't see how one produced the other, but I could plainly see that in both cases, the numbers were small.

"Hmm." Scrawled helpfully at the bottom of the page were the words 'Try the Petite Miss section.'

"What do those mean?" Sobely asked, pointing a finger at the marks on the pages. *I guess that answers the question of whether or not she can read.* I noticed that the particular line her finger rested upon was the one labeled 'BUST.' Though I knew it was only a coincidence, I still felt my cheeks grow warm. *And a moment ago you were all fire and steel...*

"These are numbers. They will match the tags on the clothing. These numbers indicate what size clothing would fit you best." I explained.

"Oh... Tim?" Her voice grew soft.

"Yes?"

"Are the marks on my back... are they why I have to wear all these clothes? Do you think... Do you think they are hideous?" Her eyes glistened, lips trembling, and I was at a total loss for words. The urge to kiss those lips, to confront her fears with tenderness... it was nearly overwhelming. She had suffered, and even though they had erased the memory of what they had done, the blank slate still bore traces of what once was.

"Sobely..." I began, still unsure of that to say. I drew her in close, pulled her into a tight hug while searching for the right answer in my mind. But nothing came. All I had was the way I felt. And I didn't think she was ready for that yet.

"Sobely... you are very special to me. I know we've only just met... but I cannot... Somebody *did* hurt you badly. They tore into you for who knows how long – that is why you bear so many scars. But they do not lessen you. They are nothing to ever feel ashamed of. Do you know why?"

"I don't know *anything.* Why?" Her voice was a whisper.

"These scars mean that someone tried their best to break you down. And they failed. You are alive. You are here, with me. You should not feel shame, but triumph, because all those scars prove is that someone failed. I do not know why it is you were sent to me. But I do know that there isn't a person in this whole world that could ever take you away."

"But I am nothing. Why would you care about something that is nothing?"

"You are everything to me."

Once I showed Sobely what to look for, I decided to let her pick out her own clothing. She browsed with uncertainty, flipping through the racks delicately. When she would find something she liked, she would bring it to me. I would smile at each selection and add it to the pile slowly growing in the basket. A pattern soon emerged – nearly everything she picked was adorned with flowers. Mostly roses, but with the occasional lily or moondrop. Color-wise, much of the clothing she chose was black.

After we had acquired what I deemed to be a decent amount of shirts and pants – with a few pair of shorts and skirts thrown in to prepare for the coming summer – it was clear that I could stall no longer. It was time to push the half-laden cart into the section labeled 'delicates.' I guided her across the aisle, unsure of how I was going to explain the necessity.

"Now we need to pick out some underwear you like."

"Underwear?" She wrinkled her nose. "More clothes?"

For some reason the expression on her face made me chuckle.

"You know, you aren't like other girls."

She tilted her head, puzzled.

"Normally if a guy took a girl out shopping for clothes, with no limit on how much to spend, the girl would disappear with the cart for a few hours. With you…"

"I guess I just don't understand the appeal."

A girl that would choose to be a nudist out of a sheer lack *of vanity.*

Many guys would jump at the situation. After all, the easiest way through would be to pick out everything myself. To be fair to her, I would then be obligated to at least imagine how each piece would look on her. Dressing her to suit my tastes would actually be an acceptable solution to our unique situation.

Morally… the best thing for her would be to nurture her self-identity. To that end, shopping for clothes was a perfect exercise. After all, they say it's the clothes that make the man, or in this case, woman. So far, it seemed as if she wasn't too attracted to anything wild or crazy. I imagined the dark colors were less confusing to her. Her preference for roses was likely something left over in the recesses of her mind.

The trick now, would be in convincing her that underwear was necessary.

I held up a pair of black jeans. The right leg of which was covered in a cascading pattern of embroidered flowers.

"These are very beautiful." I began.

"I like the… I don't know the word. But I like them." She reached out and traced the embroidery with a finger.

"They are flowers. In particular, this kind of flower is called a rose." I explained, momentarily side-tracked.

"They are pretty." She replied, entranced.

"Well, can you feel how the material is a bit rough?"

"Yes."

"These *jeans* will look great on you. They were made to accent your figure. Which means they will fit a bit snugly."

I dropped the jeans back into the basket, and next pulled up a shirt. An embroidered vine traced in a spiral around the waist, terminating with a spread of blood-red roses that would cover the right breast.

"This is very nice. But it places a lot of rough thread over an area of your body that is very sensitive."

"Oh. Should I pick something else?"

"There is no need. There is a possibility that this shirt, and those jeans could cause some discomfort. As you move, the fabric will also move, but differently as it is pulled in different directions. This can cause blisters and chafing." I was using the extreme case, but I felt it was the easiest explanation to go with.

"I'm not sure what those are. But they sound bad."

"Underwear is designed to prevent that problem. It provides a buffer over your sensitive spots. It fits in a way that is snug to those areas, moving *with* the skin rather than against it."

"Oh. Why don't they just make all the clothes like that?" And image of Sobely in a tight-fitting cat-suit threatened to flit across my mind's eye, but I quashed the notion before it could fully form.

"Well... that sort of outfit wouldn't really be much better than just going naked." I answered.

"So... it would be a bad idea then?" Sobely looked at me with an expression of pure trust. She would believe anything I told her.

"It would be a bad idea to wear it in public, at any rate."

"Hmm." She turned to survey her choices. I had successfully guided us to the section marked for her size. Being a more upscale boutique, they did not stock anything that was plain or ordinary. I found it a bit hard to concentrate or even breath looking at some of the choices on display, my mind automatically picturing how each set might look on her.

Some of the pieces really lived up to the term 'delicate.'

"Well, they seem pretty. What should I get?" She turned back to me.

"Umm." I cleared my throat. "This is the size bra you need..." I pointed the symbols out to her. She studied them intently, being a longer stringer of characters than those for her shirts and pants.

"But what should I choose?" She looked me in the eyes again.

The big temptation was to run through finding the most conservative things on display and quickly remove myself from this part of the store. A smaller temptation was to grab more revealing pieces and then remove myself from this part of the store. However, neither temptation won out.

"Pick whatever you like. I would suggest you go for pieces made of softer materials, but other than that... it is truly up to you to choose. You will be wearing it, after all." I only stammered a little, my voice shaking only slightly when my eyes caught sight of a lacy piece that I was pretty sure wasn't designed with modesty in mind.

"Oh." Sobely turned again. Apparently, the piece that had caught my gaze found hers as well, because she walked straight towards it.

"This is pretty." She took it from the rack. "Hmm." She stared at the tag intensely. Judging from the soft smile on her lips, the symbols were a match. At least this piece wasn't black, instead an angelic shade of white that would be barely discernable from her skin...

For some reason, I found breathing to be difficult for a few minutes, and it seemed as if they had cranked the heat on in the store, despite it being the middle of May.

Through the next fifteen minutes, Sobely browsed the racks, returning every so often to deposit her selections in the cart. I told her to be sure and pick out plenty and did my best to not gawk at every piece that fell into the basket.

Sobely seemed to be utterly fascinated by flowers. By the time she had finished searching out treasures, it seemed as if she had found every design that included them. Lace, embroidery, patterns... flowers represented in every conceivable way. The second common theme, again, was the color black. I wondered why it was she seemed to shy away from anything that was bright. Why so few choices lightened the color spectrum of her new wardrobe. To peek into the cart was like staring into a dark void into which a vast array of blooms had been thrown.

04

"Why is it you do not look at me?"

"Umm…" *I thought we had already covered this subject.*

"I know why you *should not,* but it seems like this would be easier if you looked at what your hands were doing." At this comment, I looked down and realized that if I continued to hook the bra together in the manner I was working, it would pretty much defeat the purpose of wearing one.

"My goodness! I am so sorry. That must feel terribly uncomfortable. I'll fix it straight away." I loosened the garment, pulled it off, and straightened the twists in the delicate fabric. My face burned with shame. Again

Society had done a splendid job instilling me with the deep belief that any contact with someone of the opposite gender was automatically something dirty and wrong. In truth? I was just being a complete idiot. A sheep blindly following society's rules in a situation that clearly didn't warrant them.

Time then, Tim, to grow up.

Feeling myself become composed at last, and finally able to handle her unabashed nakedness, I started over.

"How about we start with your lower half? You're probably starting to feel a bit chilled. It might take a bit to figure this thing out." I said, holding the freshly untangled bra aloft.

"Alright." Sobely nodded, crossing her arms as a slight shiver roved over her flesh, raising goose-bumps in her pale skin.

I picked up the pair of panties from where we had set them on the bench and noted that it did indeed actually match the top piece of lingerie quite well. I felt a slight sense of relief that her tastes in clothing meant that there would be some ease in the coordination of her outfits. It would make things much easier later on. I carefully removed the price tag so as not to damage the fabric. As I helped her step into the black undergarment, I could not help but appreciate just how smooth her frail-looking legs were. Perhaps the fingertip I rested on her skin as we pulled the fabric into place was unnecessary, but it could do no harm.

Other than the disturbing pattern of scars at her ankles, her skin was flawless. The muscles beneath felt like steel wrapped in silk. Though she had seemed unused to exercise, she was also a lot stronger than she appeared. If she had been bound in place, her muscles should have waned in strength. It made sense that she would possess little stamina.

The panties hid the very bottom of some of her oldest scars, and if I were to judge correctly, the lashings had been administered over the course of several years. They seemed as faded as the scar on my leg where an errant tree branch had once pierced it after a slip from a tree, and that accident had happened when I was nine.

The fabric was of a high thread count cotton. The fine tracery of needlepoint roses justified the price listed on the tag. I would have commended the designer on their fine work of drawing the eye right to the pleasing places they wished it to go.

It did not seem too far-fetched to imagine that her beauty might also have been by design rather than natural providence. *Chosen perhaps. Not* made, *surely. Who could accomplish such a thing?*

"I like it when you look at me, Tim. It... it makes me feel warm. I think I was cold for a very long time. I do not think anyone has ever looked at me the way you do."

Her voice was quiet as I picked up the pair of jeans. It was the pair from before, so heavily embroidered by bloody red roses. When I glanced up, her near-translucent skin was tinged red. The full implication of her statement hit me then.

Is it possible that she might feel for me what I feel for her?
Could she be in love with *me?*
She feared my rejection.
Has complete trust in me.

When I dreamt of her, did she also dream of me?

I chose my words carefully as I helped her into the pair of jeans, showing her how the long row of buttons worked.

"Sobely I... I am so very sorry." I slipped the straps of the confounded bra up her arms, and then gently spun her around so I could face the complex-seeming clasp.

"For what?" I spun her again to make sure the thing fit properly. My unpracticed eye judged that the clerk's estimation must have been correct.

"I've been an idiot." I picked up the blouse, a dark charcoal button-up of something soft, patterned into the dark fabric was an even darker array of even more roses.

"What does that mean?" She asked. I helped her slip the shirt on, and then stood back to survey my work.

For a long moment, I was unable to answer, unable to even breath, having been rendered so by the vision before me. Everything had come together to present a Goddess to the world. *Brush that hair out a bit...*

"The way we met was unusual. The sudden challenge you represent made me feel off-balance. Your extraordinary beauty and being in such close proximity to it; I just wasn't prepared for you. This sort of situation doesn't happen to people very often."

"Oh." Was her reply, uncomprehending, but also distracted by trying to decipher the purpose of the buttons on her blouse. I stepped in close to her to help.

"The thing is – you pop this bit through the hole in the opposite side – The thing is: I am madly in love with you."
Sobely slumped, making herself very small.

"You are? Why?" She sounded so vulnerable, and her voice wavered. As if she were standing on a precipice, waiting for the wind to do what she could not. I finished the last button, and cupped her chin in my hand, tilting it upward so I could stare directly into her eyes. Those wondrous green globes, strange, yet so very beautiful. Her too-large irises were flecked through with so many shades of green, to stare too deeply was to face the danger of losing oneself within them. They brimmed with tears now. Rose petal lips trembled. I had no more words for her. Instead I leaned in.

Her arms raised, clutching my shirt as our lips met, as if afraid I would pull away from her. I could taste the salt of her tears on my tongue as they spilled from her closed eyes. Time slowed to a standstill – the only sound I could hear was her heartbeat. For the eternal moment of that kiss, it was as if nothing else in the world existed. With futures now uncertain, our hearts beat as one.

Stepping out into the bright afternoon sun, I realized that we had spent a long time inside the brick building. Time seemed to pass differently now, as if it could be ignored altogether.

"Where do we go now?" She asked.

"Well, you need some other basic stuff. The best place to find everything would be Wal-Mart, so I guess we go there." I hoped that it wasn't too crowded today.

We walked in comfortable silence to the enormous blue and white building. Luckily for us, the parking lot was nearly empty. Oddly so, for a Saturday.

Inside, we browsed quickly, finding her a brush, and soaps. We got her a toothbrush and paste as well. *It should be fun to show her how to brush her teeth.* On the way to look at shoes, I also grabbed her some socks, some plain white T-shirts, and sweatpants.

"We should find you some pajamas, too." I said, half to myself.

"What are those?" She asked.

"Clothes you wear while you sleep." I answered. She made a face.

"Do people watch you when you sleep?"

"Not usually." I thought of an explanation. "But if Mom looks in on us in the middle of the night, it will be less awkward."

"Oh. I *guess* that makes sense. She should not see me naked." I turned red at her incorrect assumption. *No, more like she shouldn't see you naked, and me in the same room.* Sobely wouldn't understand that unless I explained it to her. Even if I *were* ready for such a conversation, I sure wouldn't explain it at Wal-Mart!

We found her some soft pink flannel pajamas and headed into the shoe section. *First, we'll need to know her size.* I led her to the sizing chart on the floor, glad Wal-Mart thought there were adults that needed one. *Glad that Wal-Mart is the number one shopping destination for rednecks everywhere.*

"Ok, take off a shoe, and place the back of your foot on this line." I indicated the heel line. She complied, and her toes just barely reached the six-and-a-half mark. *She does have small feet.* I showed her the number to look for and let her browse on her own.

Moments later, Sobely came back, looking a little dejected. Her hands were empty.

"They only have three different shoes in my size, and I do not really like them. I can choose some if I have to though." She said.

"No, that's all right. I should have known better than to try to find decent shoes at a Wal-Mart. We'll just have to stop at a shoe store before we eat. Let's go pay for our things, and we'll be on our way." *What was I thinking, shoe shopping at Wal-Mart. They would probably all hurt her feet anyway.*

"What does it mean to pay?" She asked as we wheeled the cart to the checkouts.

"When you go to stores, you must pay them money for the things you want." I explained.

"How do you get money? Is it abundant?"

"Not really. You usually get money in exchange for work you do."

"So you can buy clothes?"

"Yes, and other things. It is a pretty good system and has been around for a very long time." *A lot easier than carrying around a bunch of chickens, too.*

"I must be costing you too much. You should not buy me so many things." She said, indicating the laden cart.

"Don't worry about that. When my Dad died, he left me with his bank accounts. I have plenty of money to spoil you with." I assured her. She blushed prettily, and then asked another question.

"So you have a lot of money?"

"Yes, but I'm not much of a big spender. I doubt Mom even knows how much Dad left to me. So don't worry about the price of anything you want, it really isn't a problem."

"Alright. If you are sure..."

We went through the line, and I paid cash for the purchases, showing Sobely how stuffed my wallet was. The cashier was not impressed. I gave the unhappy woman a big grin and grabbed our new bags. Sobely and I then left Wal-Mart, only to enter the shoe store next door.

Once inside, Sobely went straight to the shoes in her size and began to browse. I sat on a bench, waiting to see what she would choose, hoping there was something here that she liked. The clerk had the sense not to pester.

Naturally, it did not take her long to come back with her choice. In her hands was a shoebox containing shoes made of soft black leather. Deep red embroidered roses flowed over them, the detail exquisite. There was no heel, and they laced up pretty high. The brand name imprinted on the sole gave me confidence that this store only carried the best. High quality build, expensive, and completely worth it.

The shoes would go with everything else she had picked earlier, though it was little surprise she would pick this particular pair over any other they had in stock.

She sat on the bench beside me and started to pull on a shoe. I put my hand on hers to stop her. The new shoes weren't laced, and she had no socks on. I picked them up from the floor, and laced them for her, and then reached into a Wal-Mart bag for a pair of socks.

Then I knelt in front of her. *She can learn to tie them later.*

"Let me have your foot." I said. She raised one foot and placed it in my palm. I started to slip a sock on her, when the foot shook. Giggles sounded from her pretty head. Unable to resist the temptation, I traced a finger lightly under her foot, causing it to jerk from my hand, and then a gale of the heavenly laughter escaped her throat.

The shoe store clerk just rolled her eyes and turned away.

Serious now, I put her socks on, and carefully helped her into the shoes. I tied them securely for her, aware of her eyes watching me work. I was secretly hoping she wouldn't figure it out too quickly.

"How is that?"

"They feel a lot better than your Mom's shoes." She replied, flexing her foot.

"These may be a little uncomfortable for a bit. But once you wear them a while, they will feel better. Come on. Let's go eat now."

With all the bags weighing down my arms, I had to be content with her placing her hand into the crook of my elbow. A distinct kind of torture, now that I *had* other options.

Realizing how tired she must have felt, I chose a restaurant that was closer to home. The good old universal McDonalds. Inside the red-and-yellow building, I set our bags at a table, and let her sit while I ordered for us.

When I set the burger in front of her, her nostrils flared at the smell and she immediately scooped it up. I was I glad had thought to remove the wrapper for her, since she practically inhaled it. Finishing it faster than I could even believe. I was quick to finish my own, but she was already half-finished her soft drink when I was done. She munched a few fries and then sat back in her seat.

"Do we have to eat this all here, or can we take it with us?"

"No, we can go. Let me dump the fries together." I said. I dumped the two boxes into the bag and gave her my soda to drink while I collected our things. By the time I had it all in hand, the second drink was gone, and she was happily munching fries at a more reasonable pace as we headed outside, and on to home.

"Your bed is ready. Sit down, and I will help you with your shoes. Then you can change into your new pajamas and go to sleep." She sat, and I knelt. Off came the shoes, and then the socks. I inspected between each of her delicate toes, gently removing the lint. Sobely looked at me strangely.

"Why are you looking at my feet? Is there something wrong with them?" She asked.

"Nope, nothing wrong. This lint has to be removed or it will turn into fungus, and fungus can hurt your feet. I am just making sure that nothing will hurt you. That's in my job description." I joked.

"Oh. That is good then, because I like it when you touch my feet like that. It feels really nice. Can I... go to sleep now?"

"Almost. Let me get your pajamas out for you, let you can change into them and then you can go to sleep. Okay?"

"Okay." She yawned again.

I pulled the pink pajamas from the Wal-Mart bag, and pointed her to the bathroom.

While I waited, I closed the blinds on the windows, and shut the curtains tight. The light disappeared but for the glow of the lamp on the desk. I set my alarm in order to catch Mom early, and then locked the door for good measure. *How long can I keep Mom from discovering Sobely? Will it be long enough to get Sobely ready for it? Long enough to come up with an explanation that isn't as crazy as the truth?*

Sobely reappeared, looking as if she hadn't slept for a week. I noticed that the pajamas were on more or less correctly, her only error being that the buttons weren't lined up in the correct holes. I went to fix them, and she whispered,

"What are you doing? I am not wearing underwear now."

Oh. Yeah.

"The buttons aren't quite right. Put your hands over mine and follow what I do." I said, determined to teach her. She felt my hands, and I kept my eyes on her face as I lined the buttons up carefully. Turned out they were two holes off. She blushed, though whether from embarrassment from her mistake or from my gentle hands, I did not know.

Done, I spoke softly into her ear.

"Okay. Climb into bed. I will stay up for a while and watch over you. Keep you safe."

"I have never doubted that." She said. She started past me, and then stopped, a smile coming to those enchanting lips.

"What's up?" I asked, seeing a thought that was obviously pleasant form behind her green eyes. She turned to look into my face. Her ears had reddened.

And before I could blink, she was kissing me. I managed to stay upright, but only because I caught myself on the desk. My eyes closed, and my free arm hugged her close. Soon enough, we were both forced to stop to gasp for air. *Curse that mortal weakness!* I could feel a smile try to split my mouth past my ears. Truthfully, the kiss had left me more than a little bewildered. *I wonder what brought that on.* She smiled just as widely.

"There. Now I can I can sleep. In my head, a phrase had come to me. I had to act on it."

"A phrase?" I asked, still a little slow.

"Yes. I thought of the words 'Good-night kiss.' I have no idea why though. Was it wrong?" She was so quick. I had thought before that I could never feel any happier.

I was glad to be wrong.

"Well," I began carefully, "If that was something wrong, then let's not be right. Your good-night kiss felt pretty wonderful to me."

Her smiled was cruelly ended by a huge yawn. I heard her jaw creak from the force of it, and a little wince crinkled her eyes.

"I guess I will go to sleep now." She climbed into bed, slipping under the waiting blanket. I pulled it over her, and tucked her in, kissing her quickly on the forehead, lest I get caught up in it. I sat in my desk chair to watch her sleep, turning the light down low.

Sobely couldn't seem to get comfortable. She tossed around, twisting in the blanket. I let her rustle for about twenty minutes, before asking.

"What is wrong?"

"It is these pajamas. I cannot sleep in them. They bunch up, and the buttons press into my skin. It kind of hurts. Do I *have* to wear them? It would seem that the blanket is already covering me up quite well."

She sat up, waiting for my answer. I was already in trouble up to my ears if Mom found her like *this.* If Sobely wasn't even dressed, then I might not ever be able to calm Mom down. However, Sobely had to sleep, and it was obviously impossible for her to do that with the pajamas *on.*

Then a possible solution jumped out at me. It would make it a slice better situation to be in, but I would still be walking a very thin line. I wasn't going to let anything make her uncomfortable, but I had to do my best to keep us both out of hot water.

"Let's try something else first. If it doesn't work, then you can sleep naked. Go and put on the softest underwear that you have. That would be better than no clothes, and you might be able to get comfortable then."

"Alright Tim. They did all seem so soft. I did not pick out anything that was rough. They should not wrinkle up, either. They fit me better."

She slowly got out of bed and rummaged through the bags. She found the bag she wanted, and took it into the bathroom, remembering to close the door. *I hope she can get comfortable, so she can get some sleep. I don't know why I was so nervous. I was going to sleep in this chair anyway...*

Out she came again, clad only in her new panties. The set was adorned with more roses, inviting the eye. I did not let my eyes be invited, only watched her as she slipped back into bed. Watched as she finally got comfortable and promptly fell asleep.

It did not even take her five minutes before she was writhing again.

She was murmuring, and I could feel her terror radiate across the room as she tried to escape something in her nightmare. I glanced around nervously, unsure of what to do. Then she screamed, coming awake abruptly. She sat up sharply, panting, sweat glistening on her brow. The terror I had not seen since this morning was back in full force.

I was already by her side, and she clutched at me frantically. Wailing openly now. I held her helplessly as she cried. She murmured that something was hurting her, and that a shadow was dragging her away to hurt her more. The darkness laughed, and she did not like the things the man brought from the tray...

It broke my heart.

It was worse than anything I had ever before experienced.

I needed to remain strong for her.

"What can I do, honey? How can I make it better?" I would have stopped time if she requested it. I did not know how to help her, but she did.

"Hold me. Please? I... remember darkness, and it hurt so much. No one ever held me then. No one loved me. It was only... pain." Her voice sounded broken. This time I didn't try to stop the hate that coursed through my blood. Someday I would make everyone who ever hurt her pay.

Every. Single. One of them.

"You want to feel loved? Then feel it in my arms. *I* love you. I will hold you as much as you want. Forever. Let me change into my pajamas, and I will hold you all night." *And every other night, for the rest of our lives.* She reluctantly let go, and I reluctantly got up. I quickly grabbed a pair of sweats and a T-shirt from a drawer, and went into the bathroom to change, leaving the door cracked open to listen for her. I managed to not to run back at her every sniffle.

Once changed, I scooped up all the clothes, and deposited them at the foot of the bed. Sobely had grown anxious but relaxed a little when she saw me. I smiled as warmly as I could to relax her more. I climbed in on the other side.
She pulled the blanket over us both, and then nestled into my side. Relaxing into the crook of my arm.

Strangely, I was perfectly relaxed as well. As if I had slept with her in my arms for years. She murmured her thanks before falling into a deep, untroubled sleep. I had much to think about, but...

I was very relaxed.

Sleep soon claimed me, too.

05

"Tim? Is everything alright?" A muffled voice called. I woke up so fast that the room seemed to spin for a moment. When I *could* finally read the numbers on the clock, I groaned. I had slept right through the alarm.

Sobely looked frightened.

"It's okay. Just my Mom." I whispered to her. Louder, I said, "I'm okay Mom. I was only sleeping."

I glanced around the room and felt relieved that I had remembered to lock the door. Evidence of a female occupant was everywhere. We had spent the day before inside my room. She had wanted to try on all of the clothes and had questions about every little thing her curious eyes found in the room. Except for ordering a couple large pizzas – both gone – we had closed ourselves off from the rest of the world.

The night before we had stayed up late. She munched on pizza crusts, and we talked about nothing in particular. And even though I had stamped down on 90% of my urges to kiss her, the remaining 10% still amounted to quite a lot. My head had been set to spin, and just when I thought I couldn't stand it further, she'd have a new question to interrupt with.

Just now I spied a bit of rose-embroidered black cloth, and I made a conscious effort to avoid looking at Sobely. As a matter of fact, I found myself upright, out of bed, and halfway to the door before my brain even registered fully what that bit of clothing *was.*

Which is why when I shoved myself through the door to the waiting bright sunlight and my mother, my head was down. My face the color of Kool-Aid. Not the best position to be in when preparing to lie to my mom.

"Oh! Tim? Are you feeling alright?" She asked. Inspiration struck. I wouldn't even need to lie.

"I guess I'm not quite as okay as I thought when I woke up. Everything seemed to spin, and my legs feel a bit weak." I looked up, hoping the sudden bright light of the morning sun would give my eyes an appropriate amount of watery-ness.

"Well, maybe you should come in and lie down on the couch, so I can keep an eye on you. I will call in."

"It's okay, Mom. You don't need to do that." A fresh surge of panic raced through my veins.

"Nonsense! They can get by without me for one…"

I spotted the glint of black steel in the tree line at the same time the sound of thunder deafened my ears. Something hot and wet splattered my face, my clothes, the door behind me. A sharply keening cry followed the thunder like the wail of a banshee. It felt as if I were falling, a heavy weight crushing me against the door. My hands found the doorknob, removing the obstacle that had halted my descent.

The cry was my own. The thunder started up again, this time rapidly repeating. Thuds as projectiles struck the bricks, a few even piercing the darkness of the doorway. The muzzle of an automatic weapon erupted with flame and cold fury, wielded by a sinister man dressed up like a 1930s gangster. I realized I had become drenched with the color red. The flecks of bone and brain matter stuck to the bare skin of my chest. Cooling drops dripped across my vision, creating a crimson haze in which to see the mad world through.

The top of Mom's head was gone. A faint gurgle could be heard, like the stage-whisper in some macabre play. I was still screaming wordlessly.

Instinct forced my body into motion. I pulled my mother inside the threshold, and then kicked the heavy door shut. Bullets thudded against it, failing to penetrate it. Yet it seemed as if the whole building shook under the violent assault.

I crab-crawled to the bed, leaving Mom where she lay. Her blood spread on the oak floor, an expanding lake of crimson against the dark grain. With a short yelp from Sobely, I yanked her from the bed, and then shoved her beneath it. My mind raced frantically, trying to think about what I needed to do.

For precious seconds the realization of what was happening threatened to shut me down. Completely through the sheer force of will, I managed to shove the despair down into my stomach. Shattering glass from the window polarized my emotions, and I began to formulate a possible way to escape the onslaught.

The flash of bright metal caught my eye. My mother's arm bent in an impossible angle, the elbow a shattered and bloody mess. In her hand were her keys. With the bark of gunfire growing louder – as if a second gunman had joined the first – I scrambled forward. I snatched the keys up and rolled myself under the bed to where Sobely was. I had stopped screaming. Sobely could only manage weak whimpers of terror.

"Stay close." I growled, before rolling out the opposite end. I led Sobely to the space beneath my father's hardwood desk, wanting as much dense material between her and the gunmen as possible. From our cover I yanked open the small unlocked safe on the floor under the desk, stuffing the pockets of my sweats with cash. A picked up a shirt that had somehow fallen behind the safe and passed it over to Sobely.

The thuddering gunfire grew louder yet, and the walls were starting to let in light. The brickwork was crumbling rapidly under the combined fire.

Moving like a machine, I emptied the rest of the safe into the backpack that had been on the desk. We were going to get out of here somehow, and I knew going to a bank would be a bad idea. Something told me that if we survived this, our troubles would only be just beginning.

"Stay put." I commanded, crawling forward quickly from the relative safety of the massive desk. What clothes that were in my path I stuffed into the bag. Staying low, I pulled the drawer out of the nightstand, pulling it back with me to the desk. Most of the contents I dumped into the bag, unsure of everything the drawer contained. One small box I kept out.

"Now, get to the bathroom." This I had to shout, as the gunfire intensified further. Whoever was shooting at us was advancing towards the brick building.

Sobely, to her credit, obeyed instantly. As we did a fast shuffling crawl to the bathroom, I managed to get the small box open. The wooden grip of a snub-nosed .22 revolver found a firm hold in my right hand. A glance confirmed that it was still loaded. I even managed to scoop some of the spare rounds into my pocket before discarding the box.

Once inside the bathroom I kicked the door closed. The gunfire muffled a bit.

Blood and fury pounded in my ears.

I got to my feet, and then immediately doubled over, throwing up all over the floor. The animalistic terror on Sobely's face churned my stomach further, causing me to heave a second time. Again, instinct kicked in. Instead of curling into a ball on the floor to wait for the end, I scrambled to the window and peered out cautiously. Nothing glinted in the bright sunlight, so I turned around to look Sobely over. She got the shirt on, and miraculously was unhurt. I felt a sense of relief at this. With so many rounds chewing up my room, it was a wonder that we both hadn't been reduced to hamburger.

"You need to stick very close to me. Do you understand?"

Sobely nodded, limbs shaking visibly.

"I am not going to let anything happen to you. Do you understand?"

Again, a nod.

I scooped up a towel and wiped at my face, letting it fall without a second glance. In the other room I could hear the door finally splintering apart. Finally succumbing to the gunfire. Once more I sprang into frantic instinct-guided motion.

Revolver in one hand, bag slung over my shoulder, I grabbed Sobely's arm near her shoulder and hauled her to her feet. I hit the imposing window shoulder first, shattering the safety glass into a shower of sharp confetti. Bare feet crushed against the broken pieces and slicked with blood. Yet we did not even pause in our flight. There would be time for bandages later.

Out the window, and then we were sprinting across the overgrown grass infested with thistle. Sobely kept up as we somehow made it mostly unhurt to the corner of the garage. The gunmen were in the room behind us, battering down the bathroom door. If they had still been outside, they would have easily been able to cut us down as we sprinted over the open ground.

Sliding along the building to a dusty window, I used the butt of the revolver to smash the glass, hauling Sobely over the threshold and into the dark garage. The sounds of a door being knocked off its hinges wafted from the bedroom, and then quiet.

I didn't stop moving. I popped open the back of the waiting SUV, tossing Sobely inside, followed by the bulging backpack. From a utility shelf I snatched up a large heavy duffel bag and tossed it in as well, before slamming the hatch closed and scrambling into the driver's seat.

I felt a lazy droplet of something thick drip off my chin. *I'll never be clean again.*

"Hang on!" I shouted back, somehow getting the key into the ignition without dropping it from trembling fingers. A pause – only long enough to catch a breath, and I cranked the engine over, bringing the vehicle to roaring life. I stabbed at the garage opener but did not wait. Instead, as the door began to move, I yanked the shifter into gear and stepped hard on the gas pedal.

With a jarring jolt of impact, and the screech of metal twisting apart, the big automobile freed itself from the garage. Onto the street, moving away from the carnage. In the mirror I could see four gunmen, all dressed exactly alike. All with the same hard face and glittering eyes. All four raising their antiquated Thompson sub-machine guns simultaneously.

We careened around a corner before they could open fire.

A few blocks later, I realized we were going to have to get a different car. As safe and reliable as the SUV was, *they* knew what it looked like. The plates were registered to my mother. Despite the 5-star crash safety rating and all the other little design features that made it such a safe car, to us it would be a death trap. With that in mind I began to wind my way through town. Hoping we weren't being followed somehow. Hoping that by reaching out to the few friends I had left in the city, I wasn't dooming them to the same awful fate as...

I couldn't bear to think the words, even. Regardless of the risk, what other choice did I have?

We turned onto a farm road, and I slowed so as not to kick up the gravel. I stopped the white SUV next to a row of other vehicles of many different makes and models. Looming over the scene was an old farmhouse, complete with a sagging roof and cloudy windows. The house had been the home of my best friend – his parents still lived there. I also knew that the blue Dodge truck I planned to take ran perfectly. *But if it's reported stolen, then it won't be any good to you either.*

"Sobely, I need you to go and get into that blue truck. Grab the smaller bag. Stay put and lie down – I'll only be a minute." I instructed, pointing to the vehicle in question.

"What are you going to do?" She asked, terrified.

"I'm just going to go get the keys from my friend. It won't take long." I reassured, opening my door. Sobely followed me out, clutching the backpack tightly. The cool breeze raised gooseflesh on her bare legs, her feet bloody from the glass. Though she moved swiftly, I could see her limping, too. Grabbing the duffel bag, I followed her closely, tossing the bag into the back of the truck before opening the door for her.

I ran to the door of the house, glancing around. Hoping the shadows did not conceal monsters. I knocked three times, as loud as I dared, and waited the agonizing seconds it took for the door to open. A wizened old man stood in the jam, squinting up at my face.

"Tim, it's good to see you. You know our door is always open to you, there is no need for you to... What's wrong?" Dan finally recognized the pained look on my face, as well as the blood that had dried and was beginning to flake off.

"I can't come in, Dan. I just need the keys to the Dodge. I'm gonna need to cut across the south field to avoid them." I knew it wasn't much, but it was the best explanation I could come up with.

Without hesitation, he took the key ring from his belt loop and removed an old brass key.

"What's going on? If you're in trouble, maybe I can help."

"You are helping me. I wish I had the time to explain everything, but I have to get her out of here before they catch up to us. I'll owe you one." I said, taking the offered key.

"You owe me nothing, boy. Your daddy saved my boy. The least I can do is save his."

Almost overcome by emotion, I gripped Dan up in a hug.

"Tell Molly hello, and that I love you both. The keys are in the SUV. Do me a favor and move it into your barn and destroy it."

Without waiting for his reply, I leapt from the stairs and raced back to the waiting truck, and to the girl waiting within.

Sitting inside the pickup, I tried my best to clean off most of the blood with a grease-stained rag on the dash. I pulled a shirt from the backpack and pulled it on, and then put on the dull brown work coat that lay on the floorboards. Finally, I scooped up a cap and some faded sunglasses that hung from the gun rack and put them on as well. Sobely watched in silence.

"Lie down and hang on. It's going to get a little bumpy." I said. She complied obediently, stretching out the best she could on the seat, her feet in my lap. *They are looking for a teenage boy and girl in a white SUV, not a farmhand in an old blue truck. Let's hope they don't look too closely.*

I cranked the engine over, and the truck came to life with hardly a cough, eager to move. I was only too happy to oblige it.

We crossed the bumpy farmland, carefully following a path laid out by countless trips to tend the crops. With a short sprint across a strip of grass, we came to a stop. The highway dissected our path, leading north and south.

South would take us back to the city and would invite further disaster. North would lead us to freedom, however temporary that might prove to be. Not a single car passed, to wonder at our decision. The choice was predetermined, and therefore not a choice at all. Like everything else, the path was one forced upon us.

The crossroad seemed as a mocking proof of Fate, cruel and petulant. The tires gripped and rolled, pulling us onward. I slowly let them accelerate us toward the uncertain future, the past lying in shattered pieces behind us. With the taste of blood in my mouth and unspeakable horror burned forever into my brain, our trial had fully begun.

Thirty, fifty miles down the road, and I told Sobely it was safe enough for her to sit up. She scooted across the seat and wrapped her arms around my right bicep. Her tears had come to a full stop, yet her face remained red and puffy. At that moment she was so vulnerable, fated to trust me with her life. Unbroken, yet weak. The slightest betrayal would end her. Yet, I would never commit that crime.

She was now all I had left.

Mom is dead.

I shoved the thought away angrily. Something must have flashed across my face.

"I'm sorry Tim. So very sorry." She whimpered. Anger flared like a flash-fire. I pulled the truck to a screeching stop by the side of the road, throwing us both forward. I turned, and she shrank away from the hatred that was in my eyes.

She feared me. She was right to fear me.

"Don't you ever say those words to me again! Don't you *ever* apologize." My tone was acid, and my voice not my own. I struggled within, trying to muscle the unleashed Beast into an iron cage of willpower. I had to make her understand that I wasn't trying to scare her. That I did not want to hurt her. She wasn't the monster in the truck.

"This is all *my* fault. *Mine!* I should have put us on the road on day one. You were given to my care for protecting. I was even warned that somebody would come looking for you. HOW COULD I BE SO STUPID?!" I was screaming the words, and she seemed to shrink back even more. I wished she could know just how much I hated myself for the fear in her eyes.

"Tim... I..."

"My mother is dead because of me. *I* screwed up. Do you see that? Please, I'm begging you. Never ever blame yourself for this mess. Blame me. It's is my mistakes that caused it. Some *guardian* I turned out to be."

The fear vanished from her face, to be replaced by understanding; and I was in her arms. Hot tears began to leak from my eyes as she squeezed tighter, rocking us gently. An animal howled nearby, alien voice of rage and pain. Only, this creature wore my face. My arms gripped her as just tightly as she held onto me. Shame at my failure swallowed me whole, ripping the air from my lungs in gasping sobs.

I knew that it was my naiveté that had killed my mother; that I might as well have pulled the trigger myself. This wasn't a game to be played by children. It was a war that we were doomed to lose. We could not fight back, only try to survive as long as possible. The only real question left worth asking is how many casualties would be tallied to their side. How many more people would die because of me?

Would Molly and Dan be safe? Would they simply destroy all my friends in punishment for our running? *What choice did we have?*

Eventually my tears dried up. My voice gave up, and I sat in silence. I slowly became aware of my surroundings and of our current circumstances. Slender, loving arms held me in an embrace that reminded me of the promise I had made.

Reality was like a slap to the face.

You haven't failed her *yet. But if you just sit here crying like a little baby, you will break your oath. Then her death would be for nothing.* I had snap out of it fast. Sobely needed me unbroken right now.

Somehow, I pulled away from her, and got us moving again. We only needed to keep traveling. We needed no destination, just the open road before us. The empty highway was all the security I needed for now. As long as we drew breath, I had to hold on to hope.

For her sake.

The countryside passed by the windows in a golden blur of afternoon sunlight. Though it was only early summer, the weather had already turned to the perfect golden brilliance that all children look forward to at the end of the school year. For most of them, they would need to wait one more week, maybe two, for their joyful freedom to begin. That last bell would ring, and millions of jubilant children would flee their brick buildings and shed the worries of attending school. For three months, they would be free of their burdens.

In three months' time there was a strong possibility that I would be dead. Dead, and a failure.

I glanced at my passenger, sleeping beside me. The golden rays lit up her face, making her near-translucent skin glow. Her black hair shined like onyx, flowing over her shoulders in a slight tangle. Behind the eyelids drooping with heavy lashes, I knew her brilliant green eyes were still. For a time, she was free to sleep without the burden of her nightmares. I wanted to pull her to me, to rest her sleeping head on my shoulder. To feel her breathing, and to know that she was safe. To trace a finger along an ear.

Instead I contented myself to watch the gentle rise and fall of her chest.

Eyes back on the road, and another car was coming our direction. *No, not a car.* I realized. A panel truck, painted a seafoam green made garish by the grime that coated it. As it drew nearer, I tensed. When it pulled close, I could finally read the name nearly buried under the filth. 'Bert's Mobile Slaughtering' it read. The cartoonish pictures of a hog and a cow beneath, framed by sausage links and a T-Bone.

I shuddered involuntarily. Images flashed in my head. And for the 100th time in the last few hours, I relived the nightmare that had been unleashed on my life.

I shook the memories away and refocused my eyes on the yellow lines that separated my car from the other lane.

By the time the sun was crawling back up the horizon the next morning, we had crossed two state borders. The truck was now operating on fumes and wishful thinking. Reluctantly I pulled the

Dodge off the highway and into a sleepy little nowhere. The single-pump gas station stood closed. Whoever ran it was probably still in their bed.

I brought the truck to a shuddering stop, switching off the engine. My eyes burned from the long night spent watching the yellow and white lines pass us by. I shut them against the harsh morning light and pulled my sleeping angel into my arms. *I'll just rest them for a moment...*

The light was terrifying in its brilliance. It was as blue as glacial waters. It shone from everywhere and nowhere. The light served to illuminate every flaw, every fear. Every decision was bathed in shadow. Every moment warped and twisted.

As terrible as it was, the light was only the silent companion of the beast that prowled shadows that sprang from nothing. The Beast growled and cackled, mocking me with the knowledge of its own superiority. No matter how hard I tried, that cruel thing would still take her. I was helpless against it, hopeless in fighting it.

It laughed because I knew the truth of it. The Beast would always be there because it was only a reflection of myself. One day I would find it a necessary evil to rely on. I knew those shadows it pounced upon. The thin veil between madness and the edge of reason.

Blood sprayed the air, spouting from a shadow that held the face of my mother. The screams turned the rest of the shadows into monsters that cackled at my despair. The face of pooling blood morphed until it was *her* face, mouth open, pink froth upon her lips as her scream became a wail.

06

A hand thumped against the window, pulling my splintered mind back to full alertness. I jerked upright, a short yelp tumbling from my lips. Loud laughter pierced the thick glass, pealing from a man in coveralls, doubling over from the force of his mirth.

The sudden flash of anger made the Beast grin within its cage.

I rolled the window down and tried not to glare at the big man.

"About time you people decided to open up." I said curtly.

"You should have seen the look on your face. It was like somebody had shot you." He chuckled, oblivious to the gravity of his statement.

"Just fill our tank please. We have a long way to travel."

"Sure, sure. I'll gas you up boss." The attendant went to it, oblivious too of the terror still on Sobely's face. Just as well. If he had noticed her, he probably would have done more than a double-take.

"We're okay. It was just a rude old man who decided to have some fun at our expense." I patted her back. I hoped the gesture was comforting. It was synonymous with trying to hold onto a lifeline. Trying to pull back on a chain.

"We are not safe yet, are we?" She asked. I considered her question a moment. True, we had come a long way already. It was easy to allow ourselves to think we had escaped the danger. However, I didn't think any amount of distance could make us safe now. This was their game. If they were that easy to defeat, then they would not have bothered to take the trouble in the first place. The best we could hope for was that they would grow tired of playing before they caught us.

"We aren't safe yet." I agreed.

I paid the old man for filling up the truck, and then pulled it forward into a parking space. I hesitated a moment, and then retrieved her bandana from the floor.

"Let's go inside and see if we can find something to eat."

"Okay. I think I need to use the restroom, too." She replied.

I opened the door of the truck and we went into the little convenience store. After pointing out the restroom to Sobely, I turned to the task at hand. The choices on display were dismal. While the shop had a somewhat shiny microwave for patron use, the pre-made sandwiches were all missing their sell-by stickers.

The dry goods area looked as if it were several shipments shy of full capacity. Clearly, I wasn't the only person who wanted to forget this place existed. This wasn't all that surprising, since the inhabitants hadn't exactly been welcoming. As I moved about the store trying to find something for sustenance, their eyes followed me. The only thing I could find worth paying for was a couple of juice bottles, and even these were a few days past their expiration. I took these up to the register. Hotly aware of the stares. Hoping that we hadn't made it into the news yet in these parts.

Several more minutes of uncomfortable silence went by before I began to realize that something must have been wrong. Sobely should have been done by now. I shoved the juice into my pockets, and then knocked on the worn restroom door.

"Are you alright in there?"

"I... do not know." Came the barely heard reply. Panic bloomed, like a detonating bomb.

"I'm coming in." I announced, opening the door. The sight that awaited me froze me in place for a moment. Something most definitely was wrong with her. She was crumpled on the dingy floor like a doll tossed aside by an angry child. Her jeans were still around her ankles, as if she had fallen when she had stood up from the toilet. Her face was as red as a beet, and her skin glistened with the shine of fever.

"I am sorry Tim." She whimpered, her voice weak.

I sprang forward, scooping her up from the floor. With a gentle tug, I pulled her underwear back up, and then picked up her jeans. She felt lighter than air as I carried her back out to the truck. Her skin felt cold, despite the red glow it exhibited. Her head wobbled feebly from my quickened gait, dislodging the red bandana I had fashioned into a makeshift hat. I saw the attendant's jaw slacken as he caught sight of an exposed ear, but I didn't even bother to slow down.

I cursed the necessity of having to stop in this miserable little town.

Panic threatened to shred the bars of the cage that held the Beast. *If she gets sick, what do we do? A hospital would turn us in, and if we went to Greg, they* will *kill him.* My breathing became nearly as ragged as hers.

I got her into the truck without incident, and then covered her up with my coat before climbing inside.

Then I tore out of the parking lot as fast as the lumbering machine could manage. Once we returned to the interstate, some sanity was restored to me. I realized that she hadn't eaten since yesterday morning, when I had pulled through an empty drive-thru for a breakfast platter. *With her appetite, it's no wonder she's not feeling well. Her tank had run as dry as the truck's.*

I dug a juice bottle out of my pocket and opened it, handing it to her.

"Drink this. I've got another one as well. You must be starving."

Wordlessly she managed to sit up, slumping against my shoulder. She gulped the juice from the first bottle down greedily, didn't slow down through the second either. Her color faded a little more towards normal as the last drops of juice slid past her dry, cracked lips.

"I am so tired." She whispered, lying back down in the seat, her head now in my lap. "I tried to be strong like you, but I am so tired."

"Hush now. It's alright. You will be okay. Just rest now. We'll be okay." I said, trying as much to convince myself as her. I placed a hand on her shoulder and felt the now-steady rise and fall. She had already fallen asleep, very faint snores escaping her pale throat. I wished fervently that we hadn't had to abandon the SUV, with its reclining seats.

"Soon." I promised, whispering so as not to wake her. "Soon we will be safe enough to rest awhile."

But for now, the road beckoned and warned of distant threats.

By mid-day we had entered yet another small town, this one a stark contrast to the last. This place was cheery and bright. Trees lined the street, casting friendly shade against the coming summer. I decided that it was a good time to refuel, and to finally eat a proper meal. Sobely's weakness seemed so obvious now, when I realized just how little we had eaten since the house. I had been so concerned with keeping one step ahead of whoever might be trying to find us, food had been all but forgotten.

About halfway through town was a brightly lit gas station. Next to this was a little hole-in-the-wall burger stand. After filling the truck's tank with gas, I crept forward until we had parked beside the restaurant. Despite the fading paint on the building, the smell of cooking meat had both our mouths dripping with saliva. *Maybe not the healthiest place to stop for a meal, but we could both use a few extra calories anyway.*

Inside, the faded red paint was brightly lit by what seemed to be a million tiny bulbs. Classic Rock played in the background, adding to the timeless feel of the stopover. A bored looking waitress showed us to a booth and then took our order. Even with the dour look on the woman's face, I decided that I liked the place. It was comfortable and had its own enduring sense of charm.

Sobely had regained almost none of her vigor. Though her smile had returned. I knew it better than my own now, yet I could never tire of the heart-breaking beauty of it. I felt some of the tension relax its grip on my shoulders as I soaked up her smile like one would soak up the rays of the sun. *Surely we have come far enough now that we can relax for a little bit.*

"You know, I think I am in love with you." I said, lightly dazzled.

"Really? Is that why you kiss me so?" She teased. "Though it has been a little while..."

"Hmmm." I leaned toward her, glad that we were sitting side by side. She leaned as well, eagerly meeting my lips in the space between us. Well, she found my nose, anyhow. I gently adjusted my angle.

Even after everything we had been through, I would have been lying if I said that fireworks didn't go off every time her lips met mine. Truth is they only got brighter, *more* dazzling with every embrace. I was beginning to learn that love was a bottomless thing. It was so impossible to fathom that all a person could really do was jump in it feet first.

How could you fear something that had no end to it? Better to fear the sun. The sun would one day die, and yet true love never could.

Time hadn't really stopped for us. Of course not. Which is why, though it seemed as if we had only just begun, our kiss was interrupted by the sound of two plates meeting the table. The waitress was attempting to be discrete, but the smell of the food was too much of a pull for Sobely, who turned away.

I caught the smile upon the waitress' face.

"Uhh. Sorry. I wasn't trying to disturb you two lovebirds." She apologized.

"It is okay. I am hungry." Sobely chirped, before lifting the massive burger for the first bite. *That's the great thing about these privately-owned burger stops. They are always generous with the food.*

The waitress smiled sheepishly, left a bill on the table, and went back to her stool by the door. We both fell on our plates like wrath, taking each bite just as fast as we could chew and swallow the previous one. As expected, the food was delicious. I suppose I might have been biased just a tad. After not eating for so long, I was actually *craving* spam. And cheese whiz. Swimming in gravy. *I wonder if they'd serve that?*

In mere minutes, both burgers, both plates of fries, and both large sodas were gone. We leaned back and patted our full bellies at exactly the same time, causing us to break up in laughter. Which was only slightly colored by the panic that ever waited in the shadows of our minds.

"By tonight I think we will have travelled far enough that we both can catch some real sleep, provided we can find a quiet spot to do so."

"That will be nice. I do not understand how you can stay awake for so long. You must be very tired..." Her remark was punctuated by a deep yawn.

"It is easy to stay awake when *your* safety is at risk. Tomorrow we will get our bearings. I'm not sure when it will be safe to stop travelling, but perhaps it will be easier on us if we knew what direction to take."

"Alright. Perhaps we should buy some things so we will not have to keep stopping to eat in town every time we get hungry." Sobely smiled, and her eyelashes batted rapidly. My over-tired brain fought to keep control of my hands, as her unconscious flirting set off sparks. I wanted to kiss her now more than ever. Wanted to keep on kissing her until the world ended. If I gave in to that feeling though, it wouldn't take very long before the world *did* end.

Instead of kissing her and running my fingers through her hair *(what a fine pickle that would leave us in)* I stood up and laid thirty dollars on the table to pay our bill and to tip the waitress. When Sobely stood, I could see that the color had returned back into her cheeks. That some of her strength had returned to her limbs. *She was only hungry. No wonder, the way she eats. I've got to feed her better.* My full stomach made my eyes droop with fatigue. *No time for that yet. We have to keep moving. As far as we can.*

As we left the burger stand, I felt strangely giddy. The colors of the world seemed to vibrate faintly, to switch back and forth between dull and bright. Almost like watching a TV that was losing its picture. Distantly I knew that this was because I hadn't slept in days. My reserves were running low, and the last traces of adrenaline were left miles behind. But I couldn't sleep yet. I couldn't pull in to the little roadside motel. There were hours yet to go before resting, and many more miles to put between us and *them.*

If we hadn't been subjected to torturous terror, and rushes of frantic adrenaline, I probably would have had a lot more energy; would have been able to push on a lot longer. As it was, I was feeling as drained as if I had spent a week running around a track. Longs hours spent in the driving position even made that notion convincing to my heavy legs.

As we left town I turned the truck onto a different highway. A different direction. If we were being pursued, a course change couldn't hurt. The giddiness made me feel especially proud of this small bit of cleverness, and I fought back a gale of laughter that would have frightened Sobely. It would have betrayed the fraying state of my mind.

I needed sleep in a bad way.

No rest for the wicked. And no rest for me either.

I couldn't help but wonder what life could have been like if we had been left alone. Here we were: I was driving down the darkened highway while she slept in the seat beside me. The gas tank was full, and we had nowhere to be. We might have been out on a little adventure, with plans to return once we had seen what there was to see. Only, there was nowhere for us to return to. Home no longer existed for either of us. All the people that had tied me to a particular place were gone.

I only had her left. Our home had become the open road.

I peeked at my watch, and again tried to wrap my over-tired brain around the colossal changes that had occurred over the last few days. I had sworn to protect this girl, without hesitation, and perhaps a little naively. I had no clue as to how I would be taking care of her. No hint of the danger we faced. She had been left in my care with nothing.

If I had known then what sort of jackals waited for us in dark places, we would have left that first day. My mother wouldn't be left on the floor with most of her face turned into a fine red mist.

A voice within my head spoke up, and more importantly, it was absolutely correct. *It is wrong to blame yourself. How could you have known?* I was pitted against master manipulators. They would do anything to cripple my thinking ability. *You acted on the information you were given.* That inner voice again spoke the plain truth. They had led me like a sheep, almost to my doom.

To them it was nothing but a game. We were pawns, being moved about the board. The fact that we seemed to have given them the slip could be nothing but artificial fantasy. Theirs was a long game, with no rules, and no consideration for those swept up in it. My father had desired that I protect her. Had he known who I would be protecting her from? Did he know the cost?

If he did know, does that mean *he* was responsible for Mom's death?

One thing seemed certain. We probably weren't meant to go and fall in love. They had meant to leave her as nothing but an empty shell. Perhaps, in that small mistake, our salvation was confirmed. I might be scared. I might have to fear for her life every second of every day. But I would not let any harm come to her. I acted out of much more than the simple desire to see a thing through.

I acted out of love.

Yes, I still seethed with anger. I still wished fervently that I could bring destruction down upon those inhuman creatures dressed so ridiculously. Yet I knew that I would be pushing myself hard just to keep her safe. Even with everything I was capable of mustering, that single task might just be beyond my reach. I still had no idea of just what they were capable. Their opening bid had been horrifying enough.

You don't know what you *are capable of either...* That inner voice whispered, the voice velvet madness.

I took one hand from the steering wheel and gripped hers with it. I stole another look at her before returning my tired eyes to the road. Despite everything, or maybe even because of it, I did not hate her even a little bit. I was incapable of turning my fear and anger on her.

My life now began *and* ended with her.

Up ahead, as if in response to my heavy eyelids, or maybe just my heavy thoughts, I spotted a barn. It looked intact, despite the charred remains of a house nearby. The driveway was overgrown, abandoned. Somebody might still own the barn, but it was clear they didn't come 'round often. Surely they would not visit it tonight.

I pulled into the driveway, and then eased the truck through the open barn doors. While Sobely slept on, I got out to see if the doors still worked. Luckily, they still rested solidly on their rusty old tracks. Carefully, and with the slight squeak of disuse, I pulled them closed. This shut out both the late afternoon light, and any prying eyes that might wander by.

Returning to the aging truck I found my green-eyed beauty awake, stretching like a sleepy feline. Her ears even seemed to stretch with the motion. She looked at me and smiled that perfect smile. I smiled back at her and wondered who could ever harm such a sweet girl.

"Are you feeling hungry?" I asked.

"Oh, yes!"

I rummaged in the back of the truck for the small cooler of groceries we had purchased a few hundred miles back. This I took back to the cab.

"Can we eat outside, please?"

"Okay." I would deny her nothing.

She unbuckled and then got out. We found a pair of old milking stools, and set them up by a barn window, the cooler a makeshift table between us. I made a couple of sandwiches; glad I had thought to buy mayonnaise. The bread had gotten a little dry riding in the back of the truck though.

"How are you feeling right now, Tim?" She asked as she licked the remaining crumbs from her fingers. Automatically, I began to make her a second sandwich.

"I'm a little tired. We've been driving for a very long time." I smiled, hoping it was genuine enough. She frowned in sudden anxiety, her lips trembled, and tears formed at the corner of her eyes. Whatever dam she had formed to keep her emotions buried broke wide open.

"You must hate me. How can you smile at me, when It is I who have ruined your life? If only we had never met!" A tear escaped to roll down her smooth cheek.

"Do you love me?" I asked, quietly and firmly.

"You know that I do. I do not think I could ever feel this strong for anything else in the whole world." She answered, just as quietly. Her voice began to waver with the trembling of her lips.

"You love me so, and yet you wish that we had never met?" I almost whispered. She thought about this for a few seconds, realization beginning to dawn upon her features.

"No." She whispered. "I do not wish that. Yet, I ruined your life! It would be easier if you *did* hate me."

I could see her point, her confused conclusion. Somehow, she had decided that everything was her fault. As if it had been her choice for all this to have happened.

"If you could believe for even a moment that I hated you... No. That is lunacy! If you believe that I would be better off without you in my life... That's madness. Don't you see? This was something done *to us*. *You* did not choose this. You did not decide to kill my Mom. *They* did."

I let the words sink in for a moment.

"Sobely?"

"Yes?" She answered timidly.

"I love you. Next to that, nothing else matters. You are precious to me. More precious than my own life."

"Oh Tim!" She cried, flinging herself on me. I could hear her breath hitch as she fought back the tears. I wrapped my arms around her and rocked gently. I was glad that she could no longer see my face, as an unpleasant thought began to course through my mind. *I would very much like to beat every one of them with my fists until I can't feel them anymore. And then skin them for good measure.*

"It's alright. Let it out." I pushed away my anger, locking it away. I let her hear how much I loved her. How much I wanted her to be comforted by my arms.

"Please don't... don't leave me alone. Please... I'll be a good girl." Her tears fell to my shoulder.

"Never. I won't ever. I don't want you to ever give that idea another thought." I reassured, disturbed by the way her voice had shifted to something monotone, robotic. What had she been put through?

Finally, she cried fully. She shook with the force of her gasping sobs for a long time, her tears soaking my shoulder. All I could offer her were my hands, and all they could do was gently stroke her back. I tried to somehow knead strength into her muscles. I forced myself to not imagine those hands around the necks of those that hurt her, lest my rage be revealed.

Nearly an hour later, her heart-rending sobs subsided. She pulled out of my arms. Her beautiful eyes were swollen, and her perfect lips trembled uncontrollably. I wanted to kiss them, just to still them.

"You do love me? Even though I am so weak?" She asked, some of the fear remaining.

"You aren't weak." I answered. She waited expectantly. *Oh.* "Sobely Blossom, I love you with all of my being. All of my heart, all of my soul, is yours. I will never stop loving you. I would move the very earth itself to keep you safe."

She let me pull her into another embrace, and whispered,

"Thank you. I love you, Timothy."

A silent moment passed. Her trembling lips stilled, and again I wanted to kiss them.

"Do we have to leave yet? You need to sleep, Tim."

"We will stay here tonight. It should be safe enough."

"Can we sleep out here?"

"Yes. I will go get the blankets." I stood, and went to the truck, retrieving the brand-new blankets we had bought.

She cleared our picnic area as I removed the packaging from the two blankets we hadn't even used yet. The one in the cab smelled of her. The light was failing, so I went back for a flashlight. This she held while I spread the blankets on the bare dirt. *We'll need to get a camp mattress tomorrow. Sleeping on the hard ground won't be good for her.*

When I finished, she set the light down on a stool so she could remove her shirt and jeans. After folding them carefully and placing them on a stool as well, she sat on the makeshift bed to remove her socks. She began to diligently check between her toes as I had shown her, while stealing glances at me.

Her sleeping habits no longer filled me with anxious uneasiness. But I would have been lying if I said that the sight of her sitting there in only her underwear didn't have some effect. She was beautiful, from her toes all the way to her mysterious eyes. To not admire her long, graceful legs and the soft perfect swell of her breasts would have been a crime in itself.

She turned to get her feet out of the dirt, exposing the ragged scars on her back to the harsh light thrown by the flashlight. In my sleep deprived state, even they seemed hypnotically beautiful. Not for the brutality they represented, but because of the soft skin they traced across. I felt a stirring low down in my body and fought it. *You just need to sleep.*

She completed her check and crawled beneath the blankets, but even they seemed to enhance her curves as it settled around her shape. She smiled up at me, no doubt in response to the sheepish look of awe on my face.

I shook my head to clear the spell she had unknowingly worked upon me, and crawled into bed beside her, kicking off my shoes as I went. She quickly settled into her place in the crook of my arm but did not fall asleep yet. I could feel her eyes on my face in the darkness.

"What is wrong?" I asked, concerned.

"Where *will* we go? Will we have to live like this forever?"

I thought her question over carefully, with no result.

"I don't know. I have no idea what direction to take, or where to go. It doesn't matter though. I know that I won't let anything happen to you, and that is enough."

Her hand found mine.

"That is enough for me, too." Her head nestled into my shoulder. I wanted to kiss her again. *Would she still love me if she remembered who she was?* I wondered idly. After a few moments, I decided that she probably would.

I knew that I would still love her. How could I not?

She was in my dreams, after all.

I fell asleep, the warmth of her love filling me. That light illuminates the soul, and leaves contentment.

Even in the blackest dark.

07

A shriek alerted my over-tired brain to the danger.

My eyes snapped open, and then abruptly shut as a powerful beam of light hit my face. *No, no, no! How did they find us?* Her arms squeezed me like a vise, desperation granting her enormous strength.

We were doomed this time. There was no way we could run before the bullets hit us. *I failed!*

And then, a minor miracle.

"Turn over onto your stomachs and put your hands on your heads! You are under arrest!"

My awareness snapped back, now that there was hope. I sat upright, pulling us both into a sitting position.

"Wait! Don't shoot!" I opened my eyes, and in the light cast by the flashlight I could see a man in a dark blue uniform. A sheriff's badge was affixed to the neatly pressed breast pocket of his shirt. His face was red, and it took my half-asleep brain a moment to realize why this was.

Swiftly, I pulled the blanket around Sobely's shoulders. I had to hold it in place, after the force of her terrified shaking made it slip off again.

"Do you want to explain to me why you are trespassing on private property?" He sounded as if he already had a good idea of why were there.

"We are lost, sir." I answered, trying to decide what to tell him. The adrenaline surging in me was making it a little hard to think straight. *Just because he is a cop, doesn't mean he is safe.*

"Really? Or did you just decide that this was the perfect spot for a little privacy? A little nookie away from where your parents will catch you?" He sounded amused by this prospect. I had to admit, it was a reasonable assumption to make.

"No, sir. We really are lost. Just take a look at our license plate."

The Mag-Lite shined onto the bumper of the truck. I could see the sheriff shake his head once, and then whistle.

"Wow. You two are a long way from home. A little far to go for a little alone time. Runaways your age would think to get a map, so... you're running from something." The deduction was exactly right.

"Yes sir. We got a world of trouble after us. They... they killed my family."

"And hers?" He asked, now staring intently at me.

"She is... an orphan."

"So? Why is she with you, instead of somewhere safe?"

"I am safe, wherever he is." Sobely's voice was fierce, daring him to contradict her.

"Sir, I am not leaving her anywhere. She is under my care, and they want her dead, too. She... needs me." I banked everything in hoping that the sheriff was kind enough to understand. If he wasn't, we were dead anyway. I suddenly could not remove my eyes from the massive revolver on his hip.

The sheriff tipped his hat back.

"Hmm. I'm guessing that you're... nineteen, right?" The sheriff was good at this. I nodded.

"Well. She wasn't mentioned in the news, or in the fax. She has some pretty identifying features, too." He said, whistling again.

"What?" I was taken by surprise.

"You haven't seen the news? Heck, it was on the national radio, too."

"The radio in the truck is broken." I replied numbly.

"You are Timothy, right? Timothy Kines?"

I nodded slowly.

"You are wanted for questioning regarding a shooting in Oregon."

Oh no! If he reports us... if we are arrested...

"Please, sir. Don't arrest us. They'll find us, and we'll be dead by morning." I begged. Sobely began to tremble again.

"I know you didn't do it. I won't turn you in, either. You sure don't look like a pair of killers, though I imagine you would kill me if I threatened *her*." His voice softened.

"Yes. I think I would." I whispered. *I know I would.*

"Nope, it just didn't make any sense to me. I even talked to a colleague over there and asked for some of the particulars, just in case you happened by. He told me that he had several eyewitnesses report that four identical men in trench coats opened fire in a residential neighborhood with old tommy guns. Even as crazy as it sounded, it made a lot more sense than the details coming in over the wire."

I started to shake. Each of the details the sheriff recounted fell into my brain like a drop of mercury.

And apparently, *they* had access to the police.

"Please... They'll kill her..." The fear twisted, like a swallowed shard of glass.

"Relax, kid. I ain't gonna tell nobody about you. I promise."

I focused on breathing slowly, trying to calm the rapid-fire beat of my heart.

"If you could tell us how close we are to a town, we will get a hotel room. You can forget we were ever here." I tried to put some confidence into my shaky voice.

"Well, the nearest town is about ten miles on down the road. I'm the sheriff there. The nearest inn, though, is in the next town. Seventy-five miles beyond that."

"We'll be on our way then, if you'll excuse us." I started to stand, but Sobely was holding me in place, her arms a vise constructed of terror.

"Nah. I reckon I can't do that." He said, still kindly. The shard split, and I felt the sharp twist in two directions. My heart sped up again.

"Why not?" My voice was quavering. My eyes were fixed on the revolver. The drops of mercury pooled in the center of my brain.

"Uhh... I didn't mean to scare you, kid. I just meant that you look dog-tired, and I would hate to have to clean up the mess if you veered into a light pole. I'll take you back to my place and put you up in our guest room."

He sounded kind. But he was still the one with the gun.

"We'll follow you in the truck, then." *And slip away when we have a chance.* The sheriff laughed.

"Those plates would stick out like a sore thumb around here. I thought you were trying to lie low. My, but you do look real tired. By my reckoning, you must have driven two days straight to come this far. Come on, I won't hurt either of you."

We had no choice. He had the gun. If he was a bad man, we were doomed. *And you left your gun back in the SUV.*

"Fine. Please, some privacy, so she can get dressed." I struggled to come up with an escape plan.

This time, it was handed to me. Literally. The sheriff unbuckled his gun belt and offered it to me.

"Here. I know if I were in your shoes, I wouldn't trust anybody with a gun, either. So take this, and be careful – it's loaded." I took the offered belt and checked the big revolver. True to his word, it was loaded. He had decided that the reports of our misdeeds were false and was genuinely trying to help us.

I guess I could trust him for now.

A real bed *would* be welcome.

I stood and put the belt around my waist. The weight of the gun was oddly reassuring. Surely, the sheriff was no threat now that I had his gun.

"I will remove the truck's plates while you get dressed. Tomorrow, we will bring it back to my house, and try to figure out what to do with it." The sheriff turned.

"We're leaving tomorrow." I said, firmly.

"You've done really well to get this far, kid, but I think you'll be needing a few pointers about the rules of the road. Besides, Mildred will be delighted to have some company."

He walked off before I could reply. I held up the blanket behind me and watched as Sobely sleepily got to her own feet. She didn't seem to understand what I was doing though and wrapped her arms around my neck in a hug.

This time, I did kiss her.

"Hey. Don't you think you should get dressed?" I whispered. She smiled.

"Oh. That is why you got the blanket all stretched out like that. So he cannot see me. I thought you were going to wrap me up in it." Her eyes twinkled. She stepped back, out of her embrace.

A big yawn forced her smiling jaws apart. The chain reaction started, and my own yawn sounded as if I had bent the frame of the truck. My adrenaline reserves must have still been low, because the boost had already worn off. Leaving the fatigue to crash on down on me like a ton of bricks. I felt more tired now than ever.

With a slight wobble Sobely twirled to fetch her clothes from the stool. She struggled into her shirt, as if wrestling with something alive. When she managed it triumphantly, although inside out, I couldn't help but smile in response.

When she lifted her foot to put it inside her jeans, though, her balance disappeared. With a yelp of pain, she landed on her rump, slipping enough for her head to be thrown back to hit the stool. The blanket dropped from my grasp.

I knelt beside her, adrenaline impossibly flowing again, lifting her head into my lap. Panic choked off all possibility of speech at first.

She was crying.

"Sobely? Are you okay?" My voice was small.

"Ow. That hurts! Why am I so tired? I have had more sleep than you – I should be more awake!"

I could see that her tears were more from frustration than pain.

"It's ok. You have been learning a lot, and stress can wear you out faster. Let me help you." I quickly, gently, kissed the top of her head.

While she sat, I helped her into the jeans, as well as her socks and shoes. Mine were still on in case we needed to get away quickly. Now I could see how much of a joke that would have been.

She helped me clean up, until she nearly fell again. I made her sit on one of the stools. I then folded the blankets, packing them and the small cooler back into the truck. The Sheriff had finished removing both license plates, and he was now taking a cable and lock from the trunk of his cruiser to lock the barn up with.

I did not feel frightened of him, or worried of his intentions. Something told me that the portly sheriff *was* a good man. Maybe a little bit of my father's intuition dwelled within me.

Besides, a real bed would be most welcome. Definitely.

"Tim?" She whispered, nudging me awake. I had fallen asleep in the back of the police cruiser. Shame burned in me, stinging worse than my bloodshot eyes. I was supposed to keep track of where we were going.

At least we were here. The cruiser was parked next to an older sedan. In the dark, I could just barely make out the dim outlines of the sheriff's house. In the dark, everything looked sinister.

We were let out, and I felt slightly better to be out of the stifling confines of the car. The chilly night air helped to bring me some semblance of wakefulness. At least, I could actually feel Sobely half hugging me as we followed the sheriff up his porch steps and into the dark house. She was warm.

Odd that for once, she was leading me.

Once inside, a light snapped on, and an old woman confronted us. At the same time both hugging and berating the sheriff.

"Jack, you are far too old to be going out on middle-of-the-night calls. That is why you have deputies... who are these people and why does that boy have your gun?"

"Mildred, these two have come a long way and are very tired. Now, would you be a dear and go make up the bed in the guest room?" Jack's words made Mildred's eyes widen.

"Did you go and make us hostages?" She stage-whispered.

"No. I gave him my gun so he would feel safe enough to come home with me. These kids need a bit of help, and I didn't want them running off before we could give it. Now, everything else can wait 'til morning, so go get their bed ready, you *old bat*."

"Fine, fine, you *crow,* but you owe me an explanation." Mildred's banter was almost cheerful, and the emphasis placed on the words 'old bat' and 'crow' explained why. It was probably a code for 'all clear.'

Mildred disappeared into another room.

"Sorry for my wife. She's a little ornery but has a heart of gold. She'll take care of you for now — I have to go file a false alarm report. You'll be fine." The sheriff left before I could manage to get my tongue to work. Everything seemed to be moving both as slow as turtles, and lightning fast. *At least he left us the gun...*

When Mildred reappeared, I was already leaning on Sobely a bit. I fought to stay upright, but it was a losing battle. The two days of panic, adrenaline, and driving through the night caught up in a bad way. Somehow, she managed not to collapse under the weight of my arm.

"Come on, my little dears, you look right dead on your feet. Right this way is a real comfortable bed. My, but don't you look like a sight." Mildred was still chattering, but my mind only had enough focus for one thing, and that was following her to a waiting bedroom.

Once in the bright room, the only fact I registered about it was that the bed was easily big enough for four of us. Without further thought, we had settled under a faded quilt, the room swirling into utter darkness.

The next day was painfully bright. My body wanted more sleep, but I had woken up because there was something wrong. The familiar, blessed shape at my side was gone. My eyes snapped open against the painful light, panic jerking me to a sitting position. Sobely was pulling on my T-Shirt. I didn't remember taking it off.

"Sorry. I was not trying to wake you. I just need to use the restroom." Her smile was apologetic. "I will be right back."

My own bladder made its presence painfully known.

"Wait, I got to go, too." I staggered from the bed and followed her out. Once in the hall, Mildred called from somewhere.

"You guys up already?" I hoped we wouldn't have to be.

"No. Umm, where is your restroom?" Sobely spoke first. Mildred appeared around the corner, drying her hands on her apron. Her face was thin, like the rest of her, but grandmotherly. Silver hair curled elaborately on top of her head, and her smile was easy. Lots of little lines traced from the corners of her mouth, a testament to a lifetime of chatter.

She looked us both up and down. Probably taking in our bedraggled condition.

"Right this way, kids. When you guys do get up for the day, I'll make you some breakfast. Maybe you can tell me why you two are here." Her words flowed together with hardly a space between them.

"Hasn't Jack told you?" I asked, as she opened the bathroom door for Sobely.

"He hasn't been home yet. There was a stampede at the dairy. Some kind of animal on the loose. Some folks got hurt, and there are cows all over town. He did say to tell you hi, though." Mildred was interrupted as Sobely opened the door. She, at least, looked well rested.

I stepped into the bathroom, listening to the old lady start up the conversation with Sobely. Jack had been right – she did like company.

After I relieved myself, and splashed a little cool water on my face, I found the hall empty. I quickly repressed the wave of panic this caused. *She is either with Mildred, or in the bedroom. These people won't hurt her.*

When I opened the bedroom door, Sobely *was* there. Stark naked. Her back was to me, but this made very little difference. She was just too flawless. Even the terrible scars could not change that. There wasn't a model alive that wouldn't kill for a figure like hers, scars and all. *Get a grip.* Quickly, I shut the door behind me, paranoid that someone else would see her like this. Maybe even a bit jealous? She turned at the sound.

I could honestly say that she blushed from head to toe.

"Uhh..." She pulled the quilt from the bed and wrapped it quickly around her. All the sleepiness had left me, and I wasn't exactly proud of the reason. *Come on, who wouldn't have a reaction to that?*

"Mildred wanted to wash our clothes because they are all dirty. We do not have anything else to wear. I am sorry – I just liked the way the sun and the air felt on my skin." Her bright color faded a little. A shy smiled played upon her lips.

I noticed then, that not only were the curtains wide open, but so was the window. The window looked over the front yard, and a house could be seen across the road. With surprising speed, I seemed to have teleported across the room, and shut the heavy brocaded curtains, plunging the room into darkness.

There was a knock on the door. But before I could say anything, Mildred had opened it, mouth open to begin her chatter anew. She took in the room in a glance.

"Oh! I hadn't thought about the window, though I think most people would have shut the curtains before they stripped down to their skin! Glad you're back, young man, I need your clothes too. Might as well wash them all at once. Fresh..."

"I'm fine." I said quickly, realizing I would have to interrupt her to say anything.

"Nonsense. I'll give you some privacy, and you can get undressed. I can smell you from here. Later, we'll get you both a shower or bath or whatever you prefer. Just don't worry, get a little more sleep, and we'll sort it all out later." This time, she stopped on her own. I looked down, turning red again. *I'm not getting undressed with Sobely right here. I am having enough trouble...*

Suddenly, I saw us from Mildred's point of view. We *did* share the same bed, and Sobely *did* sleep practically naked. The *old bat* must have thought we...

The old lady was waiting, practically biting her tongue to keep from talking.

"Ok, then." I nodded. She stepped out of the room.

Calmly, I pulled the flat sheet from the bed to wrap around me as I undressed. I was determined to be responsible. There were things she couldn't understand, and I wasn't going to explain them to her. Sobely watched me, as I struggled from my pants while keeping the sheet in place.

"You know, I do not mind if *you* see *me* naked. It kind of feels a little... I do not know. But it is nice. I only got red because of the look on your face. It made me remember that you said you should not see, and... I was sorry I messed up." I tried not to think about how her words made me feel, but the sad tone at the end couldn't rest.

"You didn't mess up. I should have knocked."

At this point, all my clothes were piled on the floor. I smiled at my little success.

"Oh. Still, though, I forgot you did not like to see me naked." Her voice was so innocent, I slipped before I could bite my tongue.

"I like it, in fact I like it very much..." *Oh crap!*

"It is the scars on my back, correct? They make me ugly." For a full minute, I was speechless. *If I tell her the truth, she'll have more questions. If I tell her nothing, she'll think she isn't good enough. What do I do?*

I swallowed my irrational fear. In my head, I firmly held on to the fact that in many ways, she *was* a child. She needed reassurances. Besides that, I enjoyed every glimpse I got. It made me a pig, and I felt guilty to admit it, but I couldn't lie to myself any more than I could lie to her.

"You are the prettiest, most beautiful woman I have ever seen. Scars can't change that. It's not just your... body that is gorgeous, Sobely, but you shine from within. You shine like the sun!" *Good grief. That wasn't awkward at all... Coward.*

"Oh, Timothy." She suddenly crushed against me, kissing me with a fierce happiness. With the world exploding in a good way, I was barely aware of the door opening quietly behind us.

"I'll just grab these and leave you two alone..." For the first time, Mildred was quiet. She kept her eyes on the floor as she gathered my clothes, and quietly shut the heavy door behind her.

The fire in Sobely's lips erased all conscious thought for a little while.

At long last, and much too soon, Sobely pulled away. A very puzzled look on her face. I found that I had been squeezing her just as tightly and had to be quick to catch the thin sheet. The puzzlement scrunched her eyes a little, and her lips were pursed to one side.

She was also trembling.

And in the four inches between us, I could feel the heat radiate from her.

"Why am I trembling? I am not scared. And I feel very hot. Is there something wrong with me?"

Every fiber in me screamed at me, to explain exactly how right everything was. Not just say how right everything was, but to show her, to let her *feel* how right it all was. It was like agony, that she had pulled away in the first place, and her words had ignited me like a pyre.

Honor still won out, for now. *Stress can do all sorts of things to the brain.*

"No, you aren't sick. I'm trembling too, and also pretty warm. Sometimes kisses can do that." I *was* trembling. *Amazing. Your voice even sounded pretty calm. You are a nitwit, though.*

"Oh. I want another one, then. That was... awesome." She leaned. *Distract her!*

"Hey, how 'bout we get some breakfast?" I choked. There was no way I could stand calmly and endure another one of those. No way I could sleep now, either. Or ever. Lucky for the shreds left of my integrity, the distraction worked. Her eyes lit up, and she quickly turned to pick up the quilt.

"I am so hungry, I could eat two of those hamburgers we had the other day!"

It would be a little awkward eating, clothed as we were, but not nearly as awkward as trying to stay in this room another minute.

I already longed for her to be in my arms again.

At least I had the courage to hold her hand when we exited the room. Since going right would have led us only to the bathroom, I turned us left, and we soon found ourselves in a kitchen. Mildred stood at the sink, washing a pile of dishes, a strange sound coming from her. It took me a moment to realize that she was talking to herself in a low voice, at a speed that a hummingbird wouldn't have been able to match.

I cleared my throat.

"Oh... let me go get you two a couple of bathrobes. I... didn't think you would need them yet. You two... must be pretty hungry."

Sobely nodded eagerly, oblivious to the undercurrent in Mildred's words. My face turned scarlet, all too aware of her hidden meaning.

Mildred made a quick exit down a different hall, coming back with two burgundy robes. Embroidered on them was one word. Guest. The lady smiled. The effect this had on her wrinkles was amazing and worked well as a distraction. My mind had begun to wander back into the bedroom.

"Used to run a bed and breakfast, till my arthritis got to be too bad. Oh, how I miss all the company." She handed the robes to us. *Despite all the chatter, I bet her regulars miss her, too.*

Quickly, we made our egress back to our room. *Calm.*

"Wow, Tim, I do not even understand half of what she says. Why did she think it would take longer to come to breakfast? Did she think we wanted to sleep some more?"

"Something like that, I'm sure." I replied. I turned around to give her privacy to change. It was a simple robe and it didn't take long.

"Alright, Tim. But there are no buttons. How is this better? I still have to hold it around me."

It wasn't simple enough. Of course, she doesn't know how to tie a knot. I told myself sagely. I turned to help her, thankful that she was at least holding the terry-cloth shut. But I needed both hands.

"Turn around while I get mine on, and I'll help you." I said.

"Alright." She chirped, spinning around, robe twirling along with her hair.

I was in my own robe in a blink, hoping she would/wouldn't peek. I still did not want to have this conversation with her. I wished things could have been different for us.

I wished Mom were here.

I grabbed her shoulder and spun her to face me. My fingers fumbled for the sash, as her eyes had hypnotized me. Somehow, I got a hold of both ends and looked down to start the bow.

"Oh!" She exclaimed. To my credit, I managed to continue what I was doing.

"Do you think she would make pancakes?"

It was lucky I had finished the bow. The anxiety, lack of sufficient sleep, and crazy tension broke, and I started to giggle madly. Sobely was instantly confused.

"What is funny?" Her question only made the giggling worse, because the look on her face was priceless. *If I weren't laughing so hard, I would kiss her.* This thought also made the laughter worse. *You wouldn't stop at just kissing her, either.* Eventually, she started to laugh too, which made my own redouble. She had to hang on to my shoulders to keep from falling over, she was shaking so hard.

The guilty part of me was gleefully taking note of what the mirthful shaking did to her lithe body.

"What's all this about?"

While we did not notice Mildred enter, her question actually made us laugh so hard we both had tears running from our eyes. If we hadn't run out of air we probably would have kept going until they locked us in the funny farm.

The human body has strange ways of dealing with trauma.

We were in as much danger as two people could be in. Murderers were after us, with unknown capabilities. Neither of us could really sleep well, because of our fear. We both panicked when we did not know exactly where the other was. For all we knew, the men in trench coats could be walking up the driveway right now. Maybe it wouldn't even be them, but some*thing* even worse.

Our bodies cleansed us by making us laugh. And now that we were done, I could feel that all the tension built up in my muscles was gone.

Again, I felt a pull to kiss her until nothing made sense. My brain calmly informed me that whatever happened as a result would be perfectly natural. Between two people who really loved each other.

The shreds of my decency had its own argument. She was like a child. She was innocent of all things. I could not, I would not allow anything like that happen until...

Until what? My rational side argued.

Until the right time, maybe! Anything now would be born from desperation. My consciousness rationalized.

You're hopeless. Rational shut up. Mildred was still waiting.

I did kiss her. Quickly. It was too hard to resist that pull completely, and kissing *was* still legal.

All's legal in love.

"Nothing, Ma'am. We've just been through a lot. Laughter is nature's defense against depressed desperation." I put an arm around Sobely. "Do you have pancakes?"

"Umm. Sure. I haven't cooked anything yet. What all would you like?" Puzzled, Mildred was far less chatty. And her question was the only opening Sobely needed.

"I like hash browns, and pancakes, and um… so-sage, and bake-on and… those yellow squishy things and orange juice and umm… malk? Mulk?"

"Milk." I gently corrected.

Mildred was speechless.

"She could eat it all in one sitting, too. She's got the metabolism of a squirrel." I explained, apologetically. *Listed nearly all the breakfast items she's ever had.*

"I suppose I could cook you all that. My goodness!"

"Well, I'm sure we could make do with pancakes and bacon. We don't want to put you to too much trouble."

Sobely's face fell a little.

"No, no. I love cooking, that's no trouble at all. Just, normally ladies are… uh… dainty eaters? Could I start you off with some toast and jam?"

"Sure! What is that?" Sobely's enthusiasm almost made me start laughing again.

"You're kidding. How can you not know what toast is?"

"I have never had it." Sobely answered, matter-of-factly.

08

"Right." Mildred gruffed, shaking her head and walking back to her kitchen. I kissed Sobely's cheek before we followed – the inferno was containable that way, though it in no way helped in relieving the intense pressures I felt.

Minutes after sitting at the mahogany table four pieces of toast were set before us, as well as jam. The toast was already buttered I noted as I spread some of the strawberry jam on one of her pieces. From the smell it was real butter, too.

She took one bite, and then set it back on her plate. Her nose wrinkled, and she seemed to force herself to chew what she had bitten off. I was surprised. Was there a food that she didn't like?

"Do I have to finish this? It is too… sweet." She swallowed her bite loudly. I took a bite of hers, finding the jam a little sweet myself, but then that was normal for jam.

"Try it without the jam, like I eat it." I said. She took the other piece and devoured it. I handed my second slice to her, which disappeared just as fast. I would get my fill with the spread that Mildred was preparing, so I certainly didn't need it.

I was finding it difficult to not pull her into my lap, now that the distraction provided by the toast was gone. She had sat in my lap before, but somehow things were a little different between us. I needed to get a handle on myself before I attempted such a maneuver. For her sake.

She leaned against me though and closed her eyes. Still tired from the travelling, though I was now wide-awake. By all rights I should have been exhausted, but I was wrestling with a new demon now. I loved her so much it ached.

That had always been a given.

Her touch was like a balm to me. My hurts, my fears, my cowardice. All of that disappeared when I had her safely within the circle of my arms. That, too had always been a fact. It seems that I became entirely aware of her, of her effect on me. Her exact effect. Because now, when I touched her, when we kissed...

It was like a fire. A slow-burning inferno. She was my balm, and now I knew it and craved it. Now that I knew exactly what that meant, I would have to control it. I should have been more careful from the start.

Yes, it would be so easy. She trusted me completely to always do the right thing for her. I would be a monster to betray that. Only a monster would try. She was like a child in so many ways, and needed protection, even from myself.

It was hard, though. I loved her.

"Hey, boy, would you help me carry all this in there?" Mildred called, snapping me back from my thoughts. I got up, motioning for Sobely to stay. Quietly, I put the uneaten toast in a garbage can, and took the jam back into the kitchen with me. Mildred handed me a big plate of hash browns, and another of eggs, while she handled the pancakes and breakfast meats.

"We'll come back for the plates and drinks." She said. We worked into a kind of rhythm, as we prepared the table for the meal. Sobely's mouth watered as she waited patiently for us to finish.

Once I had dished up a heaping plate of food for her, she was in a state of bliss. I was glad that the syrup was real maple. I did not think she would have liked the overly sweet fake stuff.

Say one thing about her. Nothing distracted her from a plate of food. Her skill with a fork had improved some, too.

Still got syrup on her chin. And eggs. Okay, it hadn't improved by *much*.

"Wow! You weren't kidding, she can really tuck it away." Mildred ate her much smaller portion at a stately pace. I was embarrassed by how fast I gulped my own plate of delights down. In no time at all Sobely had polished off a smaller second helping, and a lot of the juice and milk. I just focused on my own plate, trying not to laugh again at the strangeness of it all.

"I am sorry. I probably should not have taken so much, but I was really hungry. We have not been eating much lately."

"It's ok, little one. At least there is enough left for Jack."

"When will he be back?" I asked anxiously.

"Right now." Came a voice from the doorway. The sheriff was covered in mud, and he put his reasonably clean jacket on the chair before sitting down.

"Them cows were a pain in the rear. Wow, all my favorites! We should have company more often."

Jack piled the remains on Mildred's plate, stuffing the morsels in faster than even Sobely could manage. A little less gracefully, too. Sobely wiped her chin on a napkin Mildred provided.

"Jack, if you ate like this all the time you would be a fat pig." She berated.

"Already am a fat pig. Oink Oink." Jack had his plate cleared in record time and polished a bit of the mud off his badge with the napkin given to him, instead of wiping the crumbs from his face.

"Ernie Jackson, you better get in that shower this instant! And I thought these two needed a thorough wash!" Mildred hauled him up by his collar. He grinned sheepishly at me.

"Sure, sure. Hey, at least I took my boots off outside!" His banter had the feel of routine to it, and I could see the love shining in their eyes.

"My floors thank you." Her voice dripped heavy with sarcasm as she took in the mud-covered pad on the chair. The coat hadn't saved it much.

The two disappeared down the hall, still bickering, leaving me alone with my Sobely. It was so nice here, so comfortable. I suddenly wished we could stay forever.

I knew though that staying would be a mistake that we couldn't afford to make. *They* wouldn't give up that easily. We would be leaving before we put these fine people in danger. We owed them that for their overwhelming kindness. I sighed as quietly as I could, but she never missed anything.

"We can't stay here for very long, can we?" She asked softly.

"No. We can't. I think they would have kept us, too." I answered sadly.

"Well... At least I will always have you." *A happy thought indeed!*

"Of course. Forever and ever." I leaned to kiss her cheek again, but she was quick. Her head turned, and the fire erupted. How could such contact be responsible for erasing all the pain? Were her lips made to be the cure to my tortured soul? Did she feel the same?

I really hoped so.

It takes years before a child can safely bathe themselves. Helping Sobely get clean made me hope, and secretly fear, that it wouldn't take her that long. It helped that she enjoyed a bath like a child would. It helped that Mildred had a container of bubble bath. It also helped that mostly I just gave her direction, only touching her to wash her back and hair.

Washing her legs and toes was just extra.

She *was* irresistible, after all.

The real complication – because I was delighted to help her – was that when she told me she needed help bathing, Mildred had just taken it in stride. Only because she had the wrong idea of us. It was interesting to know that kind of behavior didn't bother her in the slightest, in her own house.

I guessed it wasn't uncommon for that sort of thing to happen at a bed and breakfast. It *was* interesting to find that the tub was large enough for two, though I kept from entertaining those ideas. Mostly.

The complication was this: If Sobely left before I washed, it would only create a whole cascade of questions that I would have trouble answering. Telling them any more about us than I had to was not a good idea. I figured their chances were better if they knew very little. I also didn't think I could let her from my sight for that long.

Washing with her in the room would undoubtedly make me uncomfortable. If I didn't wash, that would be noticed too. My rational side was back, asking me just what the big deal was.

My conscience told my rationale that modesty had been ingrained in me quite well, thank you very much.

Don't be a baby! You've seen her in all her glory, and it didn't bother her. Besides, if you make a big deal out of it, she'll ask questions. You ready for that *talk?*

No, I wasn't. At least there were bubbles.

Yes, there is that. Odd though, that they don't have a shower curtain.

"What are you thinking?" Sobely asked. I snapped back to what I was doing and realized I had been washing her back for almost fifteen minutes.

"Nothing important. Is the back rub helping you relax?" I moved my hands up, and gently massaged her shoulders. *Nice save!*

"Yes. I think you will have to change the water before you wash. It is really dirty." She swirled aside some of the bubbles, to show how grimy the water had gotten. *How did we get so dirty?*

"Ok, go ahead and pull the plug." She reached, and the water started to drain out. *Who cares what they think when they hear the water run again?* I actually repressed a giggle.

She stood, and I helped her step out onto the rug. My rational side had won – as long as it behaved. *Relax.* I handed her a huge towel and showed her how best to dry.

While I waited for the tub to fill with water and bubbles, I appreciated her like one would art. In that aspect, she was a masterpiece. A clear reminder of why the Greeks had tried so hard to capture the perfect-ness of the female form in marble.

Relaxed as I was about it now, I was surprised to find that nothing... dishonorable was in my mind at all. *Exactly. Rationally, she is far too perfect to fantasize about.*

Her touch was still electric fire, though.

Of course. The touch of a goddess should be.

The giant claw foot was now full. I shut off the faucet and slipped out of the robe and into the water before I lost my nerve again. The heat was marvelous. I let myself relax in it for a moment, before starting to wash. I just now found out how cold I had been.

As I washed my toes, I felt the extra sponge on my back.

"Uhh... that's ok..." I began.

"No. You helped me, and I will help you. You cannot reach your back." I couldn't refute her logic. *And if you do, you'll hurt her feelings. Don't even know how honor has anything to do with this.*

"Thank you."

So I let her scrub my back. It was nice, actually. Comfortable. Maybe I wouldn't mind helping her wash *all* the time. What was there to be worried about, really? Plus, it meant more time with her. *That is never a bad thing.*

When I had turned the water dark with the sweat and dirt off my skin, I pulled the plug, and quickly dried. Carefully, I avoided any thoughts at all. Practice was making perfect.

Or was it, that acceptance of necessity was allowing me to enjoy it, too? Was I really a monster? *I was too comfortable... I'm slipping, not getting better!*

With the robe donned once more, I turned to the task of teeth brushing. Jack had brought our bags back from the truck, and I was relieved to find that our money had not been stolen due to my carelessness.

"So, we are now going to brush your teeth. This will help prevent gum disease and the build-up of tartar. This, in turn, helps you stay healthy." I explained, having retrieved our toothbrushes from our bag. The few items of clothing we had were strangely missing. Then again, what hadn't been stained by blood had become dirty in the last few days. Most likely, it was all in the wash.

"Alright. What do I do?" Sobely asked, holding up the toothbrush quizzically.

"Umm..." I quickly realized that trying to explain would get messy. Delicately, I took her brush from her, and then led her over to the sink.

Excuses, excuses...

As she watched, I spread a layer of toothpaste out on the brush, briefly running it under the tap.

"Open your mouth, please." I whispered into her ear, suddenly nervous. I turned her slightly, so I could see what I was doing. She complied with my request, and I brought the moist bristles to her waiting mouth.

Slowly, so she would get used to the sensation, I started to brush. My free hand went to the back of her neck to steady her as I worked. An odd look of contentment crossed her face as the tiny bristles scraped back and forth over her perfect little teeth. In the silence, the sound of brushing seemed to be amplified.

Broadcasting to the world just what we were doing.

Just what are you doing. You could have simply shown her. She learns quickly. There is a mirror. This wasn't strictly necessary, was it?

I felt myself blush. As the soft brush gently cleaned her mouth, she would make small, appreciative, noises. The nylon would tickle her gums, or make a pass over her tongue, and she would relax further. Enjoying the attention I gave her.

I should have thought to turn the fan on before I got started. Suddenly I felt as if we stood within a sauna. I felt sweat break out across my skin as I watched a thin stream of frothy spittle leak from the corner of her mouth. A glance at the clock reminded me that while the American Dental Association recommended two minutes of solid brushing. Eight minutes was probably over-doing it.

I knew I was slipping up, but I still could not resist the chance to touch her. Even the embarrassment of knowing this couldn't stop me. I was going to have to try much harder to resist. *After I finish with her teeth. I'll try to figure it out while I brush her hair.*

When we left the bathroom at last, Mildred and Jack were both asleep in the living room. Jack, in a battered recliner, and Mildred stretched out on the couch. We decided to go back to our room. The glee I felt was unmistakable. However, I still had a weapon against it. I still felt reasonably sure I could fight it off. I wasn't having bad pictures fill my head or anything; all I felt was this strange yearning, this odd longing. And the electric fire whenever I touched her.

Easily countered, of course. If I stopped kissing her, if I didn't hold her, it would hurt her. She wouldn't understand why I suddenly couldn't be close. I needed to act as if nothing was different, for her sake. To keep her from feeling hurt. That was plenty of fuel to keep me from trying to do anything foolish.

Once we were behind the softly closed door, I found Sobely's hairbrush and started working on her long silky strands. She lay on her side, perfectly still. I found myself humming a tune while I brushed.

"What is that song?"

"All You Need is Love. Never a truer statement." I answered. I set the brush aside and lay beside her. She seemed to melt against me, relaxing into her accustomed spot. Even the fire relaxed a little.

"Are there any words?" She asked.

I sang softly to her, and it became a lullaby. The pull of the words lulled us both back to sleep.

Waking up in the afternoon is always a little disorienting. Of course, we probably would have slept on 'til morning if we hadn't been woken up by external forces. Seeing as we weren't in any danger, I might have been grouchy about that. But the reason was good.

It was dinnertime.

Mildred made up for sleeping through lunch by cooking a massive cheese-oozing chicken casserole, with the promise of a special dessert afterwards. To say that Sobely's eyes got wide at the wonderful smell would have been understating things.

It smells almost like Mom's.

The casserole was one of the tastiest things I had ever eaten. Sobely, who was being very careful with her fork this time, said 'mmm, mmm' between every bite. Her face had stayed clean, even though she ate two plates of it all by herself. The plates weren't small, either. I could tell by now that she really liked milk, too, since she finished off the half gallon served up in a stoneware pitcher.

I was a little worried that she would offend our hosts. However, Mildred was delighted to see Sobely enjoy her cooking. The web of wrinkles crinkled with her smile.

Dabbing her clean cheeks, Sobely complimented the meal,

"That was the best thing I have ever eaten."

So far, I had been lucky. Nothing Sobely had said had caused our hosts to ask about her memory. Mildred had let slide the little things, like the fact that she called eggs 'yellow squishy things.'

"Why thank you, sweetie. Wait until you taste dessert!" Mildred took the four plates with her when she got up to get whatever it was she made.

Dessert looked like a slab of cherry-syrup covered chocolate. It made all my teeth hurt just looking at it. Mildred gave us each a piece. Sobely took a small bite, and her delicate nose wrinkled.

"Well... I... Uhh..." She seemed unsure of what to say. She turned and whispered to me. "It is even sweeter than the jam. I do not wish to be mean, but I do not really like it."

My bite gone about as well as hers had. I thought it was far too sweet as well. Why did older people like sweet things so much? Did they not get any sweets when they were children?

"Mrs. Jackson. Not to be rude... I'm sure it is wonderful, but... I'm sorry..."

"Hey, it's ok. I suppose not everyone has a sweet tooth. Or maybe it's just sweet for something else... anyway, it's not rude to say what you don't like." Mildred wasn't offended at all. Neither was Jack – he had finished his piece and was now devouring Sobely's.

"Definitely no offense, boy. Her desserts have won so many awards, it would be silly to take offense if someone didn't like it. Have some more casserole." Jack then tried to reach for mine, but Mildred slapped his hand.

"Fat pig!" Her remark caused Jack to do an impression of a pig, which caused Sobely to start laughing joyously. *I wonder if she even knows what a pig is... I hope she doesn't ask them.*

With the comedy over, I took the opportunity to ask Jack my question.

"I was wondering if there was some way for you to help us get some different plates for the truck tomorrow. We will be needing to get on our way soon."

Sobely was leaning on me again.

"Already ahead of you. Called DMV earlier, and I just got to go and pick them up. I hope you can stay tomorrow night, at least. I would like to spend the day teaching you about some things."

"What things?"

"Well, believe it or not, I used to work WitSec. Years ago. That's how I met Mills here. I could give you some pointers on how to disappear. Keep whoever it is you're running from off your tail."

"That... would be great. How do you think we've done so far?" I asked the question casually. If the trail had been obvious, then these two were in serious danger. I had no idea what I could do about it.

"I checked with some sources, and I'd say you've done pretty well. Supposedly you're driving a white sports car. A cashier at a Target recognized you, but you've changed direction, so that is actually in your favor." His approval was a relief. *Sports car?*

"Well, thank you. Could we watch some TV?" I asked. The nap and food had given me some energy, and I wanted to start to teach things to Sobely, too. *You are deluding yourself. You are just looking for enough distraction to last until she's too tired to stay awake.*

"Sure. In fact, I'll put the old guest TV back in the room so you can have some privacy. Got the thing out in the workshop." Jack scooted his chair back and was gone before I could tell him not to take the trouble.

Big on privacy around here. What did we look like?

"Are our clothes done, by any chance?" I asked. *At least some clothing would make the privacy a little easier. I can't believe I let myself slip up so badly in the bathroom.*

I can't believe that you are choosing to be so dense, partner.

"Umm, no. It sounds a bit odd timing, but the washer broke. I was going to wash them earlier, but I fell asleep. I'm sorry.

This was maddening.

A madman cackle thundered in my brain.

"Wow. The washer broke *today*?"

"No, it broke last week. And since we hang our clothes up to dry, you'll have to wait until tomorrow to have clean clothes." Jack said, carrying a TV past us. I started giggling.

This was like something out of a sitcom.

No, it's Fate sending you a message.

The universe could not really work like this.

Why not?

At least there is a working TV to help with distraction. Fate is just making it hard to do the right thing, as it often does.

Sure. As if that even makes any sense.

Jack huffed into the hall. We could hear a few piggish grunts as he set the television up, but we all just laughed. It was just an act. He fake-stomped back to the dining room.

"There you go. Don't know why we ever closed the B and B down."

"Thank you." I stood, shook his hand, and we made our way back to our room.

I grabbed the remote sitting on top of the little set, while Sobely arranged the pillows so we could sit up more comfortably. We settled easily, and I found it easy to relish her warmth, to be very grateful for her love. I focused on that.

I turned on the animal channel and proceeded to teach her about all the cute little creatures that flashed by. For some reason, the sound did not work, but it was a lot more fun to tell her myself.

She was delighted. As I would tell her the names, she would repeat them to herself. I was now glad for the privacy. Educating her was *fun*.

I was a little smug that the distraction had worked out so well. For some reason, my psychotic rational side was a little smug too. Maybe it was because I wasn't being torn in two over the fact that she pressed in so close.

Time is on my side… yes it is…

A few hours in, there was a show on farm animals.

"See. That is a piggy. Aren't they cute?" I said.

"Yes. But Jack doesn't look anything like them. Why would Mildred call him one?"

"Well, he likes to eat a lot, and so do pigs. Plus, there is a long-standing joke, where people call policemen pigs."

"Oh. Well, I like to eat a lot. Does that make me like a pig?"

"Not at all. You are tasting everything for the very first time and seem to be blessed with a fast metabolism. Rather, you don't seem to be bothered by all the food." The science of diet was beyond me, and I hoped my explanation was adequate.

"Alright. What is that one?" She pointed. So, I told her about horses, and chickens, and many more animals. It was nice to have something so... peaceful to do. She was so eager to learn, and I didn't tire of it. Could never tire of it. *If it were someone else?*

I would never tire of *her.* Everything else did not exist.

Exactly.

09

"Hmm." She mumbled in her sleep. It was probably the thirtieth time she did this and each time it made me feel all the guiltier. *At least she's not having a nightmare...* I had to agree. She was probably having a very good dream. No doubt it was born from a *very* pleasant memory. I was a pig.

I had woken up after only three hours of rest. The robes, kicked to the floor, gave silent confirmation to what I had realized in my own very pleasant dream. *What have I done? I am scum!*

Nah... it was only natural that things would develop like this. At least you're in a safe place. Imagine if you got carried away out there...

SHUT UP!! I screamed at myself in my head.

It had all started simply enough. An infomercial had switched on, and Sobely had crushed me in one of her thought erasing kisses. The splendor, the intensity... it was quite understandable why such a glorious kiss could cause such a reaction in me. In anyone.

I would almost like to say that I had only reacted to the kiss, to the way she made me feel. I would almost like to claim that my hands had undressed her without any input from my brain. But all that would have been a lie. I had been all too aware of what I was doing. I had willingly been pulled along by the craving... or maybe I did the pulling.

Honestly, I was glad to have been aware through the whole experience. I found it to be *very* enjoyable.

This was why I was so despicable.

She trusts me. She loves me. I am weak.

Dawn was lighting the room. Sobely trembled a little in my arms. I silently hated myself for enjoying the feel of her soft skin against mine. I was torn in two, half of me ecstatic over what we had done; the other half convinced that I was a monster.

How could she even begin to comprehend what we had done? Of course she was willing... she trusted me. Somehow, with her lips on mine, everything had snapped together. Everything had seemed so perfect. But how could she understand?

If that was wrong... than why be good?

Shut up! I wasn't in the mood to listen to my rationalizing. I was sick of myself. *I must be going insane, to be having an argument with myself!*

What your problem is, partner, is that you are uncomfortable with every good thing that happens to you.

That couldn't be true. I was very happy to have Sobely in my life.

Yes, and two people in love, make love. It's not like you don't love her. Like you wouldn't die for her. Does it surprise you that she feels the same?

No. Of course I knew she felt the same about me. But she never even asked what was going on. Never questioned what we were doing.

It felt good for her, too. Why would *she protest?*

A bar of sunlight settled on her face, and her eyes fluttered open. The smile I loved filled her shining face and filled me with even more guilt. Inwardly, I groaned. She would *definitely* have a lot of questions.

What's the big deal? After that... what's the big deal? Just answer them.

First thing though, she wrapped her arms around my neck, and pulled my face toward her until we kissed. As with any other time, all the torment in my soul vanished, like she was the water for my spirit. Fire exploded, and I knew that this time, I was neither pulling nor led. I was simply enveloped.

Ah, hell. Why bother fighting it.

Exactly. You would only hurt her.

It was later that the questions came. A breeze parted the curtains, and blew across us, the cool air feeling electric on my bare skin. I turned red – I had forgotten all about the open window. With the swirl of emotions in my mind, there was just enough brainpower left to hope that our clothes hadn't been hung to dry just yet. *Just act like nothing is odd, and they'll leave you alone. Probably.*

"Is *that* why people are not supposed to see each other naked?"

Her question caught me off guard. It seemed simple, yet could not be answered with a simple yes or no. How could I explain this to her properly? She filled my silence with another question.

"Did I... do something bad? Was I a bad girl?"

Her lips trembled now. *How on earth? I'm the one who started it!*

Suddenly my shame, my turmoil, my self-loathing. It was gone. The split was gone. I could feel something else take its place, something both powerful and wonderful. Confidence. In remembering our night... and morning... I knew how right things were.

See?

"I don't see how anything that we do together could be bad. Why do you think that?" *Maybe because you are thinking it, too, bird brain.*

"Because..." Her breath hitched, and it all clicked. All of her own self-doubts, and all of my fumbling. *How must she feel, that you were trying so hard not to share an experience like that with her? She doesn't understand the rules of society. They don't even seem to make sense anymore.*

"Sobely, I. Love. You! It's not that I didn't want to... with you... I was just a coward. I couldn't explain things to you, why certain rules exist. I was too *scared* to tell you. I'm sorry if I hurt you, or if I somehow made you think I *didn't* want you."

Something my Dad had told me came to me then, distinctly. Almost as if I could hear him again. I think I finally understood his advice. *"Don't ever regret any joy you find in life. And don't run away from it either."* I promised then that I wouldn't. Now I would keep that promise.

I kissed her.

"Let's go find some breakfast." I said, trying to pull her away from the pain I could see in her eyes. Pain I had unknowingly caused.

"Did... did you think that it was wonderful?" She asked, her voice soft as the breeze.

"Yes. A thousand times yes." I answered. Her response was to smile warmly, and it occurred to me that there were other ways to erase her hurt.

It was still a *little* early for breakfast anyway.

We decided later that Cheerios were all we really needed for a decent breakfast. We had the house to ourselves, not even a note to explain where Jack and Mildred had gone. That was okay, though, because I didn't really feel like sharing Sobely just then. I was feeling unreasonably possessive at the moment.

Actually, it is pretty reasonable.

It was conceivable that Jack and Mildred had left for just this reason. I felt strangely buoyant, and not the least worried about what anybody thought about us anymore. After all, I really only cared about what made Sobely happy. Of course, had I been an observer to my behavior I would have instantly called it crap.

How many other kids my age had I rolled my eyes at because they gotten 'lucky?' I at least would be able to argue that I met all the points that I would use to argue against their stupidity. I wasn't *using* her for sex, I wasn't planning on leaving her in the lifetime of the universe, and I love her. Present. Tense. Unlike several kids I had known, I hadn't been scheming to get 'into her pants' from the moment I saw her.

I did *try* to do everything right. We had much bigger things to worry about than sex. For some reason though, that all disappeared for a while. I had known what was happening, yet...

Could it be that perhaps Fate was a little fed up with us, and decided to move things along a bit? I didn't like to think that something larger had its hand in our actions, but we *were* on the run for our lives.

Sobely was wonderful. On that fact, everything thing else revolved. I've heard sex described as a primal act, but... *primal* sounds like such a rough word. Angry even. Definitely not a word I would use to describe what happened between us. More like beautiful, or wonderful...

I realized I had floated away when I felt the rather insistent hand on my chin. *Okay... So maybe not all stories of what sex does to the brain are crap.*

I twisted suddenly, and with some kind of unconscious precision darted into a perfect kiss... if you counted perfect as missing and landing with both lips on her nose. With her, I did.

She giggled. For some reason, the sound was even more... infectious than ever before.

"A little lower, Tim. You seemed a little... um... away. I was trying to give you a kiss to bring you back to me." Her voice was a chorus of soft bells.

"I kissed exactly where I meant to. You have such a lovely nose..." I kissed it again, "And forehead... and I mustn't neglect to kiss your ears!" I darted all over her face, making her blush, all the way to the tips of those ears.

Odd that Jack and Mildred haven't asked questions about those yet.

Dark doubts about the future crept about us, but I continued to ignore them. *Of course, you realize that your resolve was seriously compromised by the tectonic amounts of stress you've endured over the last few days. The body wants what it wants, and when it's hurting it wants it all the more. If we're going to be strictly honest here.*

Shut up. You already won.

"What were you thinking about, anyway?" She scooted her chair close, the better for her to wrap her arms tight around me. And so I would have a moment to come up with an answer.

"Umm..." I panicked, "What a lovely neck, too!" I started to kiss her neck and shoulders, though I had to push the robe slightly away. I could feel the blush spread. I could also feel her relax and knew she had given up the line of inquiry for the moment. I felt slightly triumphant of that fact. Guilty too.

Looking up for a moment, I spotted our clothes, fluttering wetly in the breeze through the dining room window. The clothesline was on the opposite side of the house from our bedroom window, so perhaps some awkwardness could be avoided. *Even if they heard nothing, you'll still turn red as a cooked crab for no reason, which would still give you away.*

"Hmm… That feels nice… but I want to finish breakfast. Maybe we should stop?" Sobely murmured.

I had lost track of what my hands had been up to…

Suppressing a groan, I let her pull away, and we managed to finish our Cheerios. *Well Dad, I won't regret any joys, but I think I better learn some self-control, or I could put us both into real danger.*

We took our bowls into the kitchen and washed them. Rather, I washed them while she dried them. I took a little more time than was necessary for cereal bowls, but I was trying to make an effort to cool down. Sure, we were probably safe now, but we had start getting ready for our next move. I refused to think of what we shared as wasted time, but I knew that there were other things we needed to do with our time *now*.

So, while swirling a rag around a dinner plate from last night, (two cereal bowls just wasn't enough) I tried to put into order what needed to be done.

"We need to get our truck. Jack said he ordered us some new license plates, but I would feel a lot safer if we actually had access to our vehicle. Then we need to get stocked up on some supplies. Stuff that will keep well."

"Like jerky?" Sobely took the plate, and dried it carefully, placing it on the stack in the cupboard in front of her.

"Yeah, plus canned stuff. I think you might like Spaghetti-O's. We also need to get a good travel map. One that shows us all the back roads. I think we would be a lot better off if we could stay off the main highways as much as possible. It will be a lot easier to disappear then."

"Where will we sleep?"

"Well, that is why we need a map. Then we can find out where all the little backwoods campgrounds are. A tent would be useful too. The nice weather won't hold out forever. Plus, we can get an oversized sleeping bag. Tried to find one the other night, but it's something that we would have to go to an actual sporting goods store for."

"What is a sleeping bag?" We were running out of dishes.

"Well, a sleeping bag is like a blanket, but it zips around you, to keep the air out on all sides. We need an oversized one, because a regular one only fits a single person. With a good sleeping bag, we won't have too many problems with the cold this winter."

"I like that idea. Kind of like being hugged twice?"

"Yeah." I handed her the last fork. In a flash, it was dry, and put away.

She turned. I didn't have any good excuses for not taking her into my arms. So, I allowed my arms to wrap around her. As long as they behaved themselves.

"What can we do right now?" She asked, only casually in my embrace. She had me. There wasn't a thing we could do, without our truck.

"I guess... nothing." I answered. She snuggled in closer and whispered into my ear.

"Then, we *could* go back into our room. I bet I need kisses in other places, too."

"I like that." She said. I thought she meant what my hand was doing, but she was pointing at the mighty creature on the TV screen. I had fixed the sound, and we lounged lazily on our sides, her learning about the fearsome creatures from the Amazon. I took notice of what she was admiring. *Incredible!*

"They are... strong animals." I replied. I stopped the restless motion of my hand as it made endless journeys through her hair.

"Do not stop. That is nice, too!" She exclaimed. My fingers began to try and memorize every strand of silken goodness.

"What do you like about the crocodiles?"

"They are neat looking. And they will do anything to protect their babies. That is sweet. Plus, their babies are so cute!"

Ripping a man in half just because he happened to get a little too close to the nest? Well, I guess that's kind of sweet. But did she just say that crocodile babies are cute?

"Where do the babies come from? They have shown us all these cute little baby animals, but I do not understand it."

Here it was. Spend a day watching shows about little animals, and she's bound to ask where they come from. *That was thinking of me.* At least she understood one part of the process...

"Well. Animals, and people too, create babies the same way. Umm... Sometimes when a male and a female have... uh..." I swallowed. *This actually would have been easier to explain without her knowing anything.* I turned a new shade of red, a shade I knew would belong to her forever now. Sobely Blush.

Her eyes widened in understanding.

"You mean we will get a baby now?"

Close. *Wait. What if... What have I done?*

Thankfully, I had a few facts on my side.

Delusions, really.

"Well, uh... a baby *could* be growing in you. They aren't made every time, though."

"Growing *in me?*"

"Yes. The female is sort of designed to carry the baby inside her until it's ready to be born." I think I had a fever now. Here I had been thinking of how comfortable things had gotten. *What if she is...*

"Would that not be wonderful?" Her voice had an awed edge to it. It was the answer to my question.

"Yes. It would be wonderful. Just... Let's not worry about it right now. I promise I will explain how it all works later, but I'm not really ready right now."

"Oh. I see. I guess having a baby would be difficult for us. Maybe when we do not have to run anymore we can... wait. We should not... do that again. That is why people shouldn't see each other naked." The disappointment dripped from her voice.

Wait a minute here! Didn't that commercial say...

"Actually, I don't think we have to worry just yet. You see, there is a narrow timeframe during the month that a woman could become pregnant. There are things we can get to prevent pregnancy, too. As long as we acquire them as soon as we can, we ought to be okay for a couple of days."

You always hear about how hard it is for couples to get pregnant. A few days shouldn't matter... right?

Yeah, right. Sure. Nothing at all to worry about.

"Pregnancy?"

"That is what it is called when you have a baby growing in you."

"Oh. So... I probably do not... It is safe for us to..."

"Yeah. I think so. I'm not really an expert." *And I slept through sex ed, the one health class most students pay attention to.*

"Well that is good, then." She was pleased. Or at least she seemed pleased.

Eager to end the conversation, I started kissing the back of her neck. I resolved to pick up a book on the subject at the next opportunity, to better educate the both of us.

"I wonder where Jack and Mildred went." Sobely pondered. She tilted her head so more of her neck was exposed to me.

"I don't know. Jack is the Sheriff, so he is probably working. Mildred probably had errands to run or something." I spoke in a rush, not letting her distract me from my newly self-appointed job.

"It is kind of nice to have a safe place all to ourselves, do you think?"

"Mm-Hmm" I mumbled. The buzz of my lips made her shiver. *Home had been* safe *too.*

With speed that I hadn't expected, she rolled around to face me.

"We really *should not* waste the little bit of time we have. Tim?"

She was trembling. Despite her words, her tone wasn't playful. Instead, I could hear... terror in her voice. *You aren't trying hard enough, buddy. You vowed she would always feel safe.*

I sighed. Sadly, the comfort I had already been intending *was* only a temporary fix. I still had no idea how to make her feel always safe. *Maybe time will help with that.*

"Yes?" I asked gently. I resisted the urge to pull her close, to close the distance. She needed other comforts as well.

"How much time is there? I do not mean here at Jack's. How long are we going to remain safe? How long before they find us? I do not..." Her voice got very small then. "I do not want to die."

I rejected the automatic response. I wanted to tell her 'Forever.' Instead, I stared into her eyes, and tried to find an answer that wouldn't be a lie and would also be acceptable to me.

In her arms, it was easy to believe we were invincible. That we *had* forever. I truly believed that love would get us through our trials. Yet, it also occurred to me that getting through our trials together did not mean we would also survive them. We had already passed the only one that really mattered, anyway.

And it was with this that I foolishly answered her.

"I strongly believe that we have already won. We already know that nothing will ever tear us apart. We already know that we will never give up fighting. From our standpoint on their sick game board, we have achieved our goals. It doesn't matter what they throw at us — we won't break. I don't know how much time we will have before... before the game ends. We were never meant to be a winning side, just the pieces."

"I am scared. I know... what the greatest pain *would* be. I want more, Tim. I want more time with you. I want forever and ever."

Tears spilled over from her eyes. They stopped me cold. I was such a fool. *You said the wrong thing again.* I had meant to comfort her and said the wrong things. *How does 'giving up' comfort anyone?*

"Sobely, listen to me. I... was just saying foolish things. I am an idiot."

She shook her head. Her mouth opened, as if to protest.

"Maybe today it looks like we can't win, but I promise you that we will find a way. Because there are so many things I want to do with you. So many places I want you to see. So many tasty foods for you to try. And one day, there is another promise to keep."

"What is that?" She asked. I could not bear her tears any longer. I pulled her close to me again and whispered,

"Someday, we will have a cute little baby of our own. And *you* can rip anyone in half that gets too close."

She laughed, and I kissed the tears out of her eyes.

Before long, the darkness lifted again, leaving us free to find our own temporary bliss.

A rapping on the door boomed into the light slumber we had fallen into. Somehow the world seemed as if it were cast in a strange, magical light. As if everything were cut from gossamer. The only thing real was the beauty beside me, who had also come awake at the odd noise.

Nothing seemed real. My brain seemed to have been left behind. The rap came again. Somehow, I was able to have the presence of mind to pull the quilt over us before answering,

"Come in."

Jack opened the door cautiously.

"Hey there, kids. Come on out and have some lunch. Mildred went out grocery shopping, but there is plenty of casserole left. Besides that, I need to get started teaching you some survival skills."

Jack closed the door quickly. His face was red.

"I do not want to get up just yet." She whispered, snuggling closer to emphasize her claim. I understood perfectly. I wanted it to always be like this.

"We probably should though. He could teach us a lot of useful stuff. We will need every trick we can get when we get on the move again." I said, defeated. *Will it never end?*

She sighed.

Carefully, we slipped out of bed, pulling the two robes back on. Again, I demonstrated the simple knot needed to keep it closed, but I could tell she was still confused by it.

That was fine with me. Any chance at all to touch her... *Focus now!*

We joined Jack in the dining room. On the table waited two plates of steaming leftover casserole, as well as three glasses of cold lemonade. Sobely, for once, did not seem very eager to begin eating, and instead picked at her food.

While we ate, Jack talked.

Information poured out of him. I wished for a time that I had thought to grab a notebook, because I did not think I could remember all the little details that he described. Things to do and also things not do to stay ahead of anybody. Hiding was a lot more complex that I had thought. All you needed in the movies was a good disguise.

In reality, though, changing the color of your hair did little to hide you. There were so many things he spoke of, I could not help but be lulled into a kind of hypnotic trance by his voice.

And then I realized it. I saw the pattern to what he was saying. The Golden Rule for staying ahead of your enemies. In a break of his constant talking, I decided to voice my discovery.

"Basically, you are saying to have no habits. Don't be routine about anything. Right? All the little things mean, to keep *changing* the little things."

Jack was silent for a moment.

"Hey. That's pretty good. I should have thought of that summary years ago – would have saved a lot of time. Would have had more time for questions, and more time to answer them correctly."

"Yeah. Where are we going to get new IDs, so we can keep changing cars? Wouldn't it create a paper trail with all the titles being filed, and the car insurance? That would give us away."

Again, Jack was speechless for a moment.

"I hadn't thought of that, either. In the agency, we would always give them new ID cards, so that was never a problem. That was Mildred's job."

Jack hung his head in thought.

"Well, they don't know the truck. Maybe we'll change the paint or something every once in a while. You don't need an ID for that."

"Good point. Besides, a classic like that ought to have a better paint job. Engine is perfect on it."

"You checked it?" I asked.

"Yep. Right before towing it back here to put the plates on it. Would have brought you along, but you were… uh… busy."

I turned red again, at exactly the same speed as Sobely.

"You two are in perfect harmony, aren't you? Even better than before." Jack said. His voice was light, but I could feel the weight of conviction behind his words. The rightness there. Maybe it was just because it mirrored my own feelings.

He had noticed the new ease between us, the complete absence of awkwardness. I wondered if he suspected just how it came to be, and then realized he understood perfectly. I felt a fierce affection for this man and wondered at how great things could be found even in the midst of hardship.

Before, I would have passed him on the street, and not even look twice. Would have never wondered who he was. Did it take crisis to understand people, or had it been her?

She was the reason that I kept living, though I had lost so much. She was also the reason I had started living. The hole in my heart was filled, yet I had never known it was there before. Yes, I mourned my family. But I could live as long as I had her.

Anything she gave me beside her companionship was icing on the proverbial cake. Her love, her heart, I would have lived without, just to be near her. She had given it all to me without reservation, and with perfect understanding of what she was doing. Love was not taught after all; love teaches you.

I would have thrown myself from a cliff if it would have been able to guarantee her safety. As Jack had pointed out before, I would kill anyone that threatened her life. I would love her every minute I was awake, and every minute I slept. A coma could not take her from me. Every fiber I was, every pulse of my heart, was hers.

Now, I had actually accepted that. I accepted that she could feel the same. It was *wonderful* to be alive and in love. I had waited all my life to live, but I would have waited an eternity for her.

Harmony? Is that word strong enough? It was not cliché to say that she was my other half. It was truth. Or perhaps, it was closer to say that she was everything.

To Jack, I simply nodded.

Supper that night was a somber affair. No one spoke, forks were used with such care that they didn't even tinkle against the plates. Mildred hadn't spoken since she had arrived home and tended to avoid both our gazes. When she did look up from her plate, her eyes shined with unshed tears. Even though her cooking was perfect, I couldn't taste it.

This place had been our safety, and we would be leaving it. Never mind the reasons why, never mind that every minute here put them in even greater peril. They did not understand what our danger was, or how tenacious our enemy. I didn't have any idea of the scope of it myself. At least they believed me when I told them that we must leave in the morning.

Jack was strangely still. I hadn't noticed before, but Jack always fidgeted. He was always restless. Tonight, though, he was still as stone, the only movement being the occasional bite taken from the plate. Even that stopped, with only a quarter of the food gone.

They could feel it. Plain as day.

Sobely's plate, too, was barely touched. She had taken only a few bites before clinging to my arms as if I were going to blow away in a breeze.

I was the only one to finish what I was given. I ate the rest of hers, too. Not because I was hungry, but because I would need to stay strong tomorrow. Who knew where we would stop again. The pasta would be a good long-lasting fuel for a good long drive.

After dinner, Sobely and I washed dishes again. Rather, I washed, and dried, while she clung to my waist like a child. She could feel the terror as well as I could and was far less able to handle it. I felt angry with myself for being unable to do anything to soothe her. Temporary comforts faded all too quickly. The knowledge that we would be on the move again brought up the ghost of what had put us on the road in the first place.

When Mildred came in to the kitchen, it was to wish us good night, and to make sure we wouldn't leave before saying good-bye. Her tears made me a little angry too – she had no idea what she was asking us. The best thing would be to leave them right now.

I promised her that we wouldn't, so long as they were up early.

I could not stall, even for them. I had delayed my instincts before, and we nearly died as a result. My mother had paid the price and had never even known what was going on. *The last thing you ever said to her was a lie.*

Knowing we would never get to sleep unless we were relaxed, I decided that we should take another bath. Only this time, I joined her in the oversized tub. Truth be told, she wouldn't let go of me. I washed her gently while she clung and wept. I wasn't enjoying it like I had thought I would. Probably because she wasn't.

Why couldn't I make her feel safe?

Or, is it that she feels the new weight pressing in? Does she feel that something has changed? We had disappeared, and they were bound to escalate things.

Perhaps they wouldn't find Jack and Mildred, but they probably would. We doomed them the moment Jack shone his Mag-Lite on us. Sobely's terror was for them. She could feel it just as well as I could. In the morning, I would tell them to run. They knew how to hide, better than we did. They had a better chance to be safe.

The rest of the night passed in passion rather than slumber. I had been right; we couldn't sleep. The moonlight made the curtains glow, and her pale skin seemed to be a light, holding the darkness at bay. The world only existed here, for us.

In the darkness, shapes moved in and out of being with fluid grace. Nothing was given to harshness; all was soft in that strange glow. In this little world, nothing could be evil. Evil was what prowled outside, looking for a way in, and failing. For now. But it would always come back to try again.

Terror and desperation collided, forming an illusion of perfect safety, bound by our love. There was no need to agonize over parting – for we would never be without the other. Nothing would touch us. We were safe.

If only the lie could remain the truth.

Like children, we clung to each other, afraid of the dark. We found a comfort and clung to that too. Like children, we feared for the monsters in the gloom. We feared that they would eat us if the light went out.

Love *comforts* all.

10

"Here, Tim. You may need it. I've got others."

I stared at the revolver a moment before accepting it. The holster had been placed on a different, less official-looking belt. This one designed to hold a number of extra bullets. The similarity it had to something from an Eastwood movie nearly made me giggle.

The monster was loose, somewhere. *One revolver versus the world...*

"Thank you, Jack. For everything. Please – you must heed my warning. Run. They *will* come." There was a desperate begging in my voice now.

"Don't worry about us. We'll be fine, dear."

Mildred patted my shoulder. Her gift had been a larger cooler, stuffed full of food. The presumed reason for her sudden shopping trip yesterday. She had also purchased comfortable clothing for travel, large sloppy-knit hats, and a couple pair of sunglasses.

Neither of them seemed concerned with the death that hung over them like Grim's Scythe. *Why won't they listen?*

Sobely still hadn't spoken. Her silence was beginning to worry me. She had been pretty... vocal in the dark, but since we had woken to the cold dawn, she had not even said that she loved me. Her tears now shook her body, and me, yet there was no sound.

Mildred had tried to fret over her since we emerged from our room, but she was pushed away, and Sobely clung tightly to me. Afraid.

The terror was catching up to her.

"Good-bye dear friends. Thank you both so much." I whispered, unable to produce any volume.

"Good-bye." Jack said. Mildred looked down, unable to speak.

Gently, I pulled Sobely into the truck, setting the gun on the floorboard. The engine roared to life, a dependable noise. I paused before putting it into gear, staring at Jack and Mildred, exchanging my thanks to them silently.

And we pulled away from those that sheltered us. The terror wasn't in parting, or even in the knowledge that they were no longer safe harbor. The terror I felt was something that had begun to build since that very first day. It had finally broken free.

Something was let loose.

The prelude was truly over. The game had really begun.

"Tim?" Her voice quavered. After not hearing it for hours though, it was still a slice of paradise.

"Yes, my love?"

"I feel even more afraid than before."

I squeezed her gently with the arm that was around her, willing her to feel safe. I let the truck come to a stop in the shoulder.

"I'm here. I will always be here. No matter what happens. I know you are scared, but I promise you that I will *keep you safe.*" I stared into her eyes intently, trying to imbibe her with confidence I didn't entirely feel. *You do feel it. Deep down. You swore it; therefore, it will be so.*

"How? I feel... Now it is like I *know* that there are monsters after us. Before... I had not actually thought about it."

"Don't worry. I promised you, and I always keep my promises." *You don't know what is out there, or how to save her from it.*

"It does not matter if I die." She whimpered, her voice a cruel mockery of my own thoughts from the day before.

"Don't say that!"

"If they got me, they would still come for you. I feel... happy about that. It gives me a reason to stop thinking of a way to face them alone. To try and save you. It would not matter. It means we can stay together always. It means I can hear you tell me all the wonderful things after we..." She smiled a little, "You still have not told me what it is called."

I felt tortured. She had thought of facing them alone? Had thought it would somehow protect me? Didn't she see that my life would have no meaning without her in it?

"Making love. That is what it is called. I wish you would stop blaming yourself for this. You never chose for this to happen." My tone was gentle.

Her face grew bitter.

"I don't remember *what* I chose."

Tears spilled from her precious eyes.

Oh. It was something I had never considered. That she may have somehow chosen all this. That she may have had a hand in planning this. *But do you really believe that's possible?*

No, I do not.

"Your memory may have been lost, but they couldn't erase *you.* Somehow your will, your spirit endured. You could never have chosen for this to happen. Can't you see that?"

Her head sunk in shame at my words, and I wished I had chosen them better. Still, I could not let it rest. Slowly, I lifted her face, and kissed her. Trying to make my love erase her fears, as hers did mine. I think I was at least partly successful, because when I was able to part, a small smile spread her lips.

That smile was enough to give me some hope. Hope enough to put the truck back into gear and continue our journey. This time, she rested against me and slept, satisfied for the moment that she was safe.

If only I knew *how* to keep us safe. If only her arms could provide the answers I so badly needed. If I could just shake the feeling that something monstrous *was* on our tail. Her safety was my greatest fear, and the revolver on the floor did little to reassure me. How could I save us from the unknown?

By nightfall, we were both too ravenous to ignore our hunger any longer. We parked the truck in a rest area and proceeded to devour a container of pasta. We didn't even bother with the plastic forks that had been thoughtfully packed for us, just stuffed the cold food in as fast as we could.

Fear makes you hungry.

Fear is just another greedy Beast, looking to feed.

Afterwards, we spread our blankets in the bed of the truck for our bed. I had wanted to continue driving, but the full day of on the road, the full belly, and the sleepless night before left me much too tired to continue driving. Instead, she lay in my arms, and we gazed up at the millions of stars we could see in the cold night sky.

I could tell that she was still fearful.

"Before I met you… well. I don't really know exactly how to say this." I murmured, trying to distract her, and trying to share with her the joy I truly felt.

"Say what?" She asked. I swallowed once, to clear the dryness from my throat, and began.

"I used to just drift along. I thought I had been doing okay. I thought life was okay. I didn't understand. I didn't realize the numbness I felt inside."

"Because… of your Dad?" She squeezed me gently, as if to ward off the pain his memory usually caused. A pain that I did not feel this time.

"No. I… I was happy when he was alive, but I was drifting then, too. Perhaps I was searching. Maybe I would have begun wandering on my own."

"Drifting…" She whispered sadly.

"To be perfectly honest, I feel as if my life began with you. As if it was as empty of meaning as yours is of memories."

"Because… no. You said I should not blame myself, and I will try." Her voice was sad, still. I had to endure the momentary pain, so she would understand.

"Don't you see it? The reason is obvious. *You* are my reason for being alive. Before, I had just been moving through life. I did not see it; I did not really enjoy it. Sure, there was happiness, but… it had no meaning. Nothing had meaning. I did not notice anyone. I… did not realize how much Mom was suffering without Dad. I would have never glanced twice at someone like Jack."

I squeezed her this time and kissed her head.

"When you came into my life, I noticed that I wasn't the only person in the world."

"You are the only person in my world." She kissed my ear.

"Exactly! I was like the moon. If the moon did not have the Earth to circle, it would simple wander aimlessly in the void. I hadn't noticed my void until a planet filled it. A light filled it. Love filled it. I know now what I was missing. I... can't understand how I lived without you. So, I have decided that I didn't truly live until you were here."

I squeezed her gently again.

"What about all this? Everything we have been through? The things you have had to give up for me?"

"You are worth it. Every bit." I kissed her head again, wishing she would slide upwards a little bit. Perhaps distracting myself from the painful truth. The starkness of the thought. The cruelty. Losing Dad. Losing Mom. All of it was worth it because of her. The thought was both wonderful and horrible all at once.

"But..."

"No buts. I don't think we will have to run forever. Someday we will find a way out of this mess. We have something that they cannot defeat, not with a thousand wounds. We have our love, and with it, I know that anything can be possible. As long as you are with me."

It's not as if you think the world is better without them.

She was quiet for a long moment.

"I think... I understand now. Next to this, what can stand against us? How I feel, and how you feel is powerful enough to make anything happen."

In answer, I pulled her onto me, kissing her lips with meaning. Had we found a somewhere a little more private, I doubt we would have stopped with that kiss. So, I made sure to get plenty of them, kissing her again and again until she giggled.

Maybe now, she would stop doubting herself, or wonder why she had fallen into my life. Maybe she finally saw the same reason I did. She belonged in my life, as surely as the sun belonged in the sky.

The other problem with not having found a hotel to stay in, was being forced to get up with the sun. I suppose the early start was nice, but it just seemed so peaceful, even at a roadside rest stop. *I'm sure a good joke could be made out of that.*

Yesterday, I had been the one who had fully accepted our relationship. I had been the one who had fully accepted that Fate brought us together forever. I had thought we couldn't be more perfectly attuned to one another. That we had found our stride. I had been joyously wrong.

Today, she had found it too. I knew I would have to reassure her again – probably a million more times, but deep inside, she accepted that nothing would tear us apart. That I did not wish her to ever be gone. That I never could.

Our eyes snapped open at the same time, as we both turned our heads to look for the other. But, while our smiles were synchronized, I knew that she won hands down when it came to the beauty of the expression.

"Shall we have some breakfast?" I asked.

"Sure!" She replied.

I sat up, stretching. Briefly, I let my eyes roam for a picnic table. As far as rest stops go, this one was pretty nice, with well-managed lawns, and pretty trees. The buildings were graffiti-free even.

What my roving eyes encountered instantly turned my blood to ice. It wasn't the trees, the lawn, or the metal picnic tables that were the problem. Perhaps the pleasant surroundings helped to make what I saw all the more sinister.

Six men in identical overcoats. Peering at a map. Could be business travelers, except for what one of them was holding. Across the short distance I could easily make out pictures of Sobely and I. Disheveled clothing and bloody shoe-less feet – the store we bought shoes at had a surveillance system. I hadn't even thought of the danger from cameras.

They wouldn't just be standing there, *they* would have homed in on us and have killed us while we slept. These people were someone else. *FBI? Just calmly start up the truck and...*

"What is…" I put a hand over her mouth, and ducked back into the truck, whispering in her ear.

"Shh… There are some men out there with our picture. I don't think they're the same ones from before, but it wouldn't be a good idea for these guys to know we are here, either. Curl up into a ball, and I'll load the stuff around you. I'll try to get us out of here quietly."

Under my hand, she nodded. I picked up a discarded plastic knife.

I now wished I had Jack's revolver handy. Whoever they were, they would be armed, and they would know how to use their weapons. A plastic knife was kind of pitiful next to that.

Carefully, I got up. Pretending as if nothing was going on. I scooted her clothes under the twisted blanket and loaded the cooler and tarp into the bed. *We will never sleep out in the open again.*

The hood of my shirt was up, and I prayed it would hide my face well enough. I would have to drive past the now arguing men. I tried to hide my nervousness by whistling a jaunty tune, as if I weren't afraid that they would turn towards me.

Somehow, the act worked. I was ignored. Even the truck roaring to life only elicited the briefest of glances. I eased the truck through the lot as if I weren't terrified of discovery.

When we were well out of their sight, I pulled the truck over. My heart was now pounding, and I had to rest my head on the wheel to fight off the wave of dizziness this caused. *That was much too close!*

I stifled a yelp when the passenger door opened. A pair of jeans landed on the seat, the owner pulling her shirt over her head. Backwards.

When I felt I could speak without my heart exploding, I addressed her.

"Get in! You can get dressed later!"

She hopped up into the truck, her bottom bouncing on the vinyl seat.

I spun tires to get the truck moving again. Afraid again. The men might stop arguing and come this way at any moment. I cursed the stereo for not working, for not knowing what outside forces had been arrayed against us. Had they managed to pin us for some murder? At least if the FBI went to Jack's house, there was a good chance they would be fine. I had a feeling that Jack was very good at bluffing.

Surely government agents don't torture regular people. Right?

This changed everything. If we had a multitude of forces against us now... It was hard to swallow. We had it hard enough with our picture in the news, and a sinister, dark organization looking for us.

If we now had the whole U.S. government looking as well... The thought of agents truly lurking everywhere sent a shiver down my spine. Today we had been lucky. Tomorrow, someone with brains might actually check on their surroundings. Or they could find out about the vehicle we were driving.

Next time, we might not even wake up.

Sobely, as always, sensed the proper thing to do. She scooted in close, and carefully leaned against me. It wasn't until her still body was pressed against mine that I realized that I was trembling hard enough to just call it shaking.

How can she have so much faith in me? I might remember more of my life, but I am running out of road. I have no idea what is that we have to stay ahead of! What if I get her killed through my own mistakes?

"Oh!" Sobely exclaimed.

"What?!" My voice was a bit frantic sounding.

"I just realized my shirt is on backwards. Oops." Her voice became very small. Instantly, I realized I had snapped at her. Twice. Shame burned, and I clenched my hands on the steering wheel. *If nothing else, I should never speak to her like that!*

"I... I'm sorry. I wasn't snapping at you. I'm just on edge, honey. That... that was much too close. Please don't think I'm angry at you – what reason would I be?"

I meant my words to be soothing. I did not expect her to have an answer.

"I forget things. I do not know anything. I knew my shirt went over my head, but I forgot that the tag goes in the back. You are so patient with me, and you love me so much... but I expect you to get mad at me. All I do is make mistakes. I'm trying to be a good girl. A good girl..."

Again, that phrase.

The whole time she spoke, she clutched her chest as if gravely wounded. I wanted to stop her, but I couldn't. Because finally I could understand a part of her. She thought I would be better off without her. More revelatory, she thought that I might think the same thing.

I could not ever know what it was like to have no memories. So far, the ones she had collected hadn't all been the best. Fear was such a big part of her. I remembered her first words, when she begged me not to leave her again. I had promised her then I never would.

But that was her fear. It might take a lifetime to erase it. We ran on borrowed time. *Why can't I make her see it? Even if she understands that we belong together, how can I make her safe from her own fear?*

She had been conditioned to fear.

I pulled the truck over again. If the FBI or even Lucifer Incarnate came, it wouldn't matter. I stared hard into her watery eyes while I tried to straighten my head out. I turned the entire situation on its head, to her perspective, and genuinely considered it. Life never knowing she existed, even with my Dad.

I remembered how lost I would feel, even when Dad was alive.

I remembered how good of a person my Dad was.

I knew that if Dad knew the future, he would have chosen this.

I remembered his 'heart attack' at work.

I remembered, oddly, a smiling, but evil-looking man that had attended Dad's funeral.

Then it clicked.

Dad worked to help people. He had the connections. Was it possible he *did* know? The mystery woman said he arranged for Sobely to be in my care. Had he known what the stakes would be?

I thought of Mom. What would she have chosen? If she knew what would happen, would she still have let it unfold as it did? She had been largely selfless. A caring soul, putting one foot in front of the other for my sake.

I had been an idiot for not telling her, right away, everything that happened. To be paralyzed in thinking that I needed to find something other than the *truth* to tell her.

Had she seen the gunmen, she would have gladly stepped into the path of the bullets.

"Sobely. I want you to promise me something."

"Anything!" She cried, her voice miserable.

"I don't want you to believe that I would ever wish for any life without you in it. My Dad would have understood this, had he known what our circumstances would have been, he would have still given his life to bring us together. To stop your torture. At least we have a chance."

"You think he would?" She asked timidly.

"Yes. I believe that. He would have chosen death so we could have this chance."

"Why? Why would anyone do that?"

I smiled at her.

"Because Dad was just like that. He had his own reasons, but they were always good ones. Now, promise me."

Her lips trembled. She closed her green eyes for several precious seconds, thoughts no doubt warring in her mind. Then, her green eyes opened, and pierced mine. Intensity burned fiercely.

"I promise to never wish for a life without you in it. For as long as I live, and even if you do one day... abandon me, I will never wish that again."

As if I ever could abandon my life!

"I promise you the same. You *are* my life."

We were silent, the fresh promises hanging in the morning air. The tension slowly bleeding off.

"Don't worry about the shirt. You will get the hang of it."

Fresh tears welled up. I was trying to lighten the mood. *What did I say wrong?*

"It's not just the shirt, Tim. I... I couldn't remember your mother's name yesterday."

That *was* a little troubling. *Stress. She doesn't have much experience with it.*

"It's okay. You never got to meet her, after all."

"I also... I could not think of the name of the nice lady at Jack's house. I... I know she lives there. I remember her, but her name... Mildred. How could I forget that?"

Quickly, I dispelled the panic her words caused me. *Stress.*

"We have been under a lot of stress. Sometimes, when a person is under a lot of stress, they forget things. It is nothing to worry about, okay? Your body forgets as a way to avoid pain. You are okay honey. You know who I am, right?"

"Of course! My Tim! You love me more than anything, and you are my life."

"See, your memory is fine. It's just stress. Besides, you remembered Mildred's name after a while, and remembered that your shirt was on wrong after a few moments, right?"

"Yes. You are... You are right."

"We'll be fine. I promise you that we will be fine."

She snuggled close, content that I was right. I tried to believe I was. I could not bear the thought of any other option. The truck started forward again, pulling us along, miles away into the unknown.

Safety is all a matter of luck.

By eight o'clock that night we were checked into a small hotel. I wanted to keep going, but I wasn't about to risk another night sleeping in the open. *Easier to defend a hotel room than the bed of a truck.*

Once in our room, I locked the door and windows, drawing the curtains shut. This made me feel reasonably secure, with Jack's revolver sitting on the nightstand within easy reach. *No such thing as too paranoid anymore.*

Sobely was strangely quiet as she watched me secure our haven for the night. Her eyes seemed blank, and all my fears surfaced, bringing an ugly memory. Something the Ancient Woman had said.

She said that usually a person who has been wiped is an empty shell...

I couldn't bear it.

"Hungry?" I asked.

She nodded. Silently, with none of her usual eagerness.

"I love you!" I blurted, panicking.

"I love you, too. Very much. I am a little worried though." She spoke, and her tone was odd, but it still served to quell my fear. Of course she wasn't becoming empty.

It had been a very harsh day. She tired easily, and the surges of self-doubt and fear must have left her drained. That was probably all it was.

"What can I do about it?"

She smiled, wonderfully, but it was tinged with... fear. Then she shook her head and laughed it off.

"I am just being silly again. Please... kiss me."

I realized that I hadn't kissed her a single time the entire day. Of course she felt worried.

I was instantly beside her. I pulled her up, into my arms, and into the fiercest kiss I could muster. I felt her blush as my hands crept along her slender body.

She responded by providing her own gentle inferno, and the world disappeared to give us some time alone.

Later, we ate sandwiches in bed. We had run out of lunchmeat, so we filled the stale bread with cheese casserole. A little time in the generously provided microwave, and we had a warm, if slightly odd, meal.

She ate with none of the care she had come to exhibit, and a little of the cheese had stuck to her chin. The way she treated the messy food reminded me of a child again. She was a person at constant odds with herself.

She licked her fingers clean and used her wet fingers to clean up the crumbs that had escaped. I do not think she was even aware of the small sounds of delight that escaped her at the treat.

Perhaps it was a little bit from euphoria. I was a bit euphoric myself.

I tried not to think about the fact that she slept so much. Or how weak she seemed when she held onto me. It was all a part of her. Things we would face together.

Instead, I watched as she amused herself by tracing her fingers across her stomach, watched her fingers walk up her belly to in between the gentle swelling of her breasts. It was certainly amusing.

The wonder was in how she saw life. Others might see her actions as an act of seduction. But Sobely was oblivious to such petty things. She was fascinated by her own body. I was too... but that was beside the point. To see the world how she saw it...

No wonder she was scared most of the time. No wonder she begged to know that I would always be there for her. We had been cheated. We should have been discovering a beautiful world, and instead we were forced into this maze of horror.

I wanted to scream at that thought.

Instead, I kissed her forehead, stopping her play. The look in her eyes were both child-like and wise. She understood a few things about how to make me react to her wants.

"I am... being silly."

"Nah."

"Of course, you would not tell me if I was, would you?"

"Nah. I'm enjoying it too much to stop you." I replied. Her skin turned the color of roses.

She twisted around to whisper in my ear.

"I liked it when you kissed me all over."

It was a wonder that she didn't jump back from the heat of my sudden blush. *I was a little carried away...*

My arms encircled her, not giving her the option of escape now. If I could hold her like this forever... I kissed her, as if it could work as a magic ward against all the terrors. I wanted so badly to be able to fix everything with a few kisses!

She smiled at me, and kissed me back, slowly catching fire. The fire was low, and sweet, as it should be. Perfect.

We burned together.

I vowed freshly to always smile for her, and to kiss her at every opportunity.

When her eyes fluttered open, the smile that greeted me was brighter than the summer sun.

"Good morning, beautiful." I said.

"Hey there. What is our plan for today?"

"We are going shopping. We definitely need clothes. After that... No plan at all. Let's disappear." My tone was casual.

"Sounds good to me." She replied. Her slender arms twined around my neck.

"Do we have to get up right away?" She asked.

I kissed her, and groaned when I pulled from it, to signify that I rather not. *Already feel the wolves closing in, don't you?*

"We got time for a shower, I think. Then we have to hit the road. We really do need to get some shopping done."

I couldn't keep the sad note from my voice.

"Yes. You did say that we needed to get something that would keep a baby from growing in me."

I felt my face grow scarlet. *I had forgotten.*

"Yeah."

"You are right." She slipped away, and this time my groan was involuntary. "We should not."

She sounded so sad.

Sudden conviction filled me. I wanted Sobely to have everything. I wanted her to be a mother. I knew it would bring her happiness that she could never find elsewhere, even with me. She would have it.

"Someday, my love. You will cradle a child of your own in your arms. I promise you. Someday, it will be safe enough for that."

The promise hung heavily in the air, until the smile I loved returned to her face.

11

The days blur together. The shimmer of heat on the interstates intensifies as the summer grew. May becomes June, June creeps up on July. Our path wanders, guided by the whims of fate. It seemed as if we had been granted some reprieve.

As far as I knew, we had crossed over to the Twilight Zone. Population: 2. *Tonight's story is one of terror and uncertainty. Where every shadow hides a monster. Every flash could be the sun glinting off the gleaming barrel of a loaded gun. Join our two travelers on a highway long forgotten, as they flee the unknown.*

I wouldn't be surprised to see Rod Serling himself with a thumb out, perfectly groomed as if he had just stepped out of the dressing room...

Our path wanders, but I was ever mindful of traps. The big cities. I would have loved to share the wonders of the country – yet I knew that national parks and public monuments would be even more dangerous to traverse than the big cities.

Wouldn't want to get gunned down visiting the World's Largest Ball of Yarn, now would we?

A month passes.

We were in Arizona. I was doing my best to avoid The Big Pothole. The sun rose on the horizon. Sobely's pale skin caught the light. She slept, completely unaware of the picture she made. A blanket pooled around her, head resting on a corner that had been pulled into a scrunched roll for the purpose. She wore a shirt that was much too big. Her graceful ears quivered as if stirred by some unknown wind.

If only I had a camera. If I could only capture this moment. Something to look back on. The peace won't last. We've been lucky – but it's a numbers game. Sooner or later... Just how long can we run? How much of our time is left? I turned my thoughts towards plotting victory – though I could not imagine our way to it.

Four or five weeks had passed, with little to show for it. We were breathing. We were free. As free as the fox chased by hounds. *Sometimes the fox escapes – free to live another day. Yet, what hunter gives up so easily? Once the fox is known to be in the wind, the hunt is relentless. The hounds return the next day. And then the next. The fox lives in fear, knowing only that it does not wish to die.*

The only way to defeat the hounds, is to kill the hunter.

"I think we ought to stay in a motel tonight." I announced. Sobely turned her gaze from the passing scrub. Green eyes considered my countenance.

"Is it safe?" She asked. *Fair question.*

"I think so. It's been a long time since we've seen any sign of interest. Maybe they've found a better use of their time." I offered.

"Do you think it is possible?" Her voice had a tremble in it. *Hope?*

"Anything is possible." The response automatic. Habit. "Though I think..." I bit my lips. *Let her have some ease.* "Anyway, we'll sleep in a real bed tonight. Have a hot shower. Everything else, we can sort out in the morning."

"Mmm. That does sound like a nice idea." She murmured. Eyes half-closed, face upturned. As if she could already feel the water running over her skin already. "Must we wait until tonight?"

"Are you tired?" I asked, concerned. She hadn't been awake for very long.

An impish smile danced upon her lips. I returned my eyes fully to the road, lest I become too enchanted.

"No... I feel like... I want to move? Umm..."

"Restless?"

"Okay. Yes. Restless. I feel restless. I thought maybe... well... it is just that... Umm..." I glanced at her. She seemed uncertain, her cheeks rosy in the mid-morning sun. "A bed *would* be nice..." She whispered, half to herself. She turned her head forcibly to stare out the other window, shoulders tense. Ears gone scarlet.

Oh.

Her meaning set off fireworks in my brain. A hyper-awareness awoke in me. Every strand of hair, her bare legs. The drops of sweat as they slid down her skin, catching the hot Arizona sunlight as we drove along. The delicate sound of her breathe.

It was as if I had been over-ridden. Where before I had been thinking of how best to use our respite, now all I could do was think of her. I freed a hand from the task of steering the truck, and let it find her knee.

"I suppose there is no harm in an early check-in. I *have* been driving a long time. Probably a good idea to stop early today. How about we see what's in the next town? Maybe stop somewhere for a bite of food."

Her head snapped back around. A serious expression on her face now.

"Only one bite?"

I chuckled.

"What is funny?" She asked, bewildered.

"I mention food, and you become so serious! It's only a saying. 'Grab a bite' means 'to get a meal.' I won't starve you – I promise." I raised my hand from her knee to tousle her hair affectionately.

Though it hadn't been easy, I had now mastered the fine art of carrying on an animated conversation with her, without steering us into a ditch or something worse. If left to wander, my eyes always found their way to her. The real trick was to keep from becoming entranced.

I pulled my gaze away from the contented look on her face. Before returning to the road, my eyes located her sweatpants on the floor. Tucked neatly within were her panties. A delicate bit of lace with the power to send all the blood in a body rushing about.

I shook my head to clear the spell. Mindful of how my face burned a little hotter than the fierce sunlight warranted.

Flashes of memory arced through my brain like lightning. My mind surged with temptations, filling me with no small amount of shame. Her world was so much simpler. Her mind free of societal rules and roles. Her thoughts unfettered by impropriety. She did not understand her own primal instincts. She did not know the affect the glimpses of bare skin had on my brain.

She hugged my arm, humming tunelessly. Blissfully oblivious.

My desires weren't for my own pleasure, though. I longed to see her face in ecstasy. To erase the world of uncertain terror in a wash of blissful, blessed *joy.* To have her know only the pure, aching delight. *You don't understand it any more than she does, partner.*

There was much to be afraid of, and I would trade a piece of my soul to grant her immortal happiness. Given the choice between preventing a nuclear strike against the White House, and the guarantee of her safety, I'd press that button myself with no remorse.

"I think you should probably get dressed now. We can't really go into a restaurant without pants." I said. The truck still rolled along. I had triumphed over the Beast.

Her arms moved up to encircle my neck. I could feel her breathe on my ear as she bent closer. Whispering.

"How about we find one of those 'drive-in' places, and get two 'bites' we can take with us to eat at the hotel?"

"Well, that was good." She said, scarfing a fry.

"I guess fast food is the same everywhere." I replied. She giggled, her hair a rippling wave to tickle my chest.

"The food was good, too." She kissed me on the shoulder.

"Hmm. I see." I let a finger trace along her spine. She shivered slightly and nuzzled deeper into my side. She yawned and stretched.

"I'm stuffed now." She remarked, eating a pair of fries. She yawned again mid-bite. "I'm also very sleepy."

"That's understandable. I think you should probably take a shower before you go to sleep though."

"You are probably right. A nice hot shower. I do feel all sticky. Although..." Her lips spread into a heart-wrenching smile.

"What is it?"

"The last time we stopped at one of these places, there was not enough hot water for both of us. You had to wash in cold water. Maybe…" She bit her lip, suddenly shy. "Maybe we should share it this time."

For some reason, I felt guilty again. It still felt as if I had done something wrong by her. A sense of unfairness. Or maybe I just wanted her to be able to understand everything. It seemed to me as if I had her life unspooling all out of order. She didn't even know how to write her own name yet.

"Did I say something wrong again?" Sobely asked. I sat forward in the bed, buying time to get my thoughts in order. I found an exposed toe and ran my thumb down it. Applying gentle pressure to the arch in her foot.

"No, I think that's a very good idea. I was just thinking about… things."

"Bad things?"

For all the guilt I might have felt, I did not feel *regret.*

"Not really. I guess maybe… I miss being home."

"Oh." Her eyes clouded over.

"Although…" I let my fingers moved up to her ankle.

"What is it?" She echoed.

"You."

"Huh?" A confused look on her face.

"You are my home now."

She smiled once again.

"Tim?" Her voice was raspy.

"Yes?"

"Are we doing what is best?"

There was more than a hint of pain in her question. The moon lit the room through inadequate curtains. Though I couldn't see the clock, I knew we both should have been asleep long ago. I regarded the question carefully. Considering the motivation behind the question.

"What do you mean?" I finally replied, uncertain.

"Maybe it is bad."

"I'm still not understanding you. What do you think is bad?" I asked.

"Me..." She whispered.

"What?"

"I mean... should I be... in love?"

"Why shouldn't we be?" I asked. It was the same response I had given myself, whenever I considered the same question. It was usually enough to interrupt the cycle of doubt. It wouldn't work so well now.

"I... I am not even sure what it means. You make me feel so wonderful. Safe. I do not deserve... " She whispered, the words catching in her throat. The moon hid behind a cloud, turning the room pitch dark. I did not have a ready response for her. Instead my fingers found her chin, held it steady so my lips could find their mark in the dark.

"Tim?" She pressed, pulling away. Outside, I could hear the wind begin to blow.

"I'm thinking of the best way to explain what I'm thinking."

"Oh. I thought maybe... I..." She choked. The red glow of the bedside clock provided just enough light for me to see the wetness on her cheeks.

"I must admit that I have wondered the same thing. What have I done to deserve you. The circumstances were beyond our control. Before I had even come to grips with everything that had happened to us, I had become completely, deeply, in love with you. I don't even know how to explain what that means. I could recite everything I've ever heard about the topic, and it still wouldn't be enough to properly explain to you what love *is*."

"Oh." She repeated. Maybe it was just a trick of the light, but I thought I could see a quiver in her lips. She fought back tears. She fought to be strong, every action one of defiance.

"I think, maybe, that is a part of it. It's confusing, and it is also clear. I can't tell you it's exact definition, but I could tell you that just as surely as the sun rises, I love you."

She rose up on an elbow. We had learned that her eyes did better than my own in the dark. Her enlarged irises caught just enough of the light, seeming to glow in the darkness. Her pupils had slitted to a narrow line. Her regard absolute. Trying to obtain a deeper *meaning* from the lines on my face.

"You say, 'just as sure as the sun rises.' You believe that it will rise tomorrow. Yet – this is not so certain to me. The sky could just as easily remain dark. I do not *know* anything." Her voice was sad, her words illuminating.

To me, the universe was a constant. It had been long before and would remain long after.

"What do you feel?" I asked gently.

She shifted, sitting up. Her legs tucked under. One hand steadied her, the other curled and clutched to her chest.

"I feel this. This thing within my chest that you call my heart, it pounds." Her arm reached, hand now resting on my breastbone. "I feel it beat within you when I rest my head against *your* chest. When you smile, it beats faster. When you kiss me, I can feel it stop. It leaps about when you tell me how you love me."

I sat up, to kiss her shoulder.

"I think it would not move at all if you were to go away."

"That... *That* is love." I held her so she could hear my heart beat. The heart that belonged only to her.

At once, she pulled away. Fear filling her delicate features. The moon peeked out, just for a moment to illuminate her face.

"Do you promise that it will always be so? That you will always..." Fear colored her voice. The moon hid itself again. The wind howled sudden; a banshee's wordless scream. I wondered at what things had been done to her. I worried that she should still feel so afraid.

She pressed against me, a frightened child once more. Fearing that she might be swallowed up by the darkness that surrounded us.

"I will always love you. It is a promise easily made. It is not even something I *could* change. As you have already said, this heart that beats within my chest is yours."

Almost imperceptibly, she relaxed in my arms.

"I just wonder if it's... truly alright. Would it not make it so much more terrible for us, in the end?"

Her voice cracked. Again, she fought her own tears.

"How can you be so sure that you are even supposed to love me?"

The Beast raged, and then cowed. This wasn't the first time her thoughts had turned to such a topic, and it likely wouldn't be the last. It was a natural thing for her to wonder if things would be better *without her.* So much pain, and she hadn't yet truly experienced what it meant to be alive.

"I do love you." I said quietly.

"But... We did not meet in a normal fashion, did we? I was just left behind. You were not given a choice."

"Neither were you."

"Even so...."

I twined my fingers with hers. She shook. Afraid. It would not be surprising if that fear was of me. I could destroy her with just a word. She was nakedly vulnerable to any suggestion I might make. If I told her that I wished her dead, she would crumble. A sand castle caught in a wave. She was so afraid I'd wake up one day and decide it had all been a mistake.

"Sobely, I was once given some very good advice. A man I once trusted more than anything. He told me that if I should ever be so lucky as to find the one person that made me happy, the one person I truly connected with. The one person I truly loved. He said I should not even hesitate. He told me what when she, *you,* crossed my path, I should grab you tight. And never, ever let go."

"But..."

I gripped her more fiercely.

"We have been given an impossible life. A month ago I had no idea you even existed. Now I don't understand how *I* existed before. Maybe we are doomed to die. They could be right outside, right now. Waiting for a signal, the order to come in and take our lives away from us. It should feel like living in some kind of never-ending nightmare, yet it doesn't. I don't care. I can never regret meeting you. I can never doubt that you belong here within my arms."

"They were after me when... they killed her. It is my fault." She whispered.

"I don't believe that. All of this – it's on *them.* Whoever they are, they hold all the blame. Somehow my father arranged it so we could meet. That I know. He must have known somehow that you would be so important to me. I don't believe he wanted us to be running in fear. I don't believe he wanted... Mom... to die. You didn't ask for that, either. You didn't pull the trigger. They made that choice. Maybe they have a good reason, but I don't care what it may be."

I took a deep breath. The moon returned.

"Don't you see it? I'm not going to ever let go of you. You are my life, and I would die without you!"

"That is how I feel, too. But..."

"Sobely. You believe I had no choice then, but that isn't true. I could have chosen to abandon you. I could have called the police, and that would have been the end of it. I chose *you.* If I could go back to that day, knowing everything that I know now... Don't you understand? I would *still* choose you. I will *always* choose you. Things might be a bit grim right now, but I still have hope, because I have you."

Sobely broke down at last, throwing herself against me. Wailing as the built-up fear finally lifted free of her heart. I encircled her with my arms, her tears soaking us both. As the sobs subsided, it was as if she became somehow lighter. Such a terrible burden, lifted away. Replaced with the buoyancy of relief.

Eventually she fell asleep. Eventually, I did as well. The moon retreated. The wind picked up.

The howl of it a feral cry, heralding the total darkness that swept across the night sky.

12

The pounding sound of the rain woke us both. The temperature had dropped dramatically and the thin blankets provided by the motel weren't doing much for warmth.

Of course, we did have our own. I was even reasonably sure that I had remembered to wrap them up in the rubber rain tarp I had found at an army-surplus store. The only thing to do was to get out to the truck, grab our gear, and hope the comforter was dry enough to do us some good. Wait out the storm.

Normally in this sort of situation, I'd want to crack open a window to hear the rain better and settle down with a good book. All that was on hand, however, was an out-of-date phone directory and a Bible. Both of which were in Spanish.

The clock read 8 AM, but the sun was not shining. I was reminded of an old cartoon about a Rooster and some sort of flood.

The single-story building we sheltered in was positioned at the mouth of a narrow canyon, just outside of town. When the first peel of thunder rolled over us, the canyon acted as a natural amplifier, and there was no more need of open windows. The sheer force of sound shook the whole motel. The rain intensified ten-fold.

I would have liked to laugh. This was like a dream – a good one. A glorious storm, and a beautiful woman to share it with. Sobely, however, was not so delighted. Her grip around my waist was absolute. She had no frame of reference for the sounds she was hearing. A loud crack; to her mind the end of the world.

"It's okay. It's only thunder. We're alright." I soothed, rubbing her skin gently. Feeling the goosebumps, the fine hairs that stood on end. It took long seconds for her to relax, if only slightly. I reached up to switch on the light, the warm glow filling the space. Revealing the terror in her eyes.

"Wha..." She shivered.

"It's called a thunderstorm." I replied gently, lightning punctuating my sentence, thunder having the final word.

"We're perfectly safe in here. It might be noisy, but there is nothing to be afraid of." I smiled. I could feel the electricity filling the air and fought back the manic sort of glee that it usually brought out in me.

"Whu..." She said again, teeth chattering. If I could have moved, I would have turned the heat on. *I really need to do something about that. I can see our breathe.*

"I need to get up now. I've got to go get our things out of the truck and get the heater on. Do you think you can let go of me, just for a little bit? Just a few moments – I'll be back in a flash."

I winced at my poor choice of words. Lightning turning the phrase into an unwelcome pun. The following thunder drowned out her response.

"What did you say?" I asked, still smiling.

"Promise?"

I hugged her, to speak directly into her ear.

"I promise. Just a few moments. I'll even leave the door open. The truck is just outside, remember?"

She nodded. Slowly, her hands unclenched. I could feel the blood begin to circulate properly again. A red imprint from her fingers remained.

I got up, pulled on my jeans. Left my shirt on the floor – it wasn't going to help much. Deep breath.

"Alright. Just a few short moments." I repeated, throwing the door open. Less than ten feet away, and the truck appeared as a dark shadow through the heavy rain. Lightning flashed again, diffusing to the point where it was impossible to tell where it had been. Blinding light that illuminated nothing. On its heels, thunder cracked. Faintly I could hear a car alarm.

Deep breath.

I tried to hurry, but the rain struck with hammer blows. Angry red welts covering my unprotected skin. I reached the tail-gate and glanced back to give Sobely a smile. There existed only a shadow where the doorway was, a pale shape framed within.

I grabbed our bags and hurried back, nearly falling when the torrent from the edge of the roof blew especially vicious. The rain had slanted through the door, leaving a puddle on the little square of linoleum. Soaking Sobely who stood waiting, perfectly naked. Frightened. I moved past her to set the bag inside, then turned to shut and bolt the door. Sobely latched on, like a sailor clutching a life preserver.

Carefully I pried her fingers free and led her to a chair to sit.

"We got to get warmed up. And dry." I explained, reaching up to switch on the aging heater. She shook uncontrollably, jaw clenched to keep her teeth from rattling loose.

I peeled off my wet jeans, letting them fall into the puddle on the floor. The heater blew chill air, no doubt trying to heat up coils that were currently being pounded by the cold rain.

"Well, that's not going to be much help for a while. Come on, I think I know how to warm you up faster." I said, pulling her to her feet. When her legs gave way, I caught her in my arms and then carried her into the small bathroom. The heat-lamp was blessedly quick to grant a measure of heat to the air. I opened the taps on the shower, the pipes groaning in protest.

As the water warmed, I held Sobely close. Silent. It didn't do too much to help though. I was just as frozen as she was.

Soon enough, and steam started to fill the small space. I stepped into the well-appointed shower, Sobely still in my arms. With great care, I set her on her feet. Let her lean against me as the hot water began to work a miracle on us both. I rubbed my hands over her limbs, forcing her circulation to move along. To take the warmth back into her core.

I knew the water wasn't up to full strength yet, but it still felt like a hot spring. *I didn't realize I was* this *cold.*

"Why are we in the shower?" Sobely asked, seeming to regain herself.

"To warm up. We were both frozen, and the heater…"

"No, I mean… Why are we not driving away?"

"Because it's not safe."

"That noise. Can you not hear it?"

While the shower muffled it slightly, the thunder was still shaking the walls.

"It keeps…" A gasp, "Does that not mean we are in trouble? It is just like the sound from the day…" Thunder crashed again, with extra force. "They are tearing the world apart!"

I understood it then. To me, the gunshots had the sound of thunder to them. To her, the thunder had the sound of gunfire. She did have a reference for the sound, for the bright bursts of light. The staccato blasts, the flash of muzzle fire. The walls that had splintered apart. The memory surfaced, and I found myself drowning for air. For space. For…

Deep breath.

"This isn't like that. In fact, it would be just as dangerous to those men as it is to us. That sound that you hear? It's from the lightning. Those bright flashes of light you saw. It is energy so pure and awesome, it cleaves the very air. I promise you, we are safe in here."

Sure. Nobody ever is struck by lightning while in the safety of their own home, do they? The Beast cackled.

Shut up.

I held her shoulders, rubbing gently with my thumbs as the heat of the water continued to build. Nothing I could say would really relieve the primal fear she felt, so I settled for just holding her close until the water began to cool again. I shut it off and moved her under the heat lamp. With a fresh towel, I dried her, and then myself. Dropping it to the floor and grabbing another to wrap her long hair in.

I grabbed our bag of clothing, hoping it was as 'weather-proof' as the label and the expense claimed. I got her dressed as quickly as possible, to retain as much heat as possible. Underwear, pajama pants, and an over-sized sweatshirt. Dressed myself just as quick and led her back into the main room. The heater finally blew something slightly warmer than the air around it.

I helped her back into the bed; put some socks onto her feet. As she watched, furtive glances scanning the room, I dug out our bedding. Between the weather-seal and the rain tarp, it was all dry, apart from a single corner of the oversized sleeping bag we usually shared.

Thrown over the top of everything else, it wouldn't matter. I piled it all onto the double bed, then went around the room to turn on all of the lights.

And then I was with her. She sat, knees held to chest, giving me room to sit behind her, legs sprawled to either side. I pulled the blankets in close around us and held her closer

I hummed a melody into her ear, rocking slightly. Ever so slow – achingly slow – she relaxed into me. After a time, she realized that the storm had little to do with us. So long as we let it be, it would leave us be. The wind screamed, the thunder beat endlessly, the lightning danced.

A soft sigh escapes her lips.

She had very nearly gone to sleep when the lights went out. Somewhere the lighting had won the lottery and struck a transformer, or the wind had blown something into a power line. Maybe someone desperate to be somewhere else had been driven off the road and into a pole.

Either way, the sudden drop of darkness brought the tension instantly back into her shoulders.

We could have been outside in this.

It was the exception to the rule that we had chosen to stay in the motel. Mostly we had opted to sleep under the stars when the weather was good, or in the cab when it wasn't. The temptations of a proper bed had proven to be too great for us. It was the sort of coincidence that could cause a non-believer to seriously consider that there really was something Divine at work in the world.

I vowed to pick up a proper Bible at the nearest convenience. If nothing else, the stories ought to prove amusing to Sobely.

Sobely rocked on her own, murmuring under her breath. For the first time in my life, the storming weather made me afraid. The darkness had been a catalyst, sparking a change in my own mind. The Beast began to pace within its cage, uneasy.

"It's okay, my love. It'll be alright." I whispered, somehow managing to squeeze her even closer. I realized though that it was for as much my own comfort as hers.

"Tim..."

She twisted in my arms, bringing her face close to my own.

"Tim." She repeated.

"Sobe..." She interrupted forcibly, crashing her lips into my own. I could taste the fear on her lips.

"Tim!" She gasped, breaking free of the frantic kiss. Her hands were moving. Shakingly, clenching, but with purpose.

Her intentions now clear, I joined in. In between stolen breaths and breathless kisses, we managed to shed our clothing. Cocooned within our bedding, neither one of use willing to let more than an inch separate us. I pulled the blankets up further. To muffle the storm. To shut out the hellish flashes of light.

She continued to cry my name.

I kissed her flesh wherever I could find it, even as she bit into mine. Frantic motion, providing friction; providing heat. We moved independently and together. Maybe carelessly. The Beast had taken over both of us. All that mattered was the next moment. The feel of the other. The desperate need to feel alive. To stand in defiance of the storm that raged.

As we neared out own thunderous crescendo, her cries had gone to moans. Guttural sounds of pleasure and fright. A wailing sound that increased with intensity, even as my breath came up short. Even as my pace seemed to quicken without conscious thought.

The world did seem to be tearing itself apart.

A collision of all the sound and motion. A perfect instant. The heart of the storm. She writhed in terrified ecstasy. I held onto her, unable to breath. She collapsed all at once, chest heaving. Sweat slicking her skin.

"I love you." She whimpered, falling asleep.

"I love you, Sobely." I murmured into her ear.

The silence woke me. A supernatural stillness. We had collapsed into an awkward upright position. A tentative probe of a foot from the shelter of our blankets proved the air still too cold to brave the world just yet. I settled for carefully maneuvering us into a more comfortable position.

Sobely nestled into me. She mumbled something but didn't quite wake up enough for it to make any sense. I nodded anyway, as if she could see the movement.

I am so tired of running.

The thought caught me off-guard. I wondered briefly if we could be safe now. If we could go home. Who would bother with a couple of useless kids crying in the dark?

I don't even have any sort of proof that there is anybody still looking for us.

She clung to me. My life preserver. Something warm. Something alive. Something *mine.* She deserved better. She deserved a proper home.

I wanted my Mom. Her bad jokes, her thoughtfulness. I wanted her to tell me what I should do. She would have loved Sobely as if she were her own daughter. She would have been able to explain all the little things I was too embarrassed to, and the things I was unable to.

I wanted my Dad. His easy smile. His laughter. I wanted to be taken into one of his generous hugs; no worries, Dad is here. Everything was going to be just fine. I said those words often enough. A mantra. Words to soothe. Yet every single time I said them, they felt like a lie. I didn't believe them.

I wanted to go home.

I wept quietly. She slept fitfully. The cold light that had returned with the passing of the storm slowly faded away into true night. Somehow, I doubted anyone would be around to bother us about paying for a second night.

I lay restless, only falling back asleep after all the light had gone.

"FBI! Open up! We have the perimeter secured!" I jerked upright, thinking for a moment that the TV had come on. The thudding of a fist pounding on the door proved differently.

"We know you are in there! Come out with your hands raised!"

How?

Twenty different thoughts crashed together, forcing my brain into a painful reboot. I was already rolling, rolling. Onto the floor. Sobely in my arms, now shoved beneath the bed.

"Get dressed!" I hissed, pulling likely clothing from the tangled mass of cloth. Somehow, we both managed to wrestle into our clothes while the pounding continued. Further demands were shouted to open the door.

It seemed a rather extreme response for law enforcement.

"Fuck it, Jim. Let's go in and drag them out." I heard.

I snaked an arm out to retrieve a bag. Tucked inside, the .44 gleamed.

I had just enough time to pull the hammer back when the door was knocked from its hinges. A man rapidly entered, gun already up. In that pseudo-moment of slow time, as the adrenaline hit the bloodstream, I could see his eyes sweep. The gun steady. Finger already on the trigger.

Behind him, a second man dropping a hydraulic battering ram, reaching for his hip. A flash of brass – badges hanging from chains. A perfect target in the gloom.

I moved beyond thought. I pulled the trigger. Once. Twice. Four times total. The boom of the heavy revolver deafening in the small room. An echo of the day before, perhaps.

Both men fell. If they had been wearing Kevlar, it hadn't been enough. I waited, but there was no more movement. No one else to storm through the door. There was nothing but silence, and growing pools of crimson reflecting the morning light.

Finally, a thought.

They were lying.

No shit, Sherlock.

You definitely couldn't surround any sort of place with just two people. If there had been more of them, then dropping two wouldn't make a bit of difference. Maybe I could have got one more, but then the revolver would have been empty. We'd be done. A hail of gunfire the last sound we'd hear.

Yet there was only silence. No shouts for reinforcements. No pounding of boots on pavement. We were alive.

They had come in without backup. This seemed significant somehow, but now was not the time to ponder what it could mean. I got to work, reloading the revolver first. Crawling out to peek through the door. Unbelieving. A solitary Ford Crown Victoria parked sat beside the truck. Engine still running.

"Quickly. We have to go." I called. Sobely, to my surprise, was already in motion. She had shoved her feet into shoes, one bag thrown over her shoulder. She stopped only to scoop up my sneakers, moving towards the door. I grabbed the other bags with my free hand, abandoning blankets, clothing, and plenty of evidence.

There wasn't time. I ushered her out, towards the truck. I tossed our things into the bed; the only safety now was that offered by an open road.

Wait. One more minute won't change a thing.

Somehow, I forced myself back to the room, to the man lying just outside the door. I stooped, trying not to see the blood. Stooped to retrieve the radio from his belt.

And then I was back in the cab with Sobely. I retrieved the keys from the visor, and somehow got them into the ignition. Fingers twitching now. I twisted, and the truck was alive. The engine rumbled, happy to be awoken. The drive axle spun, sending the explosive force of the pistons to the wheels, spinning tires, and sending us on our way.

As we wound through the small town, returning to the highway, I could see destruction everywhere. The shopping mall host to a collection of vehicles normally kept in big garages. News trucks, a Red Cross bus. Vans marked FEMA, and people milling about trying to look official. Residents gathered at one end of the lot looking lost.

Everywhere were people speaking into radios. The one I had captured remained silent. A quick look revealed that it had been switched off. Twisting the volume knob created a cacophony of voices, the radio skipping rapidly through channels. I switched it back off. Kept driving. Trying to avoid everyone. Trying to avoid the destruction. Hoping the road I was on didn't dead-end in some urban cul-de-sac.

Ten miles later I pulled over to throw up.

There was no going home after all.

13

The cabin was everything Mildred claimed. Quiet. Picturesque. Beautiful. A willow tree shaded the yard on one side – the edge of an old growth forest shaded the structure itself. The shoreline of a river gently lapped at the boundary of the lawn. Afternoon sun glittered off the rippling stream, casting complex shadows as it reflected through the willow branches.

The cabin was everything Jack claimed. Isolated. Hidden. Safe. The road in had degenerated into a bramble-laden path. If not for the accurate description of landmarks, we would have never found it. Tucked away in its own private copse of pine trees was a small barn. Built on one side of this was a lean-to stacked full of firewood.

After a little convincing the doors of the shed swung open, allowing room for the truck to rest, amongst an old collection of wood-working tools. The key to the cabin waited patiently in a jar of mismatched screws, right where Jack had indicated.

I hoped we would be able to find some rest here at last. At least long enough for us to get our bearings. To decide what our next move in this macabre game should be.

The constant rumble of the road beneath our tires was exacting a toll from us both. Sobely spent much of the time sleeping restlessly, while the constant blacktop had begun to blur my vision. The endless journey had caused reality to distort, where even the most mundane of items took on a darkly sinister form. Even as I scooped the love of my life into my arms to take her inside, every shadow in the yard was cast as a threat.

Sobely felt lighter than the air itself, reminding me again that one of my first priorities would be to see her fed. She deserved so much more from life than this endless compression of our spirits. The best I could offer her was to feed her pancakes.

Even those would have to wait until I had the cabin secured. I set her gently down on a comfy-looking couch of green paisley and went back to the truck. Some clothes, food, the revolver, and then I secured the garage. Back at the wide porch of the cabin, and I paused to sprinkle some broken glass in a way that would make it difficult to avoid.

Inside. Door locked. Deadbolt thrown. I secured another glass bottle with a length of string, suspending it in the air. Any quiet attempt to open the door would cause it to fall and shatter. Crude, but an effective alarm nonetheless.

Sobely was awake now and watched me work. As I similarly trapped the windows, and then set about preparing a meal, I snuck numerous glances at her in return. Despite her general lack of any decent sleep, and the completely disheveled state of her hair, her slow smile still was enough to make my throat choke tight with emotion. Perhaps with a few days of honest rest a solution would make itself clear.

It was such a strange concept after being on the run for so long. Rest. In a proper house. A bed tucked away in the wilderness where we would be safe. I supposed that was how the term was coined.

Safe as houses. Safehouse.

Soon the smell of frying oil and sweet batter filled the air, and the cabin in the middle of nowhere became a slice of *almost* home. Hundreds of miles from where we had started, in a world growing increasingly dark for us, it was all the home I needed.

I had been avoiding the cabin for a while. From Jack's house we had just drifted. Kept on the move almost constantly. Slept as little as possible in order to keep the tires spinning. One night we might stop at a middle-of-nowhere motel, another we'd lie together under the stars.

But since the storm, no motel room had ever granted us much rest. As the weather began to turn, the comforting light of the stars became obscured more and more by clouds settling in for the winter. So far, we'd only been rained on once, but the cough Sobely had for three days afterwards made me fearful of the cold months. Being as exhausted as we were, we'd have a tough time fighting off serious illness.

If she were to fall sick... Pneumonia, or worse...

I kept tabs on the news via a battery-operated radio. While we had been mentioned a few times, there was never any mention of Jack or Mildred. It seemed as if we had managed the impossible. We hadn't been tracked to their place, and the authorities hadn't discovered us since. So after several months I directed the faithful Dodge to this secluded hideaway in the deep woods.

The cabin sat in the middle of a reserve. Which meant that it was a deserted area this time of year. To sweeten the pot further it provided, paradoxically, a place to finally get in some target practice.

Beyond a slight rise to the south of the lodge, stood a gravel quarry that had been abandoned somewhere back when corporations still used Chinese immigrants for cheap labor. Due to the nature of the terrain, and this was quoting Jack himself: "You can fire off all six rounds from yon hand cannon down range – just as quick as ya please. It won't even wake the robins in their nests."

True to his word, a cupboard in the hall contained enough rounds for a small mid-sized army to wage war. Other cupboards contained enough dry goods to feed them on a year's march.

A few sheets of paper in Jack's scrawling script laid out the lay of the land, the stock of supplies on hand, and where the "wandering traveler" might discover a perfectly maintained sawed-off shotgun that had been recovered from a drunken trucker.

Some dried flowers in a Tupperware bowl had been Mildred's contribution. Following her note led to a silver pan that sat above a tea candle. A bit of water, a spark from a lighter, and the smell of her rose garden filled the room, just as it had that first morning in their house.

The smell brought tears to Sobely's eyes.

I did the dishes as she watched. So mundane a task, yet it felt so surreal. We had travelled thousands of miles, running from a force that would very much like to see us both to a shallow grave. Yet here we were, playing house. For the night at least, we could relax. As the motion of the suds and sponge worked a special kind of spell, I felt muscles loosen that I didn't even realize had been tensed.

Before I finished the plate I had been scrubbing, I found my vision blurred by tears that formed unconsciously. The heaviness that drug on my shoulders suddenly made me fairly certain that my welling emotions hadn't been triggered by the smell of the roses.

It was fortunate that the plate was of cast tin. Before I could even comprehend the pain that I was feeling, before I was aware that I had become compromised, I found myself curled into a fetal ball with my shoulders shivering. Teeth chattering.

Like a titan bridge undone by the slackening of a single cable, I fell into the chasm beneath.

Moments or hours later, Sobely was squeezing my abdomen with all the strength of an amazon. I was just coming back awake, I realized. The dreaded laughter in my ears faded away as I returned to the silent room in the woods. Things came back to focus – the drying dishes, the ceramic potpourri burner, the brown couch. For a moment I thought I had failed her.

There was this persistent image of people dressed all alike in peculiar grey-blue clothing, masks over faces. Malice in their too-shiny eyes. It was *their* laughter that still rang in my ears. Some fragmented torment that had swallowed me whole as I hit the floor, no doubt. The feeling of being bound tightly – of being trapped. The feeling still so strong that I actually pushed Sobely off me.

After a second – two at the most – I came back to myself. Back to reality, and to the love of my life. And then I was kissing her, lips desperate to taste every inch of her soft skin. I clutched her tightly even as she held onto me. I stood up with her in my arms and carried her into the bedroom at the end of the hall. I hit the walls more than once in my flight; unable to keep myself from continuously planting hot fearful kisses all over her precious lips, her cheeks, her neck.

I kicked the door shut behind us, shutting out the light. Shutting out the darkness, too.

The white morning light warmed my face. The peaceful silence was interrupted only by the sound of Sobely's sleeping breath. She lay across me, layered blankets drawn up to our chins. I opened my eyes – for a short moment the bright sun reminded me of an operating room spotlight while my pupils adjusted themselves to the glare.

Thin strands of her black hair obscured my vision like gauze until I shook my head lightly to clear it away. I freed my left arm, and ran a hand over her cheek, brushing her hair over her exposed ear. As my fingers found a familiar and favorite spot behind her earlobe, I was rewarded with her soft sigh.

This is surely *what Heaven is like.*

I yawned and wiped at the grit in my eyes. *I could do with a shave. And a proper shower.* I glanced at her angel's face again, this time noticing the dry skin and smudges of dirt earned from sleeping out on the ground. *Perhaps a good long soak for both of us, then.*

For the moment though, I was content to just lie there. For once, we had no reason to get up right away. I lost myself in the rhythm of her breath, coupled with the steady beat of her heart. The gentle rise and fall of her bosom beneath the well-worn and warm quilt. There it was; that precious thing. The fairy-orchestra playing a song just for me. Playing in celebration of the rarest occasions.

A spare moment.

I shut my eyes again. Allowed my limbs to relax again. I pulled the blanket up further, to block out that bothersome morning sun, and let the rhythm of her precious heart lull me back into a lazy sleep.

As the day wore on, we both found reason enough to get out of bed: Hunger. The air was chilly when I drew the covers back, and for a moment Sobely hung on tight, drawing close for warmth. But with a sigh and a grumbling stomach she disentangled herself. With a glance at our dirty clothing on the floor, she opted to steal the comforter from my grasp, wrapping it about herself. Then she stuck out her tongue at me. I rolled my eyes in mock exasperation and reached for my jeans.

Sobely made her way to the plush blue couch in the den, while I scooped up our clothes. I pulled my worn boots on and headed outside, leaving the small pile of laundry near the door leading down to the cellar.

I went to the garage and collected the pair of bags containing our clothes. A small one of clean clothing, and a larger duffel of dirty. The clean clothing I tossed into the house, the rest went with me into the cellar. Fluorescent lights kicked on with a flick of a switch, and I surveyed my surroundings.

An unlit gas furnace sat along one wall. Pressing a switch sparked the pilot, and seconds later warm air was flowing into the clean duct work overhead. Along another wall sat the washer and tumble-dryer, as well as the hot-water heater. A few more switches brought the appliances online. The thin sound of natural gas through narrow pipes was reassuringly familiar. A sound that meant civilization – a thing we had become separate from. It also meant that the water would be warm enough for a shower before the first load of laundry had finished.

Satisfied that everything was operating as it should, I finally loaded dirty laundry into big, old, sturdy machine and started the cycle. As the tub filled and began its work, I headed back up the stairs leading into the kitchen.

Sobely remained just as I left her, wrapped in the sheet and lounging upon a worn recliner. She greeted me enthusiastically with a smile, which then shifted into the mischievous grin of a pixie that had just pinched some sugar.

"Are you going to eat like that?" I teased.

"Yup! I am quite comfortable, thank you. I don't think I shall move at all." She replied, seriously. With a wink.

"You'll need your hands to eat." I pointed out. At this she frowned slightly, and then brightened.

"Not if you feed me. Then I won't have to move at all." She nodded once, as if that settled it.

"What if I want to join you under the blanket?" I asked. She wrinkled her nose.

"But you're dirty!" She exclaimed, grinning madly.

"Hah! I'm not the only one!" I laughed.

Sobely peered around her thoughtfully.

"But I don't see anyone else here."

"I mean you, silly!" I responded. She opened the blanket slightly to look over herself.

"Huh. You are quite right. I got the blanket dirty." She looked forlorn.

"We have more." I pointed out. Indeed, the linen closet was well-stocked.

"Ah." She tightened the bundle once more. "Then I guess you may join me. But only after you've fed me. And…" She trailed off, mischievous again.

"And what?" I inquired, moving into the kitchen.

"No clothes! Your jeans are just *itchy.*" She shuddered, as if just speaking the word had summoned an itchy spot to trouble her.

"Hmm." I lit the stove and opened the refrigerator. Inside were packages of meat I had pulled from the freezer, and a dozen eggs we had purchased on our way up. Soon the smell of bacon filled the room, and half the eggs went into a bowl for easy scrambling.

"I counter your generous offer with my own." I turned towards Sobely, brandishing the wooden spoon.

"What would you suggest?" Her voice had gone husky, but only because the smell of bacon was stifling her playfulness.

"I feed you. Then we take a shower. And then we snuggle under a fresh blanket in front of a fire."

She grew concerned.

"A fresh blanket? Outside? That doesn't sound very nice." She was frowning heavily. I chuckled lightly.

"No, fresh linens outside would never do! I meant that." I pointed the fork past her. "That is called a fireplace. Looks like it runs on gas, which means no wood to chop. Just flip a switch, and we'll have a nice little fire in the comfort of this auspicious den."

"Oh." She answered, looking. "Well, that sounds very nice indeed. I agree to your terms. Can we have toast?"

"Well, we haven't any bread. I could perhaps toast a few of the leftover pancakes from yesterday..."

Her eyes twinkled.

"Pancakes for toast? What a marvelous idea! I approve, thou mightiest of cooks. Prepare thine meal post-haste!"

"Very well, thy lady fairest. Would thee prefer thy bacon firm, flaccid, or not at all?"

Her brow wrinkled as she worked to decipher the sentence.

"Thou woulds't mock me by withholding thy bacon? I would like it done properly, with no wiggle." I laughed merrily, the sound echoing strangely.

I did the dishes while Sobely took her bath. She had pouted a bit, but it was an old argument. Even here, I still felt strongly that one of us should maintain a watch. Besides which, I needed a bit of time to think.

Ideally, we could stay here for the duration of the winter. If we were forced to run again... we needed to recharge. To have a little bit of stability. To not have to worry if we were going to wake up with a gun to our heads.

Given enough rest, enough time, perhaps we might even be able to figure a way out of this whole mess. I had been taught to believe that there was always a way through any bad situation. It was a belief I had clung to fiercely when my Dad has passed away. The idea that no task would be set before us that we could not shoulder our way through.

He always told me that the winners are the ones who say it's never enough. *I wonder if he would have given the same wisdom if he knew the dire straits that would come his family's way.*

I had the most startling idea that perhaps it was exactly *why* he had instilled such strong beliefs in me.

As I dried the final plate, I could almost hear that same sinister cackling I had heard in a dream. As if my own psyche was mocking me.

Dad had known people everywhere in the world. He had access to just about anything, through his friends. He had touched so many lives, made such a difference. He had been a true force of nature, of God's own will. Like a windstorm, except he did not leave destruction in his wake. He was swept through the lives of people and left them better for knowing him. Touched Hope upon their hearts.

He had been like some kind of magic totem, his mere presence a weapon against the Darkness. A true superhero. While he never wore a cape, never made the news, there were countless people in the world that owed their own lives to him.

In contrast; I had Sobely. I dare not go to my best friend for fear of a repeat of what had been done to Mom. I had made unexpected friends of Jack and Mildred, though I feared daily for their safety. My resources included an ancient truck, a revolver I barely even knew how to use, and my own wit.

Paranoia had become the virtue of survival.

I knew nothing about my enemy, except that they appeared to have unlimited resources. They had influence over law enforcement agencies, and even the FBI. With all that power, they were dead set on seeing both Sobely and I into the ground. For all I knew, Sobely could be the heir to some throne somewhere, betrothed, and commanding an army of hand-maidens.

Right now I could hear her splashing a bit in the bath, content to have eaten a dinner fit for mountain men. Trusting I would keep her safe. Her desires were simple. Life as she knew it began so short a time ago. She cried for the animals that lie dead on the highways and smiled only for me.

I had become bound to her with hardly a glance.

I *must* save her.

A great pounding noise woke us both up. With my heart trying its hardest to burst from my chest and run for the hills, I climbed out of bed and pulled on my jeans. I gestured for Sobely to remain quiet and out of sight should our unwanted visitor turn out to be hostile. *On the bright side, if it were an enemy they wouldn't* *bother knocking…*With this in mind, I made my way towards the source of the pounding: The front door.

The gun hung from a hook by the bedroom door. This I pulled and held loosely at my side. While I knew I wasn't exactly a marksman with the heavy iron, I was reasonably certain I could hit anything waiting on the porch. I was also equally sure that if we had been found by those that had us on the run to begin with, they wouldn't have knocked.

Still, it was a long way off the beaten path for a Mormon.

"Hold on, I'll be right there. Coming!" I called. I motioned for Sobely to get down on the floor behind the bed, and then quickly made my way to the front door, disabling the pop-can door chime I had rigged. The gun I kept at the ready but positioned so as to be out of sight when I opened the door. For a second I wished there had been a peephole. Finally, I took a deep breath, and then opened the door slowly.

A man in the uniform of a State Trooper waited impatiently.

"Can I help you officer?" I asked, making sure the revolver was out of his sight while I raised my arm up, leaning casually on the edge of the door so I could let the big .44 drop into firing position with just a little nudge from gravity.

"That depends. Who are you? This is private property – I sure as hell know you ain't the owner." He spoke very brusquely, yet his thick mustache seemed to barely even twitch.

"Oh! Is that all?" I tried to smile but knew it must have looked uneasy. "Jack gave me permission to use his cabin for a bit." I took a gamble – if he knew that I wasn't the owner, then I reasoned that he probably knew Jack.

"Is that a fact. How about you just go ahead and call him, then. You know, just to verify." The trooper almost seemed to smile, except the expression was more fitting to a predator stalking a wounded gazelle.

"Sure! If you happen to have a phone that works. The whole point in coming out here was to be away from distractions. Don't think cell service reaches this far out, anyhow."

The trooper visibly tensed, and my finger slipped into the trigger guard.

And then he started laughing in great booming guffaws.

"I'm just messing with you, kid! You must be Jim. Jack told me you'd make it up here before the nasty weather hit. Had that ferocious downpour just about a week ago, and here you are! Nice to meet you." He held out his hand to shake.

Moving very carefully, I dropped the revolver into the stuffed chair by the door and took the offered hand.

"Anyways, my name is William Murphy. Most people just call me Trooper Bill, though. I just had to make sure that the right folks are where they ought to be. Wouldn't want any accidents." He sounded friendly enough, but paranoia warned me against arming him with too much information. Besides, I had no way of knowing what cover story Jack had concocted.

"Seems a bit out of your way for a patrol, Officer." I remarked.

"I do a weekly check of all these little hide-aways back in here. Hell, not much else to get up to 'round these parts. 'Cept maybe hunting squirrel.

I stepped out onto the porch as he talked, not wanting him to come inside to ask awkward questions. I was trying to think of a polite way to get him to leave.

"Yeah, Jack mentioned I might meet you. I hope you trust me when I say that I don't plan on causing any mischief. You won't have to worry about any strangers coming in and out — I came out here for the quiet." I smiled as pleasantly as I could manage.

"Can't say as I blame you, what's been going on these days. Anyways, now that I've laid eyes on you, I can go about minding my own business. Tell you what, though. If you decide on having some company, or any kind of emergency, Jack keeps a CB in one of the closets. Just tune it to channel nine and give me a holler. If you need anything at all, well... We're fully prepared for just about anything shy of the Apocalypse, and I'd like to think we'd ought to do pretty well then, too."

"I'll keep that in mind." I said wryly.

"See that you do." Trooper Bill tipped his hat. "And tell the little lady hello as well." Bill turned, grinning wolfishly. I felt a bead of sweat form on my brow. I had been hoping he'd think I was here alone. Especially since all the bulletins were asking for all points to be on the lookout for a *pair* of perpetrators.

I was dying to know what story Jack had concocted. *Better hope that stays just a figure of speech, pal.*

"Safe travels, Trooper Bill."
And don't come back.

You should have shot Trooper Bill when you first had the chance. You'd still be safe. You've failed. You've failed. You aren't good enough.

I've always liked the fog. The fourth day in the woods brought a heavy bank of silent mist to swirl and settle around our quiet cabin hideaway. Shadows in the gently writhing grey could have been almost anything, yet I could feel the presence of paranoia ease the thicker the fog became.

We had fallen asleep by the fire the night before. A few scattered embers glowed in the ash, casting no shadows in the same way the mist cast no sound. As I carefully stretched, Sobely continued to sleep, her head in my lap. I had slumped against the faded brown sofa, a blanket of sheepskin draped over us. We were just as snug as the sheep that had worn it previously. As snug as the cabin felt, wrapped in the woolen fog.

I sat there, mind wandering as my gaze hypnotically kept fixed on the great grey nothing. It was a moment that might have been a mere second, or long eternities. The only indication that time might have passed at all was the soft sound of breathing. The slow rise and fall of her breast.

When at last she did stir, it was as if she were waking in a dream. Her movements were that of someone unsure of their own existence. When her jade eyes flickered open a slow smile that moved the earth itself threatened to stop my heart entirely. To live in that one brief moment for the rest of time. There were far worse dreams to have.

"Good morning, heart of my heart. Did you sleep well?"

She nodded. Her hair moved in rippling waves with the movement, as hypnotic in its own way as the stillness of the fog. Her smile cracked open into a tremendous yawn, arms stretching outward like the paws of a lazy cat.

"I did. I had such nice dreams. Do you think... I wish we could stay here forever."

"We can come back someday. Maybe with Jack and Mildred..."

She shook her head. More darkly gleaming waves of spun silk.

"I want you all to myself. Forever." She whispered, her voice thick with feeling.

"Forever sounds quite nice. What would you say to some breakfast?

She hesitated.

She frowned.

"Breakfast means getting up."

"That is generally how it works. You could just relax on the couch if you like while I cook."

"Can I watch?" She asked, sitting up. Twisting around so her face was mere inches from mine.

"Hmm..." I pretended to think. This close, I could catch just the slightest tremble to her lips.

Naturally, I moved to steady them.

The day passed with the fog only growing thicker. As we conversed, washed dishes, moved around, the noise was instantly swallowed up. It made me think that perhaps we were currently in a place outside of time. Like that movie *The Langoliers* where the stillness extended even to the echo of their voices. We allowed ourselves to be lazy, feeling safe and secure at last. It would have been impossible for anyone to have found us now.

I had found a book to read, so I spent many hours with her snuggled within my arms. Some story of mythological beings and supernatural happenings. Ages of wonder and of ages past. The very nature of the atmosphere made it difficult to follow, and Sobely drifted in and out of sleep.

When twilight came, the fog turned crimson as the setting sun threw its brilliant colors into the sky far above. We ate leftovers, and I let Sobely lead me into the bedroom. The window faced south, and the room was tinged with the vermillion mist, as if the dying sun had sprayed the room with blood.

In near silence, she turned to face me, smiling shyly. Eyes hungry with her desires. I moved to her, taking her arms in my hands as I gently kissed her once again. Our fingers moved of their own accord. Buttons were undone with graceful slowness. Soft kisses caressed flesh made bare in the crimson twilight. The feeling of goose-down as it compressed beneath our weight, like slipping onto a cloud.

Her skin was the color of cream, strawberries whipped in for a pleasant treat. A feast, offered up with willing passion. Her eyes sparkling with a sense of expectant satisfaction. My fingers roamed, my lips, along with the coarse stubble I hadn't bothered to shave off. Her slender fingers slipped through my hair, perhaps grown a bit too shaggy for my own liking.

In the growing darkness, I had only her soft whimpers to guide me. Her succulence to tempt me. When at last I had my fill – whetted but never sated – I moved to meet her mounting haste. As the room darkened, we made love with no sense of urgency at all. No desperate need. Only the desire that it should be forever. Beyond forever, even.

In the last embers of light, it was as if we were moving atop a pool of blood. I shifted; she sighed; we both writhed gently.

Idly I realized that my hands had become slick. Red washed up all the way to my elbows. Blood enough now to sink in. A pool of darkness that she and I *were* sinking into, bound by a spell. Unable to comprehend.

The last thing I heard was her whimpering moan.

14

"Heart rate is increasing normally. I think he's coming around." A distant voice called. I opened my eyes grudgingly. I was in a hospital room. Green tiles, cheap art prints. The smell of industrial-grade disinfectants. A nurse stood by a doctor, both clad in grey scrubs. Only the white coat on the one marked the difference.

At the foot of the bed stood a pair of ghosts.

Mom and Dad. His arms were around her, a hopeful look on both of their faces.

"Now, I don't want you two to get your hopes up. There is still a long road ahead of us, even if he *has* managed to finally break through his delusions." The doctor was explaining. His mask scrunched as he spoke. The light was painful.

"You said that if he pulled through the operation, his delusions would disappear! I'm not sure I can go through all that again." Mom replied.

"There are a number of deciding factors, especially in cases of this severity. There could be unforeseen complications from the surgery itself. Damage to areas that we could not fully access. The neurological shifts alone could cause him to act completely different from anything you've experienced so far. Not only that, his mind may have latched onto the delusion as a lifeline. An escape from the pain he was experiencing. He may prefer the hallucinations to reality at this point."

"How could he? You weren't there, Doc. In whatever world he has been living in, he believed we were both dead. That he was on the run from some evil organization. How could he prefer that to his family? To the real world? He's terrified of shadows!"

"The file had a full account of his psychotic break. Yes, it may seem horrible to us, but there was something about some girl – what was the name he gave her..."

"Sobely. Sobely Blossom. The girl with elf ears and cat eyes." Mom sounded derisive at that. I wanted to protest, to say anything, but I could feel a tube down my throat. My wrists were bound to the bed rails. Drugs must still course through my veins, and all I could do was move my eyes to follow the conversation and pray that they would notice.

What kind of nightmare is this?!

"Regardless of how silly you might believe the notion of this girl to be, she was *very* real to him. She may still be. He was her protector. Her guardian. That need to be relied upon just might be what kept him from checking out on us entirely. We have to ease him back into reality gently, or we could cause irreparable harm."

I could feel anger stir in my blood. *Wake up, Tim. This is all just a horrible nightmare.*

"Uh, I think he's awake." My father pointed. Even though I knew this was some kind of dream, the sound of his voice was a reassurance.

After such a long time without hearing it, the sound of it now made me want to cry. I wanted him to tell me that everything was all right now. There were no more monsters – he'd dealt with them. I hadn't known how badly I had missed him.

Could *this* be reality after all?

"Ah. No doubt – he's certainly a fighter. Let's take these tubes out, shall we? See what we got, anyway." The doctor and nurse both approached. "Just relax, Timothy. This is going to be a bit uncomfortable." The doctor placed a firm hand on my chest as he and the nurse removed the tubes going down my throat.

He was right. It wasn't comfortable. It burned, the way lemon juice burns in a paper-cut. Only ten times worse. *Preposterous. You can't feel pain in a dream. It's just the* memory *of pain.*

"Hhhrgh!" I managed, coughing. An ice chip was offered, which I slurped down my burning throat. I could feel the cold sensation sooth the burn and relax my stressed out vocal cords.

"Take it easy, honey. It's been a tough day." Mom was at my other side, caressing my cheek. I wanted to brush her hand away. I wanted to take her hand and pull Mom into the fiercest hug I could manage. To tell her how much I loved her.

This is a lie. Isn't it?

"Where?" I managed, trying to learn where they were keeping Sobely. I had a flash of insight – a traffic stop that had been reinforced by the Trench Coat Men – but it slipped mostly away. Leaving me only dimly aware of the full scope of the dire situation we were undoubtedly into.

What traffic stop?

"You're safe. You're in the hospital. You've had brain surgery dear... Do you remember anything?" She asked timidly. Afraid of my answer.

"Now don't push him, Mrs. Kines. He seems to be doing quite well, but we don't want to risk too much at such an early stage of his recovery process." The doctor patted her shoulder awkwardly, and I wanted to snap his arm. The longer I was in this mind-game, the more horrible it seemed.

Yes. It is just horrible to have them both back. Terrible to think that everything might have just been nothing more than a broken brain. Hallucinations. Could it be true? Could she...

"So-be. Where... is..." I broke up into coughing. Hard enough that I could feel a very odd sensation in the back of my skull. Like a dead zone in the microwave.

"No! Not this again! Please, no..." Mom started crying. Though I was almost entirely sure that this was some kind of nightmare, I still wanted to say something reassuring. Even in a dream, I did not like to see my mother cry.

"Not quite, Mrs. Kines. The fact that he is asking where this 'Sobely' is, means that he has had a break from that reality. He can't find her, because he is here with us. In a world where she does not even exist." The nurse spoke this time. Calmly. Matronly. The head elephant, it would seem. *Maybe she's a psychiatrist. Maybe they're right, and she never...*

"NO!" I shrieked. Raising my voice only caused it to come out more in the range of a goshawk.

"Calm down, Timothy. I'd rather not have to put you under again. We need to see what physical damage may be left over from the surgery. It was a rather tricky procedure. Do you think you could stay with us, just for a little while longer?" The doctor leaned in close. His grey eyebrows were shaped in concern, the brown eyes surrounded by puffy tissue. He was either suffering allergies, or he'd been up for a long while.

I wanted to strangle him.

Instead I worked to breathe normally. I worked my jaw up and down to try and work out the lingering stiffness. I even took another offered ice chip. *Go along with it. So you can escape.*

"Where is Sobely?" I asked again. This time, my voice was somewhat more normal.

"This Sobely..."

"We can wait to talk about that, son. Just take it easy, now." Dad interrupted whatever it was Mom was going to say. She glared at him for a moment, but then seemed to give in, nodding her agreement.

They're stalling.

Of course they are. They don't want you to panic. You've had a long day.

It was hard to form statements. Questions. All the phrases I knew I needed to utter were locked down, escaping only in tiny bits. Relying upon my fractured psyche to put them together properly. First and foremost, though...

"Where is Sobely? What have you done with her? Who the hell are you people?!?" I tried very hard to stamp the anger down. I'm not sure I fully succeeded.

The doctor again.

"Mr. Kines, I'm afraid you've had a bit of a shock. There was a tumor..."

"Where is she?"

"There was a tumor growing inside your skull. We've had to remove it, and there is good chance for you to recover most of your brain's function in time." He continued, gamely.

"What have you done to Sobely?"

The doctor sighed.

"Just tell him! Why bother playing this game?" Mom demanded.

"Tim. You've had a psychotic episode. The best we can reckon is that the pain had grown so intense, your mind had constructed some kind of fantasy world for you to escape into. As much as I would love to produce this 'Sobely' woman for you, I'm afraid that it just isn't possible. She doesn't *actually exist*." The doctor held in his breath.

It was amazing how much these newer beds weigh. I tried to thrash, to hopefully break free. All I managed to do was set off some kind of alarm.

"Now, I can't let you do that! You need to try and calm yourself, young man. Or else I'll have to put you under anesthesia again."

In spite of the fact that I wanted to continue until he *did* 'put me under,' I did not have the strength. Besides which, thrashing was just making my head hurt. I forced myself to relax. Mostly.

"This... can't be real." I muttered. Mom's crying grew in intensity.

"It's okay to feel that way. It's going to take some time to adjust." The woman I reckoned to be a shrink patted my restrained arm. Unsurprisingly, the touch wasn't at all comforting.

"They're dead." I whispered.

I didn't want it to be true, but it was. I knew it.

Are you so sure?

My inner voice didn't sound right. It wasn't the usual Beast, but a spider whisper of doubt. Lies whispered into my ear, to make me doubt.

Mom uncovered her eyes to stare at me. Her irises were shot through with red. Her makeup had become runny.

"How can you still think that? Do you really wish we were dead?" Her voice was jagged.

"I..." I didn't know how to respond. I wanted to tell her how much I missed her, but somehow I knew it would be wrong. This was *not* my mother.

"It's not that he wishes it were so, Marie." Dad pulled her back into his arms. I got the impression it was to keep her from attacking me, more than to comfort her. Even in this dream, he was the voice of reason.

"I... It's just the truth. You're dead. Both of you. This isn't real. It cannot be. If she is not here, then this is not the real world!"

Mom stormed off, crying. The doctor adjusted the IVs, and I could feel myself gently going under. Like a man enchanted by sirens, sinking into the ocean.

Take me back to her.

We had been running for a total of two and a half months, near about. After the incident at the motel, we opted to ignore them as much as possible. A brief pop into a post office to see whether or not our pictures still hung on the bulletin boards. Each check found the notices for our capture becoming increasingly buried under all the other requests piling up. As good an indication of any that we had fallen lower in their priority.

So it was logical to think that the roadblock ahead wasn't meant for us. Likely, they were trying to catch some miscreant that escaped his chain in a work line, or some such. Still just to be as safe as possible, I pulled a hat on. Threw on my shades. Quietly told Sobely to wrap the blanket around her as much as possible and lean against me.

The revolver was within easy reach, yet still tucked where the questioning officers would not be able to see it. It wasn't a big truck. Surely, we wouldn't be asked to get out so they could search it more thoroughly? Not when they already had two trailers pulled alongside the road, officers in one, another looking after the small crowd of people that probably belonged to the two caravans.

I carefully reached down, and pulled the hammer back, into the ready position. Just in case.

"Alright, let's try this again, young man. Do you know where you are?" A different doctor. This one didn't wear scrubs. Instead he had a white blouse, black trousers. A pinstriped tie. The look in his eyes that screamed PSYCHOLOGIST.

"I am somewhere that I'm not supposed to be. Somewhere that doesn't make any sense." I replied. Hoping to be vague enough, that the lies wouldn't come.

"It will make sense in time. You had quite the traumatic experience, you know. It's perfectly normal to feel displaced." His tone was friendly enough. Practiced. A line he's said a thousand times already. A small detail, added to the countless others. Proof that I wasn't just asleep. They were doing something to me.

They got us.

More proof that this was all a lie.

The Beast agreed. The Spider, crushed.

"You don't understand..." I said, cutting off the thought unfinished. *Almost slipped there.*

"I suppose I don't. Not fully. The brain is so extraordinary. Faced with terrific pain, it can create its own way out. Believe in something strong enough, and even the impossible can feel as real as I am. Though I suppose right now you probably don't trust that I *am* real, do you?"

"You can stop this now. I'm not buying it. You are sick bastards, aren't you?" I felt the venom in my voice.

"I'm afraid you still aren't yet ready to face the truth." He gestured to an RN, who unclamped one of the lines feeding into my arm.

Once we were in the trap, it took them less than a second to spring it. The rear-most truck reversed swiftly, pushing the trailer behind us. The cruiser pulled forward, blocking the road. The small crowd of campers either ducked for cover or pulled weapons.

A man in the uniform of the State Trooper's office stepped up to the window, gun drawn.

"Hands where I can see them!"

I wasn't going to give them any more advantage. I pulled the revolver up and aimed it at the trooper. He fired his own weapon — which turned out to be a Taser. I felt electric fire course through me. Somehow, I got the gun pointed in the right direction anyway.
Though my feet wouldn't cooperate to push down the gas pedal, I still manage to squeeze off a shot. Had the satisfaction of seeing it enter the Trooper's cheek.

As he sank to the ground, I read his name plate. 'Trooper Bill Gordon.'

Too late, I saw the approach of the Trench Coat Men.

"The swelling has all but subsided completely. He ought to do better this time, Lord willing." I heard the sound of that first doctor's voice.

"Though he does seem rather attached to his delusion." The second added.

"Just let me talk to him." My father, this time.

I could hear the door slide open, and then shut with a pneumatic hiss.

"Don't open your eyes. I know you can hear me." He soothed.

"Why are you doing this?" I whispered.

"Son... I need you to fight. Harder. You know the truth – fight for it!" He responded. It was something my Dad would say in a situation like this. In fact, I think I had heard him say those exact same words somewhere before.

Is this some kind of memory, then? Or constructed of memories. A dream that won't just end?

"Yes. I do know the truth. But every time I insist on the reality, they just dose me again." I sounded bitter. *You're arguing with a ghost. He's dead, Tim.*

He's still Dad, though.

"It's all a part of their process. They don't want to overload your cortex. They're gonna draw it out as long as they can." I felt his hand on my shoulder. Like I had felt dozens of times before.

He was always my voice of reason. My internal dialogue always sounded like him.

"I… wish it could be different. But… I cannot exist without *her*. Please, make this stop! I can't face a world where she is not in it!"

"You have to keep fighting, son. Don't give up."

We were surrounded before Trooper Bill's body hit the ground. Hands were reaching in. Pulling away the gun. Pulling open the doors. Removing the seat-belts. Removing her. *I swung my arms like a windmill, trying to claw my way to her. It couldn't end like this.*

In the end, they were just too many. The Trench Coat Men were supported by a throng of men and women. Badges glinted from their places, swinging from thin-linked chains around their necks.

I had failed her.

I wouldn't go down without fighting.

Again, I was too late in noticing the man carrying a syringe that approached. A tall man, wearing gloves of black vinyl. A dozen or more hands held me still as he plunged the syringe into my arm.

"I'm curious to see how well he fares. If the fight he puts up is any indication, he ought to provide some nice data points.

I could hear her scream my name as my body rapidly went limp. Soon, I was awash in a sea of pain, slipping underneath.

"Tim? Are you awake?" The psychologist again. *Way to mix things up.*

"Yes." I answered.

"Good. Now, I'm going to ask you some questions. All I need is a yes or no to them. Should be simple, right?" He was kindly again. His voice the same as the man with the gloves. The viper from the dream that was reality.

"Yes." I responded, willing to play along. All the while trying to think my way out of the nightmare.

"Your name is Timothy Kines?"

"Yes." I answered. That much wasn't a lie.

"Your parents are Jonathan and Marie Kines?"

"Yes."

"I am told that you did very well in high school. Going off to college?"

It threw me. *You were considering them before she came into your life. Back when it was all so mundane and simple.*

"Thinking about it." I answered.

"Now, a yes or no. Let's not strain ourselves." He chided.

I remained silent. Thinking frantically.

"Fair enough. Too soon for that one. However, you consider yourself to be completely sane, correct?"

Here, he didn't even try to hide the answer he would prefer to hear. Knowing that I hadn't gone crazy at all, I was able to answer.

"Yes."

"You do well with chess. That implies that you think and act in a more logical manner. Is that correct?"

"Yes."

"Okay, now just listen to me for a moment. You *have* had a terrible brain injury. A rather large tumor lodged in the back of your skull. A few days ago, the pain of it drove you to shoot yourself, which is actually rather fortunate. If you hadn't, we might not have found the tumor. The bullet lodged in the one spot where it could do no harm, but the x-ray picked up the mass. If we hadn't gone in, you'd be dead by now."

"Bullets do tend to have that effect on things." I glibbed.

"Shush. I'm not done yet. Over the past few years, and even more so in the past few months, you've been developing a deep psychosis. No doubt a side effect from the mass pushing on your brain."

"That isn't true." I stated.

"Nevertheless, it is fact. Now, in this altered state, you have constructed a whole world for yourself. It's time for you to return to the real one."

"Yes." I responded. It was true enough. The longer he talked, the more time I had to think. The more time I had to buttress myself against this construct. Every new detail became fuel. I spent the time trying to think of where in my psyche the objects around me come from. The particular fade to the lettering on the doctor's stool, for instance. *Which visit to the hospital did* that *particular detail come from?*

"I get the impression that you are humoring me. So let me return the favor. Your story is that your father is dead. What's it say here…" He consulted his notes. "Ah, yes. A sudden heart attack. You believe it wasn't an accident. You think he belongs to some sort of underground cabal, running malicious experiments."

"He was probably trying to stop them. He was a good man."

"Of course. The crusader, shining the light from the inside of the shadowy underworld. I forgot. Now… Yes, in your version of events, this happened three years ago. Well, nearly four now. You believe that just *two* months ago, a strange naked woman with glowing eyes just happened to drop off another naked woman with elf ears. And ever since, you've been on the run, protecting her."

"Ever since the Trench Coat Men came. They shot Mom." I corrected.

"Ah, correct. How silly of me to forget that. Now, where have you been these last few months? Can you name places?"

Truthfully… I couldn't. For the life of me, I could not remember a single name of any of the dozens of towns we had travelled through. Only the name of Trooper Bill.

"I wasn't sightseeing. I was keeping her safe." I whispered.

"Of course. After all, she was completely dependent on you. Can't even tie her own shoes."

"She's getting better at it."

This is a trick. He's manipulating you, partner.

"Yes, thanks to your teaching. Now, I want you to do something for me, Tim."

I stared, not willing to so readily agree to any task set before me by an apparition.

"Think about that story. Honestly, if you read it, would you expect to see it in a newspaper, or some kind of comic book?"

Put that way, it does seem a bit absurd… But that's life, isn't it?

"That isn't a yes or no question. I won't be tricked by you, you bastard. Poke me with your needles, ask me endlessly stupid questions. It won't matter. I know this isn't real. My parents are both dead because of you people. NOW LET ME SEE SOBELY!" I roared that last at the man. He shrank back for a second, then reached over to adjust the fluid lines.

We tried to ignore the thought of the cabin. A warm, safe, hideaway in the woods. It only took one day of Sobely coughing to change my mind. A few hours after we go tucked away in the cozy cabin, I started to relax.

Of course, time moved funny there. The whole thing seemed like some kind of dream.

This isn't right, either. This was your dream.

I snuggled with Sobely on a couch that had been recovered with recycled denim. An odd choice, but appropriate, I suppose. We felt the heat radiate off the cast iron wood stove. We could rest here a while.

You've got to snap out this, Tim. She needs you.

"What?" I muttered, coming back awake.

"I said, you need to snap out of this. Sobely needs you." My father stood over me. His face was pale. Like the day I found him, on the floor of his downtown office. I had come to borrow a couple bucks for lunch. I don't think I ate anything for three whole days after that.

"You aren't real." I stated.

"No, I really am not. I told you earlier – you know what the truth is. You have to fight, son."

"FIGHT WHAT?!" I shouted. Every detail a lie, yet just to have him here in a nightmare reminded me of what he had meant to me. My Dad was my hero.

"This!" He gestured the space around us. "This delusion. They want you broken. I need you to *break free*."

It occurred to me then that if I *were* to construct some kind of escape route from this elaborate nightmare, Dad would undoubtedly be the big clue.

"How do I break free? How do I save her?" I begged the ghost of the memory.

"You have all the answers. You have the truth. Let it be your sword. Your shield. The BFG 9000 you use to blow this charade sky high."

I could feel myself smile. Dad never played Doom. *Gotcha, pops. Good advice.*

I shut my eyes and remembered that this was all *just* a dream.

I tuned out the sounds, knowing they were constructed of my own memories.

I knew there would have been no ice chips for me. I should taste the nasty flavor that goes along with dry mouth. When I concentrated, I knew this was actually true. Whatever they were hoping to accomplish, they failed.

In the true world, all I had was Sobely.

To choose a reality of sorrow over a comfortable lie. Pity.

15

"That's odd. A voice in the murky nothing. The space between the dream and reality. Or maybe the space between a dream and another dream.

"What's that?" A second voice. Like a second anchor, pulling me back.

"His brain waves just spiked. Almost like he was waking up."

"Don't be ridiculous. Look, the binaural monitor got dislodged. He's probably just reacting to the smell of your breath."

"Shut up! Look, he shouldn't be able to move. How could he dislodge the headset?"

"One of the nurses... Wait. His heart rate is rising. Temperature returning to normal... That's impossible."

"Better get the Director."

"No. Not yet. Fix the head set and check his lines." The second voice had a note of alarm in in his voice now. Muffled sounds turned acute as something was pulled off my head. I could hear machinery, and those that tended to it. Quiet reports whispered with urgency. Briefly I considered that perhaps I had become trapped by another dream.

"Shit! That... isn't supposed to happen."

Muddy darkness swapped with intense light, causing my eyes to squint even though they had had been taped shut. I could feel a prickly sensation in my right arm. Sounds continued to sharpen, now to the point where it hurt my ears. The light impossibly bright.

"Get the Director."

"He's busy. We're getting a visit from the head office soon."

"You better go quickly then. He'll want to see this. Looks like Subject Six is going to be more interesting than we thought."

The lie of my memories was suddenly and completely laid bare. This was no cabin in the woods. No safe refuge. That place had never existed. A drug-induced fantasy to mask the reality. It wasn't nearly winter time, either.

"He's still in session with subject five. Won't even let us in to provide refreshment for him." A third voice. A woman.

I struggled to move. To peel the tape off my eyes. To get a look at my surroundings.

"In this case, I think it's better him than us. If Lot found out..."

A multitude of murmurs in agreement flooded the room. Followed by unspoken silence.

I wept, memories flooding back. Ugly truth shielded by pleasant lies.

Less than three months, and I had already failed her. For my failure, I had earned my own room in hell.

The leaking tears loosened the adhesive on the tape, allowing me to finally take in the truth in all its stark horror. Bright light, sanitary white, surgical steel. Machines that went bing! And beep! Or quietly wheezed in the corner. Men and women in gray wearing hair caps and sterile masks, only their too-shiny eyes visible of their faces. In every pair of onyx regard I saw only unattached malice.

The only truth that had existed in my memories had been Trooper Bill. He had set up a roadblock on the outskirts of some prairie town we had hardly paused to pass through. A glance in our window, a word spoken into his radio, and the truck had been neatly surrounded by the trench coat men, policemen, and the plain-clothes unit of FBI agents. Before I could throw the Dodge into gear to take our leave, sharp barbs had bit into the flesh of my cheek. I got the satisfaction of seeing Trooper Bill crumple before they had me out of the truck. With spasming muscles, I hadn't been able to retain the firearm. After everything, my rage had amounted to neutralizing exactly ONE threat to our existence.

You ARE still alive.

So?

So man up! If you're alive, then so is Sobely.

With sobering realization of the possibility, I put myself into motion. A concerted effort against the restraints, pulling so violently that I could hear my joints pop in their sockets. I growled low in my throat and twisted the best that I could. Trying to throw all my strength into a single buckled strap.

The buckle snapped with a suddenness that caught me by surprise. Momentarily driverless, my body continued to writhe. The freed hand clawed at the restraint on the other side. The belt began to loosen.

Then everything washed away in a flood of nausea and pain. I flailed uselessly, my arm connecting with men and machinery with equal abandon. I howled my fury untamed.

With a sharp prick in my neck, my strings were cut. A rag doll, helpless while restraints were replaced. Vision swimming again as the door opened to admit a tall man in black goggles, an old-fashioned reflector attached to a wide band around his bare forehead, his bald head reflecting light nearly as well.

He took in the room and then clapped his hands once.

"Splendid! I am pleased to see his spirit is yet unbroken!" He chuckled to himself.

The best I could manage in response was another low growl.

"I can also see why Lot ordered his execution. I, however, am not so afraid. Not of this *boy* or that miserable whelp he fights so hard for. Such a fascinating pair. That I would agree, yes I would!"

He strode over to the table I was strapped onto. They had reclined it back to an angle that would keep me from utilizing gravity again.

"Who knows, if he is a good little boy, I just might feel inclined to spare the girl, I just might. She'd make a pretty piece for my collection. So soft. When she cries out his name, I almost feel moved. So much more... fun than the whimpering orphans I usually have on hand to play with."

Two things became certain then.

One: Were I capable of moving, I would have broken the restraints and strangled the fiend at my side, standing with hands clasped before him like an excited child.

Two: He *would* die.

For the moment the drugs they had pumped into my raging system pulled my aching bones back into darkness.

Please don't dream this time.

"Do try and restrain yourself now, Mr. Kines." The Director waited as my senses slowly returned to me. Seething anger writhed like a living thing in my gut. Instead of struggling against my restraints, I struggled to smooth my face into a mask of calm reason. If it couldn't be done, I hoped to at least appear as if I were in control of myself.

"I'm going to kill you." Despite my efforts, my open declaration came out as a predatory growl.

The Director just smiled.

"Still unbowed, I see. I wouldn't expect anything else." Like before, he clapped his hands together once. Like he had been offered a brand-new toy. The expression twisting his lips was gleeful, but somehow I doubted that any emotion *ever* reached his eyes. The dark goggles seemed a part of him; as if he were some kind of insectile predator. Merely trying to pass himself off as a man.

But we must wait to leap until we are sure of the kill.

"I doubt you would be so thrilled if you were to remove these restraints. Care to find out?" This time I managed something close to the commanding tone of voice my father had always possessed.

"The data points would undoubtedly be of some interest. Perhaps another time, hmm?" He spoke with genial cordiality. No different than a co-worker making a rain check for dinner plans.

"Any time your curiosity needs closure, Director."

Another clap and grin.

"Splendid! Let's get started tracking today's data points, shall we?" He pressed a button on the wall, a small buzzer sounded, and the door opened.

All my hard-won calm was lost in an instant. Three of the grey-clad men wheeled in an upright square framework structure of PVC. Sobely's limbs were stretched tight to the four corners. Her head hung low in defeat. Blood wept from dozens of tiny puncture marks.

Naked, bleeding, and limp. Like a side of beef in a butcher's barn.

I gasped her name, straining my already bruised limbs. Wanting desperately to hold her. To save her. For the effort, a club struck my abdomen, forcing all the air out of my lungs. I heard a sharp crack from the impact.

Her eyes lifted. Recognition flickered across her ragged green eyes. A glimmer of hope sparked to new life.

"Ah. How amusing! Let's give them the room for a moment, shall we?" The Director and his minions filed out, shutting the solid door behind them. They watched from the hall through a viewing window that had likely been installed for just such a purpose.

"Sobely?" I whispered.

"Tim! He told me... Is it truly you, or just another trick? My head hurts so much." A tear escaped her right eye, though it was plain she was trying to maintain some semblance of composure. Her left eye was swollen nearly shut. She set her jaw rigidly, the spirit of defiance still alive within her.

"It is truly me, my heart."

If I could have had my hand free, it would have reached for her. Forsaking even escape. The need to touch her, to be sure this wasn't still part of a nightmare was nearly enough to drive me to madness.

"How can I be sure?" She whispered, her voice heavily laden with emotion unshed.

I tried my best to smile.

"Do you remember the very first promise I made to you?" I asked gently. Her tears began to flow in earnest.

She managed a weak nod.

"We are going to make it out of this. They haven't won yet. Hold on for me." I pulled again at my restraints, wanting only to brush her tears away.

"I am scared, Tim."

The door opened to admit the Director and a single club-wielding orderly.

"How very touching. Trying to inspire hope where there clearly is none. To what end? You'll never leave this place alive. Any hope you spark will only be crushed by your failure to deliver. In a way, my boy, that makes you a rather cruel person. The question now..." He touched a device to Sobely's skin, causing an instant reaction. She screamed as her muscles involuntarily moved in spastic motion, flexing from heavy current.

"The question is how long you endure before you expire. Six months? A year? That data will be quite insightful. And a pleasure to record."

Sobely continued to writhe in agony, even as the device was removed from her skin. As for myself, I became filled with a murderous calm. I strained again, could feel my joints swell with the force, and yet I remained silent. Nothing I said would make any difference to the inhuman monster before me. I remained silent, staring into her eyes. Willing what strength I possessed to transfer to her. To help her stay strong.

Somehow, she managed to quiet her screams. Blood filled her mouth from a bitten tongue. The Director frowned, pressing the device in again. Sobely barely even shook, even managed a smile.

"How very peculiar. Hmm..." He dropped his hand once more, turned, and snapped his fingers. Sobely was wheeled from the room. The lights shut off, leaving me alone with my rage and the ticking machinery.

She is alive.

I had no idea how much time had passed. I might have dozed off a dozen times. I might not have slept at all. The noise from the machines my only clue that time passed at all – and that had grown into a cacophony unbearable.

Periodically, and with extreme care, I would pull at the bonds. Singly, and without making any noise. Perhaps it was only wishful thinking and a touch of madness, but I felt sure that I could feel the straps slip. If they did, it was only in amounts so miniscule that is could have just been my imagination. Sensed, more than truly perceived. I wanted to yank at them. To somehow summon the bear-like strength that had allowed me to break free before.

I restrained such urges, however. I somehow knew that the time was not right. Better to prepare for the right opportunity. Better to get what little rest was offered, so I might recognize the opportunity when it came.

The machines tittered, counting each breath I did or didn't draw. Each beat of my aching heart. A dozen cold sentinels chattering away in the dark. Unwavering and oblivious. A tale I had read in high school returned to me then, and I allowed myself to remember it. A world without people, where the automatons continued their chores until the very last electric motor turned its very last revolution. Bradbury, I think it had been. A darkly fanciful tale, the perfect poetry to accompany my own slow descent into the whispering of the dark.

Surely the strap on my left arm – one of the ones that they had to replace after my earlier wild tantrum – had loosened. I gasped as if in fear, hoping to hide the excitement that threatened to make my pulse quicken. I willed myself towards calm. To rest. To not trip the sensors keeping tabs on my triumphs, and to do my best to look as if I had given myself over to despair.

It wasn't much of a stretch. I wallowed in that feeling and awaited my chance in the chuttering darkness.

When the lights came back on they heralded the arrival of a multitude of grey-clothed orderlies. With rapid and smooth movements, they unhooked all the machines and wheeled them from the room. In mere moments I was alone in the bright light, heavy silence broken only by my gasping breath. A broken rib had forced me to stifle a cry of pain with each inhalation, and to grimace when I let the air out again.

From a grated speaker set into the wall above the door:

"Do you promise that you will behave yourself?" The crackling voice was the Director's.

"I don't exactly have a choice, now do I?" I called back.

"Oh, there is always a choice. If you promise to reign in that temper of yours and be a good little boy, I have something nice for you."

I did my best to give an impression that I was thinking it over, though my mind had already been made up. There were other ways to remain defiant.

"Alright." I answered. Whatever was being offered, it was a change of the variables. Any change had the potential for possibility. Raging now would offer no hope of escape.

"That is not the proper response, Subject Six." The Director admonished. I gulped down the spike of anger. *Was he the engineer of her undoing?*

"I will be a good boy."

"Splendid!"

The lock clicked, the door opened, and Sobely was gently pushed inside. The door shut, and the lock clicked again.

Surprisingly, there was no audience at the window. In fact, someone had shut the internal shutters, blocking us from the view of anyone that happened to wander the hall. Granting us at least the illusion of privacy.

Sobely wobbled unsteadily to where I lay, her ankles swollen. Her darkened eye had puffed out further, completely covering one of the glorious green irises I had so often found myself drowning in. Otherwise she had been cleaned, dressed in a hospital gown, and was almost completely unrestrained. She teetered at my side, and then managed to lay across my chest, weeping. Calling my name. Planting urgent kisses wherever she could reach. I fought the urge to free my left arm – to just put a comforting hand around her shoulders. I bore no illusions about our privacy. Such places were bound to have cameras embedded into the masonry of the walls.

Instead, I murmured, "I wish I could hold you, my love." This whole set-up was an obvious trap, and I endeavored to do all that I could to make the Director's life more difficult.

"Oh, Tim!" She struggled to be free of the one safety measure they had taken with her. Her arms had been tied behind her back with an elaborate ladder knot. Impossible to loosen from pure effort. Impossible to untie without the use of both hands. They were pulled together severely at wrist and elbow, and I imagined the position was very uncomfortable. The tension on her shoulders was visible through the sheer fabric.

"Calm. Save your strength." I whispered into a nearby ear. I longed to bend forward, just a little. To plant kisses of my own on her delicate and bewitching earlobes. I'd kiss every inch of her once we got free of this place, just to celebrate our continued existence. No matter what was thrown at us, we still had *us*.

She settled down, then. Managed to climb onto the table, somehow. The feel of her body pressed against mine served to instantly calm my raging heart. In a moment of maddening clarity, I knew we would somehow be all right. We would make it through this nightmare. *Dad reminded you that you know what the truth is. We will be free.*

I hummed a song for her as she settled into weary slumber.

It was very likely the only sleep she'd gotten since our capture.

How long have we been here?

Before much longer, my vigilance slipped, and I too fell into the velvet darkness of the sleep you can only get when the love of your life is safely beside you. As long as I could feel her heart beating, the world would continue to exist. Together we were unbreakable.

And 'ware to thine enemies.

"Splendid!' The Director cawed, forcing my eyes open. Sobely slumbered on.

"I'm *glad* that you're so *happy*. I have an offer for you." I kept my voice down, so as not to wake Sobely yet.

"Hmm?" An amused grin settled on his face like it was unwanted. The black goggles promised that the eyes behind them were only full of malevolent madness.

"Let us go." I kept my tone even.

"And why would I ever do that, my dear boy?"

Imagine you are the lion, regarding a baby gazelle.

"I would think that your data points would be useless to you if you were dead." I answered, ice in my veins. Bound? Beaten? Tortured? Yes, I was all of those things. Broken? Not even close.

"How very generous of you. Normally I might even be inclined to entertain the notion of your release. However, you see... I'm in a tight spot just now. Yes." He tapped the end of his pen to his lips. Seeing no clip board, I had a feeling it was the only reason he carried the stylus.

I swallowed my contempt for his theatrics.

"Perhaps I can help with that." I kept forcing down the bile that threatened to come up my throat. *Keep him talking.*

Every syllable, down to the last nervous half-chuckle, was a piece of valuable information to me. I harbored no illusion that the man was even capable of coming to any sort of arrangement with me. My father might have had the power to talk his way out of a den of vipers — but the best I could hope for was to keep breathing long enough for opportunity to arise.

"Now, that would certainly merit consideration, if only it didn't equal an immediate death sentence. Unfortunately, my employers would be very cross if I acted in such a unilateral manner." This time he tapped the pen on his cheek, thinking himself a cat with a mouse.

"There is always a choice, Director." I echoed his earlier words.

He sighed. It could have been genuine.

"Yet they can always be stripped from us without warning. Orderly? Grab the girl" A burly man yanked Sobely up, pulled her away without compassion. Another man stood at the door cradling an automatic weapon, curiously fitted with a silencer.

"Together, the two of you are quite formidable. Lot was correct to feel afraid. I would be remiss if I didn't try and learn from his mistakes. Especially with hard data points to back up my supposition." He snapped his fingers, and a third orderly came forward to hand him a needle filled with something dark.

"Now, I did say that if you behaved that you would get something nice. You've held up your end, and so I shall spare her life. You, however..." He approached. Sobely screamed, pulled at her captor. The ferocity of her movement neatly yanked the burly man from his feet, and she surged forward. With her good eye full of thunder, she intercepted The Director, bowling him forward to crash into my table.

He spun on her and smacked her across the face with his free hand. Fresh blood flew with the spittle as she fell to her rump, teeth snapping together audibly. Dazed for the moment. Long enough for the orderly to reacquire a grip on her arms and haul her up. The Director turned back to me, face grim.

"Wait!" I commanded. To wonder, the Director halted.

"I will entertain you a moment longer. Her... spirit has inspired me to notions."

"I thought you wanted to see how long it would take you to break us. Giving up so soon?" I made the question a taunt. Holding him in contempt for his apparent weakness. At least, that was the impression I was trying for.

Another sigh.

"My hands are forced. As you mentioned yourself, no data has any value if I am not around to extrapolate its secrets. So while I would enjoy breaking you at my leisure... I simply do not have the time any more. It's risk enough just to leave her alive. The both of you? Just unthinkable. Feel grateful for the generosity I've granted."

He began forward again, placed a gloved hand on my shoulder.

"I could help you. Don't you desire to be the one calling the shots?"

He paused again.

"Hmm... Well, you are Jonathan's son. Perhaps..." He strode to where Sobely stood, still trying to free herself. She had managed to head-butt the orderly, bringing forth a fountain of blood from a badly broken nose.

"If you in insist on acting like some untamed beast, then you shall be treated in kind!" He slapped her again. Hard. Then he yanked the sickly green gown off her.

It was only with the greatest effort that I managed to remain calm.

"I won't help you if you hurt her." I stated. He spun on his heel once more.

"I've decided. You are just too dangerous. Nothing to be done for it. No incentive to bring you properly to heel. As long as you live, you pose a threat to me. Now, girl, watch as I kill the thing that makes you strong. The source of your insolent, ungrateful, defiance. Watch carefully as I rob your life of all hope." The Director moved with the theatrical surety of a stage magician. The needle stabbed into my neck. Cold poison spread with electric pulses of chemical fire. Sobely wailed.

I was out of time, and I only had enough strength left for one thing.

"Sobely! Listen!" I called. She quieted – or the world started to grow quieter. Neither mattered.

The Director watched intently. It was clear he expected me to behave very differently. Already I could feel the darkness sweep in. My muscles burned, begged to spasm in death throes. I was determined to not break. With my final breath I would grant her all the strength that remained to me.

"I love you, Sobely. You are my hope. My life. Please… remain…" I struggled to think, to breath. The poison acted like an anchor, pulling at my ankles to the depths of a black current.

"Please… stay… Please. Be strong!" I gasped, struggling for every whisper of breath. In the dimming light, I could still see her face. She nodded once. Weeping silently. The Director cackled.

"I love you, Tim. Forever." Her chin rose in defiance.

As my vision swam in and out of focus, I was granted the vision of one final slow smile.

"Forever." She whispered, a tear running down her cheek.

As always, her smile stole my breath away.

Forever.

Eternity in her arms. A short wait, perhaps, and then infinity. To surrender to salvation's army – to meet her again in that heavenly paradise. Perhaps that had been the point of our misery. Without such terrible hardship, would we have appreciated paradise as much?

When the concept of Faith had been explained, she eagerly accepted it. She knew everything I told her was truth, so convincing her the reality of Salvation had been as simple as telling her that it was so. A Bible had found its way into our pack, and several nights under the boundless sky had been spent reading her stories of lions and prophets. Of a Savior's journey to fulfill His promise.

She had wept like a babe when I read to her of the crucifixion. Locked within the confines of her missing past, I believed she knew just how Christ must have felt at Calv'ry.

My eyes opened to a field of wildflowers. Daffodils, daisies, lilies and poppies bright. An endless horizon of glorious color, under-lit with intimate red-leaf clover blooms. I reached to cup a delicate blossom, and my hand came up bloody.

My eyes refocused, looking for the thorn. The sharp rock. Looking past the blossoms cheerful. The red of the clover seemed to flow like wine, moving gently in a breeze un-felt.

With horror growing with every second, I discovered that the leaves were all coated with blood. Darkly warm, flowing through the flowers like a bubbling brook of red. I followed that red flow upstream. Crushing petals, bare feet squishing into a ground muddied with the endless stream of blood.

I crested a hill, and then sank to my knees. Below, resting serenely in a crimson pond, was Sobely. No rise or fall of her bosom. No silent mutterings of a dream moving her lips. As still as a statue, carved from alabaster and ebony.

"NO!" I cried, stumbling forward to take her lifeless body into my arms.

"I don't want eternity! Not without her." I cast about for something sharp. A blade to plunge into my heart. Let me lie as still as her, together in an eternal sleep.

"Don't make me suffer your paradise, if it is to be without her!" I screamed into the perfect blue sky.

I sobbed, no tool to help me escape this Eden. All that I had were the flowers, and the blood.

16

This isn't heaven or *hell.*

No burning torment. No pleasant bliss. Just an itch. Eyes stuck with a heavy build-up of a yellowish crud. A crud that trailed down my cheek, causing the itch. A positive sensation, overall – proof that I was still alive. An uncomfortable ache in my joints served as confirmation. I was still held fast to the steel table.

I am still alive.

The room was dark. Shades down. I could hear the murmur of voices approaching in the hall. Silhouettes in the window. Somebody tall; most likely the Director. He stopped a moment to face his companion. A shorter shadow in a flat-topped hat. Speaking in a voice like the sound of a blade cutting through silk. An image flashed of the creepy shadow-man that had attended my father's funeral. Lot.

There were so many people there that day. People from all walks of life. Businessmen rubbing elbows with burly bikers. Yet, he *had stood out, didn't he? The only one that didn't seem to belong.*

"This facility has outlived its usefulness. See that you do not do the same." Lot said. Dry leaves caught in a breeze.

"It's just the data points from subject five are so fascinating. Lot, her capacities are extraordinary, and with a just little more time…" The Director now a child wheedling for an extra cookie.

"That is precisely why I am here. Finally, your *data points* have yielded something useful. I shall remand her to the care of my facility back east. It is now your duty to close this site down. Abandon it fully, Director. Failure to obey will be dealt with severely."

"But all my research!" The Director exclaimed.

"My people have already archived it. You will be granted a generous office suite and full access to the databases. If you manage to turn all that gibberish into something useful, I may have more exciting work for you. The board wants to reign in our excesses a bit. The hunt for the boy... never mind. He is dealt with, and we can now move on to the next phase. He is... *dealt* with, correct?"

"It was a bit messy, but Trooper Bill was most helpful. Pity he was unable to be properly rewarded for his effort." I could hear genuine regret in the Director's voice.

"The boy did us a favor. Such gross incompetence... No matter. No one outside our direct control has any inkling of the near-mishap we suffered, though since that mess in Arizona our federal contacts *have* become quite nosy. Jonathan's son proved his resilience to the very end."

"I should have liked to have studied that one. If we could determine the source of such resolve..."

"It would lead to nothing but trouble. Our units need to be obedient, not resilient. I had... other plans for the boy. Just the same, I will take their bodies for further analysis."

"That may prove difficult. They were both cremated." The Director sounded genuinely apologetic.

The magician trying to sell the audience on a lie.

"I gave you the task of apprehending the pair *alive*, and you're telling me that not only did you fail in this, but that you had them *both* cremated?" Lot's voice was sharp. No more silk.

"The FBI wanted full autopsies on them. It took some effort to get the paperwork changed so they'd go into the oven, rather than put under an unsanctioned microscope. Failed prototype or not, I imagine her genetics would bring them knocking on our doors rather sooner than we'd like, yes?

There was a pause, I could sense a small power struggle between the two. The Director was clearly the inferior, yet he chafed. He hungered. For that reason alone, he had elected to capture us and bring us to his facility in secret. Lot did not seem like the forgiving type. If I had the power to pop out and go "BOO," Lot would probably shoot the Director first.

Lot lowered his voice. I strained to listen.

"The personnel that have proven useful have already been loaded onto the transport. I shall leave a few soldiers behind to prepare her transfer, and to see that this site is scrubbed thoroughly. Once complete, you will personally escort Subject Five to our Alpha Quarters. Understood?"

"That helicopter couldn't hold even a third of my staff!"

"Fortunate, then, that so few of them were deemed to be of any value. You might consider cremation for their bodies as well. Purge the entire campus. It would speed things up."

Lot spun on his heel and strode off. The Director remained where he was, speechless. Four silhouettes moved past him, moving in the same direction as Lot. From the shape of their hats, and the lack of definition to their shape, it was clear that these were the Trench Coat Men.

The Director turned at last and slowly walked out of view.

I discovered that the left-hand wrist restraint had come loose. With great care I quickly freed myself and dropped to the floor. Part of me worried that this was some sort of trick. The Director was a madman. The radical change of his behavior was obviously because of Lot's impending arrival, but that didn't mean he had been through with me. His theatrics might have been just an attempt to break her spirit. If he knew he'd be handing her over to Lot, it stood to reason that he would try to make her as pliable as he could.

It was possible I had been drugged and left to stew while Lot was around. To keep me quiet. If that was the case, I wouldn't have much time to escape. If this whole thing was a trick, then I had to make the best of it.

Lot believed I was dead, and that was a start. Wiggle room.

As it ever was, nothing was certain. Sobely lived still – though it was apparent that Lot had his own designs on her. The last image I had of her was one of defiance. She would not make things easy for him. If the Director wanted her broken, he'd fail.

She will cry when she sees you.

Of course she would. Imagine if Juliet had woken just a bit sooner. Romeo would have bawled like a baby. There was no shame in it.

Where will you go?

Anywhere would be better than here. I removed the replacement straps from the table and wrapped them around the knuckles of my right hand, leaving the buckles to swing free.

You don't even know where you are...

And so what if I didn't? Was that a reason to just give up?

No. Not while breath remains in your chest. Just be ready for anything.

They ought to put that on a tee shirt. I'd be wearing it all the time.

Maybe you ought to be concerned about the fact that you are having a conversation with yourself.

I pondered that for just a second, and then shrugged. Couldn't be helped. I needed all the helpful advice I could get.

This is true.

I approached the door on tip-toes and paused. From the other side, I heard the crackle of a radio.

"Kilo-two. Prepare Subject Five for immediate transport."

"Copy." A voice answered. I heard his boot steps as he turned. Apparently, a guard had been stationed in the hall just outside my room. Out of view of the windows. *Too bad for him, then.* I eased the door open and peered through cautiously. His back was turned away from me.

With an agility that surprised myself, I sprang at the man. Adrenaline was ever so useful. When I had woken up, I had difficulty just breathing. Now I was a lion, an unsuspecting buffalo before me.

I crashed into the man, striking him at least once with my make-shift flail. He rolled beneath me – but that proved to be a mistake on his part. From the new position, all I had to do was push my knee into his throat.

I felt his windpipe collapse. A pathetic gurgling sound now all he could manage. Hands clawed for his ruined throat as if that could help. If he had tapped the call button on his radio, he might have at least been avenged. Instead he only gurgled and stared, disbelieving. He could have been screaming in fury or begging for mercy.

My response was to wrap the straps tighter, buckles across my fists, and punch him repeatedly. Even when he ceased to make any noise at all, I kept striking. To be able to finally *do* something to one of Lot's men. To be able to physically stop one bad guy from ever hurting her again...

As lovely of a mess you're making out of his face, don't you think you should start moving?

I shook my head to clear it, now moving with more deliberate purpose. I removed the Kevlar vest he wore, the belt with a militaristic-looking sidearm and combat knife, and then his boots. The automatic weapon he wore on a sling I also claimed. Both weapons were curiously fitted with noise suppressors.

Before I stood to continue on, I snaked his wallet from his pocket, and slipped it into my own battered jeans.

The boots were too small, but I wasn't the only person that would be needing shoes. Quickly, I tied the laces together and slung them and the vest over my bare shoulder.

Halfway to my feet, and I stooped once more to pick up the radio from where it had fallen on the plastic tiles.

Only then did I get a good look at the hallway. On one side, a door with the number '7' stenciled on it. To my left, a door with the number '5.' I went left. Quietly I moved to the door and eased it carefully open. Wary of an ambush.

I involuntarily groaned in dismay. The occupant was female. She hung by her wrists in a rig like the one that had been used to secure Sobely. However, her hair was auburn, her eyes a clear grey, and blank of life.

Desperation over-rode rationality. I ran to the next door.

Empty.

To the next.

Also empty.

In the final room at the end of the hall, across from a door with the word 'Director' stenciled on it, I peeked inside and felt my heart stop with relief. The desperate animal calmed; sated by the sight of *her*. They had put her into a fresh gown, but she was bound at hands and feet. Gagged with a purpose-made strap and blindfolded with heavy cloth. Fresh bruises on her bare skin bore testimony to the terrific fight she had put up.

"But you're dead!" A startled voice called behind me. The Director's door must have been well-oiled. I stood straight, snapping the rifle up as I turned.

"One correction, Director." I squeezed the trigger. A burst of muffled shots sprang forth. Red blooms spread across his chest, and he slumped against the wall, sliding to the floor. A look of shock on his features. His goggles came loose to reveal eyes of ice chips.

"You're dead." I finished. I watched the light go out of his eyes. His jaw slacked, shoulders drooped with gravity. A dark pool of blood spread, seeping beneath the door of his own office.

I turned back to Sobely. Rushed to her side, yanking off the blind-fold when she started to struggle against me. I carefully untangled her gag as she cried my name over and over. The knife made short work of the rest of her restraints. For an eternal moment, she just stared, still repeating my name. Still as a stone. Complete disbelief of what she saw filled her soft features.

She saw me a ghost and must have been considering the thought that she had gone insane.

Joy soon chased this away, and then she was upon me. Kissing me fiercely. Wrapping her arms around my neck. I returned her embrace, but only so I could ease her enthusiasm to a halt.

"We have to leave, my sweet blossom. There will be time for kisses later." I smiled gently at her. She burst into tears, unable to even speak my name anymore.

I told you so.

"Put these on." I passed her the boots. She obediently complied, clumsy fingers forgetting how to tie the laces together. A near-silent mundane moment while I tied the laces for her. Once completed with the task, she clutched my neck again.

"Put this on, too, please. I know it is kind of heavy, but it will help protect you, okay?"

She nodded, taking the heavy Kevlar vest and slipping it over her shoulders. With hands that shook, she managed to connect the

Velcro together in a fairly straight line. It was much too big for her, of course. The body armor made her seem even more frail than before. She shook – the adrenaline surge from before fading despairingly quickly.

She rose to her feet, and then leaned heavily against the wall. Breathing hard from the strain. I looped an arm around her waist and began to half-drag her back down the hallway. Back the way I'd come.

My legs moved like the pistons of a machine. Unfeeling, efficient. My own adrenaline reserves had long since been tapped. The last time I'd gotten some proper rest nothing more than a memory of a memory. The Director believed I was dead. It hadn't been a trick, then. For whatever reason, his poison had failed to do the job.

My intent was to carry us both to the end of the hall. To the double-doors of the waiting elevator. To continue outside, and to not stop ever again. Yet, when we passed the open door leading to room 5 – Lot's Subject Five – a voice called out. Sobely slowed to turn. The movement seemed to take an age to perform.

"Please. Whoever is there. Take me with you. Please?"

I hesitated. The facts of our situation were painfully uncomfortable. Sobely was hardly able to move on her own. This other girl was probably no better off. Taking her along wouldn't be much safer than leaving her here and would increase the danger to Sobely as well. The choice seemed obvious.

Yet Lot desired her. That factor weighed heavily but was hardly decisive.

Put a bullet right between those grey eyes. It would be mercy.

I actually felt my arm begin to rise with the gun, when she spoke again, breaking the silent spell.

"Please?"

Dad would have saved her.

Hmph! I guess taking one more person along on this loony ride won't make the target on your backs any bigger.

"We have to help her." Sobely murmured, leaning against the wall. Freeing me to move. To act.

"I'm... not sure how we can. I can't carry two of you. I'm barely moving as it is." I whispered back.

Valiantly, Sobely straightened until she managed to stand entirely on her own two feet, and with minimal shaking.

"I don't need to be carried. We can't leave her here." She swallowed visibly. "I'd rather die." Her chin rose stubbornly. I whistled through my teeth, all too aware that the unbelievable image she made was terrifying – and made the love I felt for her swell even more.

"Inside, then. While I free her." I said. My mind had been made up for me.

I approached the new girl, quickly undoing the blood-stained straps. The evidence suggested that she had been held captive for a long time, and yet she managed to keep her feet with scarcely a wobble.

Maybe we'll be alright with another person in our doomed little group after all. Clearly, she possesses a considerable inner strength of her own. There is a reason Lot wants her after all.

"Alright, miss. Are you able to walk?" I kept my voice low, straining my ears to listen for the approach of danger. The woman nodded.

"Okay. That's good. Follow, and try not to fall behind." I turned away. A hand brushed my back.

"Wait, sir." She quietly pleaded. I turned back around to face her, gesturing for her to continue.

"Please wait..." She repeated.

"Um... We are. What is it? We really do need to get out of here soon..." While I tried to keep my tone gentle, I also let the urgency bleed through.

"Yes, of course. It's just..." She pointed at her face. At her unfocused grey eyes. "I'm... blind." She shrank slightly at the admission. I moved closer to the woman and took a really good look at her eyes. They were extremely clear, and the grey color swirled with the proper patterns of the human iris. Yet there was something off... perhaps the color was a tad more muted than any I'd ever seen. The divisions within the pattern were pale, rather than dark.

And then I felt like kicking myself for not seeing the obvious. The room was darkened. I hadn't turned the light on. My eyes had adjusted well to the gloom. Her pupils were like pinpricks. Like those of someone trying to stare next to the sun.

At least she says she can walk.

I gently took her by the hand.

"Come along, miss. Let's get out of here. I got you." I glanced at Sobely, who smiled encouragingly at the woman. Not that she could see the gesture.

The woman came when I pulled her towards the door. Sobely put an arm around her and tried not to lean too much. But as they turned to enter the hallway, they both sagged towards each other. Arms entwined tighter to keep their balance. Certainly awkward, but at least we were now finally mobile and moving.

Down the hall, down an elevator, around a corner, down another hall. Our progress halted by an electronic security door.

Luckily for us, the security room was on *our* side of the bullet-proof portal. Frantic seconds looking for the over-ride, rewarded by the sound of a lock releasing, and a subtle whoosh of doors opening elsewhere. I hesitated another moment, and then sprayed the security console with automatic fire. Something shorted, and the station caught on fire.

If we were really lucky, it was a closed-circuit system. With no data backups. Maybe our escape would be a mystery.

The reason for the silencers had become apparent once we got outside. The compound was in the middle of a bustling city. Noise and vibration and thousands of people going about their lives, mere feet from a place run by demons. Some of the grey-clothed orderlies were likely employed from the surrounding cityscape.

Could you imagine how that job interview went?

I managed to not laugh at the thought.

A grey wall was the only barrier between the mundane world, and an outpost of Hell. All those noises I had imagined had come from muffled machinery working within the bowels of some sinister laboratory within a forbidding and desolate bunker squatting like some malevolent toad within the desert... The building had contained nothing more than grim hallways, the occasional room with scientific equipment in it. From the conversation I had overheard, there was likely some kind of central server down in a chilled basement.

The rumbles, the strange honking sounds, all of it; nothing more than a thriving metropolis heard through decaying walls of mortar and concrete. Traffic went by. Street-workers dug into a sidewalk. Cars honked warnings to wayward pedestrians paying no attention to the world around them. I shook my head. Hard. The experiences throughout the hour had become a jumbled mess in my already scrambled mind. To come out of the place where a tall man in black goggles reigned as king to find such an *ordinary* setting... it was too much.

Most of these people would never know fear of the scale we had already conquered. Many of them would live out their lives. Work. Find people to spend time with. Have children, raise them. Have ulcers because of nagging mothers-in-law. Retire from jobs they had spent 20 years secretly despising. Spend their final years fishing and trying to find some enjoyment to make up for all those years of denying such simple pleasures in order to punch a clock and live an ordinary life.

We huddled by the wall as I tried to get some sense of bearing. Even the simple step of determining north was impossible. The sky was a bit grey, the air slightly chilly. Were these people going home, or going to work? *The gunman you took out might have had a watch.*

True, but I didn't think to grab it, and I wasn't going back into the building. Part of me feared that we had somehow managed to escape to such an ordinary place by magic. If we went back inside to try and improve our appearance somehow. To try and find clothing and shoes and watches and maybe even a cell phone, we might walk back outside to find exactly the sort of place I had believed to have been held in all long.

We can't stay here. You can smell the smoke start to waft out of the building. Maybe they had set up their fire on some sort of timer – Lot said something about 'purging' the site. Maybe that surveillance console found a little more fuel to spread to. Either way, it won't take long before someone else smells the smoke. Eventually it will become visible, even to those wrapped in their little worlds. We can't stay here.

I took a hold of myself, and then looked us over. I felt the sunlight, and decided it was afternoon. The gate out of the complex was to the north. I wore jeans crusted with blood, a gun belt, and had a militaristic rifle tucked under my arm. Sobely wore a plain white hospital gown, a massive Kevlar vest, and combat boots. The blind woman had just a thin medical gown and her vacant stare. As oblivious as most of the people bustling down the sidewalks were, I doubt we'd get very far if we just took a stroll down the street.

I looked out at the traffic, a rudimentary plan forming. A man was approaching a parked car, pulling keys from his pocket. From his attire and the near-lifeless slump to his shoulders, I imagined he worked in a plain cubicle in one of the tall offices all around. No kitty-cat poster to cheer up his day.

A little excitement will be good for him.

"I need the vest." I stated.

Sobely quickly tried to comply, but the effort of pulling the Velcro apart unbalanced her. Only the wall and the steady grip of the blind woman kept her from the falling to the concrete. I stepped close and got the vest free. Donning it in a flash, and then quickly kissing her cheek.

"Here. Hang on to this. I'll be right back." I pressed the rifle into her arms. And then I ran to the sedan. The tired worker didn't even notice my approach.

"Sir." I called. He didn't look up, just pulled the newly unlocked door open and began to sit down in the driver's seat.

A typical office drone, looking forward to meatloaf and a few hours in front of a T.V. before going to bed. Lucky bastard.

The pistol rapping on the glass of the windshield got his attention.

"Move over." I commanded. Wordlessly, he complied. I sat in the newly vacated seat and plucked the keys from his startled grip.

"I would very much appreciate it if you would sit still and stay quiet. This will all be over soon, I promise. All you need to do is cooperate." I tried to sound friendly. The man trembled anyway.

I started the car, threw it into gear, and pulled it into the empty lot, parking near the girls.

"Please don't move. I'm a bit desperate at the moment, and I'd rather not have to use this." I waved my arm with the restraint still wrapped around it. Only after a moment did I realize I was also waving the gun right in his nose. *You're tired, Tim. Besides, I think he gets the idea, anyhow.*

The man nodded, dumbstruck.

I jumped out, leaving the engine running. So far, I seemed to have avoided the attention of anyone besides the bewildered man.

Typical sheep.

I opened the rear door and moved to help Sobely and the blind woman in. To her credit, Sobely managed to look fairly intimidating with the rifle. An attempt to stifle a yawn almost looked like a menacing growl. *She's still adorable, though. Blood stains and all.*

I think the Cubicle Worker had gone into shock. He hadn't even fully shifted into the passenger seat yet. He sat motionless, staring the way a cow might stare at a bolt gun. I moved to the passenger side of the car and opened the door.

"You're gonna have to drive, friend. Do you think you can manage that?" The man scooted back across, patiently waiting for me to get in and get everyone settled, before putting the car back into gear. Then he looked at me questioningly.

"Umm... Where to?"

I smiled at him, suddenly finding myself with an urge to giggle at the absurdity. He shrank back from me. I couldn't blame him.

When the wolf smiles, the sheep knows he should fear.

"Well, I don't exactly know where we are. How about we just start by driving *away*?"

The sedan began to move, leaving the lot. Joining the flow of traffic. We were on the road again.

Our unwilling driver got us out of the city without incident. Our captors had brought us to Colorado – three states away from our encounter with one Trooper Bill. So many miles away from home.

It seemed sad that I could still consider anyplace *home* still.

Ten miles out of the bustle of the city, with nothing around but postcard-perfect mountains, I felt it was time to make some introductions. Though I had enlisted his help with the pointed menace of a gun, I felt it was important to prove to our driver that we meant him no harm. That *we* weren't the bad guys.

"What's your name?" I asked. I made sure the pistol was tucked safely at my side. It wasn't his fault we'd been captives, after all. No need to frighten him any more than necessary.

You father would have already made friends with him.

Shut up.

"John." He answered nervously.

"Irene." From the back seat. I had almost forgotten the presence of our extra passenger. She had kept so quiet.

"Well, John. My name is Timothy Kines. You may call me Tim, if you like. In the back are the ladies Sobely and Irene. I apologize if we have frightened you. We were in dire straits and I really couldn't afford to be polite about it."

John glanced at me then, for the first time seeing more than just the threat of the gun. From what little I was able to see in the rearview mirror of my face, I knew I was a fright just to look at.

"I can understand that. I guess."

"I hope so. I'm afraid this will likely prove to be a very stressful day for you. Are you married?"

John nodded,

"Six years."

"Kids?"

"Not yet. It's been... a sore subject at home. I think maybe I've been an idiot about the whole thing... but I don't know how to tell *her* that."

This time my grin was genuine.

"Take it from me, John. There truly is such thing as a wrong time for kids." I glanced back at Sobely, who nodded solemnly, and perhaps a bit sadly.

John looked me over again, glanced at Sobely in the mirror.

"I'm thinking you have a point there." He sighed.

"I would also think that having a home to return to, a job to put food on the table, and a wonderful person to spend the rest of your life with... well, that would seem like ideal conditions." I looked around the car. While it wasn't new, it wasn't a rolling wreck, either.

"Besides which, you don't have to *say* anything to admit defeat. I would think that *actions* would be more appropriate." Irene said, leaning forward. Smiling mischievously.

I laughed at that. Whoever she was, she certainly had a sense of humor.

John blushed.

"How far to the next town, John?" I asked, getting back to the matter at hand.

"Maybe another fifteen miles?" He replied.

"Is it as large as the last?"

"No. It's not small, but... It's more like an extended bedroom community."

"Good. Any stores there?"

He nodded.

"They have a Super Center."

I concentrated on slowing my breathing, shut my eyes, and tried to figure out what our next move ought to be. The next few hours would be especially dangerous for us. The odds of running into Lot's forces so close to his facility were pretty good. Especially since we had left the place with a few bodies, a few bullet holes, and slightly on fire. We weren't exactly in any shape to just blend in somewhere, either.

The guns were both an asset to us, and a liability. The car – and its driver – would be missed quickly.

And what would you have considered if he weren't married?

All the cash we possessed consisted of whatever had been in the wallet of the gunman I had taken out. None of us would even pass the lax requirements of entry into a convenience store. *No shoes, no shirts, good Lord is that a gun?*

I snapped my eyes open, coming to a decision.

"Pull over John, if you would." I commanded. The gun lifted almost on its own to rest in my lap.

The car slowed to a stop in the shoulder of the mountain road.

John's day was about to get a little worse.

"Cell phone?" I asked. John passed it over in silence. I turned it off and tossed it into the glove compartment.

"I am sorry that I have to do this. You seem like a decent fellow." I apologized, feeling wretched. *It* has *to be done.*

"We all have our choices." He answered tiredly.

"Step on out of the car with me, please."

John opened his door cautiously, face contorted into a thin mask of calm. The lie evident through the terror in his eyes. *Better that he fears you. Better for us. Better for him.*

Alongside the road, I led John perhaps fifteen feet behind the car. His shoulders tensed, as if he expected to hear the gun at any moment. *At this range, he'd never hear a thing.*

"All right. I'm going to need your clothes. Your wallet. Your shoes. Everything."

He began to unbutton his shirt, his eyes glazing over. A weary acceptance of his Fate heavy in his motions.

"I'm not going to hurt you, John. I just don't have a lot of options right now."

He nodded, unbelieving. I didn't really fault him for it. In moments he stood in his undershorts. I was relieved that he was the type to wear an undershirt. It was damp with sweat of course, but muggers couldn't be choosers. I was also relieved that he had thought to remove it with the rest. I wasn't sure I would have had the heart to actually ask for it.

"Don't move." I ordered, taking the clothing back to the car. The work shirt and pants I passed through the window.

"Do you think you can help Irene get these on?" I asked.

"Yes." Sobely replied. I plopped the vest into the front seat, pulling the white A-style shirt over my head. As Sobely helped Irene get dressed, I split my attention between getting John's shoes on, and keeping an eye on the man himself.

Soon enough I was able to take the now discarded robe from Sobely and took it back to the helpless-looking man standing on the side of the road in his underwear.

If this is the worst thing to ever happen to him, he should consider himself blessed.

"Here. Sorry I can't do any better for you, John. You've been decent about all this." I offered the gown. John took it gingerly and pulled it on.

"You're not... I mean... I thought... with the gun..." He gulped. His nervousness made him shake more than the chill air warranted. His gaze was fixed on the sinister-looking black pistol in my hand.

"This was just a precaution. Just in case we were somehow followed. I already told you that I wouldn't harm you. I am a man of my word."

Maybe the tiniest bit of relaxation to his posture.

"I am... glad."

I sighed. I was now about to take the *real* leap of faith.

"It would be a good idea to forget all about us. A random mugging – and you didn't see any faces. Got it?"

"You rob the clothes from my back, and then ask me to forget about it? What would I tell my wife?"

"Report being robbed, if you like. Just forget the details. I'll try my best to leave your car in the next town. Wallet too, though I'm going to need to take the cash. It would be better for us if you didn't report anything at all, but I don't expect you to do us any favors. I just ask that you don't give them too many details. Or any, really."

"Why would I help you at all?" The question was asked without any avarice. Genuine curiosity, really.

"Because, John. Those that are after us think for the moment that we are dead. The longer they believe that, the further we can get away. Besides which, if you did tell the whole story to the authorities – or to anyone else..." I swallowed, finding it hard to say the words. Needing to say them anyway.

"If you tell it, you'll very likely receive a visit from some *very* bad people. The sort of people that would ask questions."

I was now skirting the edge of how much I wanted to share.

"How bad could they be?"

I shuddered, stricken with a slow-motion replay of my mother's face coming apart in a messy splatter of bone, blood, and brains. For a moment, I could feel the warm rivulets of her life run down my cheeks again. I resisted the urge to scratch my head. To seek out the bits of grey tissue and bone I had found in my hair later.

"All I dare say is that there are those out there in this world that *are* truly evil. What little you know would be too much for their liking. I want you to go home, John. I want you to apologize for being an idiot to your wife. To see your first-born's first-born. To one day find that everything you've worked for, everything you've lived through, has granted you boundless joys. For the sake of your loved ones, just trust me. They've already taken far too much as it is."

"Huh." John thought carefully over my words. His eyebrows knitted together, his head bowed.

A passing car would be very *inconvenient right now.*

"I get this feeling that if we were to sit down over coffee and compare life stories, I'd find nothing at all to complain about, and go straight home to make love to my wife until the even the stars went to bed." He finally said, sheepishly.

"She's all I have, sir. Sobely. We don't even have our own clothes anymore. If there were any other way, John, I would have taken it."

"Well... I *could* have you come over. We've got closets full of clothes. Shoes. Food. Even got my father's old truck running a week ago. I'd let you take it. Considering you've robbed me at gunpoint, you've been downright decent, too."

I felt a weary sigh escape.

"No, John. It has to be like this. Just this much puts you in far more danger than you could ever know. I don't want you to find that out, either. That's what I'm trying to tell you. Forget us."

"Two, seven, three, five." John recited.

"What's that supposed to mean?"

"It's the pin number for my bank card. I'll report it missing in the morning, but nothing else. I'll tell my wife I went for a drink with the boys and ended up out here."

"That's... very generous. You don't need..."

He shook off my protests.

"It's alright, Tim. I'll get quite the tongue-lashing from the wife, but she'll believe it. I don't handle alcohol very well." He smiled ruefully.

"I wish you luck, then." I tilted my head.

"Well, you'll have my info. If you ever manage to get out of whatever mess you folks are in, maybe look us up? My father used to tell me that you'd find friends in the strangest of places if you just keep your eyes open."

I started at that statement. My own father had told me exactly the same thing, on more than one occasion. I tucked the gun into my waistband, and shook John's hand, before turning back to the car.

"Don't be a stranger, Tim."

17

"Now hear this: We are approaching your final destination. Welcome one and all to beautiful Oakland California. Careful when you step off the bus, folks. It's a hot one out there. Thank you for choosing *Cross-Trek Express* for your travelling needs. God Bless."

God bless indeed.

I gently shook Sobely awake, triggering a fit of coughing from her. The ice pack on her forehead slipped off into my lap and could have easily passed for a hot compress. Not for the first time during the trip, panic threatened to overwhelm me.

A bus would not have been my first choice out of Colorado. While I would have liked to believe that Lot thought us all dead, practicality warned me otherwise. We got lucky, plain and simple. Hopping onto public transit seemed ludicrous. Taking an express route directly towards the home of someone they would undoubtedly be monitoring just pure *lunacy*.

It would have been better for us to hotwire a car. Something non-descript. More than a million of them went reported missing every year. A few crossed wires and we would have been gone. Just another random crime in a world full of them. No doubt we could scrounge up enough spare change to get something to eat. Watch out for friendly and anonymous soup kitchens. Not an ideal lifestyle, surely, but one we could have managed and maintained. Relatively safe, too.

But then Sobely had started to cough. Hard. So hard in fact, she passed out right in the middle of the store we had been securing a few essential supplies from. I quickly scooped her up into my arms and got her outside, lest somebody call for an ambulance. She woke up long enough to throw up the meager deli-provided dinner she had barely touched, and then collapsed back into my arms.

Her face was a lot hotter than it should have been.

I carried her over to a pharmacy and settled her onto the bench generously provided outside. Irene somehow managed to keep up, though in my panicked flight I had forgotten her. She settled onto the bench as well and held Sobely to her chest while I rushed into the store. Cold compresses, Tylenol, a thermometer and cough drops. The desperation was free of charge.

While I tended to Sobely the best I was able, which wasn't nearly as well as I would have liked, my brain happened to send a flag through the concentrated buzz of panic. The bench appeared to be the entirety of a local stopping point for a bus, with discount express services running between Independence, Missouri and – like some impossible joke – Oakland, California.

It did not seem to be entirely outside the realm of possibility that this was part of the game Lot had been playing. In my current state, however, paranoia reigned supreme. Perhaps we were meant to escape. Maybe the whole thing had been planned out – and we were playing a part in some magnificent and malicious comedy.

After all, the odds of coming to *this* particular bus stop, with *that* particular destination was absurd. Surely the universe couldn't work that way. And then reading the rates of our fare, I nearly laughed out loud, instead choking it down to a maniacal titter.

We'd have just enough for three riders.

I had debated the choice up until the bus pulled up. Was this the work of God? Providence made real? While it was true that I hadn't exactly been in *constant* prayer of late, I certainly knew that He was up there. This was certainly just his kind of miracle, too.

Yet it was also just as easily the work of the infinitely evil Lot. The devil, as it were. Further effort to break my willpower and plant us scarcely deep enough to nourish the roots of a lonely willow tree.

Part of me, though, dared to hope. Despite the pure insanity. Despite the risk I could be placing all the other riders in. The destination had dredged up a name from my memory, with a whole host of the unresolved emotional turmoil that inevitably accompanied the name. The Dodge had belonged to his parents. He once had been my best friend. My hero, even. The dependable older-brother figure. Everything had changed since then.

On the very day my father died, he had moved. He wouldn't even be bothered to delay his departure long enough to attend the funeral. The news had been given that very day – though one does not simply move 610 miles away just on a whim.

We hadn't spoken since. When I had needed him the most, he disappeared. Here, years later, when things couldn't get much worse... I was given a path that would put me practically on his door step. Like the whisper of some holy ghost, I recalled the fact that he had left to start his new practice.

In the end though, it really wasn't a decision at all. I carried Sobely aboard the aging bus and cast about for a seat. Near the back, an older black man sat next to an unoccupied seat, the next available seat across the aisle. I set her down, Irene taking the seat across, and went back up front to pay.

On the way back, the older gentlemen was up, carefully moving past Sobely. Doing his best to not jostle her as he passed. He met me in the aisle, and something seemed incredibly familiar about him. He nodded.

"Thank you, sir."

"No problem, son. I've had to move seats for far less important reasons. At least here I'm moving forward, eh?" He chuckled and moved past. Gratefully I took the seat beside Sobely. She began to shiver. I pulled her to me as best as I was able and rocked her gently.

Then the bus began to roll forward, onward, towards my past. Towards the only hope for a future.

Gregory H. Liet. Savior – or enemy? Safety, or certain doom? Lord, if you are watching...

"It's time to wake up, my love." My lips brushed her exposed earlobes as I whispered. This in turn caused a bit of a twitching motion that threatened to dislodge the knit cap. Green eyes opened. Glassy, unfocused, yet still breath-taking. The cat-like pupils were dilated wide, reducing the brilliant green color to a narrow band. They came to focus on my face only with obvious effort. A slow smile parted her dry, cracked lips.

"We are there?" She stammered, and then started coughing. I quickly passed her one of the hard, lemon-flavored lozenges and held her to my chest. Patting her back gently until the coughing subsided.

"Almost. I think we'll need a short walk once we get there. Maybe another short bus ride." I replied. I would have to find his address once we reached the city.

"Do you think we will be in danger?" She asked.

Briefly I imagined that a whole platoon of Trench Coat Men would be waiting at the bus depot. I clenched the grip of the pistol tucked into my waistband, felt a fierce determination harden my resolve. We'd come this far.

"I think we are always in danger."

I raised her chin, kissed her gently. Slowly. Mindless of the heat coming off her face. Of the sickly-sweet taste on her lips.

"I will always be here, though. Right here, right next to you. I will keep you safe, no matter how many they send. Death couldn't stop me."

A startling moment of clarity as my own words fully registered with me.

They would break long before I ever will.

As it turned out, there wasn't another bus to catch to reach Greg's home. According to the phone book and a map, Greg's house sat in a newer neighborhood. No reason to send buses around when all the residents were driving Mercedes. Taking a taxi also wasn't an option. A city bus was a lot more likely to take on a trio of broke passengers than your average yellow cab.

So I slung Sobely onto my back. Irene kept a hand clenched on my shirt, the cheap backpack containing all our worldly goods on *her* back, and we walked. A two-mile hike on a sidewalk that was questionable at best. The temperature floated somewhere just north of 100 degrees. Despite that, Sobely was still noticeably warmer. I could hear the rattle in her lungs with each breath. Every step on the uneven ground carried the threat of causing a fit of coughing.

The only goal worth having was that next step. The motor traffic rumble was distant. Other pedestrians only obstacles to avoid. Dimly I was aware that I hadn't slept since our escape, and even then, I didn't consider that final 'rest' as being very rejuvenating. The last stop the bus had made for food, I had focused on getting soup, cough drops, and instant ice packs. Irene, thankfully, ate like a bird. As for myself, I had forgotten to eat entirely.

I knew that the combination of events over the last week should have dropped me, yet I also knew that I wouldn't stop until our destination reached. I should have been in a coma. *Hell, you've already died once, Tim. What's a little thing like sleep deprivation and minor starvation next to that?*

Those two miles easily stretched into ten in the heat, and I became very aware of muscle fatigue. The burning sensation that filled every fibrous strand, settled even into the bones themselves. The part of me that might have wished for despair seemed to have borne the brunt of the exhaustion, leaving me with nothing but a singular purpose.

One more step.

There was no energy to wonder how Greg was going to react. Only enough to *have* the question, and the response: *Out of your hands anyways.*

We must have stood out. Each passing moment, the odds that a policeman might stop us to ask questions rocketed upwards. That one of these moving obstacles might wish to ask just what it was we were doing, ever more likely. Considering our luck, it could probably be said that at any moment, Lot himself would put a hand out to halt our progress. Yet none of that mattered.

One more step.

Then another.

Eventually we reached fresh sidewalk; the shade of trees. A pleasant area for yuppie homeowners to take pleasant evening strolls. Where the wealthy health nuts might jog along with designer sports-wear and devices strapped to their arms to monitor heart rate, calories burnt, and how their investments were doing. Sprinklers ran in a valiant effort to keep the turf green. A brief consideration, a half-step slowing to a near-pause and let the spray soak us. But no willpower to actually stop. Just enough left for one more step.

One more.

Pay attention to street signs. Turn at that corner.

One more step.

The house numbers grew within the range the home we sought. Impossibly it seemed, the right number appeared on a stylishly pale-yellow house, nothing at all humble about it. More impossible; the same dark blue '73 Buick Electra that had driven off all those years ago sat in the driveway.

I would have sworn that the car smiled. A long-lost friend come to visit – how nice! The chrome gleamed, and the heat shimmer made the whole thing just seem to float a few inches above the concrete.

One more step. Onto the path. Nearing the door. This had been painted a cherry red. I looked down at the blue welcome mat. A familiar pattern across its surface, and the words "The Doctor is in." Part of me knew I should smile at that.

One more step.

The goal reaches for us. The last ebb of willpower fled back the way we came, and I collapsed against the door. Sobely slid to my side, deeply asleep. *When had her breathing become so fast? So shallow?*

Everything swam out of focus. Out of my control. I had pushed through long enough.

It was up to God now.

Still... One more step.

Irene knocked. I had the sensation that it was on the wall, instead of the door, but it didn't matter. The door opened, and it was as if it let the darkness out. Overcome at last, my eyes closed without my conscious consultation. Above me, as I sank backwards, I could make out the shape of the home-owner.

My best friend – or the last enemy I'll ever meet.

I woke up in a proper bed, which was a good sign. It was in a proper bedroom, too. Decorated in white, spacious, and air-conditioned.

Sobely is not here.

I was out of the bed and across the room before the thought fully actualized in my brain. I crashed through the door to find myself in a carpeted hall. Framed medical diagrams decorated the walls. A glass case held an antique stethoscope, reflex hammer, *Grey's Anatomy,* and a reflector. Ahead and to my left was another door. I burst through, only to find a massive bathroom dominated by claw-footed tub.

A hand touched my shoulder, and I spun rapidly. Perhaps a little more forcibly than I ought to have, because I then fell hard against the door jam. Depleted adrenaline reserves non-with-standing, my heart pounded and I was ready to take apart whoever was attached to that hand.

It took me a moment to recognize Greg. Last time I'd seen him, his hair had been a wild mess, a beard obscured much of his face, and he'd worn thick glasses. Before me now, his hair was trimmed short. Face bare. No glass warped his steel-blue eyes. Despite the drastic difference, I knew it was him. I'd recognize that furrowed brow anywhere.

Here you stand, hair going wild. Stubble on your face – heck just call it a short beard. And your vision is cloudy, surely from being so tired, but still...

"Tim! You're awake. I didn't expect you to get up for quite a while yet." He steadies me until I regain my feet, and then gripped me in a bear hug. That part hadn't changed, either.

I squirmed.

"Where is she?!" I demanded.

"Miss Irene thought you'd panic if I separated you two. Sorta standard procedure when somebody is sick, though. I guess she was right." He stood back and looked me over carefully.

I grabbed the lapels of his polo shirt. Though he was taller than my own six-foot-one-inch height, I still managed to lift his feet from the floor. *Would have been harder if he still ran around in those printed tees of his.*

"Where did you take her?!"

I felt like the Beast, long caged, and now set loose. Rage was making up for the lack of adrenaline.

"Easy, Tim! Put me down, and I'll take you to her!" Though he tried to maintain his composure, I could see fear in his eyes.

Good.

I set him back on his feet and followed as he led further on down the hall. Of course the door was at the end of it. The light from the skylights didn't quite illuminate this part of the hallway. I shuddered at the dark.

Greg opened the door and all my fear evaporated. The room was well lit. Carpet, warmly colored walls. Inside it, Sobely lay stretched out in a king-sized bed. Writhing in discomfort, sleeping fitfully. Irene valiantly trying to dab her forehead with a damp cloth. An IV was installed in her arm, as well as a few monitoring devices. Her pulse was setting off an alarm that beeped quietly from a machine in the corner.

"She's hydrating fine, but she keeps having these episodes. I can't explain it." Greg said, glancing worriedly at me.

I went to her side without a word, and took her hand. The writhing quickly subsided.

"Huh." Greg remarked.

"She was having a nightmare." I grunted. Throat suddenly too dry.

Greg brought a chair for me to sit in, which I ignored. Instead I opted to carefully climb into the bed beside Sobely, cradling her gently to my chest. Mindful of all the medical equipment but drawing her close all the same. Her breathing slowed, my heart beat lulling her tortured body into a more restful state.

"How is it..." Greg began.

"Shh!" Irene hissed, finally able to swab Sobely's face. Once complete with her task, she rose up slowly, "If you don't mind, sir, I would appreciate being shown where I might be able to lie down for a bit. I think it best we leave them be for a while." This last sentence was stated with a hint of menace.

Somehow she crossed the room, took Greg by the arm, and led him out. I only had a moment to wonder at her though. My eyelids had shut themselves without my permission again.

18

"I always find these moments to be awkward. We spend so much of our time waiting for a thing. We complain about waiting so much. The irony, then, of stalling for time, especially when the one you need to talk to has also been waiting –"

"What is it? Is she going to be alright?" I interrupted.

"What? Oh, yes. Certainly. Her body is fighting off the infection surprisingly well."

"Infection?"

"Yes. Common thing. The flu. Very mild strain this year."

I glanced at Sobely, who was still gasping for every breath.

"It doesn't look mild."

"Truth! The fact that her body is able to fight it at all is rather incredible."

Slowly, I turned my head, and stared at my friend. A well-trained, well-regarded doctor. Speaking gibberish.

"You lost me, Greg. What on earth are you talking about?"

Greg took a deep breath. And then another.

A dark thought crossed my mind.

"I feel I should warn you. Turning us in would be a bad idea."

He did admit to stalling...

I felt vulnerable without the gun. Well, *more vulnerable* was probably closer to the truth. I had no idea what had become of it after I had passed out. Something told me that asking about it right now might not be a great idea.

To his credit, the look of hurt on Greg's face at my suggestion seemed sincere.

"I wouldn't turn you in, Tim. Even if all that nonsense they reported about you were true. You're my best friend. Kill a dozen people – kill a hundred. It doesn't change that."

Unbidden and unwanted, the anger rose within me. I sat up fully and kicked my legs over the side of the bed. All so I could look directly into his eyes.

"When I needed you the most, you left. Three years, and barely a word from you. How can you claim your friendship *now?*"

"Then you really *don't* know. That explains an awful lot." He said quietly.

"Better clue me in. Buddy. I'm getting really tired of that phrase."

"First, let me finish telling you her prognosis. There is more you should know."

"Fine. But you aren't off the hook."

"Don't I know it." He muttered under his breath. "Well, from what information I was given, the common *cold* should have proven deadly to Ms. Blossom here. Jonathan said it would all work out, but this is still rather remarkable. She ought to be dead, yet she's not. For that matter, with what you've been sweating, you ought to be dead yourself. Just... remarkable."

"Been there. Done that." I tried on a grin. It didn't settle easily, but I carried on gamely. "Death cannot stop true love. It can only delay it for a while." I quoted. A moment of puzzlement on Greg's face, followed by a broad grin. Genuine and brilliant.

"Princess Bride. Nice. There is more truth in that sentiment than you know, my friend. You're the reason *she's* still alive. The reason she will recover."

Too many questions left to ask. I picked one at random.

"Why don't we start with you explaining to me why a simple cold should be something to worry about?"

"Well, she possessed no natural immune system. No anti-bodies in her blood. Essentially, she should not have been able to survive very long outside a completely sterile facility."

I flashed upon a statement the strange woman with the glowing eyes had made. *"Poor thing. She may not have much time here. Treat her well."*

I forged onward.

"If that's true, then what changed? You stated that she *had* no immune system."

"Pretty much true. Every germ would have been a potential hazard."

I thought about Sobely's weakening state when we had first gone on the run. Her collapse at the gas station, the startling way she would shake for no apparent reason. I had believed she was just run down. Under-fed and over-stressed. Not enough restful sleep. I had thought she simply adjusted to it, because she hadn't had a repeat episode.

"Again, what changed? How could I fix her immune system when I didn't even know that it was broken?" *And how is it that you seem to know more about her than I do? Just who the hell are you, anyway?*

Greg hesitated. Almost as if he had heard my thoughts. More likely, he could just read them on my face. I was *trying* to be patient. But he'd always been observant to the point of annoyance, and I was never very good at poker.

"From the tests I ran, I'd say that sometime right about two months ago, you triggered an event that caused her immune system to kick on. Like flipping a switch. The body started producing anti-bodies. Benevolent bacteria. A natural reaction, but not one that she should have been capable of. At least, not according to the file I was given."

"How could I trigger any natural process..."

It clicked. Around two months ago. That was right when she seemed to recover. She started to get stronger. I hadn't noticed the exact time – I had been distracted by her. And by the guilt I felt. Now my head spun. It had all been a chain reaction, caused by stress, hormones, and my complete inability to resist her.

A natural process. More than just the act itself. If I hadn't lost self-control, or if...

"Are you saying that because we... had *sex*, it kicked on her internal defenses?" I knew better – it wasn't that easy. But I had to ask. For clarity.

Greg smiled sheepishly. He rested a hand on my shoulder and met my gaze. He didn't have to say anything else – his body language confirmed what I already suspected.

"I'm saying, my friend, that she is pregnant. The boost of hormones, the beginning of the pre-natal cycle, even the infusion of fresh healthy DNA, all of it started the process of correcting her imbalances. With proper rest and hydration, she'll be fine."

I sat down hard, even though I had already been seated.

Pregnant.

This changes everything.

The thoughts cluttered. They jammed. They bound. Too many questions. So much uncertainty. The future lay grimly before us all. It was clear to me now that Greg had been somehow *involved* in all this. I had no clarification on the matter of his alignment, but at this point the issue was rendered nearly moot.

I had promised Sobely that one day we would know the joy of children. I had also promised that at such time we would be safe. I had whispered the promise into her delicate and lovely ear. I felt reasonably certain that to have a child *now* would not be in the best interest of anyone. I had taken steps, trusting that Fate would not be so cruel as to render those precautions irrelevant.

And then I had gently nibbled on that ear, and we had celebrated the possibilities of *someday.* Yes, we had been careful, though the sheer need for the other's touch had put us in precarious situations at times. I could recall the scrutiny of a drug store clerk, worried that Sobely's unique features would be remembered from some news report, and our *need* would be the end of us.

I remembered how her hand had trembled inside the safety of my own.

To think that it hadn't mattered one bit.

To think that that clock had been running out on us this entire time.

And now? To know that my one moment of utter weakness, of losing myself to my desires... That weakness had saved her life. Even as it threatened to put another life into harm's way. Impossibly mad. Clever lunacy.

You made her a promise. You will keep that promise.

The clutter cleared. The questions ordered themselves. Resolve settled in my stomach. We had wandered with only a solitary purpose. To get away. In that goal, we had failed. We had survived my failure this time. There would not be a second time.

I rose from bed. Found Irene in the hallway, sitting a blind vigil. I sent her to Sobely's side with a touch and looked for Greg. I found him in his garage, door open. Hood up on the Buick. He sat on a tall stool cleaning an engine part.

"Wouldn't do to have a leaking valve cover, would it? Makes such a mess. Burns through oil. Best to correct such things as soon as possible, before they compound into something bigger. Wouldn't you agree?" Greg didn't look up from his work.

"Some things can be mended easily. Others are beyond even the help of Duck Tape." I replied.

At this, he spun on the stool to face me, indicated a second one currently bearing the weight of an old TV. I lowered the heavy set to the floor and sat. Facing Greg. Resisting the urge to stare him down. To glare at him until he spilled all his secrets. *Friend or foe?*

"I'm taking Lot down." I said quietly, meeting his eyes. Greg sighed.

"A person waits years for such a moment, and then when it arrives... I wish I could hold it off just a little longer."

"Time is a luxury I have been doing without." I answered.

Greg pondered that for a moment, wiping at the already shiny valve cover.

"I suppose you have. What would you have me say?" He finally queried.

"Where does all your information come from?" *Best to determine loyalties first.*

"Your father. Mostly. I've haven't much, either. Only what the man thought would be good for me to know."

"My father died three years ago." I said, flatly.

"It'll be four years in November." Greg corrected softly. Mournfully.

"Why didn't..." I could feel my anger rise. Fought to stamp it back down. It wasn't helpful to me.

"The last thing I wanted to do was abandon you, Tim. Never the way it was done. You *have to* believe that. You know who I am. The kind of man I am. You have to know." Greg pleaded.

"Yet, here we are." I responded. Bitterly.

"Precisely."

I looked up from the crack in the concrete I had been inspecting. Anger flared, and then faded. Understanding did much to cool my fury.

"*This* was his plan? To leave me friendless? Was it also his plan for my mother to take a bullet through her skull? To have us running for our lives, without any inkling as to *why?* Here I believed he was a hero."

"He is. Tell me. When you ran, did you know the name of your enemy?"

"No. I only learned it by accident. I was supposed to be dead at the time."

"And I knew that you *would* know your enemy. Rather, your father knew it. He knew you would learn it all on your own. Somehow, he knew what your future would bring. He sacrificed his life to affect the outcome. Maybe he sacrificed Marie's as well. It is entirely possible that none of us will survive this. He believed in something great. A dream. His ultimate goal. The single thing he felt was worth *all this.*" Greg spread his arms for emphasis.

"And what was that? What use is having a goal that you can never achieve?"

Greg seemed taken aback.

"You've come all this way, and you *still* don't see it? Did he really leave you with no clue at all? Yet, here you are. Just as he predicted." I could hear the awe in his voice and was irritated by it.

"We've been *his* pawns this whole time! Just pieces on a board. I'm tired of the manipulation. I'm tired of this ridiculous game. I mean to end it, Greg. So help me, you better not get in my way. Cut the hero-worship bull shit! It seems my father was the type to use his own *family* to further his own agenda. Whatever it had been."

I felt immeasurably tired just then. I wanted nothing more than to go back upstairs. Crawl under the covers. Hold Sobely close to me and await the end.

But that lasted only a moment. My resolve returned.

"You're no pawn, Tim. You *are* the goal! The reason to play the game at all. Don't you get it? He died for one reason."

"Enlighten me." I snapped.

"All of this is for *YOU!* To secure hope for *your future*. He always talked as if your victory was assured. But I saw the doubt that always plagued him. He did it all for you."

"To save me from his enemies? Awfully funny plan for that. Do you know where we spent the week Greg? No? I had the pleasure of watching faceless orderlies torture Sobely. What of her part in all this? Pawn? Motivation? Dangling carrot?"

"He kept his own council. Perhaps she..."

"I don't care for any theories! I love her, Greg. Enough for it to hurt. Her last breath would precede mine only long enough for me to destroy whatever was responsible for taking her away. She'd been kept as organic property. A lab experiment. And none of that matters. *Both* of our lives began just a short time ago. I vowed my love to her, and she gladly gave me her fragile heart in return."

"That kind of decision making *should* be beyond her. The file..."

"Faith, hope, and love. The greatest is love. No other force on the planet compares with that power."

Greg chuckled.

"Now you sound like a country preacher."

"Try death on for size. It's a real eye-opening experience."

"I've seen my fair share, my friend. First hand. I've had folks return from the other side of the veil, condition going from critical and fleeting, to stable. I've seen a perfectly healthy child expire for no reason I could explain. I've seen the hand of God at work – and sometimes he chooses to take." Greg's voice was grim.

"I've seen the green pastures. The grass pushing through pools of blood that springs from everywhere and nowhere. I did not survive all that just to throw in the towel. When we run, it will be towards victory. This will all stop, one way or another." The conviction of my words startling even me.

"What would you sacrifice to achieve that goal?" Greg's voice was quiet. Small. Afraid.

I set my jaw, realized I was unconsciously mimicking my father. Whenever I had seen him adopt that pose, further argument ceased. I hoped for similar results.

"Lot will not take any more from us. But woe to any poor bastards that get in my way."

The clock read 1:00 AM when Sobely began to stir. I took her hand. Both for her reassurance and to prevent her from pulling on the IV. Restless motion, as the drowning fights for sky, then her green eyes fluttered open. They lit upon my face, and her lips formed a quiet smile. They weren't as cracked as they had been.

They were, however, just as magnetic as always. Tenderly I bent towards her from where I sat in the chair and kissed them. I felt her free hand grab my shirt. I stifled my alarm at how weak her grip felt. A tenuous hold upon the life preserver.

"Hi." She whispered. "May I have some water?"

Luckily, I had been prepared. A lidded container of pure H2O sat at the ready, complete with a bendy straw. I held it steady as she slowly sipped. I felt like bursting. The news would certainly bring her joy, and after everything we'd gone through... well, we were both due a little joy.

Patience.

At last she had her fill. I gently dabbed at a stray droplet at the corner of her mouth. Puzzling to me, fresh droplets appeared. Dripping down. I dabbed at them with the Kleenex, but it seemed as if a torrent threatened.

Belatedly I realized that I was crying.

Her free hand reached up, wiping tears from my cheek. I pulled her up into a proper embrace, unable to conjure the words I needed to explain what I was feeling. Greater than joy. Deeper than pain. More profound than relief. Regret. Bliss. Fear... My whole world lay trembling within my arms. Her cheek pressed against mine; her tears mixed with mine. We remained. So much had happened, and we remained.

Finally, I found my voice. Not willing to release her, I whispered. I intended to tell her that we were safe. That she was going to be alright. Reassurances for things she had likely already guessed. But instead of all that, I whispered the first thing on my mind.

"Sobely... we're going to have a baby."

"Oh, Tim!" She sniffled, "That is wonderful news."

For now, it was enough. I crawled into the bed and cradled her again to me as she fell back into peaceful sleep. A soft smile playing upon her rose-colored lips.

"Are you awake?" Sobely asked.

"Perhaps. Or perhaps this is only a dream."

"Hmm." She responded. "If it *is* only a dream, then it is a pretty nice one. However, if I am awake, then I really need to pee."

Irene snorted, not as asleep as she had appeared. She had been dozing in an over-stuffed armchair wearing an over-sized Joan Jett T-shirt. Both the girls had been tended to. Sobely's IV had been disconnected, the trailing lead securely strapped in place by a clean white wrap of gauze.

"Well then, you are awake, and we shall immediately and presently see to relieving your discomfort!" I laughed, jumping out of bed to strike a hero's pose. Sobely tried sitting up, only to fall back into the sheets.

"I seem to be having some trouble getting up." She said, sounding genuinely puzzled.

Sadly, we would not be able to remain here long enough for her to get her strength back. I sighed, covering the sound with a cough.

"Leave it all to me, my heart!" I stated valiantly before scooping her up. I turned to the door as she buried her face in my neck.

"I could get used to this, you know. I love it when you carry me." She whispered. I could feel the heat in my face. Though bandages wrapped the worst of the wounds on her chest and legs, she was otherwise completely naked. The intimacy of her statement threatened to put me on overload.

Life was such a roller-coaster. Stupid hormones.

"I would carry you anywhere you desire, my Queen." I tried to cover my sudden discomfort.

"For now, I think the restroom would be fine. After that... who knows?" She answered. Irene was still laughing as I entered the restroom down the hallway. Once there, I placed her carefully, and then turned my back for her privacy.

After a time, I realized that Sobely was crying. I turned towards her and froze. She was gasping for air. Her body shook. Such sorrow as I'd never seen upon her face.

"Sobely?"

She looked up at me pleadingly, and then doubled over with pain. Her breath rattled, and I could hear her whisper.

"We should not." She shook and toppled forward. I caught her, her skin reddened by a fever renewed.

I cleaned her up and wrapped a large towel around her before lifting her back up into my arms. Her hands dug into me, clutching as one might cling to a sheer cliff. She sobbed, and in that sound, I could hear her terror. I could also hear a wet sound, as if she were trying to breath underwater.

Hurrying back to the room, I first tried to place her on the bed. However, she seemed unwilling or unable to let go. I opted to step up onto the mattress and settled down with my back against the headboard. She curled herself tighter in my lap; like a child. She burned like fire now.

Sickness, it seemed, had not released its hold yet. Irene found her way over to sit down beside us. Rubbing Sobely's back. A phone sat on the nightstand, but it might has well have been the brick it resembled for all the good it would do us.

The only option left to me was just to rock her gently. Whispering how much I loved her over and over again. Telling her that she would all be all right. Desperately hoping that it was the truth.

I could hear the clock ticking loudly. The harbinger of doom.

19

I felt a firm hand grasp my foot and give it a gentle shake, bringing me out of the light doze I had sunk into. My eyes were gummy, but I could still make out the large bag Greg held. An antique flip-top for the doctor that made house calls.

He always was a bit of a geek.

"I was worried about this." He said by way of greeting. The reality of the situation came crashing upon my consciousness, chasing the last of the sleepiness away. At the moment, she actually seemed to be doing better. The fever had nearly gone.

"Worried about what?" Irene asked, still propped up against my other side where she had fallen asleep.

"Missing out on all the fun. I leave for just a little while and come home to find all three of you in bed together."

Before I could summon an adequate response to his jest — something along the lines of *'Where the hell have you been?'* — Irene beat me to the punch.

"Doctors are nice and all, but I prefer my men to be within tripping distance."

If I hadn't been close to tears with worry, I would have laughed. Especially at her perfect deadpan delivery.

"She got sick again earlier, though it seems to have calmed down somewhat. Couldn't you have called in to work? I didn't know what to do..." I felt the words start to catch in my throat, a mad tumble to escape my lips all at once. I choked.

"Easy, Tim. I needed to stock up on a few items. She needs more fluids, anti-biotics... she's definitely on the mend, but she isn't completely out of the woods yet. She will need to take it easy for a few more days at the very least."

Irene was tracing a finger along Sobely's right ear. Briefly I wondered what she made of their strange length.

"Even so, Greg. You could have at least left me with the gun. A number where I could reach you. They could bust down your door at any moment." I wanted to be irritated, but I felt grateful that he had bothered to return at all. Relieved that I hadn't woken up to a couple dozen SWAT officers pointing automatic weapons at us.

"That... well, okay. I see your point. It didn't even occur to me."

That helped bring forth some genuine irritation.

"This isn't a video game, Greg. There isn't a reset button if we mess up. Instead there is only blind luck and desperate prayer that those foul-ups don't cost us our lives. She collapsed, and for once I had no clue what to do about it. You've got to think!"

Greg looked embarrassed.

"I'm supposed to be your lifeline, yet... I just keep messing it up. After all this time, you need me and I'm just putting you in more danger. I'm sorry, Tim. This is beyond anything I could ever imagine. Do you honestly believe these bad guys will come breaking down my door? I did set the alarm... I suppose that wouldn't really be a whole lot of help though..."

I felt a brief flash of genuine rage. The weight of the sleeping woman in my arms kept me in place long enough to get it under control. Intellectually, I knew it wasn't exactly Greg's fault. *I was this naive, once.* However, I had spent so much time running from something I could not fight, the anger that had built up was unbelievable.

Yes. Now you can rage properly. And you love all the more deeply for it.

I hadn't even given a second thought to the men I'd had to kill along the way.

Though their faces returned to me now.

"We cannot rely on luck. Or assumptions that just because it hasn't happened *yet,* means it won't happen. Every decision, hell every *step* we take, can be the difference between surviving, and the alternative. For the past few months…" My voice was ice, even as words failed me.

Greg did not respond right away. Instead, he silently moved to the side of the bed and set his bag on a clear spot on the mattress. He withdrew pouches of liquid medicine, then meticulously cleaned his hands with an alcohol-based sanitizer. Carefully he unwrapped the bandage on Sobely's arm to reveal the still-present intravenous needle. He locked together the coupler to connect the medicine to her IV, attached the pouches to a hook mounted to the wall, and stepped back.

"I'm just a doctor, Tim. I owe your father my life. I consider you to be the best friend anyone could ever have. I was given very little information, though. A file containing a bare minimum of knowledge to retain and pass on. Assurances that everything would work out. Faith that I would do right by you. I don't know what I should be doing."

I softened.

"He always played it close to the vest. Not your fault. You've been given more answers than I have, though. And…" I grinned broadly. "You're supposed to be the responsible one."

Greg grinned in return.

"Older? Sure. Respectable? You better believe it. As I recall though, you were always the responsible one. If it weren't for you… Well, there was the ravine…"

"Yeah. And Glenda…"

Greg laughed.

"True. If not for your positive influence, I might be a collection of scattered bones in the bottom of the dark gulch or married to some Gypsy woman nearly twice my age. I suppose I owe *you* my life even more than I owed it to your old man."

I found myself smiling at the remembrance of some of our misadventures. Were it to be that our reunion could not have been under a far more ideal set of circumstance. *Stories to fascinate, and a pair ladies fair to entertain.*

I disentangled myself, letting Irene take over cradling Sobely's feverish brow in her lap. Briefly I wondered about her own immune system. I still knew nothing about the woman. But that die had been cast, and for now I just had to go on faith. I gripped Greg's shoulder, and steered him out of the room.

"I meant what I said... I guess it was yesterday now. I'm done with this puppet show." I said emphatically.

"I believe you. We never really finished our conversation earlier. There is... something else. Something I haven't had a chance to discuss yet. Something that may be a help." Greg sounded slightly dodgy. His eyes shifted to look away from my face, to stare upwards. If I hadn't been guiding him already, he would have crashed right into the small table in the middle of the hallway.

"If you told me you have Lot's GPS coordinates and the keys to a missile silo, I think I would probably kiss you." I tried to edge through his hesitance with a joke, lame as it was.

"Well... I do have the keys to... something. Rather, they were left in my care. For you. Something your father left for you. Though I don't think it's a missile silo. Unless I am mistaken, I believe they're car keys."

I blinked.

"What good is a car? My father personally *knew* Lot. I think he intended me to take him down. I'd expect him to leave a bunker full of heavy ordinance."

"Maybe... he wants you to run? Maybe that was always his plan for you." Greg almost sounded hopeful.

"You don't know Lot."

Technically, you don't know Lot either. Other than as the evil maniac that doesn't just want to kill you both. He wants you broken and bleeding. And nobody has bothered to tell you why.

"I was told 'danger.' I was not given to specifics beyond that. No instructions to relay. Just a slim file, the keys, and an address. I checked the address – it's a building out in a nowhere town. Last registry to the place billed it as an auto body shop."

I shut my eyes, desperately trying to think. It was like trying to put together a 1000-piece puzzle blindfolded, with half of the pieces missing. I had the funny notion that Irene could accomplish that without much difficulty, before the issue at hand pressed.

"So… the plan was to run. Find you, and run? That's…" I struggled for the right words. Absurd. Doomed. Ridiculous. Stupid. Pointless. Something that meant all of that combined.

"Again, I wasn't told how I should advise you." Greg looked worried. I had a feeling that the anger I felt was showing again.

What the hell was your endgame, Dad? Did you want us to be safe, or to only delay the inevitable? Did you expect to still be around, or to guide me from beyond the grave? It's just me, trying to put your pieces together. Did you imagine that I might fall in love with her? Did you plan for there to be a child? What is the goal of all this? My frustration was impossible to contain, so I took the natural course of action and punched the wall.

Through it, actually.

"Forget all this! This isn't one of Dad's favorite spy novels. Not one of those old samurai films he used to watch. This is the real world. The pieces don't just fit together precisely on time, like dominoes. This is my life. Her life. I will not let this continue. I won't risk her like that." I felt hot tears on my cheeks. My hand stung, but I didn't care. I wanted to put another hole in the wall. The pent-up rage bubbled upward.

There had always been that next step to take. The idea that I had to keep moving no matter what. Keep ahead of my enemies. It hadn't been enough. Forced to stop, all I had left to keep me occupied was my anger. I felt a hand on my shoulder, and for all the wonder in the world I didn't take a blind swing. I didn't flinch away from the gesture.

I kept seeing Sobely on that sterile floor. Writhing in agony. Chained down so as to be helpless. Unable to look away. Nothing would have prevented me from shutting my eyes. Yet I hadn't. I couldn't. As she twisted, I had kept my gaze fixed upon hers. I screamed her name.

I could not let that happen again.

My fist came back to assault the drywall again but halted in mid-swing. I took a deep breath instead.

"Greg. Forgive me. None of this is your fault. It isn't my fault. We're just the pawns set between a couple of bitter enemies.

Though I'm not even sure I believe that much anymore." At this admission, I felt unbelievably tired. Soul-weary.

"What do you mean?" Greg asked quietly.

"Lot had already possessed her. She was delivered to me by this strange old woman. She said it was my father's wish for me to be her guardian. Yet... she was so empty inside. Sobely had been erased like a bad floppy disk. She didn't even know her own name."

"Yes. The file mentioned that she would not possess any knowledge that was hers. It was an odd statement. I thought it a strange thing to predict." Greg was pensive.

"Maybe it's time I took a look at this file." I suggested.

"If I still had it, I would have already given it to you."

I closed my eyes. Another deep breath.

"Who has it?"

"I followed his orders to the letter. After I studied it thoroughly, I burned it. I was told that possessing the file put me at enormous risk. I did my best to absorb its contents. Little enough there was, that was still over three years ago."

I felt my hands clench again and forced them to relax.

One more deep breath.

Then another.

A third, just to be certain.

"I am going back to Sobely. If you would please bring me my gun, I would greatly appreciate it. Then I'm going to need for you to go out. Gather some things we'll be needing. Clothes, for all of us. A cooler, food. Sleeping bags. We'll be leaving here tomorrow."

My voice sounded remarkably calm.

"A few more days of bed rest..."

"Can be had in the back seat of that Buick of yours. Maybe Dad left me another bread crumb with this car he felt I should have. After three years, the thing probably won't even start. In any case, it is a place to start. It gets us moving, for good or ill."

"I'll have to go to a regular store. They won't have that stuff at the corner mart."

"Which is one reason why I'll need the gun first thing. You should see about grabbing a box or three of extra rounds for the thing while you're at it."

Normally, I wasn't the type of person to order someone about. Yet I had sufficient proof to the fact that Greg hadn't changed a bit in all this time. He was the sort to take ten minutes just to choose a flavor of ice cream, with just two choices before him. And then order the same flavor every time. I was used to making the decisions for him. Even if I weren't, I couldn't afford to wait for his over-analysis. I imagined that trait was something that made him a good doctor.

Right now, however, he needed to learn how to be a good *survivor*.

"Well, if you think that's wise…"

"I think driving around the country with two naked women would likely attract some unwanted attention. Which reminds me – find another hat for Sobely. The one we got is too small."

"I'd been meaning to ask…"

"And you'd be wasting your time. I haven't got a clue. It isn't important in any case. Our options are limited. Therefore, we should make only the most logical decisions. Get a little breathing room. Hope for a solution to present itself, but plan for the much more likely scenario of being out there, twisting in the wind, without a clue."

"I understand. It's just… is she even human? Apart from the elf-ears… her blood was far from normal. Even accounting for the near-absent immune factors. I'd never seen anything like it, actually."

"It doesn't matter."

"It might. That she is pregnant was just about the only thing I could learn. If I had the time to sequence her DNA…"

"Then pray we live through all this. It doesn't matter *right now*. It has no effect on our present situation, other than the fact that she is sick, and is likely to get sick again. Another good reason to put a hard caliber right through the skull of the demented bastard…" I choked off my sentence, feeling some of the rage trying to surface again.

I intended to finish this fight. Do or die. I'd already had the pleasure of dying once.

Now it would be Lot's turn.

"It just makes me wonder, is all. If Lot had possession of her, why would he let her go? Just what exactly is she?"

"Someone he expected to die. Someone he believes *has* died. An empty vessel, built. Engineered. Tortured. The scars... you've seen them. Her entire life has been spent in pain. I doubt he realized that she possesses a soul. I doubt he possesses one himself.

More than all that, she is the keeper of my heart. No matter what she may look like, no matter what your science kit might tell you, she is still just that. The keeper of my heart. Lord willing, she'll be the mother of my child. Everything else is just trivial."

"What is wrong, my son? Why do you cry?" Dad asked. Even his easy-going smile was no comfort to me. People said we were a lot alike, but I couldn't see it. He was the jutting stone in the water, weathering both storms and time with the grace of a king.

I'm such a loser!

"Nothing!" I cursed. Facing a man who seemed capable of bearing the weight of the world, and still juggle a few planets besides, I found it difficult to admit my own failings.

"Come now. Don't be like that. I have told you more than once that you can come to me with anything that troubles you. Do you doubt me?" His voice was the same, only more gentle. His tone of voice the sort that might stop for a chat about the weather or talk a man away from the edge of a cliff.

"It's... not important. I'll be okay." I tried to smile, if only for his sake. If only to hide the wretchedness that I felt.

"Of that, I have no doubt. To tell you the truth, I could do with a few more conversations about things that are not important. What troubles you? Maybe a friendly ear would be an aid to you?"

I had the distinct feeling that he wouldn't let me squirm my way free of his questioning. I took a deep breath to steady my voice. I tried to sound purely conversational. Factual.

"Well... girls don't like me." Because I was a loser.

"Hmm. That is serious. You are telling me that every single female on this planet has decided to not like you? I can think of at least one girl that might disagree with that assessment." His eyes twinkled.

"Well... Mom is Mom." I answered.

"Agreed. However, I think perhaps you are just being evasive. You are a good man, Tim. If some girl chooses to not notice that fact, well then they are hardly anyone to worry over."

"But she isn't just 'some girl!' She's Reilly Tannen. She's more like a Goddess." I wiped a hand across my eyes. Hoping to regain some of my dignity. Dad had easily managed to get me to say what I'd been trying to avoid saying. It was a little terrifying

"Ms. Tannen? I'll admit that she is a pretty one. However, it appears to me that she is about as intelligent as a fence post."

I felt shock. Dad was wrong. That wasn't something that ever happened.

"No she isn't" I protested. Defending her, despite my misery. "She has a 4.1 GPA. Everyone admires her, and she is kind to everyone. Everyone... but me. I'm some kind of freak."

"I stand by my assessment. She might have folks fooled, but I sincerely doubt that she is that lovely on the inside. A girl that obviously works so hard to impress everyone around her is about as genuine as a three-dollar bill. A mask to cover the ugliness they know is inside."

"You don't know her, Dad. She's perfect. If she hates me, then I really am a loser. She's nice to everyone! Someone like that... to be the only person she dislikes..."

Dad chuckled. It wasn't mockery.

"Would you keep a secret for me, son?"

I nodded, still feeling glum.

"Your mother was the very first girl I had ever kissed. Imagine that. I'm nearly fifteen years older than her. Can you imagine what that's like?"

I shook my head.

"I was downright lonesome, 'tis what I was. I believed I was cursed. Doomed to a life where I would never know that kind of love. I travelled everywhere, you know. Just me and old Dusty. My best friend in this whole world. Yet I still felt alone, all the same."

I had seen a few pictures and could recall the smiling face of an older dark-skinned man.

"Everything changed though, when I met Marie. Our meeting wasn't just random happenstance, and I knew instantly that she was the one I had been travelling for. Do you know what the best part is?"

"What?" I was genuinely interested. Momentarily distracted. Dad did not often bring up the past.

"She knew it too. She didn't reject me. She didn't make me play silly games to win her affection. I honestly think that is how it is supposed to work, too. When you meet that one, true person. That other half of your heart – nothing gets in the way. I think it is our job to just be patient."

"You don't think Reilly is the one?"

"Son, I know for a fact that she isn't. Perhaps she rejects you because she can sense, deep down, that you would eventually see through her façade to the ugliness inside."

"Do you think... there is... someone?"

"I don't just think it, Timothy. Out there is a special girl, waiting to meet you, too. Even if she doesn't know it yet. Who knows; maybe she's hung up on Reilly, too."

Though his words were teasing, I could detect a note of sadness in his voice and wondered at it.

After a few moments of silence, I asked,

"What do I do when I meet her?"

"You grab onto her tightly, son. And don't you ever let her go."

20

crASH!!!!

The window imploded, the sound of breaking glass a catalyst that threw me into sudden, frantic motion. Before the shower of silvery shards had finished raining down on the carpet, I had rolled to the floor with Sobely in my arms. Another half-second and we were beneath the bed, handgun raised and aimed towards the door.

Sobely whimpered, and I spared her a glance. In the rush to reach safety, I had yanked the IV violently from her arm. Blood streamed from the wound at an alarming rate, staining the cream-colored carpet. I tore a strip off the flat sheet using my teeth, tying it around the wound quickly, tightly.

Just as the door crashed in. A large man in black body armor blocked the entrance, momentarily confounded by the seemingly empty room. I did not give him the time to recover. Both hands on the grip now, barrel raised. Three muffled reports, and the man dropped. One of the hasty shots hit him through the right eye.

"Wait here!" I hissed at Sobely, wrapping a second strip of torn cloth around her arm. The first had become completely soaked in crimson.

I scrambled from cover to the doorjamb, stooping to recover the small automatic the soldier had carried – just as a burst filled the air where my head had been. I turned the awkward maneuver into a roll and came up with my finger already pulling the trigger.

Which failed to produce any lead. *Safety's on!*

I dropped the auto and crab-walked back to where I had dropped the handgun. A line of splintered holes followed my movement but failed to connect. The pistol felt slow getting it lined up for a shot.

Two squeezes of the trigger dropped the second gunman, but not until I felt the hot stab of burning lead pierce my left thigh. The pain was both immediate and intense, but I did not have the luxury to spare the wound a glance. Like Sobely's arm, it would have to wait. Cautiously, I recovered the automatic from the floor. This time checking the safety, and flipping it to red.

The door to my right swung open. I flattened myself against the wall, readied the gun, and then relaxed partly when Irene stuck her head through. Her hair was a snarled tangle, her eyes as empty as ever, though a little less bloodshot.

"Stay low." I ordered. She crouched, her head swinging to stare just past my shoulder.

"What's going on, Timothy?" She asked. I collected a spare clip off the corpse at my feet, and then started past Irene. Positioning to the side of the stairwell.

Bloody footprints trailed behind me.

"No time. Get to Sobely." I stage-whispered. Listening intently, I thought I could hear the softened tread of heavy combat boots on plush carpet.

Irene shuffled out, steadying herself with a hand on the wall. Keeping low and heading straight towards an unpleasant obstacle.

"Mindful of the body." I warned, peeking carefully down the stairs.

Greg has been sleeping downstairs on his couch.

I took them two at a time, left leg threatening collapse with every pounding step. *Hurry, hurry! Please don't be too late!*

I rounded the corner at the bottom and came face-to-face with the third gunman. His weapon was pointed downward. Mine wasn't. I squeezed the trigger, satisfied that this time the gun kicked and spit like an uncooperative camel. Considering that the assailant was within punching distance, it would have been embarrassing to miss.

The impact of the jacketed shells took the thug off his feet, splotches of red streaming down the wall. Creating a near-perfect silhouette of the man now crumpled on the floor. *Feels good, don't it? Not so helpless now, are we? Burn them all down!*

The Beast agreed.

The door from the garage thundered open, and only my reflexes kept me from emptying the rest of the clip into my best friend. Greg, for his part, stood perfectly framed in the doorway, clutching an old Weatherby shotgun that I remembered well.

"Tim?" The shotgun was already pointed downward. The double-barreled gun had only ever proven to be proficient at destroying coffee cans. Neither of us had the heart to point it at anything living. *How times change.*

"Greg!"

"What's going on? I heard..." His sentence cut off as he noticed the black-garbed body ruining his carpet.

"So they *were* gunshots." He said quietly. Disbelieving. Hands gripping the shotgun just a little tighter.

"Get upstairs to the girls – and please tell me the car is ready to go." I swept the gun around to the living area. I couldn't hear any more boots moving around, but that didn't mean they weren't still there.

"Running like a top." He answered, monotone. Standing still. Transfixed by the dead man.

"Good. Now get moving. There might be more of them. We have to get going, now!" I barked this last, snapping his attention around. He started forward, then stopped again. Staring at my leg.

"You're hurt!" He exclaimed. Judging from the over-exertion of emotion, he was either going into shock, or I was.

"I'll live." I straightened. "It's only a flesh wound. Now MOVE!" I growled. That seemed to do the trick, as he finally began to ascend the stairs. I propped myself against the wall at the bottom, trying to stare at everything all at once. Fighting the urge to run up and get Sobely myself.

This was a new dynamic, and not one that I was sure that I liked. To have others to worry about. To trust. It had been just Sobely and myself for so long now, it was hard to grasp the concept of there being *more* than just us. Too many possibilities spun in my mind. Too great the risk that I'd wind up killing us all.

What choice did you have?

None. Of course. I had been moving forward this entire time *because* there had never been a choice. Nearly every decision I had made came down to that one constant. What choice did I have? The little choices – what to eat. Which turn to take. All of it had led me here. Exactly where my father knew I'd end up.

After what seemed an eternity, I heard Greg's footsteps approach. He carried Sobely, Irene hanging onto his shirt. Her free hand carrying the leather case. I felt so relieved I nearly collapsed. Already, the adrenaline was wearing off.

Carefully they started down the steps. I stepped out into the room, sweeping it once again. Watching for moving shadows. Still quiet. I stepped to the door into the garage. Nothing more threatening than an old crowbar hanging from a rusty nail. The garage door stood wide open, which I found curious.

"Get to the car. I'll cover you." I whispered over my shoulder as they reached the bottom of the stairs. Not bothering to wait for a response, I descended the pair of steps into the garage. Yelping in pain when my left leg twisted on the cold concrete. I dragged it behind me as I stumbled over to lean against the rear quarter-panel of the big car.

The yard was empty. No black vans blocked our exit. No helicopters hovered to disgorge further opponents. The sky was blue. The neighbor's sprinkler had started its scheduled routine. *After all that, and they only sent three men? What is going on here?*

Greg got Sobely into the back seat, and then took Irene's hand to help her in as well. To her blessed credit, she immediately pulled Sobely close to her. Shielding her. Those grey eyes full of tears. Sobely simply looked exhausted.

"Maybe I ought to take a look at that." Greg was beside me. Looking pointedly at my seeping leg.

"Not here. Not now. Start the car." I hissed, mostly from the pain that was now becoming hard to ignore. Also partly because I thought I had seen movement. A shadow. A tree limb caught by the wind...

"Fine, fine. I'll just…" He patted his pockets. "Shit! Keys are still inside!" He turned and ran back through the door before I could respond. Or give him the extra gun. He had left the Weatherby upstairs.

A radio squawked, and I jumped. If not for the steel machine at my side, I would have fallen from the intensified pain from my startled movement. I squelched my shout and moved to where I could listen.

"Bravo! Report! What's the hold up?"

Three men, sure. But with back-up of some sort and probably close by. *What the hell is taking Greg so long?*

For a moment, I felt like I was flying. Floating, warm and free. When I opened my eyes, I could see a play of lights moving across a cream-colored sky, and the face of an angel. It was beautiful. My head rested on a warm cloud. I felt safe.

The sensations then coalesced. My heart switched over from a slow beat to a manic pace worthy of a death metal drummer. I tried to sit up, but the increase of blood pressure in an already throbbing skull sent me crashing right back into the warm pillow that had been supporting me.

Of course, that 'pillow,' wonderful, soft, and cloud-like was really a pair of legs barely wrapped in linen. The green-eyed gaze of the angel was still the same, though.

"Hi." I tried to say. It sounded more like a groan.

"I have you." Sobely replied. The moving lights floated across her face, illuminating her impossibly glorious smile. Her eyes seemed to cast a glow of their own.

A memory flashed. Those same eyes lit by moonlight. Those lips parted in a sigh…

The memory made me smile.

"Are you in pain?"

The smile must have resembled a grimace.

I thought about her question very thoroughly. On the one hand, I liked where my head was at. On the other… my leg really didn't feel very good at all. Actually, if I were to be perfectly honest with myself, it was on fire. Not the pleasantly warm heat of a campfire, either. No, this was more the fire that sets in when the plastic breaks down and the grease catches.

"Been better." I admitted. She wobbled slightly, bringing back to mind the fact that she was still recovering from being sick. I reached up and found her arm. My grip rested on the bandage, and she winced.

Immediately I let my hand drop again.

"Sorry." I whispered. A few tears leaked from the corners of her eyes.

"It is okay. I am okay." She rocked slightly for a bit, and then regained her smile.

It most certainly was *not* okay.

Ignoring the increased blood pressure, I managed at last to sit up, scooting myself backwards with Sobely's unsteady hands resting on my back. Gingerly, I flexed the knee. A sharp pain as the skin stretched, but overall function seemed to be intact. Satisfied, I maneuvered myself into a proper seated position and then pulled her close to me.

After a few moments, the pain became useful. The sharpness of it served to burn the cobwebs from my brain.

"What happened?" I asked, quietly.

"You fell. Greg said you might have a... um..."

"A concussion. The way your head cracked... I thought it was another gunshot." This response from Irene.

"Normally, of course, I wouldn't have moved you without proper equipment. Like a pair of EMTs." Greg said, glancing in the mirror. Not being in control of the vehicle was a bit unsettling. The way everything seemed to swim in and out of focus wasn't a very comforting experience, either.

"I heard one of their radios talk. You did the right thing."

"I figured as much. We will need to stop soon, though. I need to take a look at that leg."

I shut my eyes, head tilting back. The plan had certainly gone adrift. One more night in a proper bed had seemed a reasonable thing. Briefly I wondered what had caused the window to shatter as it did. The ache in my skull made the mystery incomprehensible. Yet, I still felt a determination to put an end to it all. To finish Lot – or have him finish me. And I knew exactly how much pain I could endure in order to keep Sobely safe.

"How far away is this car my father wanted me to have?"

"Well... not too far off. If I take the next exit."

"Then take it."

"How do you know that they won't be waiting for us?"

"I don't"

"Then why risk another confrontation? We aren't exactly fighting fit here." Greg's hesitance was understandable, yet still surprising.

"Nearly four years waiting... Do you think we should wait four more?"

Greg gave me a sharp look in the mirror. Which immediately softened.

"I'm trained to save lives. Not take them. I didn't think... somehow, I thought I would be sidelined in all this. Like I'd hand over the keys, and off you'd go."

I sighed, steadying myself.

"One day I woke up to a pounding on my door. I panicked. I had no idea what I was going to do." I began.

"Tim..."

"I stepped outside my room. How would I ever explain how a girl got into my bed? How would I explain the delicate-yet-exquisite ears to her? How would I explain those perfect green eyes, with their cat-like pupils?"

"Tim..."

"How would I explain what she was doing in my bed, almost completely naked? Who would believe that she needed me to conquer her nightmares? Mom thought I was coming down with a fever. She was going to call in for a day off so she could take care of me. How was I ever going to get out of that?"

"I'm sorry, Tim." Greg said in a whisper.

"I opened my mouth to say... damn. I don't even remember. I don't remember what would have been my last words to her. I do remember that particular glint of oiled steel in the sunlight, though.

The barking sound of the gun. I remember the taste. One moment my mother stood there looking stern and worried and beautiful. The next blink, and she didn't even have a face. Whatever I was going to say was choked out by the taste of her blood. Stringy bits of hair-wrapped bone. Grey flesh flying everywhere."

"I'm sorry..."

"We have been running all this time. All summer long. I've... those weren't the first people I've had to kill. This whole time, I've avoided coming to you for help. Why? Because I can still remember that taste. Of blood and bone. Brain matter and scorched hair. The smell of it. I could not stand the thought of putting you at risk. I didn't want to be responsible for you having your head blown off in a torrent of bullets."

Tears streamed down my face. Sobely quietly shook as she cried. I could hear a raspy gasping sound coming from Irene. The memory of the last few months flashed through my mind at a blistering pace, and I wanted very much to curl up until it all went away. For a brief second, anyway.

"I don't know what to say."

"This whole time, I kept thinking 'If I go to Greg, he will help us. And he will die.' Do you know what? If you don't help me, you still die. And that is my fault. Except... I've had no choice. Seems as if I've never had a choice. Barely more than a chance."

Greg was silent. The blinker clicked to life loudly. I prayed silently this new road would lead to a way out of this madness.

"Does that hurt?" I asked, gently stroking her bandaged arm.

"A little." She answers.

"I'm really sorry."

She smiles. Backlit by the rays of the sun, shining through the crystal-clear pane of glass. Some otherworldly being to grace a lump of clay with her beneficent grin.

"We are alive."

I put my arm around her shoulders and pulled her to me. It felt odd to have her on my left. Strange to be travelling down the blacktop with somebody else at the wheel. I wasn't sure I liked it much.

We were entering a dusty little town. An outpost along the highway that was nearly identical to the countless others I'd seen over the last few months. Names of such places were forgotten almost before the traveler has left, if the township has bothered to put up a sign at all. A last place to stop before entering the long desert.

A wind-beaten sign declared this small burg to be 'Flatland's Pass.'

The businesses seemed to cater to the biker crowd. Dilapidated repair barns, a small truck stop with a lot full of motorcycles. There was an army surplus store with a variety of leather goods on display in the window. The gas station – last gas for 175 miles! – had a collection of Free Air! stations and was framed by a motel that was reasonably presentable.

Greg pulled up to one of the many free-standing garages. No signs. No lights. A quick glance over the other structures showed this to not be out of the ordinary for Flatland's Pass. A heavy padlock secured the door. The service-entrance was an older single-panel style garage door, also padlocked.

"This is the place." He announced.

Though the garage looked abandoned, it was obvious that it was also cared for. None of the windows were broken. The pavement was cracked, but relatively weed-free. The locks both glinted lightly of oil.

"What kind of car is inside?" I asked. Considering the setting, it was entirely possible we'd find nothing more than a pile of rusted parts inside. If we found anything at all. Besides that, the mode of transportation itself might indicate what my father expected me to do.

"No clue." Greg answered.

"You had the location, and the keys. Didn't you think to maybe find out what is out here? To check to see if there is anything here at all?"

"I was strictly instructed not to. I was informed that everything would be ready for you when the time came."

If there was one thing I could count on from Greg, it was that he would always follow directions. Procedures. He never cut corners to save time. Never let his curiosity control his pace. I sighed.

"Let's get this door open. There's enough room in this place for six cars. Best to get inside as soon as we can."

"I don't have anything to numb the operation site with, though I do have a couple flasks of bourbon." Greg was rummaging in his bag. I was lying down on a low steel table that looked strong enough to park a semi-truck on. Judging from the scuff marks, that might have actually been its purpose. Still, it was remarkably clean and had been covered thoughtfully by a canvas tarp.

As was my father's mystery car. That tarp had been tied to various bits of heavy debris, and stretched, presumably to obscure the shape of what was beneath. With the grime coating the windows, the curious peepers might not have even been able to see the shape at all. We had opted to leave that tarp alone until my leg had been taken care of.

Well, Greg opted. I was too light-headed from blood loss to argue with him.

Instead I wondered at who the caretaker of the garage was. More of the green canvas covered chairs. Despite the layer of grime on the windows, the place was remarkably free of dust. The chairs had proven to be in good shape, giving Sobely and Irene a safe place to watch Greg work. Or listen to him work, as the case may be. I glanced over at the pair. Sobely was tilted forward in her seat, hand linked with Irene's. I smiled for her.

Wait...

"Bourbon?" I queried. Greg hadn't been one to drink.

"Yeah. It was less conspicuous then grabbing the heavy-duty painkillers from the hospital."

I blinked.

"That's actually really good thinking."

"I told you I had studied field medicine. I find the history of it to be quite fascinating. It's amazing how much of it is derived from techniques that are centuries old."

"If it was good enough for the cowboys and indians, I suppose it's good enough for me."

I rolled my shoulders, mentally preparing for what was to come.

"This isn't the first GSW I've treated, you know." Greg proceeded to lay his tools out with precision. Each one he pulled from a brown glass container, drying it with a cotton towel that had been sealed in plastic.

"I imagine not." I replied. I kept my breathing calm. If nothing else, I hoped to influence his state of mind. His movements were glacier-slow, which wasn't doing much to quell the anxiety building within me.

"Normally there are nurses. Anesthetics. Anti-biotics. The beep of monitors…" He paused. "When I threw together this kit, well. I'm fully prepared for most kinds of 'field surgery.' I didn't really believe I'd actually need to perform it." He tittered nervously.

"You mentioned that you studied it."

"Oh yes. Adamantly. Even continued to read about it after I finished with school. I have the knowledge, it's just…"

"What?"

"Normally, you would be under right now. We don't have the patient awake for something like this. I'm not sure what to do, other than offer the bourbon."

"We don't have the time for me to get drunk enough to black out. Think about it. Any less than that, and you'll have trouble getting me to hold still."

"You're a mobile drunk, then?" He paused in what he was doing, inquisitive.

"I wouldn't know. I don't drink. I'm not going to start today, either. Can't we get on with this?" The delay was giving me time to think. Time to contemplate the purpose of each of the tools he placed on the steel tray.

"I didn't plan on digging a bullet out of you."

"I didn't plan on getting shot. Yet, here we are." *Steady. Calm.*

"Yes." The tray of tools was ready. Gauze and a number of other things were spread out on my chest, lying atop clean linen. The jeans were hanging off the Buick's door. Modesty wasn't exactly my first concern, yet I still felt some relief that Irene couldn't see me at the moment.

"This will hurt." He whispered.

"I hear gangrene isn't very pleasant, either." I did my best to relax.

"Point taken."

With a deep breath, he lifted a scalpel from the tray. Then I felt a gentle hand take mine. I looked up at Sobely and smiled. She dazzled me back.

I felt the presence of the scalpel, felt my cheeks tighten, my eyes water. But they never left hers. The warmth of fresh blood was only a minor distraction. A strength flowed where our fingers were intertwined. A physical component of the unbreakable bond between us.

Clink! The sound echoed in the silence.

"Hold here, while I get the irrigation bottle." Greg commanded. I placed my free hand over a wad of gauze, felt the dampness grow as it soaked up blood. Greg jogged to this trunk, coming back with a sports bottle.

"This will sting. It's got grain alcohol in it. The clerk at the liquor store told me that drinking it would be very bad for my health." He moved my hand.

"If the clerk at the liquor store said it's bad for you... what did you tell him?" I felt that was an important point. Or maybe not.

"I told him 'I'm a doctor. I'll decide what's good for my health!' and purchased some bourbon to chase it down with."

A coolness mingled with the red heat where the bullet had lodged. The sharp-smelling fluid washed away the blood handily. Then I felt it hit raw nerves, open flesh. It didn't sting at all. I stifled a cry. Greg kept squirting the boiling magma into the wound. Sweat broke upon my brow, and I reconsidered the bourbon.

I hadn't seen her move. I had let go of her hand, lest I crush it. She dabbed at my forehead. Butterfly touches against a molten inferno.

"Extricating the foreign object now. It looks to be intact."

A scrape of a utensil being lifted from the steel tray. The pressure. A tow truck had attached itself to my bone and was gently trying to pull out my femur. The dull ache where the lead had buried itself became a sharp reminder that I nursed more than a bruised muscle.

Sobely's lips were at my ear, whispering comfort. Her hair tickled my cheek, becoming damp with the tears that were leaking without my consent.

An eternity had passed over the course of a few seconds. Ended by the sound of a chunk of soft metal impacting on steel.

Clunk!

"Irrigating." A cool rush, chasing out the fire. A different bottle, then. I unclenched a fist, reaching my arm over her neck. A kiss on my cheek; a second on my lips.

"Stitching."

She was my strength. My calm center. With her by my side, I could stare down the devil himself.

And in that crystalline millisecond, I faced the awful truth.

I would need to send her away. I gasped, choked, kept the keening cry of pain from escaping. Pain that had nothing at all to do with the impromptu surgery taking place.

I would be leaving in search of Lot. A hunt for the Devil's favorite uncle. She could not hunt with me. More was at stake than just *our* lives now. Irene, Greg, and the baby made four.

As my friend finished carefully placing sutures, I drew upon the love that passed from her tender gestures into my skin. I found the calm voice in the storm. I would be going alone; there was no doubt. Yet her love would ride with me.

21

I tested my weight on my newly mended leg. A sharpness, yes. As if I had been running too long. It did not seem as if it wanted to collapse which I took as a good sign. I flexed my toes, bare on the concrete, and was thankful someone had taken the time to sweep recently. Briefly I closed my eyes, finding my center. Sobely, Greg, and Irene waited patiently.

My patience had run through. Briskly I walked over to the hidden car, undoing tie-downs as I circled. As the tarp went slack, the shape revealed beneath enticed with graceful lines. Yanking back the cover, I was hardly surprised to find the Charger my Dad had once cherished.

What was surprising to me was the shape that it was in. The last time I'd seen the car had been almost a year prior to my father's death. I remembered being disappointed when he had returned from a trip in a new car. I had always thought I'd get the Charger. I was nearly old enough to have a permit, and it was no secret that I had loved the old beat-up muscle car.

I heard Greg gasp, though whether in recognition or appreciation I couldn't tell. I hadn't decided which was the more demanding emotion in my own being, yet. The car had originally rolled out of the factory in 1969. It had been owned by a friend of my father's, who must have led a dubious lifestyle. The doors hadn't matched the body. The driver's seat had been a completely different color from the passenger seat. The rear panel behind the tattered back seat had been riddled with holes, and my father had always been evasive as to the story behind the car. All I had known was that he loved it. Despite being more than wealthy enough to have it restored, he had left it alone.

He claimed it was a rolling tribute to a friend he'd never see again.

I had spent many hours beneath its hood, spotted with rust. The trunk had been secured down with a tough rubber strap. Yet still she purred. Now... it was hard to reconcile the differences. The doors were the same – I believe they had come off of a car a year older – but now were properly aligned. Paint as black as an oil slick transformed the rusting hulk into a gleaming thing of absolute beauty. Broken only by a trio of perpendicular stripes on the rear of the car. Two thin silver lines sandwiching a wide one of crimson.

The hood sported a pair of intakes, black chrome that barely stood out from the rest of the car. Stainless steel pipes vented the exhaust to each side, angled out just ahead of the wide tires. The windows were all tinted dark. A shadow. The promise of speed. The aging relic had been transformed into the ultimate driving machine.

"She'll stand out a bit..." I said finally. Trying to sound nonchalant.

"Whoa." Greg said.

"Who are we talking about?" Sobely asked. She stood beside me, peering all around the car, as if expecting to see someone magically standing there.

"Boys and their cars..." Irene teased. Sobely seemed to understand the meaning, and looked over the slick, sleek blackness.

"How do you know it's a girl car?" She asked, still confused.

I laughed and drew her close to me. Her hair tickled my bare chest. I really ought to do something about the general lack of clothing between us. She wore the T-Shirt that would have been more suited to my size, and little else. Irene wore a button-up that had to have been Greg's. Only he was fully clothed, though my blood stained his pants, speckles forming a pattern on the blue cotton shirt.

In the presence of the magnificent car, I felt we were under-dressed. For long moments I forgot all about the danger we were still in. Forgot my present goal of putting an end to the running. Looking over the triumph from the heyday of Mopar, I felt like maybe a good, long, drive wouldn't be such a bad idea after all.

"Guys tend to always think of pretty cars as women." I explained without explaining.

"Oh." She responded. "Why?"

"Because the good ones are more than we deserve, and contain more power than we could ever handle, just like a proper lady." Greg answered.

"Just an excuse, really. A man would find just about anything sexy, in the right conditions. They need hardly any reason to personify the things they desire amongst inanimate objects." Irene chided. She stood staring at the wall on the eastern side of the shop, speaking in our general direction. For a moment I felt sorry that she couldn't appreciate the sleeping beast within our presence.

There are other ways to see...

"Keys, Greg." I said, flicking my fingers. He handed them over. Reluctantly.

I removed the single car key from the ring, and then passed it back.

"Better open up that door, my friend. Wouldn't do to asphyxiate ourselves." I gently pushed on his shoulder. He shook his head, breaking free of the trance. As much as I would have liked to stand and stare at the car myself, I knew that time was never one of our luxuries. Greg moved over to the garage door and lifted it partly. Letting in dim light.

I unlocked the driver's door, gestured for Sobely to climb past. At once I was in awe at the beautifully detailed leather interior, and the shape of her rump as she scrambled past. The pair of greasy buckets had been replaced by a single bench seat, whereas the rear bench had become a pair of bucket seats. Centrally mounted was a rack for weapons. A hanging tag held a list of firearms, and a list of dates pertaining to maintenance.

From the steering column; another tag. This one logging vehicle maintenance. I laughed at the last service date. September 3rd, 2001. Less than a week ago. It was possible that it was a coincidence. The record showed that the vehicle had been in proper maintenance for the past three years. But the fact that the last service date filled in the last row on the tag...

Somehow, he'd known. I was beginning to believe that fact more and more.

I slid beside Sobely, yanked the tag free. The key slipped into the ignition with a soft click. A promise of exciting things to be explored, if only I'd light the fires... The whole car seemed to tremble slightly, as if in anticipation. Perhaps it was only me.

A hum as the key clicked into auxiliary mode. The dashboard lights up. Black with white lettering. A set of needles, chrome-edged crimson. The tank showed full. Battery fully charged. A light flickered from red to yellow beside the tachometer.

A switch illuminated. Since the key refused any further forward motion, I pushed in the switch. The LED switched to green. A second attempt to twist the key yielded a slight cough of a noise – and then one of the sexiest sounds a man could ever hope to hear. Though she sounded healthy as factory fresh, I knew the timbre of that engine. The 8-cylinder, 426 cubic-inch, Chrysler-made Hemispherical combustion engine. Generation II. Fed by gasoline as pure as you could find it. No rattily roar from a busted-up exhaust. Instead, as I applied just the barest touch to the gas pedal, the car merely purred more forcefully, the sound sending a tingle into my bones.

Probably pushing more than 425 ponies, too.

"Okay, Tim. Forget what I said. That *is* sexy. And most *definitely* feminine." Irene panted as the vibrations filled the air. To her ears... for a moment I felt a bit envious that she could hear things I never would.

Greg laughed, and then wouldn't stop. Had I sounded so maniacal, when I had first begun this trip?

I sighed in pleasure, closing my eyes. Feeling the shape of Sobely pressed into my side. The feel of hand-stitched leather wrapping a wheel that had been cast during the height of the Vietnam War. Tilted my head back against the rest and felt leather and sheepskin. I could smell him. My father. I could smell a hint of oil, a touch of mint, and the strong scent of the exotic chocolates he had kept in his pocket.

I laughed a little then. I reached back to haul the coat overhead, and into my lap. Too many zippers, for far too many pockets. Dark leather, stained with oil and diesel. He had called it his driving coat. A Tanker's jacket from the war, lined with sheepskin. Buckles around waist and neck, though it had been decades since they could actually clasp.

And sure enough, when checked thoroughly, a pocket revealed a vacuum-sealed pouch full of the sweets he'd share by way of greeting. "Chocolate?" He'd ask. He advocated that it was an important supplement belonging in every person's diet. "Made from goat's milk, so even you lactose-free lads can get a dose!"

I lingered in the past for a long moment. With care I broke the seal on the pouch, handing a piece to Greg. His grin must have matched my own. In tandem with unwrapped candies, we popped them in our mouth, flicking the treat up into the air to catch it on our tongues. Just the way he always had.

We'd practiced, though I don't think he ever knew. He'd always been the hero to both of us growing up. Cooler than James Dean, tougher than Steve McQueen, smarter than Eastwood. As suave as James Bond (The Connery Years) but without the booze and endless women. You would believe any story he'd tell you and argue if he told you later it had been made up.

The anger I had been feeling evaporated. Anger at the universe. Anger at my father. Even the anger for the deathly hounds that chased us. The taste of the velvety chocolate was like magic. The magic to be all that he was, and even more. Because he had believed it. And whatever Dad believed, was always the truth.

"Ummm... Could I maybe have one of those? I'm starving." Sobely interrupted. I tousled her hair and grinned affectionately. Infected by the nostalgia.

"I definitely smell chocolate. Don't hold out on a girl, now. Haven't had any of that... for a long time." Irene's voice first came out tough but ended with hesitation. Just thinking back had reminded her of a past that must have been unpleasant.

"Of course!" I said, first passing a piece to Greg who passed it over to Irene, and then unwrapping another. Pretending to eat it, so I could see the pout on Sobely's face. With her lips slightly parted, I placed the treat between them. Delivering it to her with a kiss. I saw her eyes light up before they closed. Satisfaction pulling her cheeks out in a smile.

The rest I tucked back into the pocket, before pulling the jacket on. A valiant steed, a magic cloak. Now all I needed was... My eyes lit upon the tag hanging from the gun rack. I stepped out of the car, startling Sobely. Belatedly I realized she had still been leaning in from the chocolate kiss. She managed to catch herself before she fell flat on the seat.

Sure enough, the trunk possessed a lock far more robust than any factory hardware, which explained the purpose of the final key on the ring. Greg passed the keychain back, standing at my side. Nearly fumbling, I got the complicated looking key into the innocent-enough looking lock plate. A twist, and the panel slid aside. Revealing a faintly glowing keypad. I entered in the date of the last day my father had served. It was what he had set the combination lock he used to use to secure the door of his safe at home.

The latch released, the trunk popping upward perhaps a quarter of an inch. I grabbed the bottom edge, noticing the feel of smooth hydraulics assisting a heavy door. The trunk had been transformed into a reinforced gun locker. Clearly the suspension had been reworked, as the rear frame sat the perfect height from the axles. Never betraying the presence of extra weight in the rear end.

It was then that I realized that the driver's door had worked far too smoothly as well. I glanced in the framework of the doorjamb to find extensive reinforcement, and discrete hydraulics to assist in getting it open without a fuss. I had been too distracted by other views when I had first opened it to notice.

Never mind the open road. This car had been suited up for war. The arsenal in the back enough to assault the gates of heaven itself. A steel box clasped with a simple lock, key inside it. Further crates undoubtedly containing ammunition. The first box, when opened, was full of cash. And a note. I handed this to Greg, uncovering another case. The emblem on it... I instantly teared up. A box I had made him in woodshop. I remembered carving it. I spent a much longer time on that carving than the whole rest of the box. Two trimesters working on it. The last gift I had ever given him.

A stylized Destro skull, from *G.I.Joe*. A mistake – I had looked up "Marvel Skull" on the internet and printed the first one I found. He joked, "Destro probably sold him all his guns!" and then tousled my hair like I was still 7.

Inside, tucked in straw-filled burlap, was his service weapon. A Colt 1911, .45 Caliber. The same emblem I had painstakingly carved into the box now adorning new grips. The message and the meaning were clear.

He didn't want me to run. He knew all along exactly what state of mind I would be in when I finally made it here. There would be no maps to secret hiding spots. No pleas to keep my head down. He knew when I made it this far I'd be pissed off and ready to do battle.

The note was simple. It directed that I put on the coat and go across the street. Talk to Jack. The surplus store had been called 'Jaxboots.' I had wondered at the spelling. A generous wallet tucked in the largest of the jacket pockets held most of the cash, easily. The leather coat hid the holster I had also found wrapped in the burlap. Under my arm, the cold steel on my skin was a reassuring reminder of the veritable cannon being held in place. The Excelsior. It wasn't until after he had died that I had figured out the reference.

I handed a short-sawn shotgun to Greg. He checked it, grabbing a box of shells.

"You stay with the girls. Get loaded in the car. If there's any shooting, you put the hammer down and get the hell out of here." I instructed.

"Do you think it will come to that, so soon?" He asked, nervously.

"I've no idea. I think we entered the final stages of this thing the moment we escaped in Colorado. They could be preparing the charges now, deciding to just put a crater to the lot of us and be done with it. I'd like to think that Dad wouldn't lead me into danger. I have some faith now, that he knew what he was doing."

"But… just to be safe, then?" He said, meaning the gun. I gestured him towards the driver's seat.

"Yes. Just to be safe."

He ushered Irene into the back seat, before swinging in to take my place behind the wheel. I knew he'd hate to leave his Buick behind, but this was beyond mere sentiment. I passed out the door, pushing it up and over in its track. Giving the Charger an unimpeded exit. Then I sauntered across the road. There was no traffic. The lights of the shop were on, but dim. It would have been my luck if the shop had been shut down weeks prior, due to tax evasion or something.

Yet when I pushed in the door handle, it swung inward. I stepped in, checking corners. Finally bringing my vision to rest behind an old grump of a lady sitting behind the counter. There, an open door dark enough to hide any number of dangers.

"May I… Oh, but of course it's you. I knew today was going to be special." She smiled, and it did wonders to her tame her fierce disposition.

"Umm… I'm supposed to talk to Jack." I said. Wishing I hadn't sounded quite so timid. I had hugged myself against the cold on my walk over, but also to bring my hand close enough to draw the gun in a hurry.

"You're him then. Jon's boy. Aye, I see him in ya. I was hoping this day would come before I shuffled off. 'Soon' is a relative term to a youngster!" She harrumphed, still smiling.

"You're Jack, then?"

"Who else would I be?"

I imagined the economy of the township was likely too weak for a shop such as this one to support an employee. Still, I was a bit surprised. All this hardware, watched over by one old woman. I re-evaluated my opinion of her. She couldn't have gotten by on fierceness alone. More than likely, she was the town favorite; woe to any that tried to mess with 'Jack.'

"I suppose it makes sense to find the proprietor in their own store, Ma'am. I must admit that I was expecting to find a man, though. No disrespect, of course."

"That's quite alright, young'un. When this place opened… well, calling it 'Jacqueline's Army Surplus' didn't seem to be very respectful. Went with Flatland's Surplus for a few years, but... a lot of hard-types on Harley's would come through. Mostly looking for boots. Especially old German ones. Big fella started calling the place 'Jack's Boots' to his friends. I took a fancy to it. Saved a bit by shortening it some, and the sign hasn't hardly even seen a good scrub ever since."

I found myself smiling unexpectedly. Here I was on grave business, and the cosmos seemed to deem that I needed one more character in my life. Her speech was just queer enough to be slightly hypnotic. You wanted to hear what she said next.

"It would seem, ma'am, that I have been found fortunate enough to meet the good ones called 'Jack' in this world. I've another friend that prefers it to his given name." I laughed, thinking of Jack and Mildred's bantering. "I think you'd get along with him, and his wife."

"Any friend of yours, can count on my own sweet disposition, should we be well-met. But my, mustn't forget my manners! You're here. After all these years. Such a fine young man you've grown to be. I spoke true – there is a touch of your father in you. Especially those eyes... The man before me though... you are your own kind of man. The nobility in your bearing is all you. Your father was right."

"He was rarely ever wrong."

I pulled the packet of chocolate out and offered the lady a piece. This she took and plopped into a mouth that had long since given up on teeth. She closed her eyes as the treat dissolved on her tongue. When they popped open again, another change had occurred.

"You've had it rough, far rougher than he wanted. He used to tell me about how destiny worked. That there was little choice when there was work to be done."

"When's there's work, it should be done. Whoever it falls to see it done is the right person to do it." I quoted. A line from a Samurai film, and one my father often recited.

"Aye. Spoken true. To say such a thing, even to believe in it... 'tis far different than actually living through it. You've lost so much for someone so young. It doesn't seem fair." She frowned, the expression directed at the hands of fate.

"A greater injustice it is, to see a job that needs doing; to walk away." The conversation reminded me of the ancient woman that first brought Sobely to me. I still didn't know the scope of everything, only now I knew I was meant to fulfill a purpose. Not planned to do so – *meant* to do so.

"You aren't alone, are you?" She asked.

"No."

"Yet..." She trailed off.

"What is it?"

"Not my place. I have a job, and I certainly won't walk away from it. Arthritis set in decades ago." She grinned, only her eyes remained haunted.

"Very well. I was given the instruction to talk to you. I've had less than breadcrumbs to guide my way, yet I still somehow ended up here. The road was long, the..." I searched my brain for a word, "The trials were great. I've got blood on my hands. I don't think I'll be lucky enough to escape further bloodshed."

"For once, vengeance, justice, and security all have the same solution. The trick, young one, is to understand which it is that drives you." She crossed her arms. She had posed a test, and I had to carefully choose my answer.

"I intend to do what is needed. A well-placed domino set to tumble and complete the pattern that has been laid out."

She seemed stricken for a moment.

"You're... incredible. You have to see how extraordinary you are. You have a choice. You always have a choice."

"I choose to be true to who I am. In this way, I fit into the pattern that was set. True, theoretically I could choose differently. But I won't. I don't believe there really is another choice for me. I am who I am. I didn't know exactly who I was when this all started, but I know it now."

"And who might that be, exactly?"

"I am expected to be one thing, yet I am another. I was devoid of life, but now overflow with it. I understand it now. There is at least one more bullet to fire. More if there are obstacles set in my path. All of them are necessary. Should I succeed, then I won't ever have to fear again. She would be safe. If I fail, well... none of it will have made a difference if I fail."

The woman had gone through the darkened door to retrieve something, gesturing towards the racks of clothing. Military surplus mingled with a certain 'tough-guy' style. I gathered clothes for the girls, a change for Greg. Black jeans and a plain black t-shirt for myself. Wool socks, and shoes for everyone. For a moment I was reminded of playing pretend as a child. Wearing my father's coat and tromping around in his boots.

The jacket had been a bit too big for Dad. I realized that I must have grown taller than he had been. The sleeves reached the wrists properly, not obscuring my hands as they did his. For a moment, my head spun. For a moment, I could believe he was still alive. That he was just outside, or just around the next row.

Like a soap bubble, the feeling vanished quickly.

At the counter, Jacqueline stood ready. A small package sitting on the surface. I took a deep breath, let the world fall back into proper order. There was business to conclude. Another road to travel. A *final* destination to reach. In my moment of dizzy surrealism, I understood what steps I would need to take. I readied myself for them.

There are very few things in life that can improve one's perspective in an instant. That distinguished list contained such experiences as a sincere smile, the birth of a newborn, a kiss in the rain. Auspicious to be sure. And humble on that list – a pair of new shoes. Or, as the case may be, a new pair of steel-jacketed combat boots.

When your only option for clothing is what you can find in an out-of-the-way army surplus store frequented infrequently by bikers, one should just be happy that nobody died wearing the boots in question.

Jacqueline, being a bit of an enterprising sort, had run out of the standard German-issue 'jack boots' favored by her clientele long ago. Her solution was elegant and straightforward: Find a supplier willing to put a few antique designs back into production. As much as bikers might insist that they prefer aged war boots, nothing really beats a pair of *new* shoes.

Color choices for clothing were various shades of camo, and various shades of black. And various black shades. Mentally I added Mad Max and The Punisher to the list of things I would introduce to Sobely. Then I congratulated myself for believing that there was a point in keeping such a list in the first place.

Why stop there? A Mel Gibson/Dolph Lundgren movie marathon would be just the thing, wouldn't it?

Irene and Sobely managed to get dressed on their own. With extra-large aviators, black jeans, half-boots, and a short coat, Irene looked as if she belonged on the back of a motorcycle. Perhaps blowing bubbles with bright pink gum.

Sobely, on the other hand... Nearly the same kind of get up, she simply managed to look cute. Adorable, really. The pants I had found to fit her were made of heavy leather. Too many buttons, and a fly that crossed diagonally to her hip. Her coat sported a rabbit-fur-lined collar. If Irene looked the part of biker babe, Sobely looked as if she belonged on the magazine cover of a publication pandering to the 'weekend road-warriors.' A work of pin-up art to be duplicated on the nose of a fighter jet, or tank. If anything, the clothing contrasted with her delicate features, emphasizing them.

I had a substantial urge to take her somewhere private, where I might enjoy her beauty a little better. Maybe it was the leather and stirrup-boots. Also, there was a fair bit of neediness in my thoughts, tempered by a sudden bout of despair. Yet, I would always need her. Would always despair at the thought of us being apart. For as long as I lived, she was my source of life. The cool water in the desert.

I had an address. I had a target. For once, I knew where it was I could go; that it would most definitely be a dangerous place. To consider anything other than sending her someplace *else* was sheer madness. To keep her at my side would be for my own purposes – pure selfishness.

Yet I wavered.

Her eyes found mine. My hands found her shoulders. I leaned, ran a finger along the length of an ear. Watched them tremble and warm to the touch.

"I love you." I whispered.

"Yes. And you are sending me away." Her voice was heavy. Eyes brimmed, but the tears did not fall.

"How did you guess?" I asked. No point in denial.

"There is... a distance. Even now. I am at the end of your arms, rather than within them. You lean to me, rather than hold me close. Touch my ear with fingertips, rather than kiss my lips."

"It is quite the opposite of what I want to do."

"I know. If I begged... would you stay?"

"No. I cannot. To take you where I'm going would court disaster. To run from what I need to do would ensure ruin. I must go, and I must go alone."

She wept a little, and I felt my heart breaking. I wanted to... there was no point in considering all the things I wished to do.

"Could you... for just a little while? Could you hold me, let me believe it was forever?"

"I will return to you. I swear it." I answered. Still holding her at arm's length.

"Please? Just a little while?"

Unable to deny her desires, I pulled her close. Her hands curled in my shirt, and she cried. Inside, I felt a little broken. Wretched. She sobbed, and I stood still as a monolithic god. To move would only invite further pain – in either direction. I would send her away – and it would take every bit of courage I had. She had been constantly at my side ever since I woke up to a strange light in my room. Ages ago. So much had happened, and yet there was still one more stretch of road to travel. A lonely highway for both of us.

Her smiles filled the day. Her kisses filled the night.

"I will return to you, my love. I will." I whispered, and we continued to stand there. For the moment, I would give her forever.

22

"Greg. I need you to leave now." I stated calmly.

"What are you talking about?"

"I need you to get them somewhere safe. Hide until this all blows over. It won't be long."

I kept my voice calm. Placid. Irene and Sobely sat in the car. Irene had found a brush and was working it through Sobely's hair. Sisters of circumstance.

"I won't leave you now. Not now. Hell, not ever again. I ran away once, and..."

"You aren't listening. I'm not asking you to run."

"No? It sure sounds like it to me. You're planning a one-way trip into hell, and you don't want me along for the ride. Isn't that what you're saying?" He grew angry. Still, I kept my voice calm. My features relaxed. I tried to exude the control that I wished I could feel. To be the commanding presence my father had always been.

"Please."

"Why?" The word was a barb. An accusation. I wanted to be angry with him — he had no right to be indignant now.

"Irene. She should be taken somewhere safe. I don't think that applies to where I'm going."

"Alright. What about Sobely? Does she need to be there when you go to war?"

My breath caught.

"No. She does not." I whispered.

"What?" He repeated. Unbelieving.

"It's simple, Greg."

"Not to me. I told you, I *am* ready to fight. To stand by my friend. God, it killed me to just leave you like I did. I had all the right reasons for doing so, was drilled on how important it was, yet none of that changed the way it made me feel inside. Never again. I'll follow you to the bitter end." His whisper was louder than I would have liked.

"That's good. You're ready to fight; that's excellent. It may even come to that. I hope not. Your hackles are raised, which means you are more alert to danger. Go ahead and be angry with me if you wish. It will give you an edge. You *have* to do this for me."

"I could refuse."

"Would you? Do you think I ask out of idleness? That the thought of it doesn't threaten to knock me down? I fear drowning, Greg. I fear drowning, and *I am asking you to take away my life preserver.* You have to understand what I'm asking you to do. What I am trusting you to do *right*."

Greg stared, his anger slowly softening to a certain degree of surliness.

"I still don't like it."

"I know. You don't have to like it. You just have to do it."

He stared at me for long moments. He must have seen the fear lurking behind my façade, for his features softened. He took a deep breath, exhaled it slowly. His head dipped, defeated.

"Yes. I will take her. And I will pray fervently that you won't be far behind."

"I don't know how I'm going to be able to take one *step* without her. How I'm going to have the courage to do what I need to do. I know now that I will have to manage, though. It's the only way."

"What if… I don't mean to sound pessimistic, but what if you *don't* make it back to us? I know your father believed that you were going to succeed at everything, yet I don't know what it is he expected you to do. I mean, why *you* in the first place? If this was his problem, why didn't he deal with it?"

The thought had echoed within my own sleepless nights. I had found the answer at last.

"He did. He put all this in motion. I'm a cog in the machine used to destroy his greatest enemy."

"A pretty damn big cog, if you ask me!"

I smiled tightly.

"That's the funny thing. If you remove even the smallest gear, the watch no longer winds. The size of the piece has no bearing on its importance. Remove any of them, and it is nothing more than a broken lump of metal."

"What is that supposed to mean?"

"It means, Greg: Your purpose is to do as *I* say this time. To take my heart and soul and to keep her safe. To make sure my child has a chance to be born. It is something only you can do. Without you, my task now would be impossible."

"You sound as if maybe you won't be coming back." He crossed his arms.

"Maybe I won't. But I will succeed, nonetheless. If I fail, it won't matter who is by my side. It won't matter how far you run. So, I simply will not fail. Even if that means I never come back."

There are an infinite number of silences.

With her, the silent road was broken up with smiles, with her warmth. The noise of the tires tooling along the tarmac was a white-noise counterpart to the song of a heartbeat. A sleepy sigh. Miles that were passed in silence were filled with love.

It was just me, now. I was enveloped in silence, just as solid as the leather seat. The road waited on me. The task was now nigh, but the road itself wasn't going anywhere. A new feeling squeezed into my chest. Unfamiliar at first.

It had been months now. I had forgotten about loneliness. A feeling I hadn't missed until it came back. A new texture to it this time – the cold reality. The grinning skull of the grim reaper reminding me that I had a greater chance of meeting him, rather than ever seeing her again.

They would be safe with Jack and Mildred. I had called them from a phone at the surplus store. First, I considered sending them back home, to Greg's parents'. Of course, I thought better of it. If they had thought to send a team of killers to Greg's house, they would be watching Dan and Molly. Especially when the hit squad was discovered dead.

I was careful not to tell Greg of my fears. He might not have been able to control himself. He'd call them, or worse, go straight home. Even now, the Trench Coat Men might be sitting in his father's barn. Just waiting patiently with the farm equipment. Machines all built to fulfill a singular purpose.

They had left nearly an hour ago. Sobely had stopped crying, being brave for me. She had smiled sweetly, sadly. The image burned into my retinas.

It could not be the last time that I would see her. No matter how the next few days went, I *would* return to her.

It didn't matter how many men with assault rifles got in my way, either. I had plenty of lead to pay the toll with.

I turned the key.

The road waited.

The engine purred with a special kind of menace. The sound simultaneously raising the hairs on your arm in fright and triggering an exhilarating spike of adrenaline. Dangerous. Yet beckoning. The Charger hadn't sounded nearly so good the last I'd seen it. The transformation of the rusted clunker was more than just visual. Before it had run reliably, like a horse on the verge of being sent to pasture. Now it was a Beast. Hungering for the open road.

Maybe it wasn't just the car, though. There is something to be said of having a purpose in life. Where I had been wandering aimlessly before, now there was a goal. A destination. Perhaps my final destination. Somehow just the idea that this would be the end of it all – one way or another – made me feel relieved.

The nicely appointed handgun tucked beneath my arm in its holster might have had an effect on me, too.

For the first time in my life, I was *dangerous.*

I revved the engine carefully, felt the car shake slightly. A barely contained predator lived beneath the hood, spoiling for a fight. Despite the gravity of the situation, I felt a smile form on my lips. I ran my tongue over them to moisten them and could still taste her tears. A flip of a switch, and cool air vented inward. A bit of adjustment to the mirrors, and there was nothing left to fiddle with.

I hadn't driven much manual, but this was the kind of vehicle that made no apologies. It was a tiger. Meant to be driven by the bold. No pandering to the weak-willed. No mercy.

Gently I popped the stick down into gear, released the clutch slowly. Felt it catch. The open garage door rapidly grew. The road called, and the beast was eager to get moving. A tap on the gas to merge with nonexistent traffic. The power pressed me into the seat. The truck had lumbered, Greg's Buick rolled along smoothly. The Charger leapt ahead, just begging to prove how much rubber it could leave behind. How much road it could eat up. Like a wild animal – roaring with the sheer glee of finally being free of the concrete prison. A warhorse yet unbroken.

Months of running, fear of bullets in dark places. Fear that she would be taken from me in a thunderstorm of gunfire. No more.

The end of the road beckoned.

"Either you will protect her, or you will fail."

A few months ago, life had seemed to be such a simple thing. Get up, move about a routine. Think about what I would do with my time, now I had graduated. Find work, though I didn't need to bother. Buy a car. Buy a house. Start a family. Routine. Millions of people went through the same process, the entire world over. While I never considered myself special, part of me wondered if life could be just a little bit more... *interesting.*

To tell the truth, I had always been a bit aimless. Without purpose, you might say. I didn't know what kind of man I had become. I had no clue as to what work I might fill my life doing.

I think that I might have liked to become a cop. A detective, rather. Solving the tough cases – or whatever passed for it in my town. Keeping order, upholding the law. Sounds nice. Not too boring, just a touch of the interesting thrown in.

Sure, one might wonder what the point was. I had no guarantee I would survive the day. However, I did have it on good authority that I would either succeed or fail. There was no middle ground. Failure was death. Maybe it would stop with me. I knew it now – I'd been the goal all along. The gruff woman that went by the name "Jack" had confirmed as much.

The words of another friend resurfaced. He had also gone by the name Jack. It wasn't *his* first name, either. *"Whenever you leave the room she just stops. She waits. She would wait on you forever, I think."*

"I will be waiting for you." She had said, when I finally convinced her to go. It hadn't been a declaration. No bold proclamation. Just a simple statement of a fact that was true. Two plus two equaled four, and she would wait on me forever.

"Either you will protect her, or you will fail." The words rang through my thoughts. A strange woman had spoken them to me, on the morning my life first found purpose. She had said little else – only to run and to never stop running. I had gotten hung up on that second idea. Never a moment to catch our breath. To think things through. Always the open road to travel, boogeymen in our wake.

Running hadn't protected her. It didn't grant her safety. It just wore the both of us down until I was blindsided by my own inadequacies. The two of us versus an infinite madness.

Dealing with the problem head-on was the only play to make. Put a bullet through Lot's skull, and maybe his cronies would find something better to do. The maddening aspect was how the entire thing had been arranged. This wasn't a game of chess between two masters – no. Dad had always preferred to play solitaire with dominoes. He used to sit for hours creating intricate patterns that wouldn't be revealed until they were set off, to tip into one another. To cascade neatly in the pattern of his own design. He had been quite good at it.

It was coming down to just two final tiles. Two final pieces left to crash together.

It was dark when I reached downtown Los Angeles. A bit lighter when I found the address. Dawn was threatening.

Right in the middle of an industrialized zone, stood a garage without a house. The remote that had been clipped to the visor of the Charger suddenly became relevant. I pressed the button, watched as the door revolved open. An ordinary garage, if empty. Against the far wall; a door.

I eased the car inside and shut the engine off. Another tap of the button and the big door closed behind me. Sealing me in. Headlights illuminating the next step. I switched them off, retrieving a flashlight from the glove compartment. The bright beam of the Mag-Lite played against the wall as I made ready to open that door. The gun secured, extra clips where I could find them through touch.

I considered the automatic rifle in the trunk briefly, and then decided that the way ahead might be too narrow. I had more practice with handguns, too. No, a rifle would be a risk, best to stick to what I knew best.

As I had seen in movies, I held the gun at the ready, steadying it with a hand that was busy holding onto my light source. Both items would make getting the door open an awkward task, yet both were necessary.

I transferred the flashlight to my chin, deciding the risk it. My freed hand twisted around the doorknob, yanking the door open as I jumped clear of it. Quickly I got the flashlight back into my fist, got the gun back into a ready position.

Nothing but silence. More darkness.

The proverbial backdoor into the devil's playground.

The hall on the other side was wide enough to drive down, and long enough to be impossible. The darkness swallows the beam of the flashlight, revealing walls, the glint of windows, and little else. What was clear was the gross sense of scale.

The garage was a free-standing structure. Surrounded by industrial warehouses. I had circled the block, had seen clearly that the garage didn't even touch the other buildings. Yet, here was a space that defied that entirely. The floor didn't slope downwards; I had not gone down any steps.

Questions prickled at my consciousness, but they were hardly of any importance. Sound echoed eerily, lost to a ceiling that stretched far beyond the reach of the Krypton bulb. Against the heavy veil of darkness, the bright beam was pathetic. The infinite blackness whispered of untold horrors.

When I was younger, I had avidly read the works of Edgar Allen Poe and H.P. Lovecraft. This hallway could easily have been the focal point of one of their stories. The oily gleam of windows promised rooms – where one might regret shining a light. It was said that to tread the dark spaces in search of monsters was to court insanity.

I stepped forward.

I kept my footsteps light; my breath to a whisper. Listening intently for the trap, even as I neared the first of the windows. I was struck all at once at the discordant similarity to the facility Sobely and I had been made captive. Where the Director's lair had been painfully bright, confining, surgically sinister, this place left you alone in an ink-black void. Though the path was straight, one could not help but feel as if you had gotten all turned around somehow.

I peered through the first window. No creature of tentacle and blood stared back. Instead I caught the sterile gleam of surgical steel. The room had been intended to hold a single occupant. Steel slab for a bed. Steel toilet. A complete absence of anything comforting, compounded by an utter lack of privacy for whoever had been locked within. The ceiling was studded with wired-meshed fluorescent lights.

Across the hall, the same. As I continued past more windows, cell after cell was briefly illuminated. Beside each was a heavy door, with a heavy lock. A rail to slide an identification plaque into mounted near the top of each. Every room was empty – not even a particle of dust. No spiders dwelled here.

Then, larger windows. Doors with mesh-reinforced viewports. The red lens of a light fixture above each. Inside each of these was a cabinet and a table. Both of the same darkly gleaming steel. A dozen of these exam rooms, six on each side of the hall.

Then there was nothing at all. For a while.

It became clear to me that there *was* no ambush waiting. It would have been impossible to arrange – every sound magnified greatly. Every flicker of light was painfully visible. It was also clear that this was not a facility to hold captured subjects. There was too obvious a purpose. Too much the sense of a laboratory within a production line.

This is where she was born. Where she had lived.

The thought was errant yet rang with truth. Disturbing to me now was the total emptiness. Whatever production that had once filled the rooms with light and noise had ceased long ago. Where, then, was the product?

I reached another row of windows. These all looked into the same room. The vast space contained row upon row of glass containers capped with more steel. Ports for hoses, and mysterious equipment panels. The door plaque remained, proclaiming the room to be The Nursery.

Across the hall the plaque read: Environment. Racks of combat armor hung inches from the floor, disturbing the illusion of life. It would have been easy to image an entire army standing at attention in there. I did not need to take measurements to know that these had been built to fit exactly one body type. A person that was, perhaps, a tad short. Slender. Feminine. Elongated helmets – the better to accommodate ears that were a stretch too long.

I continued. The next set of rooms resembled torture chambers. Heavy chains suspended from the invisible ceiling. A row of monitors and assorted equipment mounted to the far wall. *Testing chambers?*

The last room on the right stopped me cold. The chains here were rusted – *no. Not rust. Blood.* Splatters of the ochre color covered the floor, leaving a pattern. A gap large enough for a small body to hang. A black glove lie forgotten on the floor. The monitors and equipment replaced by a simple rack. I looked within the room with intensity. Unable to turn away. Unwilling to enter. Wicked knives kept company with a black whip with too many tips. Objects that belonged in an exhibit on the inquisition era, displayed here in a torture palace. A device studded with valves and vacuum tubes hung beside the more archaic devices, electric probes dangling at the ends of heavy-gauge wire.

Here was where Sobely has been un-made. This had been her prison. A cell of loneliness and pain. A view of an abyss, brightened only with the approach of her captors, come to play with their toy.

The hot rage that had fueled me now turned cold. My veins filled with ice water, my mind clear as a glacial lake. All questions were washed away. Fear, doubt; gone. One single purpose left to inhabit. *Make them pay.* I turned from the glass. In the distance I could see the end of the hall. One more doorway – a light escaping from beneath.

Time had stretched. Shifted. Leapt and crawled. Now, it was nearing the end.

23

"You came in through the old garage. That was your father's entrance. We each had our own, you know."

He didn't turn. I glanced at the corners before shutting the heavy door behind me. A flick of a lever, and a heavy bolt slid home. At the least, it would slow down anybody that wished to gain entrance. *With what you saw out there, they could go right through the walls if they wanted.*

Full attention on the man before me, I leveled the gun; keeping the sights centered on his back.

"You've got his car – I wondered where it went. You wear that silly coat he insisted on. I dare say it agrees with you more than it did him. He played the part that you so easily inhabit naturally. Hero. You've got his gun pointed the correct direction. Right at your enemy. Smart lad. You've learned the lesson he never seemed to be able to comprehend."

He wanted a reaction from me. Spouting facts, and lingering allusions.

"I am not the same man as my father." I replied. Lot spun crisply, perhaps a trace of surprise in his steel-blue eyes. In his hands was a pen – the old-fashioned kind – and a leather-bound journal.

"Why of course you're not! I apologize if I gave the impression of such an implication. Your father had this funny notion, you see. He believed that by always acting honorably, and treating even your enemies with respect, the same would be returned in kind. You've learned better, though. Haven't you?" His tone was teasing.

I resisted squeezing the curved piece of steel against the spring.

"As I understood it, he didn't have very many enemies. Seems as if they *did* respect him."

"Oh, I certainly have a great respect for the man. He was a fool to think that respect would cause me to be anything other than what I am. He expected me to be honorable, just on the basis that he, himself, was honorable."

"You have no honor."

"Precisely my point. Worse for your father; he actually *trusted* me. He never betrayed his word. Not once. Somehow, he believed I would keep mine. Despite plenty of evidence he had to the contrary. Where did it leave him, in the end? Hmm? What did his life matter? Given foolishly, I say. It was too late for him to learn guile. For one such as myself, his motives were so clear."

"What do *you* know of his motives?" I asked. Wary of his treachery, yet... Why let me get this far?

"I know that it is your tenacity that has saved you from them. The soldier as well, I suspect. You've got her tucked away, don't you? Sent her with the good doctor. Back home? No matter, not anymore. She's out of reach, while you've come to settle your father's accounts."

"I come to settle my own. I was never privy to my father's business. I have reason enough to settle the score with you – and certainly have plenty to justify the toll you'll pay." I gestured to an armchair, "Why don't you sit down? It's more dignified."

Lot laughed. The sound was dry. Dead grass against a grave marker.

"A bit fatigued, are we? Is that a bandage I spy, under that red-stained hole in your trousers? Did you have a bit of an accident, perhaps? Get nicked by some poorly placed lead?"

"I can stand just fine. I can stand here until the end of *your* life, at any rate. I simply extend to you the courtesy. A gentleman discusses things sitting down. Civilized. Only animals stand around to bark at each other."

"The gentleman with the gun always sets the terms of the discussion."

"I don't believe you to be unarmed."

"Good boy. I'm not." He set the pen within the book, and with deliberate caution removed a short revolver from within his wool jacket. This he set on his desk, before crossing the room to the armchair I had indicated.

I sat on the desk.

"Do you mind?" He asked, lifting a cigar from a box. I shook my head. He deftly chopped the end off with a device pulled from a pocket. "Bad habit, I know. Yet, I do not see any point in resisting it. Do you?"

"How you choose to pollute the air is your concern."

He chuckled. From the stand, he picked up an oil lighter. A few moments, and a thin trail of smoke drifted upward. A contorted look of contentment on his face as he slowly exhaled. It would be his last cigar. I didn't think he'd even be finishing it.

"Where were we? Yes. Your leg. Shrapnel? Knife? A bit of broken glass, perhaps?"

"They were your men. You ought to know."

"I wish that were so. My men would have been more efficient. Those were hired help, I'm afraid. I would have much preferred to have been able to send my own. Their style may be dated, sure, but they are quite effective. And loyal. Never did get word back from those..." His lip curled. "Mercenaries. Not even notice of their obvious failure."

"Good help is hard to come by, I suppose. It's no concern of mine."

"Of course it is! That is another matter entirely, though. You know, I actually thought that maybe the doctor got them all. I still thought you were dead."

"And your Director killed by a beaten blind girl?"

His eyes lit up.

"Is she still alive? Marvelous. I thought maybe the fire got her. Terrible way to die, or so I'm told."

"Fire?" I slipped. Betrayed curiosity. "I put a few rounds into your security console. I didn't exactly have a torch to take to the building." I covered.

"That must have been enough. Electrical short, in a building so very old. A spark in the walls... makes one wish they hadn't replaced all that asbestos. I had other suspects. Plenty enough foes to wish me failure. However, I realized it must have been you. It seemed far-fetched that the doctor could have disposed of the team I sent to kill him. Just too much coincidence. That the Director lied was no surprise, certainly. I must admit he was rather convincing. Sold me on your death."

"He did try."

"I have no doubt. If my resources hadn't been... liquidated, I would have killed him myself. Such gross incompetence. I figured he still had the soldier. He was the best qualified to study her, and I would have gotten what little I needed from her soon enough. Her use was practically at an end, as far as my own personal involvement went. Even with the data in hand... What would I do with it? Without my prize."

"You keep using that word. Soldier."

"Yes. Last of her particular batch, I'm afraid. Did you not have a look around on your way in?"

"I saw."

"You saw the combat suits?"

I nodded. *Let him talk. Even if he lies, that can still teach much.*

"Fully pressurized. The idea being that if one of them were captured, she would succumb to disease before being a liability. Your father's idea. Millions spent on the design. He was rather convincing himself. I wanted to dispose of the whole lot when we encountered the first flaw."

I smiled grimly, determined not to let his cavalier attitude bother me.

"Sounds like he took you for a ride."

"Yes. I thought it didn't matter. Disposal was still called for when further complications arose. Years wasted. We could not develop a new batch *and* pay to equip such a specialty class. Not that they weren't a decent product, mind you. Just one we couldn't sell. Not even as B-stock. The problem was in housing."

Thoughts swirled. I betrayed none of them with action.

"Seems like you might have underestimated them. You missed one." We were discussing the mass execution of hundreds. All of them like Sobely. Discussed it like one speaks of weeding an overgrown lawn.

"Your father's bargain. Save this one. Deliver her to you. Leave you both alone. All in trade for his life."

I don't know how, but I kept the gun steady. I did not allow myself to show the rage. The Beast waited at the bars of his cage, impatient. Knowing it's thirst for blood would be sated, and ready to get on with it. To hear so plainly the terms that led to my father's death... I felt nausea. I felt a titanic struggle within to keep my finger from clamping down on the trigger.

Not yet. He's still talking. He might not be the end to this.

Outwardly calm. A tempest raging in my heart.

"Seems like a good bargain. For you."

"Yes, it did. Too good, in fact. Any number of ways he could have leveraged a wench for his son. Besides which, what was the point? She'd die within months, even if we boosted her immune-factors as much as we could. It seemed a cruelty done to you, and a treat for myself. To have the pleasure of watching my old friend breathe his last, and then get to watch as his son suffered the debt of his final bargain... It didn't fit his character."

He played you like a fiddle. Dominos.

"Did you think he wouldn't expect you to be suspicious?"

"With him out of the picture, it didn't matter. Why would I keep my word? Who would hold me to it? As much as I might have enjoyed watching you find destruction, it was far less trouble to just dispose of the soldier and be done with it."

Doesn't he realize how close he skirts the edge? Shouldn't he be bargaining for his own life? Or does he realize that I would not grant such a request and speaks just to hear his own voice.

"What stopped you?"

"Curiosity, of course! After I found his journal, well... seems our Jonathan was far more active in the program than any of us realized. He was always so keen on relying on proper human beings, so none of us suspected. His plan, though, was flawed. Maybe it is better to say it was incomplete. Sure, your hormones might have been powerful enough to get the experiment under way. The young man I saw, however, was raised better than that. You wouldn't dare. And the whole thing would be for naught."

"So, your plan was to wait for me to outgrow those hormones? Wait until I had better control of myself?"

He smiled. I felt sick. He drew in a long puff from the cigar, let his lungs stew for several seconds, before replying. Smoke escaped around his words.

"I understood it would take something more... drastic. And even then, a gamble. I had nothing to lose, however. At least, that's what I believed. I put together a better plan. The pay-off would be worth it."

"Doesn't seem like your plan panned out as you hoped."

"It did fine. Stress, you see, can over-ride a lot of things. A bit of conditioning to set the trap. A tragedy to get the adrenaline pumping. Then, a bit of quiet for you both to stew in. If it didn't work, it wouldn't matter. She had days to start the process, or else I'd get to enjoy the privilege of watching you go mad."

"You didn't consider the idea that I might fall in love with her."

"That didn't matter, either. I suspected that was your father's play. Why it had to be *this* particular unit... Your father counted on you to fall head-over-heels for a killer vegetable. A doll. Empty as if she had been made of porcelain. I suppose he had the right of it, then."

"You don't know what you are talking about."

"Don't I?" Lot opened the leather-bound book. Flipping pages nearly to the beginning of the volume. He showed me the page – I recognized the handwriting of my father.

"The solution was under my nose. Not me. Not Marie. Our son. Timothy plus Lot six dash four-two-A-six-nine-six equals the key to the whole bloody problem."

The words hit like an anvil falling from the sky. I could not contain a gasp of shock.

"He refers to her as 'Project Blossom.' A pretty name. He numerically chose a name to give her. Something otherworldly. It's all here. Of course, he taunts me as well. I feel privileged to be given any thought at all in these pages." He flipped a few pages over. "He will beat you, Lot." He read.

"Did he lie to you?" A taunt of my own. Lot's fate was determined the moment I had been given his address. He might by lying, even now, but he had little reason. The truth was enough of a knife to twist. A few weeks ago I wouldn't have bothered to let him speak at all. A few days ago, even.

Only now did I understand patience. Even in deceit, Lot could reveal much that was still hidden. My life had been nothing but mysteries and questions since the day my father died.

"It would appear that he did not. Huh. Strange, I hadn't thought of it before now. Yet here I am. Beaten. You've won the prize, my boy."

The conversation was turning. Lot chose his words with care. He was leading me along. Perhaps just buying time. Manipulating.

"Where did you send them off to? Your Trench Coat Men?" I questioned.

His fingers clenched suddenly, violently. Destroying the still-burning cigar. He didn't even seem to notice.

"They said I was out of touch with reality. Me! They sit alone in their towers and think they own the world. They dare say that it is *my* methods that are too old for the game. Every turn, they take more and more. I couldn't even track down one idiot boy and a mindless automation! Excuses! Lies! They set their own plan in motion years ago. But I kept their secrets! I did their work! And how am I repaid for my service? This *empty* place. This grave. My own men turned against me. So close. So close! A few weeks wouldn't matter. Damn them. Damn their impatience!"

His eyes had glazed over, madness disrupting the mask of calm he had worked so carefully to present. Evidence at last that a screw had come loose. The toll my journey had taken on his sanity beginning to show.

"Surely, you aren't entirely without resources..." I goaded, hoping he would reveal the information I still needed to know.

"Money is always easy. Power? Everything I have accomplished, thrown back in my face. All that I have done, laid to ruin. Because of that damned Jonathan and his schemes. It would take years..." He stopped. His eyes narrowed. He seemed to come back to himself.

Calm now, he brushed the remains of the cigar from his jacket. The remaining stub, he lights, sticking it into the corner of his mouth. A deep draw, and the smoke coiled.

"The past deserves no more concern. We've come to it at last. You are here. I left the door unlocked, and here you are."

"Here I thought it was because you didn't know how to throw the bolt. No minions to scurry and dance to your whims." Anger was useful, but this time he did not rise to the bait. Instead, he smiled.

"Minions can be purchased or made to order. I've had my fill. No, what I need is something else entirely. I can adapt, and well I should. You've proven yourself a worthy foe. Your tenacity unmatched. You didn't come in here gun blasting, either. That shows that you aren't the idiot I imagined. Everything was a risk, but we have certainly borne some fruit, haven't we? We'll sweep away all the morons in their glass towers."

That manic gleam returned.

"You have the key we need. I have the facility. Money. A perfect genetic specimen growing within subject 6-42A696. We'll bring the whole world to its knees!"

His audacity was a blow unto itself. A mad king with an empty throne room making mad declarations.

"You expect me... to work for you?" I could not keep my voice from going a little shrill.

"Not *for* me. *With* me. Partners. Together, we'll topple the old world, and build a new one to *our* liking."

All of it made sense now. Why he had kept talking as if we were old friends discussing business. It had all been the wind-up for the pitch.

"Was that your hope? You thought I would look past all of your sins, that I would be flattered?"

"Why else? You've run a good race. You have proven your value to everyone. With nothing, you have destroyed one who had everything. Just imagine what you could accomplish with *my* resources at *your* disposal."

"And Sobely? Where does she fit in with your plans?"

"You want her? Keep her! Keep whoever you like, in fact. The doctor, the blind girl. You can have them all."

"What of my child? Your precious key."

"Well, naturally I would leave the care of the infant to you. It would have the finest of everything. It will take some time to prepare things. To restart production. Time enough for a child to grow. To test all the possibilities. You could spoil the thing however you wish – I'd even bow to the brat and kiss its feet as if it were a holy emperor."

A deep breath. Lot took a last draw off the cigar, before crushing it out.

"So this was all a test."

"Mostly. Part of me did want to watch you suffer, I admit. Yet... your father spoke often of your potential. When the Director informed me of your death... I nearly shot the smug son of a bitch myself. He had instructions! He disobeyed. You've dealt with that, and good on you."

Another deep breath. Hands steady.

"You offer protection, then? I don't imagine your... superiors would tolerate a coup."

A final prod. I had to know. If shooting this man would only see him replaced with something else, something *unknown...*

"From the very beginning, they did not give a flea's ass about you. Any danger out of those old men would come much later, and by then it will be too late." He smiled. Believing that I was considering what he offered.

"What of the woman with the glowing eyes? I didn't get the sense that she saw me as inconsequential."

"Jon's legacy, I'm afraid. This whole time I believed the witch a loyal servant. So very useful. The moment those chains came off... oh, she did as she was asked. Brought the... girl to you. The fastest way, and time was ever short. Then the bitch disappeared. No matter, though."

The iron at her wrists had been used to bind her to him. Like an animal.

"Why is that? Seems like she's... something not to trifle with. Powerful. She wanted me to be kept as far from you as possible. I don't imagine a partnership would please her."

"As I said already, it doesn't matter. Listen." He leaned forward. A co-conspirator divulging precious secrets. "The blind girl. Her potential... I already had her half-broken. You could have anything you want."

"Anything I want?"

"Just say the word." He beamed. Confident that I had seen the value of his offer. A devil with a deal, surely too good to pass on. Worth anything. The cost of a soul, no more than that.

"Her smile." I said at last.

"What?"

"Her smile. I live for it. It's all I want. She grants it freely, and I feel as if I were the richest man alive. No deals. No expectations. Soft. Simple. Wonderful. You can't offer me that."

"What are you..."

"Don't interrupt me, Lot! You've had your say, and now I will have mine. You tried to take her from me. You tried to crush her spirit. You tried to take her smile away from me. No, I don't think we shall be friends. You have made yourself my enemy. You toyed with our lives. Your dogs killed my mother. The hounds drove me to kill men who didn't have anything to do with anything. But worst of all, you tried to take her smile. You are my enemy, Lot, and you could never be anything else."

I stood. Lot shrank in his chair.

"Wait! Even now, you aren't free of that man. You stand there in his coat, exactly where he placed you. His specialty was always in getting the pieces on the board to move of their own accord. Unaware of the hands of the invisible master sliding them across the squares."

"As if you are any better." I pulled back the hammer.

"I've been trapped in *his* game. *His* manipulations! Just as you are. We are two kings, face to face at last. All of the pawns have been swept aside now. Just you and I, alone. Yet we are both here not through our own doing."

"You should have quit playing." I raised my arm, rolling my shoulders. Flexing toes within my new boots.

"I thought so, once. He knew my nature so well. He knew how my madness worked. But don't you see? We are free now. We don't need to remain his puppets! Think of what we might accomplish. Kings! We could bring down those lofty towers and rebuild this world just as we like. Free, forever!"

"No thanks. I think I prefer being on my own."

"So did your father. We were friends once. Even when he decided I was his enemy, we still we worked together. Years of work. We accomplished so *much*. You don't know what it is you're discarding. You could shape the world, just as he did!"

I crossed the room. Planted the barrel on his forehead. His eyes crossed, body quavered with fear. The mighty manipulator, revealed to be nothing more than a rat in wolf's clothing.

"I am shaping the world."

I squeezed. The sound was deafening. The silence more so. His body slumped, slipping further for the mess. I retrieved the journal from the table and turned away.

It was done. Or nearly so.

I turned back, lifting the old glass table-lighter. I sparked the flame and threw it against the bookshelf. Glass shattered, oil spreading the flame quickly across dusty books and bone-dry oak.

Now it was done.

On my way in, the facility had seemed spooky. With the silent machines, and the rows of empty cells. Waiting. Everything pristine and clean, in anticipation of someone throwing the switch that would bring it all back to life.

On the way out, I could see it more clearly. Not a monstrous laboratory, awaiting new subjects. Not a facility of pain. Surely it had been both of those things once upon a time.

Now it was a mausoleum.

The fire would spread. Authorities would arrive and try to unravel the mysteries within. Maybe they'd find the truth. More likely than that, the entire thing would be covered up. Swept under rugs.

It didn't matter to me anymore. As the dark madness faded from Lot's eyes, so too did his hold over me. This 'council' had deemed him mad, his quest a fool's errand. His hatred for my father had led him astray. We were insignificant, and that was a wonderful thing to be.

I returned to the Charger, spun the tires. A thin tendril of smoke was clinging to the sky like a phantom kite-string. Perhaps a camera would reveal the black Dodge leaving the scene, when reviewed.

That wouldn't matter, either.

I was returning to her.

The sun had long passed its zenith, halfway through the graceful dive into the horizon. Soon enough, the burning embers of the day would be at my back. The engine rumbled agreeably. Every minute, every mile, and I could feel the weight lift. The relief, the knowledge; it was done.

The only task remaining was to return to her.

~**End**

The sky was the color of faded denim. Geese arrowed south overhead, the maple trees were turning crimson in the yard. The sort of day people wrote songs about. The sort of day that would send most normal people outside, to enjoy one more lingering day of sunshine.

Those people don't have her.

She sat in my lap now. A plate stacked high with breakfast foods sat before us. I was taking great delight in feeding her. I was reluctant to let her go, even for a moment. I had driven through both nights to return to her.

And she had been waiting. As the Charger pulled to a stop in Jack's driveway, she had come running. She had forgotten her shoes but didn't seem to notice the gravel digging into her heels. I had not dared to call ahead.

She leapt into my arms, covering my face with kisses. I had scooped her up, just as I had on that first day together. I hadn't put her down since.

There were pancakes, of course. Eggs, bacon, and a heap of fresh vegetables. Jack was getting ready for work. Mildred was outside hanging clothes – the dryer was still broken. Greg and Irene were asleep in one of the guest rooms. Apparently, she hadn't wanted to be alone. I spared a moment to consider what her story might be. What nightmares did she struggle with?

"I love you."

"Mmm mm, hmm?" She answered, mouth full.

I chuckled, wiping the corner of her mouth with a napkin. She swallowed the obstruction and took a big drink of juice to clear away anything remaining and tried again.

"You promise?"

Before I could reply, her lips were against mine. I could taste the maple lingering. Like frosting on a cake, really. I returned her affection, lingering to taste the sweetness beneath the sugary glaze.

"Keep that up, and the food will be long cold before you finish it." Jack entered the dining room, sitting down across from us. Helping himself to a plate piled high. Mildred really had gone a little overboard.

Sobely broke away in order to respond.

"Cold is fine, too." So in saying, she snatched up a crust of toast, sopping up egg yolk. This, of course, dripped down her chin before she could get it past her lips. I dabbed at her chin, if only to keep it from dripping further. I was quite reluctant to let her go, and now there was no longer any reason that I had to.

"It *is* good to see you eating. You had us worried, little miss." Jack ate with the pace of a marine. Technically he was already late for work.

"I did not feel like eating before. I am hungry now, though."

Mildred appeared from the kitchen, wiping her hands on a cloth.

"Are you still here? And here I thought I married a professional." She said dryly.

"A man's gotta eat."

"What an impression you must leave with your deputies!"

Sobely's eyes moved back and forth through the exchange, even as she continued to eat. I reached for a strip of bacon, chewing thoughtfully as they continued to banter.

"I called Marsha an hour ago and told her I was running a bit late. Are you in such a hurry to get rid of me?"

"Where you take your nap is no concern of mine." She sat, eyes twinkling.

Jack sputtered.

"I don't take naps! I might rest my eyes a bit from time to time, but I'm not so old as to be caught napping on the job!"

"Uh-huh. Right. You're the only man I know with a thousand-yard *snore*."

Jack's face reddened. Sobely giggled. I realized I was grinning like an idiot and worked to smooth my face.

"I'll take a look into those addresses you gave me." Jack changed the subject.

"I would appreciate that. I'm at a bit of a loss as to what to do next. I cut the head off the snake, but perhaps there may still be consequences left to deal with."

"We'll figure it out, son." Jack rose, finishing his coffee with a giant swig. "In the meantime, eat. Rest. Make sure you have your doctor friend redress that leg. Everything is going to be fine now. I have a good feeling."

"I believe you may be right."

"When it comes to matters of the gut, Jack is always right." Mildred quipped. Jack opened his mouth to reply, and then thought better of it. Patting his stomach unconsciously, before turning to head out the door.

It was a beautiful Tuesday morning. Soon, kids would be climbing into busses on their way to school. Adults would breathe a quiet sigh of relief before sports and other activities borrowed on their time again.

Just now, everything was bright and beautiful, just as it should be.

www.ingramcontent.com/pod-product-compliance
Lightning Source LLC
Chambersburg PA
CBHW061918130726
47908CB00017B/1956